Praise for *Around the Squ*

I just finished the delightful/suspenseful *Around the Square*. I found myself walking through the architecture I was raised in or near. I don't believe I have ever read a book that used so many facets of the community, church, schools, libraries, all the businesses on the square. The cooperation of groups, churches, quilters, teachers, townspeople, youth, and parents make an event worth remembering. Hayward is a place where business is done on a word or a handshake. There were eccentric and interesting characters like the dark, mysterious man giving away brownies, never knowing, but hoping he was on our side. Thanks for an exciting trip through the past.

—Verneine Gebbie

What a refreshing feel-good story Mary Ann Seymour has written about small-town life. I'm ready to pack my bags and move to Hayward. Who can't remember someone in their life like these characters? Wouldn't it feel nice if people everywhere helped and had a sense of community that these people do?

—Dian Huss

Around the Square by Mary Ann Seymour is a wonderful novel that involves you in the appealing story of a small town filled with colorful, unique characters and an unlikely crime. Her writing includes an excellent balance of suspense and foreshadowing, delicate humor, and vivid details. She leaves you anxious to read more about Claire and the town of Hayward.

—Kathie Hagen

Around the Square takes you to a place anyone would love to be, a small charming town with wonderful characters who are true friends. Yet there are those who are full of mystery and with questionable backgrounds. I loved Mary Ann Seymour's descriptions of the daily routines. It made me feel at home. I look forward to reading more of her work.

—Ann Crane Harlan

Butterfly
Messages

Butterfly
Messages

a novel by
Mary Ann Seymour

TATE PUBLISHING & *Enterprises*

Published by Tate Publishing & Enterprises, LLC
127 E. Trade Center Terrace | Mustang, Oklahoma 73064 USA
1.888.361.9473 | www.tatepublishing.com

Tate Publishing is committed to excellence in the publishing industry. The company reflects the philosophy established by the founders, based on Psalm 68:11,
"The Lord gave the word and great was the company of those who published it."

Published in the United States of America
ISBN: 978-1-61566-826-7
1. Fiction: Christian: General
2. Fiction: Family Life
10.01.26

DEDICATION

For the hundreds of five- and six-year-old children who have enriched my life over the past thirty-three years.

Carmy, happy reading!

Mary Ann Seymour

ONE

Although the temperature was in the twenties with a gentle wind, Claire stuffed her half-eaten bagel in her pocket for a snack and headed out for her almost-daily walk. Ever since her move to Hayward, Iowa, she had tried to keep up her exercise routine. She had made it through most of the winter vowing to walk unless there was ice or too much snow. She liked walking in this kind of weather since hardly anyone else was out who might notice that she often carried on a conversation with herself.

Claire bounded down the front steps, invigorated by the crisp air. When she reached the sidewalk, she turned back and looked admiringly at her house that had been built in the late 1800s, as had all of the homes that bordered the west side of the town square. The look of Hayward was one of the things that had appealed to Claire and her husband, Dennis, many years ago as they traveled around the country passing through small communities and thinking ahead to their retirement years. They had worked in the Denver area and had witnessed a remarkable amount of growth they did not like. So they had planned on finding a smaller place to call home after their working years were over. Unfortunately, Dennis was killed in an automobile accident and never had the chance to fulfill those dreams.

Many friends and relatives thought Claire was making a mistake when, after retiring from her thirty plus years of teaching, she pulled up roots and headed off to what to them felt like the middle of nowhere. Even her explanation to her daughter and two sons that Iowa was a good midway point between their homes in Michigan, Arkansas, and Colorado didn't do much to alleviate their concern that their mother was making a less than sensible decision. However, Claire had not once regretted her choice to settle in this picturesque hamlet in Iowa. She liked the convenience of almost everything she needed being across the square along Main Street. She appreciated having the chance to still be around children when she volunteered in the library of the elementary school. She felt immediately comfortable in her new congregation of the Methodist church located at the end of the square. But most of all she enjoyed the people who lived in Hayward. They had welcomed her when she first came and involved her in their traditions. Many of them had become good friends over the past months. Others she found quite interesting and sometimes even entertaining. Even though she lived alone in her old two-story, four-bedroom home, she had never felt lonely since her move.

Claire's walk took a familiar route south down her street past the homes of the town's doctor, the grocer, the owner of the Ford and tractor dealership, an elderly widower and good friend, the dentist, and the town attorney who doubled as the only real estate agent in the area. She crossed Maple and passed the impressive corner house and the obnoxious dog owned by Mayor Hayward's family, the library and St. Mary's Catholic Church, the home of the owner of the hardware store, and on to the city park on the south end of town. The park was large for the town's size. It had an extensive playground, a swimming pool, a baseball field, horseshoe pits, numerous picnic tables under old, sheltering trees, and a small basketball court.

South of the park was an expansive stand of trees that marked the location of Abbott Creek. Claire liked to walk there with the sound of water gurgling around the hunks of ice widespread along the creek. She walked around the trees, steering clear of areas of dirty snow that lurked in the shadows and had avoided being melted by the sun's warming rays. That was where she thought she saw movement out of the corner of her eye. She stopped for a moment, scanning the area. Seeing nothing, she took a few more steps when again she saw movement. "Unless it is really different here in Iowa, snow doesn't move." She looked more closely in the direction of the motion.

Then she saw it. It wasn't easy to spot since its grayish-white color blended in almost perfectly with the dirty snow. As she stared, it sensed it was being watched and crouched lower, as if in fear of being discovered. Claire stood still trying to decide the best course of action and fearful she might spook the little thing, causing it to run. Calmly and slowly she took one step forward. The white thing backed up a few paces, lowering itself still closer to the ground. Claire studied it for a moment, scanning her memory to see if she'd ever seen it before. Thinking she had not, she suspected that it was either lost or a runaway. "I'll bet it's hungry and thirsty too. It probably came here to get a drink."

The staring contest continued until she remembered the bagel remnant she had in her pocket. Slowly she took it out, not making any sudden moves. Breaking off a piece, she extended it toward the frightened animal. "Here, boy, are you hungry? You can have this. I won't hurt you." Neither budged. "Let's try this instead." Claire tossed a piece in the area between the two of them and then slowly squatted down, making herself smaller and less overwhelming. Patiently she waited. Slowly the little dog took a step toward the bagel piece. When he reached it, he sniffed it only once before gobbling it up. Claire broke off a second piece and again tossed it into the space between them. Again the dog edged forward to eat.

"Now for a real test," she spoke in a soft, soothing voice. This time she put a piece in her hand, which she held out toward the small dog. It hardly hesitated as it approached the outstretched hand and quickly cleared it of the food. Once more Claire held out a hand, but this time her hand was directly in front of her, and as the animal ate she scooped it up in her other hand. It struggled at first but relaxed when the last piece of bagel was offered. It then looked up at her as if to say, "Please, is there any more?"

It was then Claire noticed that the little dog was wet and shaking. She wasn't sure if it was from fear or from the cold or both. She carefully removed the scarf that was around her neck and wrapped it around the trembling dog. "I think you need this much more than I do." She rose to her feet, which was not easy since she had been in this position for much too long. Luckily the dog was no longer struggling and instead seemed to be relieved to be sheltered from the cold wind.

"I certainly had not planned on houseguests today," Claire said, looking sympathetically into the big brown eyes looking hopefully up at her. "But under the circumstances, I think you should come home with me for at least a while." She tucked the scarf snugly around her shivering load and headed back across the park. "At least now I don't have to talk to myself anymore. I can talk to you." Her bundle looked up at her as if it was good to hear a human voice.

No one else was out and about as she walked back up Oak Street. Everything was quiet except for the sound of the wind as it whistled past. She was almost to Maple when the loud barking from behind the fence made her jump. She almost lost control of her wrapped passenger as it tried to jump out of her arms in response to the unexpected yapping. Claire had heard the mayor's dog, Mellow, many times, but she still hadn't become used to its ferocious sounds.

"It's okay, fellow. They say his bark is worse than his bite." She was not sure if she was trying to reassure the little dog or herself. She quickened her pace as she crossed Maple. "We're almost home. At least we're almost to my home. I have no idea where your home is." When they finally reached Claire's sidewalk, she bounded up the stairs of the porch and quickly opened the front door. She didn't need to bother to unlock it since after living there nine months she had joined her neighbors in leaving doors unlocked during the day. After closing the door with one foot, she proceeded up the stairs to the bathroom. "I think a warm bath is in order. I'm sure that isn't what is on your mind, but I have no desire to have the mud dropped all over my house."

Even though the dog was still wrapped in the scarf, it managed to put up a valiant battle to free itself as Claire started running water in the tub and gathering up extra towels. She looked around the bathroom and asked, "How do you feel about White Rain shampoo?" She smiled down at the still squirming bundle and added, "You know how that song goes, 'Use new White Rain shampoo tonight and tomorrow your hair will be sunshine bright.'" Carefully releasing the scarf that had contained the flailing legs, she intensified her grip and slowly lowered the frightened dog into the warm water.

At first the thrashing increased, creating the appearance of an electric mixer in a bowl of water, but Claire's firm grip in combination with the warm water seemed to soothe the animal. The tremors lessened until it finally was calm. Either that or it was resolved to this soaking fate. Although she never completely let loose, she decreased the pressure with which she held the dog. It let out a quiet sound Claire thought was a sigh. "That's better," she spoke in a gentle, reassuring tone. "I thought you would probably like this. Be patient for a little longer while I do a quick job with this shampoo." Although a thorough job could not be done with one hand rubbing while the other was holding, she managed to remove most of the dirt. Even in a totally soaked state, the animal looked better than it had when she first picked it up back by the creek.

After a second round of shampooing and rinsing, she lifted it from the tub and wrapped it dripping, and again trembling, in a towel. "I think we're done, boy. Hey, I've been calling you a boy, but I really don't know what you are." After a quick examination she smiled. "Yup, I was right!" Claire briskly rubbed, trying to absorb as much water as possible, but as she tried to switch towels, the still wet dog managed to break her hold. Before she could protect herself, he vigorously shook excess water all over Claire and headed for the open door.

"You come back here!" she yelled as she wiped off her dripping face and headed in hot pursuit down the hall, towel in her hand. The dog, not pacified by either the tenor of her voice or the sight of the towel waving in the air, headed down the stairs. Feeling a breath of freedom at the bottom, he started to run around in circles on the living room carpet. As he ran he first put one ear to the floor and then, switching ears, circled in the other direction. Then he lay flat on one side and continued pushing himself in the circle. Within a few seconds, he flopped to the other side and again changed directions. By now Claire had caught up but just stood smiling as she watched. "I guess you prefer this method of drying." In between bursts of circling, the dog got up and ran pell-mell through the dining room and around different pieces of living room furniture until finally he either felt he was dry enough or had run out of energy. He walked over to where Claire watched in amusement and looked up as if to say, "Okay, what now?" Before she could respond, he sprang up into her unsuspecting lap.

"Whoa now," she said, lifting the still damp animal back onto the floor.

"For one thing, this is a people chair. For another thing, you are a temporary guest, so don't get too comfortable. Plus, you are still damp. I am soaked and the bathroom is a mess. I need to change clothes. Let's go upstairs and do some cleaning up." After saying that, she felt somewhat foolish talking to a dog and expecting him to understand, but as she headed up the stairs, he bounded up ahead of her and waited, tail wagging at the top. As she looked up at him, she paused. "If I didn't know any better, I would say that you are laughing at me."

Claire rummaged through boxes stored in the basement as her new four-legged friend sniffed around, becoming familiar with his new surroundings. "Ah, here it is. I thought I still had this. I have no idea why I kept it, but now I'm sure glad I did." The dog hurried over to study what she was holding, sniffing hard trying to get the scent of what had used it last. Claire gently fastened a well-worn collar around her new charge. "Now don't go getting any ideas about this being a permanent arrangement. I just don't want you to take off again until we find your real owner." The dog shook, trying to adjust the collar to a comfortable position. Then he bounded up the stairs after Claire, who also had unearthed an old leash.

After a quick trip to the backyard, the two reentered the kitchen, where Claire took inventory of possible things to feed the skinny little dog. "I don't suppose you are a vegetarian. I have a nice head of lettuce and I could add some tomatoes and carrots. Or how about some apples? Those were favorites of your predecessor. His name was Sparky. Ah, here's a piece of chicken. How about some of that for now?" Claire cut up the chicken and put it in an old bowl on the floor. It was totally devoured almost before she could straighten up. The dog licked his lips and looked up expectantly.

"We need to go easy. We don't want to put too much in your tummy too fast." She looked down at the pleading face that once again seemed to smile. "Okay, maybe just a little bit of an apple. I'll share one with you." The bits in the bowl disappeared just as fast, and the dog watched hopefully as Claire ate her part. "You can beg all you want. It won't do you any good." After she finished the last bite, the dog went to the bowl that Claire had filled with water, took a big drink, and stood with his nose against the back door. "I take that as a clue. Good dog."

Following the second trip outside, Claire sat down to write a shopping list. She was so involved in trying to figure out what she needed to get at the store that it was about ten minutes before she again thought about the dog. "Hey, where'd you go, doggie?" She visually searched the kitchen with no luck. She walked through the dining room and into the living room, again without finding him. Since there were no more hiding places on the main floor, Claire headed up stairs. She needed to go no farther than her bedroom at the top of the stairs. Looking through the door she saw a bundle of white fur curled up in a ball on her pillow. She stood and looked silently for a few minutes and before turning away said to herself, "Now don't go getting any ideas about this being a permanent arrangement."

Claire reattached the leash to the collar, which was no easy task as the dog, evidently revitalized by his nap, jumped with excitement. When the connection was secure, Claire led him through the back door. "How about a little walk, dog? I know it's cold, but if we walk fast, maybe we won't notice." The dog didn't seem to mind at all as he pulled to the full extent of the leash checking out the new smells in the backyard and alley.

The destination Claire had chosen was a very familiar one to her. She was a faithful volunteer at the Hayward Elementary School, and she followed this route at least once a week. She figured maybe one of the children would recognize the dog. Her timing was good, as she arrived as the dismissal bell rang and the children exploded out the doors. It didn't take long for some of them to spot Claire and her furry friend and quickly gather around her.

"Wow, Mrs. Menefee, that's a great puppy you have!" said one boy.

"He's sure cute," said another.

"What's its name?" chimed a third.

As little hands carefully rubbed the soft fur and scratched the floppy ears, Claire explained. "I have no idea what his name is. I found him down by the creek. I don't know who he belongs to and wondered if any of you do."

By now there was quite a crowd of interested onlookers, but the children just shrugged to an accompanying mumbling chorus of "I don't know" and "I've never seen him before."

"If any of you do hear of anyone who's lost a dog, could you please tell Mrs. Stevens in the office?" The children nodded, mumbled some more, and dispersed on their way home.

As the children left, Claire heard one say, "I think Mrs. Menefee should just keep that dog. She really needs someone to keep her company so she won't be so alone." Claire pondered that for a moment and then shook her head as if to rid it of the thought.

Since Claire was no closer to finding the owners of her new four-legged friend, she decided that continuing to feed him leftover chicken probably was not in his, or her, best interest. As she entered the Hayward grocery store, conveniently located directly across the town square, she was greeted with Bryan Graves's usual cheerful greeting, "Hi, Claire, how are you doing today? Can I help you find anything special?"

Although Claire had lived in Hayward for about nine months, she was still delighted by the sincere, friendly way the store owners greeted their customers by name. No matter what they were doing, they always made time to visit at least momentarily with whoever entered. They knew not only their customers and all their family members but their makes of cars, church membership, holiday plans, medical conditions, and probably some other things that might have been better kept confidential. But that was the benefit—or curse—of life in a close-knit small town. So Bryan was quite surprised when Claire said she was shopping for dog food.

"Dog food, you say? Well, I think that is just great. We all can use some faithful companionship, don't you know? The pet food is right this way." He led the way down one of the narrow aisles marked with one-way arrows to avoid congestion. Claire followed, preoccupied with his remark about companionship. She had not explained the dog was not really hers. "Here. Any of these would be good. Personally, I think one is about as good as another." Claire selected a bag, and Bryan carried it back to the front of the store. "Must be a pretty small dog judging by the size of the bag. What kind of dog is it? What's its name?"

"Oh, he's not mine. I am just his temporary caretaker until the real owner can be found." Claire went on to explain the whole story. After she finished Bryan held the door for her as she headed home. She had just crossed Oak Street when she ran into Jim Dunn as he turned from her door after delivering the mail.

"Oh, that explains that," he said in a matter-of-fact but still jovial manner. Claire looked at him questioningly. "The dog food, I mean. I thought I heard a dog when I dropped the mail in the slot, but I figured my ears were playing a trick. So you got a dog. Good for you. That will help keep you company. What kind of dog is it? Judging from the yappy bark, I figure it must be a little pooch. Did you just get him? What's his name?"

All of these questions were reminding Claire of her first few days in Hayward last June. Being a small community, everyone was interested in finding out about her. She had explained to the first couple of people she met about herself and why she had made the move. But after telling just a few, the word spread and everyone seemed to know all about her. Hopefully she would not have to explain about this canine caper many more times and the neighborhood grapevine would spread the word. Maybe the little dog's owner would soon be found.

Jim headed on his way, and Claire entered the front door. Down the stairs rushed a fuzzy white blur that leaped toward her from the third step, causing her to drop the dog food. "Whoa there, doggie. It's a good thing you are small, or we might both be in a pile on the floor. Were you glad to see me or the food?" She got her answer as the dog continued to lick her hand as she petted it and didn't even seem to notice the bag of food.

Claire had just entered the kitchen when there was a knock at the back door. She looked up to see a smiling Jane Dunn, her neighbor from across the alley, waving through the door's window. Claire motioned her to come in through the door that was seldom locked. "Oh, Claire, he's just darling! The kids told me you got a puppy. I think that's a great idea. He'll be good company for you."

As Jane bent over to play with the puppy, Claire's mind was replaying the same comment that everyone had made so far—even the children. "He will be a great companion for you. He will keep you company." Was everyone picturing her as a lonely old widow who sat alone at night just rocking and knitting and feeling friendless? She didn't see herself that way at all. She felt that she had done a good job of getting to know her new neighbors. In fact, she had secretly congratulated herself on forcing herself to be outgoing because that really was not how she'd been most of her life. Were people seeing the old, shy, retiring Claire coming out through the gregarious person she had tried hard to be? She was brought back to reality by the sound of Jane's voice.

"Claire, are you all right?"

"Oh, I'm fine. I was just thinking of something. And he really isn't mine." Hoping that surely this would be the last time, the rescue story was told once again.

"But he's so cute! I think you should keep him if you can't find the owner. I think he would be—"

"I know," Claire interrupted, "he'd be a great companion and keep me company."

Claire had finished washing her face and brushing her teeth and was looking forward to some time reading in bed. She walked down the hall to her room followed by her bouncing companion. Her seat had barely touched the bed when the dog was on the blanket next to her. She reached over, gently picked him up, and set him on the floor.

Patting the floor, she said, "This is your place. And this is mine." She patted the bed for emphasis. The dog took the last motion to be his cue and once again leaped onto the bed. Again Claire repeated the steps, this time omitting patting of the bed. Again the dog repeated his jump.

"This will not do," Claire said as firmly as she could. She picked him up, carried him to the hall, firmly placed him on the floor, and looked straight in his big brown eyes. "Stay! I'll see you in the morning." Claire shut the door and climbed back into bed. She had barely had time to open the book when it began. It was very quiet at first and almost inaudible. Gradually the sound grew, and what had begun as a faint whimper turned into a mournful whine. Claire turned out the light hoping that might make the dog think she was not there anymore. But the sound only got louder. The whine turned into a moan and the moan into a grief-stricken howl. Even with the pillow pulled tightly around her ears, she could not muffle the sound.

Not only was her head beginning to hurt from the racket, but so was her heart. She had the feeling maybe the poor dog was afraid that he was once again being abandoned. She knew better, she really did. But she got out of bed and went to open the door. Even in the dim room she saw white flash past her and fly into the bed. As she once again lay down, she could tell that the dog sitting next to her was smiling. And so was she.

TWO

The unseasonably cold weather had fittingly given way to unusually warm weather the week between Palm Sunday and Easter. Daffodils were getting taller, and tulips had begun to poke through the soil.

Along with the appearance of spring flowers was the appearance of relatives. Claire's son's family was coming from Michigan for Easter and to check out her new hometown. Finishing the guestrooms was the immediate priority. The beds had been made, and the final touch-up was underway with one problem—Claire's faithful feather duster, which she had used minutes earlier, was nowhere to be found.

"I hate it when I do that! How can I have something one minute and not the next?" She was looking under a bed when she heard growling. Turning around, she was greeted by the duster shaking back and forth in her face. Behind it was a growling dog who acted as if he had captured some vicious animal. When Claire reached for it, the dog backed up and shook the duster again. "I don't have time to play now. I'm expecting company any minute, and I need that!" As she reached, the dog once again backed up. "I'll get you," she said, getting up and chasing feathers and fur out of the room. Claire was saved from having to admit defeat when the doorbell rang.

"That must be them. You be on your best behavior, you hear?" she said, looking down at the dog with duster still clutched in its mouth. She rushed down the stairs and threw open the door. "I'm so excited you're here!" Claire exclaimed before looking at who was there. After the double take, she could feel the blush start.

"Well, that's quite a welcome. I'm glad to be here too," replied a very handsome gentleman whose growing red tinge in his cheeks made his green eyes look even greener. "But I think you must be expecting someone else. I think I came at a bad time. I'll come back later."

"Please come in. I'm expecting my son and his family any minute, and I assumed that's who was at the door. It's good to see you, Daniel. Please sit down. Tell me what you're doing back here—rounding up some more criminals?"

"I just took some time off for Easter and thought I'd make sure everything is still safe and sound here. But I don't want to interfere with your family visit, so I'll go now. Maybe some time we could…" The doorbell interrupted his suggestion.

Darn! thought Claire, irritated by the interruption in what Daniel was about to say. She opened the door but didn't say anything until she was certain who was there. This time it was her son, Jay, with Jill, Julie, and James. After all the hugging, Claire remembered Daniel was still in the living room and quickly introduced him.

"It was nice meeting all of you, but I think I'll come back another day. It's good to see you, Claire." Daniel let himself out, leaving Claire standing, staring at the door. Then, as if having recovered from the shock of so many strangers invading his territory, the dog bounded down the stairs and jumped on the legs of the newcomers.

"Down," Claire ordered, and much to her amazement, he actually did stop and sat on the floor with tail wagging behind him. While Julie entertained herself by petting him and he did the same by licking her arm, Jay stood little James on the floor so he too could enjoy the silky feeling of the white fur.

"Oooh, Ma, he's really cute. Where did you find him?" Jill asked.

"I found him down by the river wandering around as if he was lost and had nowhere to go. I brought him home, cleaned him up, and he's been hanging around ever since." Looks of disbelief appeared on Jill's and Jay's faces.

"Do you really think that was safe? What do you know about him?" Jay asked.

"Really nothing. I've asked around, but no one seems to know anything about him. I am beginning to think that he's a keeper. He's certainly good company and doesn't eat much." Claire laughed a little, but her humor wasn't shared. After a few awkward moments, she laughed again. "Oh, you meant Daniel. I thought you were talking about the dog!" A sense of relief filled the room, and the dog, which by now was getting used to being called "the dog," moved to Claire's side.

"Let's get your things into your rooms. Then we can visit." As Claire said those words, she hoped the subject of Daniel wouldn't come up again until she thought of a gentle way to explain how they met.

Claire took everyone on a tour of her house and yard, explaining that its builder and architect also had designed in the late 1800s many of the other homes surrounding the town square. The tour included the garage where she had, while taking over as den mother for bed-ridden Jane Dunn, held the Cub Scout meetings. They all laughed remembering some of the funny things that happened at those meetings.

Back inside around cookies and milk, Julie asked Claire what she was going to name the dog. "I guess if no one claims him by next week I should give him a better name than 'dog.' Any suggestions?"

Four-year-old Julie's dark curly hair tossed back and forth as she studied the little pup that looked up at her with big eyes. "Well, he likes to lick, so you could call him 'Licky,' or he tickles me, so you could call him 'Tickles.'" The dog cocked his head from one side to the other as if he was pondering the name choices. Julie in turn studied him and continued, "And he looks like he's smiling, so you could call him 'Smiley.'"

"Maybe we can decide after you get to know him better," suggested Claire.

"You know how I feel about dogs, so personally I don't care to know him much better," added Jay, "but I'm glad you have a dog. I think he's a good companion for you. How about a name like 'Buddy' or 'Pal'?" Again Claire was hearing those words. She wondered if she subconsciously was giving the impression she was lonely. That thought made her remember

Daniel was in town, and she wondered if he was staying at the Snooze Inn. She decided she'd call later to see if he was there.

Claire had a casserole ready to throw in the oven, and Jill tossed a salad as they caught up on things since they'd been together at Christmas. Jay kept a toddling James from getting into too many things and directed him to the pots and pans made available for playing. Julie sat at the table with a coloring book Claire had given her.

As Claire set the table she marveled at how different her two grandchildren looked. Julie's dark curls were a total contrast to James's straight reddish-blonde hair. Even their facial coloring was different, with Julie getting her mother's beautiful dark brown eyes and darker skin tones while James inherited the Menefee light skin and twinkling big blue eyes. The children did bear a strong resemblance to each other with their full cheeks, cleft chins, and engaging smiles, a genetic gift from their father and grandfather.

"So who's Daniel? He looked kind of unhappy about leaving so soon. Would he be someone you'd like to have over for dinner while we are here?" Jill asked.

"He's just an acquaintance. I might see if he's staying at the local motel. If he isn't, then I guess he was just passing through. If he does come over, he can tell you how we met. If he doesn't, then I guess I could." Claire really wanted to add that their meeting was not all that interesting or exciting, but that would hardly have been the truth, so she thought it best not to talk about it right then.

The children went to bed shortly after dinner. Jay and Jill, who normally would have stayed up late to visit, followed soon after due to their early hour of last minute packing and departure from home that morning. The dog tried to find a new bedtime companion with no luck. Claire really would have liked for him to spend the night somewhere besides on her bed but felt it would not be very hospitable to say the dog came with the guestroom.

As soon as her guests were all settled, she looked through the very thin Hayward phone book for the Snooze Inn. She was not quite sure if she wanted to find Daniel there or not. It took just a moment to get a response since, it was explained to her, there were only two guests at that time. She was connected to Daniel's room, and he answered after one ring.

"It certainly was a surprise to see you this afternoon. I'm sorry you had to rush off so fast."

"I didn't want to appear rude, but I felt that was a family time. You sure do have a couple of cute grandchildren."

"You certainly know how to get on the good side of a grandmother. Anyway, what are you doing back here? I know what you said, but in your line of business I'm not sure if that's the real reason. There was another time when you gave me an unclear reason for why you were in town."

"That time there wasn't much else I could say. This time I'm really on a short vacation. I should have called to make sure you didn't have other plans for Easter."

"It's really no problem. The kids would like to get to know you. They're curious about the mystery man they met. We'd like to have you come for dinner tomorrow night."

"I'd like that. Tomorrow would be great."

"Good, then we'll see you about six o'clock."

"And Claire, just what interesting tourist attractions are there around here?" Of course Claire could not see the big grin on Daniel's face, but she could sense it through the phone.

"There are so many to choose from. You can sit in Taylor's bakery and watch the dough rise. Or you could get a cup of coffee and people watch from a window table at Maude's. For excitement, you could grab a cart and go the wrong way on the one-way aisles at the grocery store. Oh, I know! Lila is in charge of the Easter egg hunt on Saturday. You could volunteer to help her set that up!"

The groan from the other end was impossible to miss. "Thanks, but I might just do some walking and reading. Thanks for tracking me down. I'll see you tomorrow."

Claire had a wonderful time showing off Hayward to her family and an even better time showing off her family to the town. They visited all of the stores along Main Street and happened to meet Scoop Gibson, editor of the local paper, as they left Taylor's bakery. He pointed his camera at them and said the picture of Julie munching on a rabbit-shaped cookie would be great publicity for the Taylors and cheaper than their regular advertisement. Even though Claire had written to Jay and Jill about Farley, she was glad the paranoid World War II veteran wasn't sitting outside the hardware store. Being greeted by the muzzle of a rifle would not give a true picture of the town. Instead as they browsed through the store, they found Farley sitting toward the back, rifle in hand.

"Hello, Farley, this is my son and his family. They're here for Easter weekend." Farley politely tipped his hat and gave a little grunt as he sized up both Jay and Jill. He crooked his finger toward Claire, and she bent over to hear his quiet voice.

"I don't want to scare you, but I think something big is going to happen this weekend. You keep your eyes and ears open and make sure you keep those little ones safe."

Claire whispered back, "Thanks for the warning. I'll be extra careful." She gently patted him on the leg as she turned to join Julie and Jill, who waited patiently. James, on the other hand, had grown tired of waiting and was walking through the store with the aid of his daddy's two hands.

"What was that all about?" Jill asked.

"He was just telling me that something might be happening this weekend. He's right, Lila's big egg hunt is tomorrow, but I doubt that he has it straight in his mind about just what's going to happen. He's always afraid that danger is about to befall the town."

"That must be hard to always think the worst is about to happen," Jill added, shaking her head. "That's pretty sad."

After introducing the family to Bob Simpson, the store's proprietor, the foursome continued up the street. Claire opened the door to the next business, and as they walked through the door of the drugstore, both Julie and James were surprised by the bell ringing above them. The door had barely closed when they were greeted by, "Howdy, folks, what can I do for all of you on this very fine spring day?"

Jill piped in with, "You must be Rudy! Ma has told us all about you."

"Oh my! Now that could be good or it could be bad, but judging by how Claire is one of my steadiest chocolate soda customers, I will hope it's good. Anyone ready for a soda right now? Maybe a malt or a nice strawberry shake? I could even run in back and milk old Bessy for the little one."

Julie's eyes got big. "You mean he keeps a cow right in the store?"

"I think he's just teasing you. That's what Rudy really does the best." Claire made the introductions as Julie was off to see if there was a cow, and James squirmed harder than ever.

The drugstore visit was short, and the tour continued with just a look in Feldman's clothing store. James had had it and would have preferred to be on his own rather than be confined in his father's arms. The bank was the last business on the block, and Claire was ready to turn around and head back. Jay, on the other hand, had spotted the Ford and tractor dealership and decided to walk the half block to take a look. Julie chose to walk hand-in-hand with him while the other three headed back across the square. James was allowed to walk with one hand in Claire's and the other in his mother's. Hardly anything was said as they walked, except for some babbling by James.

As they crossed Oak and headed up Claire's sidewalk, Jill spoke. "I can see why you like this place. It just gives me an unexplainable feeling of peacefulness. I'm so glad you found it." Claire just smiled and nodded. She knew exactly what Jill meant.

After lunch, everyone piled into the car, and Claire directed a tour of the surrounding area. She first took them through Abbot Creek, where Mayor Chester Hayward and his brother, Charles, owned the largest grain elevator in the area. Then they drove around Livonia, the location of the nursing home and hospital. She decided not to draw attention to the funeral home right behind the hospital so as not to cast doubt on the expertise of the hospital staff.

The last town on the tour was Kissock, where the consolidated junior high and high school for all three towns was located. High school sports were very well supported, and the Hayward County Eagles had a very large, very faithful, and very vocal following.

While in Kissock, Claire also pointed out the bowling alley, one of the few recreational facilities in the county. Hayward did have a movie theater that sometimes featured relatively up-to-date films. The other hangout, especially after football or basketball games or on a hot summer day, was the Dairy King drive-in at the west end of Hayward. She explained it was a decent place to go unless the wind was coming from the south and blew in the smell from the gas station across the highway or, worse yet, from the north and the Sewall hog farm that was over the next hill.

Jay had never been the small town boy and had seen enough, but Jill loved the rolling hills that before long would be covered with the signs of the spring planting. Neither Julie nor James seemed to care since they had fallen asleep early in the excursion. When the movement of the car stopped in the alley in back of Claire's house, the children both woke up and soon were filled with energy adults envied.

The tour had taken longer than Claire had planned, and when she realized how late it was, she began to panic. Looking at the pot roast as she took it out of the refrigerator, Claire sighed. "Darn, this is bigger than I thought. I didn't leave enough time to get it done."

"Don't you have a pressure cooker?" Jill asked.

"Never been a fan," Claire responded, shaking her head, "but Jane Dunn does. She lives right across the alley. I'll see if I can borrow it." A quick call was made, and Jay and Jill headed out the back door to get it. "Don't forget to have Jane tell you the directions for the thing," Claire yelled as they walked through the backyard.

"It's okay, Ma. My mom used one all the time," Jill yelled back over her shoulder.

Claire started the preparation that could be done ahead of time. As she was peeling the carrots, she heard a faint noise from the floor by her feet. She looked down to see the dog looking at her longingly. "Don't tell me you like carrots. What self-respecting dog likes vegetables? I don't like begging. It will get you nowhere." It was hard to resist the big brown eyes, but Claire stood firm in her resolve and tried not to look down or listen to the soft whimpers.

With the help of Jill and her expertise with the pressure cooker, dinner was back on schedule. Jay and Julie set the table. Everyone even had time to change clothes, although Claire assured them they looked fine as they were. However, she could not convince herself of it and had a hard time deciding on the perfect thing to wear. A glance at the clock told her to just pick something and get on with it. She was almost finished with her makeup when she heard the doorbell ring. She was quite relieved to know that for the first time in this house there were others who could answer the door. After a quick look in the mirror and a slight smile of approval, she headed downstairs. Jay already had Daniel seated, and Jill was pouring coffee when Claire entered the room. Daniel stood as she crossed the room. They greeted each other with a handshake, as if they were meeting for the first time.

"Ma wouldn't tell us how you two met. She said that she would wait for you to tell the story," Jill said, peering at their guest with anticipation.

"Haven't you told them anything?" Daniel looked at Claire inquiringly. Claire just smiled teasingly and shook her head. She was just as curious about what he was going to say as was the rest of the family. "Well, I was visiting in town and admiring the lovely old homes when I happened to see Claire trip on her steps and drop her groceries. I stopped to help her gather things and make sure she was all right. And that was about all there was to it."

Jay seemed content with the explanation, but a look of disappointment showed on Jill's face. She was expecting something much more interesting or romantic. Claire obviously was also, since she looked at Daniel with disbelief. "And that's all?" she asked.

"Well, they wanted to know how we met and that was it."

"Yes, but then there was a little more to it."

"Would you like to tell the story?" Daniel asked.

"I would, but I'd like to hear your version," Claire responded with a twinkle in her eye. "Like, why were you here in Hayward to begin with?" She crossed her arms and sat back in the wingback chair as if she were getting ready to test him on the details. Jill, on the other hand, moved closer to the edge of her chair thinking she finally was going to hear the exciting part she had been waiting for. Even the dog, sitting faithfully at Claire's feet, was tilting his head back and forth as if trying to understand what was going on.

"Okay, here goes." Daniel paused and took a deep breath. "I was here in Hayward because I am a U.S. Marshall and I was assigned to a couple that was living here under the witness protection program. It was on one of the visits to see them that I really did see Claire drop her groceries. Anyway, it turns out that my two charges were running a Ponzi scheme ..."

Daniel's account was interrupted by loud crying from upstairs, where James had awakened from a nap. "It seems that James doesn't want to be left out of this story. Don't tell any more until I'm back," yelled Jay as he ran up the stairs, one small dog right with him. With barely enough time to change a diaper, the three—Jay, James, and dog—were back for the rest of the story.

"The two of them had figured out there is quite a bit of money here in Hayward, so they concocted this scheme to get the town's leaders to put money into investments that didn't even exist. They were darn good at it too, for they were about to leave town with thousands of dollars. It just so happened that Claire, being the kind-hearted soul that she is, had heard that one of them had a really bad cold and took some chicken soup over the night they were planning to skip out. She walked in on them getting ready to pack up and disappear. So they tied her to a chair. Luckily, I just happened to walk in on them when I suspected things did not look quite right. And through a series of crazy events involving some of the local citizens..."

"And dog," Claire interrupted.

"Right, and dog, we were able to apprehend them as well as some mob guy that was after the two of them. It was quite an evening. Luckily, no one was hurt except for Claire, who did have some bruises and splinters from when the chair she was tied to tipped over." Looking at Claire, Daniel added, "How'd I do?"

"That was a nice summary. But while I work on dinner, tell a bit more about Farley and his ideas about the World War II codebook and Clara and her squirt gun." Julie got to work on a coloring book, and James toddled about looking for interesting new things to put in his mouth while Daniel conveyed a few more details. Then Jill returned to the kitchen to do her part with the pot roast in the pressure cooker.

The serene atmosphere was suddenly disrupted by a loud explosion from the kitchen. Julie, eyes as big as saucers, sat frozen. James dropped the throw pillow he was chewing on and started screaming. Daniel, in reflex action, quickly pulled his gun from his holster under his jacket. Jay for a split second stared at Daniel before they both sprinted into the kitchen. There they found Jill and Claire staring at the ceiling, which was covered with brown splotches and hunks of pot roast. After a few moments of silence, Julie, who had followed her daddy into the kitchen, looked up and said, "Yuck! I'm glad I didn't make that mess!"

Still in a minor state of shock, Jill said, "I guess I kind of forgot how a pressure cooker works. I am so sorry!"

Looking up, Jay shook his head and added, "I wonder how you make gravy with that."

Daniel, still being a newcomer to this group, felt it best not to say anything.

By now only one person was not looking at the ceiling. James had stopped his crying and had crawled into the kitchen with the others. There in almost silence except for an occasional, "Mmmm," he sat busily eating bits of exploded meat off the kitchen floor while the dog was gobbling up his share as fast as he could. This was the tension breaker they all needed, and as they looked at each other and the mess surrounding them, they started laughing. Now the only one not laughing was James, who was removed from the floor and started crying once again.

Considering what the kitchen had looked like fifteen hours prior, it was in pretty good shape Saturday morning. There still were very minor tan stains in a few areas on the ceiling that would scarcely have been detected by someone who had not been looking for them. Everything else had cleaned up quite well thanks to the contributions of everyone, even Julie, who seemed to think this was one of the best times she'd ever had. Even James helped by sitting peacefully in his high chair nibbling Cheerios one at a time, watching as everyone else scurried around him. Of course, the dinner menu was not quite as planned. Claire found some leftovers in the refrigerator to act as a substitute for the exploded beef. Everyone seemed equally as pleased with browned butter over the fluffy mashed potatoes as they would have been with rich brown gravy.

The peacefulness of the breakfast hour was disturbed by a sound that the citizens of Hayward had heard many times before—Lila Hayward, wife of the mayor, and her bullhorn. She was on the town square across the street and was organizing the hiding of the eggs for the town egg hunt. "Come check this out," Claire said to Jay, with James in his arms, and Jill as they walked out onto the big covered front porch. There was Lila dressed to the hilt and ordering around anyone within sight and sound. The outfit for the day was a teal-colored trench coat with matching teal-colored straw hat. Wrapped around the crown of the hat was a band of artificial flowers in spring colors—pinks, yellows, purples. On her feet were teal-colored shoes with high heels that sunk back into the soft, moist soil with every step she took. This made walking quite difficult, but it didn't seem to affect her ability to broadcast orders to her helpers.

"I would guess that is the mayor's wife you told us about," commented Jay. "I thought maybe you were exaggerating, but now I don't think so."

As he spoke, Lila spotted them watching from the porch. If they had been a few seconds faster, Claire would have yelled, "Quick! Inside!" but it was too late.

"Oh, yoo-hoo! I see you," she yelled through the bullhorn, so everyone in the square looked over at Claire's house. With labored steps, Lila walked across the grass to the street, crossed over to Claire's sidewalk, and marched up to the porch. "I'll bet this is your wonderful little family," she said, extending her teal-gloved hand to both Jay and Jill. James hid his face in his daddy's neck, and Julie, who had ventured out on the porch by now, hid behind her mother. "We are just so honored to have you visiting our little town. Aren't you just having a wonderful visit? And, of course, you will be coming to the egg hunt this afternoon, won't you, you little sweetie," she said, looking around Jill at a somewhat fearful Julie. "I know your grandmama would love to come and show off a cutie like you. Well, I must be going and get back to my workers. Sometimes there is just no time out when one is in charge. It was wonderful to meet all of you. Ta-ta!"

As Lila worked her way back to the middle of the square, Jay and Jill stood in a state of disbelief. Finally peeking out from behind Jill, Julie said, "Is the scary lady gone?" Jill just patted her hand reassuringly.

Jay said, "Wow. That was something."

"That's just typical Lila. She does take some getting used to." Claire decided to not continue her comment by adding that she doubted that she would ever get used to Lila. "I do think it would be fun for Julie to go to the egg hunt. With one of you there, she wouldn't be scared."

"I think Lila is right though. I think you should take her and show off part of your wonderful little family," Jill said. "But right now I think we all need to go in and finish our breakfast."

Julie walked across the street to the park with one hand held tightly in her daddy's while in the other hand she carried a basket that Claire had found in the basement and decorated with pink ribbon. Little James was sound asleep upstairs, as was Jill, who took advantage of nap times whenever possible. So Claire decided to sit on the porch and watch the egg hunting event. She had just settled onto the porch swing when she spotted Daniel strolling up the sidewalk. He smiled and waved when they made eye contact. When he reached the porch, Claire moved from the middle of the swing so he could sit with her. They chatted for a while before Claire issued another invitation.

"Would you like to join us at church tomorrow? We're all planning to go."

Daniel was silent for a moment then slowly replied, "No thank you." He paused again before adding, "Church and I parted ways quite a few years ago." Claire didn't say anything mainly because she didn't quite know what to say. After a long, uncomfortable silence, he spoke again. "We had a son."

Claire's curiosity was really piqued now with the word *we*. Daniel continued, "Davy was only five when he was diagnosed with leukemia. Doctors did what they could but said what we really needed was some kind of a miracle. Carol and I had been faithful church members, and we continued to be as we prayed for Davy and for a healing miracle. But it didn't happen, and Davy died three weeks before his sixth birthday. Carol was devastated. We both were. She said that I had let him down because I had not prayed hard enough. She said that God had let Davy down. I began to feel that way too. Instead of trying to be supportive of each other, we started to blame each other for everything in our lives that was not perfect. We ended up getting a divorce, and I ended up angry and disillusioned with God for letting my sweet, innocent son suffer. I have not been back in a church since then."

Claire was so stunned with what she had just heard that she truly did not know what to say. She knew how terrible she felt when her husband had died, but he was an adult who had led a good life. What appropriate words could be offered for the loss of a child, even if it happened many years ago? And then to lose a spouse too. Finally, she said the only words she felt might be appropriate. "Oh, Daniel, I am so sorry. I had no idea." She went on with the standard words of sympathy she was sure he had heard many times before. Then, never being one afraid of going out on a limb, she asked, "Why did you pick Easter week to come see me?"

"I don't know. It just seemed like a pleasant time to visit. And remember? You invited me to come back to see how lovely Hayward is in the springtime."

Yes, Claire did remember those words she had said right before Daniel had left Hayward following his arrest of the two embezzlers. Afterwards, she had thought it was a pretty silly thing to say since she herself had yet to be in Iowa during the spring, but now she was glad. She thought for a moment before continuing with her first train of thought. "I wonder if maybe deep down inside you thought Easter might be a time to get reacquainted with a church and this would be a friendly place to start. You know the minister who is very nonjudgmental, and you know some of the congregation. Think about coming tomorrow, please. If you don't feel comfortable, you don't ever have to go again." Claire was careful with her choice of words. She made sure to say "go again" rather than "come again" to leave the door open for future visits to Hayward if not to church.

"I don't know, Claire."

"What harm could it do? Come see some familiar faces, listen to some nice music, spend a little more time with my family." After she said that, she hoped she was not being too pushy. "Then you could come have Easter dinner with us. You are very welcome."

"I'll think about it, but I'm not making any promises. I did promise the Simpsons I would have dinner with them. I saw Bob at the store, and he wouldn't take no for an answer. He said it would be good for Farley to have some company."

The timing of their conversation was perfect, for it was just then that Julie came bounding up the steps. "Look, Gram! Look at all the stuff I got!" Claire lifted her onto the swing between Daniel and her, and the three of them examined the goods.

"Wow, did you leave anything for the other children?" Daniel asked.

"Oh, of course I did, but I was really good at finding things. Would you like some of my candy?"

"How nice of you! What would you like me to take?"

"I don't know what you like. You get to pick."

Claire smiled as she watched Daniel joke with Julie as he rummaged through the basket to make his selection. Then Julie turned to Claire and made her the same offer.

Everyone was dressed in their finest clothes as they headed up the steps of the old Methodist church at the north end of the square. The regular church members were there in addition to those whose attendance was too often saved for those special times like Christmas and Easter. Waiting at the bottom of the stairs was Daniel, who looked at Claire with a somewhat uneasy smile on his face. Claire walked up to him, put her arm through his, and quietly said, "I'm glad you came. So is Julie. She asked if you were going to be here."

Claire led the way with Daniel in tow. She usually sat near the front but felt a seat closer to the back would be more comfortable for all of her guests. She chose an area by the aisle so that James could be taken into the nursery if he decided he had enough church for one day. She also wondered if Daniel might at some point have those same feelings.

The church service was a pretty typical Easter service—lilies lined up along the front of the church; the choir in their newly cleaned robes, with petite Grace Carlson leading with precise guidance; less-than-petite Phoebe Peoples, the organist, pounding out the wonderful hymns in her typically inconsistent cadence; and Reverend Bill Carlson thoroughly enjoying being able to deliver his sermon to a packed house. Claire had enjoyed this church and Reverend Carlson since she had first moved to Hayward last June. She found his sermons meaningful and inspiring. But, as much as she hated to admit it, there was something else about coming to this church that always drew her attention. She was glad she now was sitting toward the back since it gave her better viewing of many of the other churchgoers.

She scanned the congregation, but her target was a bit harder to spot since many of the ladies uncharacteristically were wearing hats for this special Sunday. There was a mix of pillboxes as well as hats with small and wide brims, but they were all tasteful and rather conservative compared to what Claire was sure she was going to find. Then her eyes rested on a bright pink hat with a brim so wide that it was hard to tell who, if anyone, was under it. Claire could hardly wait until the end of the service so she could get a 360-degree view.

After the singing of the last hymn, the congregation began to leave slowly. Jay and Julie rummaged around gathering the paraphernalia they had taken that magically had kept the children's attention throughout the entire service. Claire was glad since this extra time let more people exit. And then she saw it—the whole picture! There was the huge pink hat, adorned in the front with a gigantic lighter pink satin bow that must have added to the weight of the hat. The wearer had a pink suit with a pink satin collar that matched the bow. "Now that is a pretty suit," Claire said, talking to herself as she frequently did, but luckily no one seemed to hear her. But as the suit continued toward the door, Claire got a view of the back where the silk collar continued widely over the shoulders and draped into a hideously massive bow at the waistline with tails that continued almost to the back of the wearer's knees. The bow was held in place by a large, garish rhinestone pin.

"Wow, that is quite the outfit!" Julie whispered into Claire's ear. "Who is that? I can't even see a face." Just then the hat and head tilted back to reveal Lila Hayward. "Oh, I should have guessed."

Lila glanced their way, waved, and then made her way toward them while tipping her head back so she could see where she was going and see who she was talking to. "It is so nice that you all could visit our little church. Isn't it just charming, and Bill was just as inspirational as usual." Then looking at Daniel, she introduced herself. "I don't believe you know me. I'm Lila Hayward, wife of the mayor of our fair town." Daniel took Lila's extended hand and introduced himself with nothing more than a name. Lila looked at him more closely. "You do look rather familiar. Have we met?"

"I was in Hayward last month on business, and I believe that we did meet briefly at Claire's house one morning."

"Oh, that's right. You are our little Claire's friend. It is delightful to see you again. Well, I must run. My people are waiting. May all of you have a wonderful Easter!"

"Her people? What did she mean by that?" whispered Jay.

"Who knows. Come on, we can go now." Claire led the way out and introduced her family to Bill and Grace Carlson. She also would have reintroduced Daniel, but they remembered him from his last visit. As the six of them descended the steps, they heard a voice.

"It's him. I told you it was him, but did you believe me? No one ever believes me." As they got to the bottom step, Clara Andrews was excitedly waiting for Daniel. "Hey G man, did you bring your gun? I'd like to see it."

"Hello, Clara. No, I'm on vacation, so I didn't bring any weapons."

"Drat! I don't think that's very smart. You never know what kind of trouble you might run into, especially in this town with hardly a lawman around. Well, I'm always prepared," Clara stated emphatically as she pulled her squirt gun out of her purse. "And it's loaded and ready too."

"That's good. Between you and Farley Simpson, this town is in good hands."

"Him! Don't get me started on that old coot. He couldn't protect himself from his own shadow!"

"Okay, Mother, that's enough. It is good to see you again, Mr. Chambers. I heard from the Simpsons that you were here for a little visit," said Aaron Andrews, Clara's son. Claire introduced her family to Aaron, his wife, Meredith, and Clara. "We had better be going. Our ham will be done before we get home if we visit any longer," Aaron said as Meredith turned Clara around and they headed down the sidewalk toward home.

"I'd better be heading for the Simpsons' home too," said Daniel. "Then I had better hit the road. It was great to see you again, Claire, and to meet all of you. Don't eat your Easter candy all at once, Julie," he said, bending over to her eye level. "I'll call you sometime when I'm in the area, Claire." He took her hand and shook it, just as he had the month before. Claire would have liked a little something more than a handshake, but with her family standing right there, and in front of a church besides, that handshake was probably the best way to say good-bye—this time.

THREE

The town election followed two weeks after Easter, and since this was Claire's first Hayward election, she was more interested in the politics of the mayoral selection than the rest of the town. It was slightly more exciting considering there were two candidates instead of just one, as frequently had been the case. One, of course, was the current mayor, Chester Hayward. The other was William Swan, who had agreed to have his name on the ballot only because Chester had talked him into it. William had agreed with Chester that in a democratic republic the voters should have a choice of candidates. However, he had made it perfectly clear that he did not want the job and would not serve should he, by some fluke, actually be elected.

Just to make sure that he put the best appearance forth during his campaign, Chester had done what he always did at election time. He had sent Lila out of town, this time to visit relatives in New Jersey. He loved his wife but was aware that she often irritated some constituents. Although most people knew why she really was gone, he had put a more positive spin on it by telling folks that Lila had gone to New York to check out the latest fashions.

Claire liked William, who had been the agent who had listed the house she had purchased the previous June, and felt he would make a good mayor and a fine representative of the town. Being the town's attorney she felt he had the knowledge about the workings of the local government. However, she respected his statement about not really wanting the job and somewhat reluctantly cast her vote for the incumbent.

The election had gone as most had predicted although, much to Chester's chagrin and William's surprise, William had received three dozen votes. Chester secretly attributed this to the fact that there had been some complaints about having the annual Easter egg hunt in the town square rather than in the city park where it traditionally was held. "Well, you can't please all of the people all of the time," he had told himself.

The Tuesday morning quilting group that met at the Methodist church usually did more gossiping, which they liked to think of as sharing information, than quilting.

"I can't believe that someone has already moved into Lois Teller's house. It's almost like living next to a hotel," stated Francine Simpson, wife of Bob Simpson of the hardware store.

"Whoever they are couldn't be as bad as the Brocks or whatever their real names were. Have you met the new people yet?" asked Phoebe Peoples.

Meredith Andrews jumped right into the conversation. "We did. It's not a they. It's a she, and she came over and introduced herself. She said she stopped by your place, Francine, but you weren't home. Her name is Helen something or other."

Clara offered her opinion of the town's newcomer. "Her name is Helen Crook because she is one, you know." Claire was not surprised to hear this comment since that had been Clara's opinion of Claire when she came to Hayward. And the same thing had been repeated over and over about the Brocks. Unfortunately, the latter did prove to be true, and Clara was not about to let anyone forget it. "I know a crook when I see one. A lot of people in this town still have their money thanks to me."

Meredith normally would have tried to curb her mother-in-law's comments, but she was too excited to pass on what she had learned. "She is some kind of a college professor on leave to do some writing or research or something. She picked Hayward because she wanted a quiet place without distractions."

"I wonder what Lila will think when she gets back and discovers she has a new neighbor," said Jane Dunn, Claire's backyard neighbor and wife of the postmaster. Jane was doing very little quilting since she was holding a nursing baby Jessica.

"One thing for sure, she couldn't dislike her any more than she did the Brocks," replied Ellen Hornsby, wife of Bud, the owner of the Ford dealership. "When is she due back from New Jersey, does anyone know?"

"I thought she might be back by now," answered Francine Simpson. "I'm sure we will all hear about everything that she did and probably more than once."

The timing could not have been more perfect if it had been rehearsed, for who should come down the steps at that very minute but Lila herself. Lila never entered a room in an unobtrusive manner but did it with the flamboyance of a toreador. Claire found these entrances silly, but the good thing was that Lila was always wearing some kind of hat. Claire marveled that she had never seen the same hat on Lila more than once and remembered how deep that special hat closet in the mayor's house was. Today's choice was shaped similarly to what most men in Hayward would wear, if they were to wear a hat, but the difference was that hers was made of baby blue straw. The way it sat extremely low on her forehead made it look as if it were sized for a man.

Many of the ladies started looking at their watches, and Claire had the same thought. She wondered how close it was to noon, their usual ending time. Unfortunately, it was only a quarter to twelve, so she figured for at least fifteen minutes they all would be updated on too many details of Lila's trip. She promised herself that she would try to look interested and not let her eyes glaze over like many did when Lila carried on.

"Oh girls, it was just amazing!" Lila began with a wide sweeping motion of both arms. "The clothes, the food, the culture! I just cannot begin to describe it all to you."

Claire whispered a little "thank goodness" and imagined that the others were having similar thoughts. Lila droned on a few minutes raving about the sights and sounds of the big city. Some of what she mentioned reminded Claire of exactly what she had wanted to get away from and why she had moved to Hayward.

"But here is the most exciting part. On the East Coast, couples are starting to hire wedding planners who do all the planning, so they hardly have to do a thing themselves. Now doesn't that sound like an absolutely marvelous idea? Think back to your own wedding and how you could have enjoyed it more if you had not had to deal with all the many details."

She paused a moment as if giving everyone time to reflect on what she had just assumed. Claire looked around the group and had the feeling that most of them were thinking the same thing—there was not a lot of planning when these women had gotten married—but no one seemed to offer that opinion. No one, of course, but Clara.

"What do you mean—many, many details? You get a cake, you make some punch, you buy a bag of nuts. And then you throw some rice. Doesn't sound like a lot of planning goes into that!"

Lila went on as if she had not heard Clara or else she was choosing to ignore her. "I think what this town needs is a wedding planner. And I think I am the perfect one to do the job. Oh, I am so excited. I think I should start right away."

Clara again piped up. "So who's getting married anyway? Don't you kind of need a bride and groom?"

Lila paused for a few seconds as if pondering that question. "Well, I'll just have to find the perfect couple. When I do, they will be more than happy to make use of my services."

Francine totally changed the subject when she asked, "Lila, did you know you have a new neighbor in Lois's house?"

Lila found a chair and quickly sat down. "Oh dear, I hope it's not going to be a repeat of Mike and Misty or Missy or whatever her name was. That was a disaster! Whatever is happening to the neighborhood?"

"You might like her. You should go meet her and not pass judgment without even giving her a chance," added Meredith.

"You're right. It's my duty as first lady of Hayward to welcome our newcomers with open arms."

With that comment and the church clock striking twelve, the group broke up.

Bruce "Scoop" Gibson got to the new tenant faster than Lila did and put an article about her in his local weekly newspaper. Helen Evans was a sociology professor at the University of Chicago. She was on sabbatical, researching and writing a book comparing urban to rural life. She was divorced and had no children. She liked to read, do gourmet cooking, and work crossword puzzles. She preferred classical music. Also, although she had none with her, she said she had a collection of modern art pieces by a variety of contemporary artists and thought she might miss the opportunities she had in Chicago to go to exhibits at different galleries. She added that so far she had enjoyed the peacefulness of Hayward and didn't miss the noise of the city traffic.

People read about the newcomer with interest and varied opinions. Many thought it didn't sound as if she fit in too well. Others were somewhat skeptical of someone else claiming to be from Chicago since that was what Mike and Missy Brock also had claimed. Some of the women were curious about the gourmet cooking part and wondered how well she would like their more standard All-American, heartland meat and potatoes fare. But the person who was the most curious about Helen was her neighbor, who was intrigued with the fact that she was divorced and thought perhaps she might be interested in finding a new husband.

The last time Lila had knocked on that door she had brought some of her best gladiolas to welcome her new neighbors. The reception she got was definitely less than cordial, and the gift of the flowers was received more like it was a burden to deal with rather than a colorful accent for the home. This time she arrived bearing an armful of lilacs from the large bushes that grew across the back fence of Mayor Hayward's backyard. Lila always assumed everyone was pleased to see her, and she expected that this time she would be warmly welcomed at 203 Oak Street. When the door opened, she was greeted by a smile and an invitation to come in.

Lila judged Helen to be in her mid to late forties. She found her to be friendly and easy to talk to, which, from Lila's perspective, meant that Helen did a lot of listening while Lila talked. The fact that Helen smiled and nodded in response to many of Lila's comments helped to move her up Lila's list of possible best friends. But there was one subject Lila did want to let Helen talk about, and that was her marital status and current romantic interests. When Helen said there were none, Lila was somewhat disappointed since apparently there was no wedding in this woman's future that would need planning assistance. Lila was not to be deterred and baited her further.

"I find great comfort in my happy marriage. Chester is a good provider, and he takes good care of me. I know in our sunset years we'll be there for each other, and that is a very comforting thought. Do you think you would ever get married again?"

Helen thought for a moment before again nodding in response. "I might, but it would have to be to a special man. I've always been in favor of good, solid marriages."

This time it was Lila's turn to smile and nod. Excited by Helen's comments about marriage, she hurried home while mentally starting a list of "eligibles." Helen was first on the list. Claire and her lawman were next, and for lack of his real name, she referred to him as only as "Marshall." "There's that darling Ronnie who works with his uncle in the drugstore. Rudy should go on the list too. Everyone loves Rudy! That Deputy Taylor has the most beautiful big brown eyes I've ever seen. If I were a few years younger, I might go after him myself," she said aloud, momentarily drifting off in thought.

"Oh, and of course there's the sheriff himself. Every woman likes a man in uniform.

"Cliff Wilkens, that sweet custodian at the school, would be a solid catch. What woman would not like to have her own handyman? And I can't forget John Brook. My, that man does keep in shape. It must be all that practicing with his high school teams that does it." Lila sighed, again with a faraway look in her eye.

By the time Lila reached her door, she was excited about the names she had thought of so far. She hurried to the kitchen, where she grabbed paper and pencil and quickly began to write.

Then she started to list eligible women. Her mind raced so fast her hand could hardly keep up as her list of possible future clients grew in front of her eyes.

Claire had just reached the door of the drugstore when a young redhead came storming out, mumbling something under her breath about someone being a "dumb jerk." Claire didn't recognize her and wondered if she might be the latest newcomer, Helen Evans. She couldn't imagine that Rudy, the pharmacist, or Ronnie, finishing his pharmacist internship with his uncle, would raise such ire in anyone. In fact, coming to the drugstore always made her feel good since she was greeted with warm sincerity. She decided it was best not to ask what caused that uproar, so she entered to the sound of the bell tinkling over the door and acted as if nothing unusual had happened.

"Hey, kiddo, what are you up to?" shouted Rudy from the back of the store at the pharmacy department.

"Not much, Rudy. I just came to pick up a few things."

"Make sure you look around. You know what I say, 'You don't always know what you need until you see it.'"

Claire picked up a few extra items that were not on her original list and went to pay for them when another unfamiliar person came in and headed for a seat at the soda fountain. Rudy hurried to help Claire, speaking briefly to the other person as he passed by. He had barely reached Claire when Ronnie appeared at the soda fountain to take the new person's order. In typical fashion, Ronnie introduced himself and welcomed her to the store. In the conversation that followed, Claire heard the woman was Helen Evans and decided to introduce herself. Claire explained that she had moved to Hayward less than a year ago and how everyone was very interested in her.

"I have noticed that," responded Helen. "I'm not sure that people trust me."

"That might take some time. Last summer a couple moved into your house and tried to swindle many people out of quite a bit of money. So I think people are just being more cautious right now."

"I can understand that, but I want to learn about the people and their way of life. It's research for a book I am writing. How long have you lived here?"

Claire's mind raced back to last June when she had told her story over and over and told an abbreviated version to Helen. She finished by saying she had never once regretted her decision.

"That took lots of courage. I thought I was being brave making this move for just a short time. I'm glad you've enjoyed it. It does seem a little…"—Helen paused—"quiet here. But then that really is what I am looking for as a contrast to big, busy city life."

"I'm sure that you'll find pros and cons, but I'll bet you will enjoy your time here. You might even want to stay longer."

Claire was just leaving when she ran into Meredith and Clara. Claire and Meredith visited briefly while Clara headed directly to the soda fountain. She sat on one of the red stools, plopping her purse down on the counter. She studied the customer at the other end of the counter, eying her from head to toe. "Humphf!" she said, climbing off her stool and striding back to where her daughter-in-law was still talking.

"She's a crook, I tell you! What are we going to do about it?" Clara demanded.

"Quiet, Mother. You say that about every stranger, and that is just silly."

"Silly, shmilly! What a short memory you have! Don't you remember those last two? Everyone said I was wrong about them, but look who turned out to be right."

"Maybe so, but you called Claire a crook too, and you were wrong about her."

"That remains to be seen." Clara scoffed, staring at Claire through squinting eyes. "Anyway, we need to check on her. You need to call your G-man boyfriend and see if she has a rap sheet."

"That's ridiculous, Mother. Claire isn't going to check up on anyone."

Claire left the drugstore, realizing that even if she did want to do some snooping she did not know how to get in touch with Daniel. He had always made the first contact.

That evening it was almost as if Daniel had heard Claire's earlier comment. She was reading on the couch with Lucky curled up at her feet. ("Lucky" had won the dog naming contest after it was discussed how the little pooch was very lucky to have been found, lucky to be allowed to sleep on the bed, lucky to be taken on regular walks, and lucky to have come into a household partial to dogs.) When the phone rang, Claire was so engrossed in the book she was reluctant even to answer the phone, but the constant ringing was more aggravating than being torn away from the story. When she heard Daniel's voice, she tossed the book aside as if it were the annoyance instead. When he started the conversation by saying he was in the area consulting with a client and wondered if he could drop by for a brief visit, her feet were on the floor and she was headed upstairs to change clothes almost before she hung up the phone.

While she quickly selected something more presentable, she thought about the few words he had spoken, "I am in the area checking on a client." Her thoughts rushed back to what Clara had emphatically stated earlier that afternoon and wondered if maybe she was right about Helen. She shook her head as if trying to rid her mind of the idea.

"Maybe I could at least ask," she said to herself as she brushed her hair. "The worst would be that he could tell me what he knows is classified information."

Lucky's barking alerted her to someone at the door before the doorbell even rang. "I guess no one will sneak up on me," Claire said with some degree of comfort. She added a touch of lipstick before running down the stairs. She greeted Daniel and motioned him toward the couch, where she sat close enough to him that if their hands were accidentally to touch in the space between them it would not seem too premeditated.

At first the discussion was chitchat that would have gone on between friends. When there was an uncomfortable pause in their exchange, Claire felt obligated to say something, so she jumped in with the discussion from earlier in the day. "You mentioned you were visiting a client in the area. I know your business involves secrecy and privacy, and I really don't want to pry. However, if I promise not to ask anymore about this, could you tell me if your client is within a twenty-mile radius of my house?"

Daniel looked very seriously at her while he weighed his answer. "Just how many people do you know within that area?"

Claire smiled. "Do you want an exact number? Give me a moment. If I don't count my acquaintances here in Hayward, I probably know no more than ten."

"Just between you, me, Lucky, and no one else, none of my charges are in that area."

"Some people are wondering about Helen Evans."

Daniel looked at Claire inquiringly. "Who?"

"She moved into the Brocks'—I mean the Canellas'—old house. People are wondering if that residence is becoming housing for the witness protection program."

"I don't think anyone needs to worry about that. Once a cover is blown, the chances of using the same home, or even the same small town, are very slim."

Claire was relieved to hear that but knew she could not pass on the information because of Daniel's confidentiality agreement. She also knew that even if she could pass on what she had just learned, she would never be able to convince Clara.

Daniel and Claire continued their casual conversation, and then he took it back to Easter Sunday. "I am glad that you encouraged me to join you at church on Easter. I enjoyed Reverend Carlson's sermon and the service. I was afraid it would make me feel uncomfortable, and it did at first, but as it went on I felt more at ease. I have spent quite a bit of time since then thinking about Davy's illness and death and think maybe it's time to put closure on it in a better way than what I did before."

Claire looked at him with a look of perplexity. He continued, not looking at her but gazing straight ahead as if mentally he was in a different time and place. "I felt that God had let us down when Davy died, but Carol was extremely distraught. I think she just had to blame someone. So I became her target, and I think she made me think maybe she was right. Maybe I had not prayed enough, maybe my faith was not strong enough, and maybe God was mad at me. Then I felt any God that would take his anger against me out on a defenseless child was not the kind of God I wanted. So I walked away. I walked away from the church, and I walked away from believing.

"But being in church on Easter was like opening a window again. I'm not sure that the entire door is open yet, but I figure starting with that window is a good beginning." He turned his head toward Claire. She smiled at him as she reached for his hand. He squeezed it and smiled back.

FOUR

Claire was curious, and somewhat uneasy, about the mysterious phone call that she had just received from Grace Carlson asking Claire to meet her at church in fifteen minutes. She had a foreboding feeling that made her not want to go, but she had agreed. On the way, she was joined by Ellen Hornsby and Vernina Graves, wife of Brian from the grocery store. Each had received the same call, and neither had any idea about the urgency. They were about to ascend the steps when they heard a "yoo-hoo." They turned to see Jane Dunn with baby Jessica tucked snuggly under arm, hurrying to catch up.

"Did you all get a phone call from Reverend Carlson?"

"I did," replied Ellen.

"Mine was from Grace and so was Claire's, don't you know," added Vernina.

"Any idea what's going on?" continued Jane.

The others all shook their heads. When they reached the door they paused, looked at each other apprehensively, and then entered the peaceful sanctity of the church. Usually on weekdays meetings were held in the fellowship area, one of the classrooms, or Reverend Carlson's office in the adjoining parsonage. This day he and Grace were waiting for the ladies in the sanctuary.

"This can't be good," whispered Jane as they slowly walked down the center aisle.

"Please, have a seat," said Bill, motioning toward the front pew. "Thank you all for coming on such short notice. I'm sure you're wondering why you were called, so I'll get right to the point. About an hour ago I received a frantic call from Sam Peterson."

Right away Claire was in the dark, having no idea who Sam Peterson was. Since everyone else apparently knew him, Bill had continued with his explanation. "He told me that his new hired helper on his farm was in a very serious automobile accident this morning and is in critical condition in Des Moines."

The four ladies all offered compassionate comments but still wondered what that had to do with them. Claire thought if he had died in the accident, maybe they would have been asked to help organize a reception for the funeral, but that was not the case.

Bill continued, "There's a bit more to the situation, and that's where you four come in, we hope." Bill took a deep breath. "The injured man is a widower and has children who are temporarily without a caretaker. After Sam called, Grace and I sat down to think of the best short-term solution. We prayed about it, and you four neighbors will be, we hope, the answers to our prayers." He stopped talking for a moment to let what he had said sink in.

"We would like each of you to consider taking in the siblings until their father has recovered. We thought with your being neighbors, the children would be able to see each other often, walk to school together, play in your yards, and things like that. We think you might have room in your houses for the children. We realize that except for Claire you already have three children and adding to that might be a challenge, but please consider it."

There were moments of silence. Claire broke the stillness by asking, "Are there other relatives who could take the children?"

"I asked that too. As far as Sam knows, there is no one else. They had been living with a grandmother somewhere in Kentucky, but she died not too long ago, causing them to lose the place they were living. The family moved here just a few weeks ago when Tom—that's the father's name—learned through some acquaintance that Sam was looking for help. They have been living in that old house on his property."

Ellen was the first to respond. "We could certainly help out. What's one more mouth to feed, anyway?"

"Thank you, Ellen, but it might be more than one more," explained Grace.

The four looked at each other and asked almost in unison, "How many are there?"

"Eight."

"Eight!" they responded in amazement.

"So that would mean we each would get two?" questioned Jane.

"That's right. We felt that splitting them up any more would be even more traumatic. So we thought if we kept them together in pairs it would be more comforting."

"What ages are we talking about?" asked Claire, hoping that teenagers would not be in her future. Going through those years three times was enough.

Grace took over with the rationalization of the plan. "There are six boys and two girls. Sam said that from what their father had told him the girls, who are twelve and five, had been very close to their grandmother after their mother died. So we thought Claire has that warm, grandmotherly manner that the girls could relate to."

I think that's just a way of saying that I am the oldest of the group, thought Claire.

Grace continued. "Two boys are ten and eleven. We thought that Steve would be a good role model for them, and Katie hopefully is old enough to understand the importance of having these two added to your home. Johnny can have some older companions too. Two more boys are seven and eight, and Jane was so good with her Cub Scout den we thought that would be a good match."

Thank goodness Bill and Grace forgot that I took over Jane's den before Jessica was born. I don't think I have the energy for two boys that age, Claire reflected.

Vernina sat in anticipation of what was to come. "That leaves two more and this was the hardest," continued Grace. "Then Bill remembered how Vernina had said more than once she always wanted to see what it would be like to have twins. So we'd like to give you that chance."

"How old are these twins?" Vernina asked, almost afraid of the answer.

"They are not quite two," Grace replied.

"Wow!" exclaimed Vernina. Then she added, "But that has always been one of my favorite ages, don't you know."

"I have been trying to keep track of all this. If I got it right, the kids are from twelve to two. Someone was sure busy."

"According to Sam, the twins have been the hardest for their father because their mother died giving birth. The other kids are in school during the day, but he didn't know what to do with the littlest ones. Edith, Sam's wife, had agreed to watch them until the older kids get home from school until the school year is over. Then the older kids would be in charge."

Bill came back into the conversation. "Think about it. Pray about it. Let me know as soon as possible because these children will need somewhere to go starting today."

"I don't need any more time. I'll do it," volunteered Claire, and the others voiced agreement. "But in a case like this, wouldn't child welfare want to be involved?"

"Oh, they probably would, but I think that right now it's better if they don't know. We need an immediate solution, and government red tape would only complicate things. Besides, where would they find better families than all of yours? And where would they find a foster family that would take eight children?"

As they left the church, Vernina was the first to speak. "I'm not too sure about this, but I didn't know if it would have been harder to say no to God or to Bill." The others nodded in agreement.

Claire looked at her watch. "I guess I'll go home and think about having guests. I'm nervous about this, but it's helpful to know we're all in this together."

"Pushovers, one and all," said Jane. They all laughed as they headed home.

At the end of school, the McRoberts children, Sarah, Matthew, Mark, Luke, John, and Abigail, gathered in the school library and were told about their father's accident. It had been decided that the bad news would not be delivered by the principal, Pearl Hatcher, whose tact and deskside manner left much to be desired. Instead Theresa Stevens, the school secretary who had taken a personal interest in each one since they enrolled, would tell the children. Claire watched with a heavy heart as the children clung to each other for support. She marveled at how they looked like siblings with red hair, huge blue eyes, and faces that were covered not only with freckles but also now with tears.

The temporary families were introduced and went with the children back to the farmhouse to pick up clothes and some personal "comfort" items. The foster moms were surprised to see how small the house was and how crowded the conditions were. At the same time, they noticed how clean and neat everything looked. Claire wondered how Mr. McRoberts could possibly get eight children off for the day and leave everything in the house looking as if the maid had just been there.

Picking clothes for each child was simple since there were not many. The older children's clothes were in relatively good shape, while those of the younger siblings were well into the multiple hand-me-down state. But all the clothes were clean. Claire's older charge, Sarah, chose a diary to bring with her. Little Abigail, who everyone called Abby, picked a small, pink velvet pillow with a red satin heart and a teddy bear that was so worn it would have been unrecognizable to anyone outside the family.

The ride back to Claire's house was long and silent. Claire made a few comments when they first got into her car, and the car joined in the caravan headed back to Hayward. However, she soon decided it was best to leave the girls in the privacy of their own thoughts. Sarah was much more pensive and sat with her eyes, which sometimes brimmed with tears, straight forward. Abby, on the other hand, repeatedly rose to her knees to check to make sure that the cars carrying her brothers were still in sight. She would offer a slight smile and wave.

When the convoy got to town, all the cars pulled into the alley in back of the houses. It had been decided this would allow the children to see who was going where and how close they would be to each other. By this time, the twins were much more relaxed, and it took the firm hand of Sarah and the oldest brother, Matthew, to keep them under control as they were unloaded. Claire even wondered if it would have been a better idea to have placed Sarah with the twins. But as Sarah made a mad dash to keep one of the little speedsters from high-tailing it down the alley, she was very glad that she was not in Vernina's shoes—which she hoped were running shoes. Maggie, Libby, and Ryan all came out to help corral the dynamite duo and escort them into the house.

Matthew, with Mark right at his side, and Sarah watched as the rest of the children headed into the houses. They reminded Claire of shepherds making sure that all of their lambs had been safely accounted for. Then the three of them sadly went to their appointed destinations. Abby was way ahead of Claire and Sarah as they walked through the backyard toward the door, where they were greeted by one small dog that wagged so hard and fast his long feathery tail was a white blur.

"This is Lucky," Claire said as she unsuccessfully tried to keep the dog from jumping on the girls. "He won't hurt you. He just wants to get to know you, and he hasn't learned very good manners yet." Sarah bent over to pet the dog, but Abby sat right on the floor and invited Lucky into her lap. As she tried to put her arms around him, he gave her face a couple of good licks.

"You should have called him Licky instead of Lucky," giggled Abby.

As Lucky and Abby continued to get acquainted, Claire tried to make the girls feel more at home. "I have plenty of room, but I don't know if it will be better for you each to have your own room or if you two would rather share a room."

Sarah, who previously had spoken only reassuring words to her brothers, now looked at Claire in disbelief. "You must be kidding!" Claire wasn't sure if she had said something wrong and insulted Sarah at the prospect of separating the two sisters when Sarah quickly continued, "You mean I could have a room all to myself and wouldn't have to share a bed or anything?"

"That's exactly what I mean, but would Abby be scared by herself?"

"Well,"—Sarah paused as if to postpone giving an answer—"I guess we could ask her. One thing you will find out about Abby is once she gets to know you she will tell you exactly what she thinks."

Claire helped the girls carry their few belongings upstairs and led them to the bedrooms. "You have some choices to make. There are three rooms here all ready for company. You can use whichever ones you like. You two talk it over while I get us a snack. How do you feel about cookies and milk?

"Yes, ma'am, that would be fine," replied Sarah, and after a nudge in the back, Abby, who was taking in the sight of the three rooms, agreed.

When Claire returned, the girls had made their decisions and were already lying on the beds of choice. Or rather Abby was bouncing on hers. Claire's first inclination was to ask her to stop bouncing, but she decided not to say anything and let her have a few moments of lighthearted fun, getting her mind off of why she was even on that bed. The clothes that had been folded into grocery bags were still sitting in the hall, and Claire asked the girls if they would like to hang them up and put some of their things in the drawers.

"Yes, ma'am, that would be fine," replied Sarah, again picking up her bag and carrying it into her room.

"And how about you, Abby?"

"No, they're fine in the bag."

"You wouldn't like to hang them up in the closet or put them in a drawer?"

"No, there ain't enough to bother with," she explained, still bouncing.

"Okay, but if you change your mind, Sarah or I could help you. Now, how about those cookies?"

On her last bounce, Abby was off the bed and headed toward the stairs, where Sarah joined her. Together they bounded down the stairs to the kitchen. As the girls sat eating, Claire had the urge to talk about kitchen rules but managed to curb that idea until a later time. She had the feeling Sarah wouldn't have a problem handling rules but was not so sure about Abby. Just being five years old made her the more likely candidate for rules violations. Claire imagined it would be an interesting time.

In typical fashion, word of the McRoberts family had spread. Under the guidance of Betty Nutting, whose house was in the middle of the other four, a dinner had been assembled for the children so they could be together for the first meal since being separated. The host families also were invited. One of those who contributed to the meal was Helen Evans, who stayed long enough to meet Betty and the other women. She also took advantage of Betty's offer to take a self-guided tour through the house. The turreted house had a very unique look from the outside, and people were always curious about just how the house was laid out on the inside.

Helen's contribution was the most luscious, tempting chocolate cake Claire had ever seen. "Oh great! One more woman who knows more about cooking than I do," mumbled Claire when she saw the cake. But that was only one of the yummy-looking dishes that were put out on the Nuttings' dining room table—fried chicken, homemade breads and rolls, potato salad, macaroni salad, fruit salad, and, of course, Jell-O salads. In addition to the chocolate cake, there was an apple pie and dozens of different cookies. Three kinds of ice cream, donated by Bryan Graves from the market, were waiting in the freezer.

The children roamed around the table surveying the spread. John, the eight-year-old who was assigned to the Dunns, looked at the table in wide-eyed amazement. "Is the whole town coming to dinner?"

"No, honey, just you and your new friends," replied Betty, gently placing an arm around his shoulder.

"I never seen so much food in my whole life!" John said, shaking his head. "I don't think I can eat that much."

Betty chuckled. "No one expects you to. We just wanted to make sure that there would be something you liked."

"But will there still be food tomorrow?" A fearful look came over his face.

Betty reassured him that indeed there would be and the day after tomorrow and the day after that. With that a slight smile returned to John's freckled face.

Betty's husband, Leonard, the local doctor, had called the hospital to get an update on Tom McRoberts. He gathered Sarah and the two oldest sons, Matthew and Mark, and updated them. He was as honest as he could be without trying to scare them. He also tried to be optimistic while still trying not to give false hope. Betty complimented him on his discretion. He responded with, "It was kind of like saying there possibly might be a rainbow just around the corner while it's still raining so hard you can't even see anything out the window."

Miraculously no food was spilled in the house as the children made numerous trips carrying food from the dining room to the backyard. The adults were amazed at the amount the McRoberts children ate and wondered how well those young stomachs would deal with all the food they now held. After dinner, the children had some time to play next door at the Graves.' The swing set and jungle gym had never seen so much action. As dusk faded slowly into darkness, they paired off and went to their new, hopefully short-term, locations.

When Claire, Abby, and Sarah got to Claire's house, they all sat in the living room to talk and clarify school day schedules. Lucky joined them, sitting right at Abby's feet and enjoying the taste of her legs.

"What do you eat for breakfast?" Claire asked.

"Well, it kind of depends on what day it is," Sarah responded in a matter-of-fact tone. When Claire looked at her with a questioning look, she explained. "If it's right after payday, we might have cereal and toast and juice or maybe even fruit. But at the end of two weeks, it would depend on what's left. Sometimes the kids who get ready for school the fastest might get a little dry cereal or some oatmeal, but if you're slow, you might not get anything. Dad likes to save the bread for sandwiches for our lunch. He tries to make peanut butter or jelly sandwiches every night for the next day. If he is too tired or forgets, I have to do it in the morning."

"What about them eggs?" added Abby.

"Oh yeah," continued Sarah, "Mrs. Peterson sometimes sent eggs home with Dad. But he usually scrambled those for dinner instead of using them for breakfast."

"But they were sure good," said Abby, licking her lips and rubbing her stomach.

"Okay then," continued Claire, "tell me what you would like for breakfast."

"I guess that kind of depends," replied Sarah with an apprehensive look on her face.

"What do you mean?"

"Am I going to have to fix it?"

Claire had never imagined that this thought might be going through Sarah's head, but now she could understand. "I thought I could get breakfast ready for you, unless you would like to do it yourself."

"Oh no, ma'am! I would be very happy if you would do that."

"Gee, it would be like being a queen or a princess," added Abby.

Sarah continued, "But we can certainly help you anytime. We don't want to be any trouble."

"Now that we have that established, what would you like tomorrow?"

Sarah thought for a few moments, but Abby jumped off the couch and emphatically said, "I want juice, toast and jelly, and eggs."

"How would you like your eggs?"

Abby looked puzzled. "What do you mean? I want them cooked."

"There are many ways to cook eggs. You could have them scrambled or fried or boiled or poached." Claire waited as Abby thought over the choices. Then she continued. "Would you like to have me tell you about those different kinds?"

"Nah!"

"No thank you," Sarah corrected.

"No thank you," Abby repeated. "I figure that any way would be fine with me as long as I don't have to eat the shells."

"I think I can handle that. How about you, Sarah?"

"I really could fix our breakfast. I don't want to cause you any trouble."

"I am sure that you could, and maybe sometimes, but I would like to do it for you tomorrow. So what would you like?"

"I'd like some scrambled eggs and toast with butter and juice." After a moment of hesitation, Sarah added, "And maybe could I have some bacon too?"

"Me too, me too," chirped in Abby, jumping up and down.

"I can't make promises on that one, but I'll see what I can do. Now that we have breakfast settled, let's talk about some other things—like homework."

"Oh, I don't never have no homework." Abby looked at Claire very seriously.

"You never have any homework," said Claire.

"Yup, that's what I said. I ain't never had none."

"Fine, but you and I will read every night and work on some kind of schoolwork together. How about you, Sarah?"

"I have it every night, but I feel bad that I forgot all about it tonight. I could start it now."

"I think you will be excused for not getting it done this time, but from now on it will be done right after dinner before watching any television. And I have the final say over what you two get to watch."

The girls both looked around the room, and their eyes fell on the television that sat on a small table. Then they looked at each other and smiled. Sarah explained, "We had one at Grandma's, but it wasn't very good and we could hardly see the picture. Having one will be great! Then when the kids at school talk about shows they watch, we will know what they're talking about."

"I think it's about time for my guests to be thinking about bed. What time do you need to get up?" Claire directed the question to Sarah, being quite certain a five-year-old wouldn't have a very accurate answer. "It will take you about ten minutes to walk to school." A wake-up time was selected, and after each girl was ready, Claire tucked them in and offered a prayer for the recovery of their father. Both girls assured her they would be okay in the new surroundings as Claire turned off the bedroom lights. She did have to encourage Lucky to leave with her instead of staying with Abby.

As soon as she got downstairs, she sat down hard on one of the kitchen chairs and let out a big sigh. "What have I gotten myself into?" Then she picked up the phone. "Hi, Betty. Do you by any chance have any bacon I can borrow? Oh good, I'll be right over."

When Claire got to the Nuttings, Leonard greeted her at the door and led her to the dining room, where Betty was on hands and knees looking under furniture.

"It's a little late to be cleaning the floor, isn't it?" joked Claire.

"I'm just looking for a spoon. It's a small silver jam spoon that was my grandmother's. I always keep it on the side bar with the crystal jam jar, but I just noticed it wasn't there. I imagine it got knocked off with all of the people coming through here. It will turn up. Now you wanted bacon, right?" The two visited for a while reviewing the events of the day. Then Claire suddenly remembered that she had left the girls alone. "They'll be fine," assured Betty as Claire grabbed the bacon and headed for home.

When Claire entered the house, it seemed unusually quiet since she was not met by an excited dog that had not yet gotten over the novelty of having someone come through the door. She put the bacon in the refrigerator and removed a small address book from the drawer beneath the phone. She smiled as she turned to the "D" page, remembering having a hard time deciding where to write the number Daniel recently had given her. She had started to write it on the "C" page for Chambers but then changed to "D" for Daniel and Dreamboat. Although he had called her quite a few times, this was the first time she had instigated the call. He was surprised to find out who it was since the calls he usually did get were from his clients in hiding or from the government getting another witness into the program.

It didn't take Claire long to get to the subject and tell Daniel about the events of the day. It was comforting to hear his voice, and she wished he were there on the couch beside her. She told him of her uncomfortable feeling about bypassing the social services issue and then really had a guilty feeling since he was a government employee. She wondered if he had an obligation to report their somewhat underhanded approach to the situation. She decided not even to ask in case he didn't think of that himself.

"It has been a really long time since I've taken care of children, especially young school children, and times have changed. I'm unsure how to handle rules and expectations with these children. They're one generation removed from my own children, and it was hard enough with them. I feel uneasy about trying to assure the girls that things will be fine when after hearing about the seriousness of the accident, I'm not sure that everything will be fine. And how much do I want to be optimistic and raise false hopes?

"I'm not sure what to do to keep Abby busy in the afternoons since she only goes to kindergarten in the morning and will be home in the afternoons. Maybe," she wondered out loud, "she would like to play with paper dolls or color or read books, or maybe she's the kind of girl that would rather be out riding her bike? And if that is the case, that will be a problem since I don't think she has a bike. And if she does have one, it's back at the farm. Or maybe the two of us could plant some flowers and start a vegetable garden. Yes," she continued but slowing down the flow of conversation, "the weather is probably warm enough now so we could do that together."

After the lengthy one-sided conversation, Claire paused to take a deep breath, and Daniel finally had the chance to get in a word. He tried to convince her that she was doing the right thing. "Remember, you raised three children and probably had many of the same concerns when the first one was born. Parenting doesn't come with a manual, as I recall, and neither does a situation like this." Claire, feeling somewhat better and relieved Daniel had said nothing about turning her and the others in to the authorities, said good night, hung up, turned off all of the downstairs lights and headed to bed.

She thought she should check on the girls but was afraid that she might wake them, so she tiptoed into the first room, which had been chosen by Sarah. "I guess I won't have to go any farther," she whispered quietly, for there in the bed was not only Sarah but also Abby, who was snuggled close to her older sister. Next to Abby was a white ball of fur huddled so tightly it was barely recognizable as Lucky. Bending over the girls, Claire gently kissed their heads and whispered, "May God watch over you and your father too." Then she softly patted Lucky and again whispered, "And may God watch over you too."

Lucky sleepily opened one brown eye and looked up at Claire. In the dim light he appeared to be smiling at her.

FIVE

For a gourmet cook, the choices available at the Hayward Market were quite limited. Still, Helen Evans did not complain, at least not out loud. She tried the best she could with what she found along the one-way aisles. The standard things a kitchen needed were satisfactory, but it was the more unique items that were missing. On her first trips, Bryan Graves had been as helpful as he could in trying to fill her requests, but by now she knew better than to ask for more specialized spices, vegetables, or cuts of meat. So Helen bought the things most of the other women did and looked forward to shopping trips where she could do a more thorough job of stocking her shelves.

"Howdy, Helen, how're you doing today? I'd ask you if you found everything, but I know what your answer would be, don't you know. Sorry about that."

"That's all right, Bryan. What you have here will do just fine until I can get into Des Moines."

Bryan often held the door for his customers, but the store was unusually busy at the time, so Helen pulled the door open herself and without looking immediately turned left. The scream that followed plus the sound of groceries hitting the pavement brought Bryan and the other customers rushing to see what happened. They found a very pale, flustered Helen staring at a rifle and at the person who was standing face-to-face with her.

The commotion also brought Bob Simpson sprinting out of his hardware store. He ran to his father, grabbing the rifle from his arms. "Give me that! You cannot scare people that way! You need to apologize to this lady."

Farley stared straight ahead into Helen's face. "I can't. She doesn't know the password."

"Password? What password? What's he talking about?" Helen responded in a frantic tone.

"Sprechen sie Deutsch?" Farley asked, continuing to stare at her.

"I'm so sorry for my father, ma'am. Let me help you with your groceries." Bryan ran to grab a new bag. Then he and Bob gathered the items that had rolled all over the sidewalk.

"I'll finish up here if you want to get your father resettled," offered Bryan.

"Thanks. Again, I am so sorry my father scared you. He knows most people around here, but you are a stranger to him and he overreacted. Come on, Dad. Let's go back and have a seat."

As the two of them headed back into the hardware store, Bryan quickly explained to Helen about Farley and how he mentally still was fighting World War II. "He carries that rifle—it can't be fired, by the way—because he always feels that he needs to be on his guard to protect the town. Also, he has a well-worn notebook that he thinks is a codebook, and if he hears anything out of the ordinary, he checks his book to see if it has a secret meaning. He has done some rather unusual things because of that imaginary codebook. He really is harmless, and people around here are so used to him they don't think anything about his carrying that rifle. Sometime stop in the hardware store and get to know him. Maybe next time he won't get the drop on you, don't you know."

After much debate by the adults, it was decided that on Saturday the McRoberts children would be allowed to go to the hospital to see their father. The twins wouldn't go, and Claire wasn't sure Abby should either. But Abby left no doubt about how she felt on the subject.

"I am going to see Daddy with everyone else, or I won't eat all day long. And I will scream and cry and you will wish you had let me go!"

Sarah, by virtue of being the oldest, now had become the official spokesperson for the family. She agreed with Claire and tried to dissuade her sister from making the trip. "Daddy will not look like himself, Abby. He will have bandages and probably tubes fastened to his body. He's kind of asleep, and he will not even know we're there. We all might not even be allowed to see him. I think Mrs. Menefee is right. It's better that you stay here."

"Then I'll run away and find a way to get there myself," Abby stated emphatically.

Sarah turned to Claire. "She's not kidding. Our dog disappeared once, and Abby set out to bring him home. It took all of us looking in all directions to finally find her. She was about two miles from home and was sitting by the road with her arms around the dog's neck when Dad saw her."

So Abby was allowed to go. That made six children making the trip. The problem then became how to get them there. Sarah said when they went places they all just climbed in the back of her dad's covered pickup. No one thought that sounded like a safe idea, but what they seemed to need and did not have was a small bus. It was decided that two cars would go. Helen, who heard via the community grapevine about the trip, volunteered to drive since she was planning to go on a food-buying trip anyway. It was decided that Claire would ride with Helen and three children, and Bud and Ellen Hornsby, who had built-in babysitters with sixteen-year-old Steve and fourteen-year-old Katie, would drive with the other three. Everyone thought it was a good idea to have a man along since four of the six young passengers were boys. The children were split up, so they were not in the same car with the sibling they were currently living with. That way they could reconnect with other family members. The drive was relatively uneventful except for the two stops Helen's car had to make for Abby to throw up at the side of the road.

"Why didn't you tell me you get carsick?" Claire asked.

"You didn't ask," she replied in a matter-of-fact tone.

Helen dropped her passengers at the hospital, promising to return after she gathered her gourmet necessities. The entourage entered the hospital.

Claire accompanied Sarah to the front desk, but it was agreed that Sarah would do the talking.

"We are here to see my father, Thomas McRoberts."

The volunteer, whose eyebrows had raised when she lifted her head and looked over the group of nine, said nothing but returned her eyes to her list of patients and pointed to the direction of the intensive care unit. As they walked down the sterile hallway, the children drew closer together. Sarah, who had been so grown up at the front desk, now slipped her hand into Claire's, and Abby took the other hand as they approached the ICU. At the nursing station, Sarah didn't have to ask again since a nurse emerged from behind desk and met the group.

"I heard you were on your way," she said, looking sympathetically at Sarah. "You may see your father for only a few minutes, and I am afraid that only the immediate members of the family will be able to go in."

Ellen, who was standing at the back of the group holding the hand of seven-year-old John, raised her other hand and made a sweeping motion from one side of the group to the other. The nurse just stared for a moment before responding, "All of them?"

"Yes, and there are two more who couldn't come!" spoke up Abby.

"My, we'll have to think about this." She paused, tapping her finger in the air while counting the noses in front of her. "We don't want to overwhelm your father, so two of you can go together, but you cannot stay for very long. Your father is in a…in a deep sleep and will not be able to talk or even let you know if he hears you."

The children quickly paired off by opposite ages, an older with a younger. Claire figured they had probably done this many times before. After everyone had their chance, all six children thanked the nurse for taking care of their father. Then they reversed their path and headed back to the front door.

While waiting for Helen, the children compared visits. Matthew, the next oldest, said he could hardly tell it was his father with all the bandages. Mark, next in order of age, said he could hardly stand to look at him since he looked so badly hurt. Claire told him his father was probably medicated, so he was not feeling much pain. Luke said he was fascinated by all of the equipment and wished he could have asked the nurse about everything.

Little John reprimanded Luke by asking how he could be interested in machines when their father was lying there all hurt and broken.

"I wonder if he heard anything that we said?" pondered Sarah.

"He did. I know he did," insisted Abby.

The others looked at her in a mocking way, kidding her about her comment.

"Come on, Abby, you're just saying that," said Mark.

"No, I know he did because I held his hand and told him I loved him and I felt him squeeze my hand a little. That's how I know."

The brothers started to laugh at Abby, but Sarah gave them a look and the giggles and comments stopped. Claire found it interesting how Sarah, at the age of twelve, interacted with her brothers more as if she were their mother than their sister. But then she had, after all, been somewhat thrust into that role following the deaths of both her mother and grandmother. *What a burden*, she thought.

They had not waited long before Helen returned to pick up her passengers. Everyone reloaded and the two cars headed home. Everyone was quieter on the trip back due in part to the fact that the Dramamine Claire had given to Abby had taken effect and she was sound asleep in the backseat. This also allowed them to make the trip more quickly since there was no need for emergency stops.

After dropping off the children at the Dunns,' where everyone was invited to play on their incredible backyard playground structure that Jim had built, Claire went with Helen to help her unload her groceries. Helen had insisted that she could easily do it herself, but Claire pleaded, saying she would like to see what a well-stocked kitchen should have. As she unloaded the items, she found things she had never heard of—fennel seed, chervil, lemon grass, Asian sesame oil, Chinese Napa cabbage, grapefruit citrus olive oil.

As Helen stored the items in her kitchen cabinets, Claire marveled at the variety. "These are really interesting. Maybe you could teach cooking classes. I don't mean to snoop, but all of these must have been rather expensive."

Helen just smiled. "You would be surprised how cheaply I got some of them. You just need to know where to shop. It was almost as if they were giving some of them away." She laughed.

It had been an important and emotionally draining day for the children. Shortly after dinner, Abby had fallen asleep watching television. Claire had awakened her and escorted her to bed. At Abby's insistence, she wanted to sleep in her own room, as she seemed to forget that every night so far she had ended up in bed with both Sarah and Lucky. Claire then returned to Sarah, who seemed to be absorbed in the television show. She sat beside her. It wasn't long before Sarah turned to her.

"Do you think Daddy will die? Really, tell me what you think, Mrs. Menefee."

"I don't know, Sarah. I don't know much about medicine, so I am not a good one to ask."

"But you are old and know a lot about life."

Claire was not offended at all by her comment and instead took it as a respectful compliment. "Just because I have lived longer than you doesn't mean I have all the answers. You need to know that the doctors don't have all of the answers either. Medicine has come a long way, but doctors can't work miracles."

"You mean you think it will take a miracle to help Daddy?" Sarah suddenly sat up straight and stared at Claire.

"Oh no, I don't mean that at all. I just mean that doctors and nurses do all that they can, but some injuries they just don't yet know how to heal."

Sarah sat quietly for a minute and then with tears forming in her eyes looked pleadingly at Claire. The many thoughts rushing through her head spilled out in a constant gushing stream. "If Daddy dies, I'll be in charge. I can't take care of them all. I'm only twelve. How can I possibly take care of them? How could I get a job? I'm only in the sixth grade. Who would hire me? There would be no money for food and clothes, and where would we live? I can't even drive. But then we don't have a truck anymore, so why would I need to? But then how would I take them places? I can't, I just can't—I just don't know how to be in charge of a whole family." Then with a huge sob, she added, "Oh, what am I going to do?"

Claire was not surprised that the dam had broken, but she was worried she wouldn't respond with the right words. So she answered with what came to mind and with the benefit of her old age and years of experience. "Well, to start with, look where all of you are now. Granted, you're not together, but you all are being fed and have homes to live in because there are people who care about you and would never leave you alone to carry all those burdens by yourself. I don't like to think of the worst situation, but if necessary, there are systems that would provide for you and your family. I'm sure that right now things seem overwhelming and, knowing the smart girl that you are, you're thinking ahead. But please don't worry about that now. You just have to think about your father getting well and about helping Abby and about school and about summer that will be here before you know it. Please know that you won't have to be in charge of all the others, at least not for six years." Claire put her arm around Sarah and squeezed her gently. "And besides, by then you will be old enough to drive."

Sarah snuggled against Claire as they both appeared to return to watching the television show. Claire knew she was not paying attention to what her eyes were watching and had the feeling Sarah was not either. She became even more sure of this when Sarah laid her head in Claire's lap and soon began to emit a cute, abbreviated snore. She let her stay like that until the news ended, not that Claire was one bit interested in what was happening anywhere except on her own block and in that hospital room. Although she would have been willing to carry a sleeping five-year-old up the stairs, she knew it would be impossible to do so with a twelve-year- old, so she gently woke up Sarah and guided her up to bed, where her two bed mates were already sound asleep.

"I usually go to church on Sunday mornings and would like to go tomorrow if that is all right with you. You're certainly welcome to come too. I go to the Methodist church right at the end of the square." She paused for a moment. "But we have other churches in town if you might prefer one of them. There's the Catholic church behind the library and also a Lutheran and a Presbyterian church. If those would be better, I'd be happy to go to one of those with you."

Abby was busy with her third piece of French toast, but Sarah answered. "Mama really enjoyed going to church, and God was very important in her life. You have noticed our names, haven't you?" Claire nodded as she quickly ran through the list in her head—Matthew, Mark, Luke, John, Thomas, and Timothy. Sarah continued, "When I was born, Daddy said I was his little princess. Mother always wanted biblical names for her children, and she found out Sarah meant princess in the Bible. That's how I got my name. Daddy wasn't crazy about the names she wanted for the boys, but he let her pick. Before Abby was born, Daddy said that after all of those boys another girl would be a father's joy. So Mama kept looking up names and decided on Abigail, which does mean father's joy."

Suddenly Abby jumped into the story. "That's right, and I was always his favorite too."

"No one was a favorite. Daddy loves us all the same."

"Yeah, but I was his favorite," Abby once again insisted.

Sarah, looking irritated, stopped for a moment before she continued. "When Mama found out that she was going to have another baby, they were both surprised, I remember. I once overheard them talking. Daddy said that they couldn't afford another baby. Mama said God would provide for the new one just as he had for the rest of us. But when they found out it was twins, Daddy was really worried. I know he tried not to show it, but I heard and saw enough to know that he wasn't happy.

"But Mama was joyful with the news. She pondered names and frequently changed her mind. I don't remember all of the ones she chose, but once she decided on Thomas, which means a twin, she picked other names to go with it. If Timmy had been a girl, he would have been Trinity, I do remember that." She paused again, and her eyes began to glisten as the tears started forming in her sad blue eyes. "Mama never got to see both of those boys. Daddy was so sad and kind of angry too. He didn't know I heard him, but he said those boys killed our mother, and he was not going to use any more Bible names because God had done nothing to keep Mama and he didn't owe God any more tributes by naming them with holy names. But Grandma calmed him down and made him understand those names were the ones Mama had chosen and it would not be right to go against her wishes. So Daddy named them what she chose.

"We used to go to church a lot with Mama, but after she died, Daddy said that we weren't going anymore. He said that God wasn't real and that Mama had just been a fool."

Claire almost had forgotten Abby was still there. "But I still believe. Mama always told us God would be there with us in the good and the bad times. I think this is one of them really bad times. She wouldn't want us to ever forget about God no matter what Daddy says. So I think I want to go to church. It can't make Daddy mad if he don't know about it, right? I know that Mama would like it if I went."

So the spunk that Claire had seen in Abby was showing itself again. What her mother had instilled in her for those few years had sunk in quite deeply. Sarah, on the other hand, seemed to have been more influenced by her father's agnostic attitude and politely declined the offer.

The elementary school staff was eager to do what they could to help make the situation as normal as possible for the McRoberts children. Mrs. Stevens, the school secretary, went out of her way to make sure that sometime every day she would find each child and offer a greeting or share a joke. Things seemed to be going as smoothly as possible, and the staff presented a positive face in front of the children.

The only naysayer was Pearl Hatcher, the school's principal, who not only had nothing encouraging to say about the situation but never seemed to be able to find anything at all to smile about. "I still can't believe you agreed to take on those girls. And at your age too. What were those other women thinking? Who in their right mind would let themselves be talked into adding two strangers to their family? What was Social Services thinking when they placed those children?"

"They really didn't…" Claire slipped but quickly tried to not provide the full truth, "er, ah, want to separate the children any more than they had to, and since all of us live so close to each other, it just seemed to make sense."

"I just don't understand the thinking of anyone wanting to take on more children. Children just make me nervous," Pearl added as she began to leave the library. "Oh, and by the way, if Social Services asks why and how these children were all relocated, I'll make it perfectly clear I was totally against this idea." She turned abruptly and headed down the hall.

As far as Claire could tell, the rest of the school community was very supportive, and many classmates brought some clothing for them. Claire had asked Sarah how their father would have felt about these donations. At first she said he would have seen it as charity and never wanted to accept charity from anyone. But when she saw some of the outfits that had come in for her, she couldn't resist and said that under these circumstances he would probably make an exception.

As Claire was leaving from her morning of volunteering in the school library, Theresa Stevens motioned for Claire. "I shouldn't give out personal information, but I was looking at these records and thought it probably might be all right since you are kind of involved with the McRoberts children and you have Abby and because I don't know if the others would say anything and I think that you would want to know and..."

Claire was a bit concerned when Theresa started talking, and the more she carried on, the more concerned Claire became. She finally couldn't take the rambling anymore. "What do I need to know?"

"Abby's birthday is May 15. I thought someone should know." Tears were brimming in Theresa's eyes. "No six-year-old should have a birthday that no one knows about."

"I'm so glad that you told me. It will be our little secret too."

That evening after Abby had gone to bed, Claire sat down at the kitchen table, where Sarah was working on her homework. "Do you need help with anything?"

"No thank you. I like doing homework now. It wasn't that I didn't like it before, but it was so noisy at the house and there wasn't much room and the light wasn't too good. Sometimes I was so tired. Daddy always told us all how important an education is so we can have a better life than he did. Sometimes I just wanted to yell, 'I can't do this!' but I would have gotten another one of his lectures, and believe you me, you don't want to hear one of his lectures." Her eyes widened and eyebrows rose for emphasis as she spoke.

"You just have a few more weeks of school. Then you can relax and have more free time. There is something I want to talk to you about." Sarah looked worried. Claire wondered if maybe Sarah was thinking there was bad news about her father. "It's nothing bad. It's just that I got to wondering about birthdays. I don't want any of your birthdays to slip by unnoticed. When's your birthday?"

"Mine is March 27, and Mark's is April 27. I remember his since it's exactly one month after mine. Let's see, Matthew's and John's are also sometime in April. Mom always said that starting with my birthday it was like a super special month with one right after another. The twins were born on July 1. That's a date I'll always remember since that was the day that Mom died." Sarah paused for a short time, and the faraway look on her face seemed to be taking her back to that day. She sighed, gave a slight smile, and continued. "Luke's is in July or maybe August, I'm not sure. And Abby's is sometime in May. Gee, I guess hers is probably soon. I never even thought about it."

"Let's face it. You've had plenty of other things on your mind. Maybe you and I can talk later and make some plans."

"That would be great, but I don't think she'll know when it is. And I can't remember. I don't think the boys will either. Daddy never cared much for birthdays after Mom died. I think it was because of the twins' birthday and Mom, you know."

"I'll bet I can find out. Leave it to me."

The following day was quilting group. The main topic was the McRoberts family. Everyone wanted to know about the children and their father. The temporary foster mothers filled them in as best they could.

Vernina Graves, who had joyfully deposited Timmy and Tommy with the babysitter, was first to respond. "The twins are doing fine now, although the first few nights were hard. They cried, and we all tried comforting them. Then Ryan insisted he take over bedtime, and it worked much better. He said, 'These guys are used to having lots of brothers around, and since I'm the only guy here, I think I can make them feel better.' He was right. He stuck them in their cribs, kissed them good night, turned out the light, and sat in their room for two or three nights to comfort them if they whimpered. It worked like a charm. Daytime is easier. The older children stop by after school to play with them. All in all, things are okay, don't you know."

"I really do enjoy having Luke and John," said Jane Dunn next. "They're very well behaved and cause no problems. They get along well with Jenny and

Jeff, but they are pretty quiet. They have nice manners and frequently thank me for dinner. They do their homework without being told, and both go to bed quite early. I've heard some soft crying from their room, but I figure that's not surprising, so I just leave them to comfort each other. I don't know which one is crying. Maybe it's both of them." Jane's usual cheerful look was replaced with a much more reflective one, and she gently bit the side of her lip.

Ellen Hornsby followed. "I think Matthew and Mark are doing as well as can be expected. Being older, I believe they understand the seriousness of the situation more. Of course all of them except the twins have dealt with the death of their mother and grandparents. I'm sure they're wondering if now they'll lose their father too."

"I agree with that," chimed in Betty. "I don't know if you're aware of it or not, Ellen, but Matthew has been down to talk to Leonard quite a few times. He asks lots of medical kinds of questions and frequently asks if Leonard thinks his dad will pull through and if he does, will he be like he was before the accident. That's a lot of concern for an eleven-year-old. So how are things with the girls, Claire?"

"I see the same things. The older you are, the more you seem to understand and worry. Poor Sarah thinks the entire responsibility of this family is and will be on her shoulders. I try to assure her there always will be help available, but I'm not sure how much she believes me. But Abby is so different. She's so positive and upbeat and doesn't seem to be very worried. I guess when you're five you don't look at things the same. Speaking of being five, Abby has a birthday coming up. I'm glad I found out so I can plan some type of little birthday celebration for her."

At this point Lila Hayward, who had been uncharacteristically quiet and inconspicuous, jumped up and almost yelled. "I'll do it! I'll plan a great party for her. It will be good practice for my wedding planner business. And it's the least I can do for that poor family."

Claire was a bit overwhelmed by Lila's immediate exuberant response and was not quite sure how to respond. "That's a nice offer, Lila, but remember she will only be six. She sure doesn't need anything fancy. I really think I can handle it."

"Don't worry. I was six once too, don't forget. I'll plan something just perfect. You just relax. I'll take care of everything. You won't have to worry about a thing!"

Claire smiled, but for some reason she didn't feel she could follow Lila's advice.

Claire had errands to do before Abby got home from school and first stopped at the bank. Ruby, one of the tellers, greeted her. "Things should be hopping at your house on Saturday. I hope Abby has a good time."

"Thanks. I do too," Claire answered, thinking that this party had become quite well known.

As she passed Felton's clothing store, Gladys was removing a cute little pink summer dress from a window display. When she looked up and saw Claire, she hurriedly hid it behind her back. She tried to act nonchalant as she waved, but she still looked as if she had just been caught in some secret act. Claire waved back and continued on to the drugstore.

The bell above the door tinkled, but Ronnie apparently didn't hear it as he bent closely toward a customer at the soda fountain counter. Unfortunately, Claire was well familiar with the location of the aspirin, so it was only a minute before she was back at the front. Ronnie left the other customer to wait on her.

"Not another headache, I hope," he said sympathetically. "You'll need to be in top shape for the big party on Saturday."

"I'm planning ahead." Claire laughed, although she didn't feel very jolly thinking about it. As Ronnie got her change, Claire looked back at the lady sitting at the counter. *She looks familiar, but I can't remember where I've seen her. It must be that red hair. She looks as if she belongs with the McRoberts family*, she thought. She wanted to ask Ronnie who she was, but it wasn't any of her business, so she just dropped the aspirin in her purse and left for the hardware and general store.

"Good morning, Farley," she said as she wedged her way past the chair he had moved to block a good deal of the doorway.

"Dad, you need to move over some. Customers can't get past you," grunted an irritated Bob Simpson as he dragged the old wooden chair squeakily across the floor. Farley's stare never left Claire's face as he and the chair were moved sideways. Bob took Claire's arm and walked her toward the back of the store. "It seems that your upcoming party has put Dad on alert again. He heard something about it, pulled out that stupid old codebook, and mumbled something like, 'I thought so.' He's been on edge ever since. I'll be sure to keep an eye on him Saturday, but I thought you should know just in case. Call me if he shows up."

"I'm sure there will be no problems. It's only a little party for a six-year-old, after all." Claire said the words, but she could tell by the look on Bob's face he wasn't sure whether to believe them. She was not sure she believed them herself.

"I hear there's going to be a birthday party at your house pretty soon," said a grinning Bryan Graves as he bagged Claire's groceries.

"That's what I hear."

"I loved birthday parties when I was little. Matter of fact, I still love them, don't you know. All the presents and the cake and ice cream. And those funny party hats. I just loved those. My dad put on two of them once, and they looked like horns. They made him look like the devil." Bryan laughed as he enjoyed his memories. "Lila's been a busy little party planner. She even placed some special orders. Speaking of orders, I'm under orders not to say anything to you about it. She wants it all to be a big surprise."

She kind of shuddered as she left the store and headed home. Even in the short time that she had lived in Hayward, she had seen Lila in full action more than once. "That woman has no sense of simplicity. Why does she have to go to such extremes?" She had phoned Lila more than once, and Lila had insisted things were going to be low key and very appropriate, but she had admitted she'd planned some fun surprises. Claire wanted to call the whole thing off and throw the party herself, but she knew it was too late. She was kicking herself for not having said no to Lila when she first volunteered. Now she would just have to live with whatever happened.

The doorbell rang Friday night, and Abby rushed to the door. However, she did not recognize the man standing there. "Well, who are you?" she boldly asked, looking up into his face.

"And I might ask the same of you," the stranger replied.

"Well, I live here and you don't," Abby sternly responded, placing her hands emphatically on her hips. "So I guess that makes me in charge, huh!"

"I guess it just might. So, little lady of the house, would you please tell Mrs. Menefee that she has a visitor?"

"Well, I ain't tellin' her nothin' if you don't first tell me who you are."

"In that case, will you please inform her Mr. Chambers is here?"

Abby turned her head away from the door and, in a voice much louder than a petite little girl should have, yelled, "Mrs. Menefee, there's some guy here to see you." She quickly turned her head around as if to make sure he wasn't going to sneak by her.

Claire came into the living room, where she could see the standoff at the door. Her heart did a little flutter when she saw who it was. She took a deep breath and somehow managed to not run toward the door. Instead she maintained a calm demeanor as she crossed the living room.

"Well, Mr. Chambers. What a lovely surprise! Won't you come in?"

"That's kind of what I had in mind, but this young lady wanted to make sure I was really okay."

"You can never be too sure, you know," Abby said, turning to Claire.

Clara would like this girl, Claire thought before she introduced the two. Then Abby went back to drawing a picture for her dad.

Daniel followed Claire to the couch. "So that's Abby. She does seem to have a mind of her own. How are things going by now?"

"As well as can be expected. The children are all very polite and well behaved. As far as I know, there have been no major problems. The girls have been fun to have around. Sarah and I have lots of heart-to-heart talks about her family and her life. Abby talks a lot too, but most of what she says is about school or things we do together. She takes naps many afternoons, which is good for both of us. When she's awake, she always finds things to keep her busy. She likes to help me with the housework. She's young enough to still think cleaning is fun. She's really interested in some knick-knacks that have been in my family for years. I have two tiny blown glass swans she is fascinated with. She said she's never seen anything so pretty. My own children certainly never found them very interesting.

"I'm so glad you came today, and I hope you can be here tomorrow too. We're having a birthday party for Abby, and I'd love to have you come.

There's nothing as exciting as a six-year-old's birthday, you know." The minute the words fell from her mouth, she desperately wished she could gather them up and stuff them back in. But it was too late, and the look on Daniel's face told her all that she needed to know. "I am so sorry. That was not very thoughtful of me."

"Don't worry about it. You just told it like it is. Being five is good, but being six is even better." In trying to soothe over the somewhat uncomfortable situation, he continued, "Believe it or not, I can remember my sixth birthday. I got a football. I don't know who was more excited, my dad or me. He always wanted me to grow up to be a famous football player. Things sure didn't turn out that way."

Claire squeezed Daniel's hand, thinking it best to not say anything further until she was sure she wouldn't stick her foot in her mouth again. Luckily Daniel spoke next.

"I have a visit to make this evening, but I'll make a point of being back tomorrow morning. I can help you get things set up."

"I appreciate your offer, but Lila Hayward has graciously volunteered to organize the entire thing." Claire really wanted to say Lila pretty much forced herself into the situation and she was concerned about just what her plans were, but she decided to say nothing more.

"You mean that mayor's wife is planning a party for a six-year-old? This I have to see!" That comment didn't help make Claire feel any better about the situation. In fact, she was now more worried than ever. "How in the world did she get involved anyway?"

"Lila has this crazy idea of starting some business where she does all the planning for weddings. She thought this would be good practice."

"I cannot imagine there would be a need for something like that here. Are there really a lot of weddings?"

"Not that I know of, but I have this feeling she might try to do some matchmaking to stir up come customers. So I'd avoid her if I were you." Claire could feel color rising in her face and wondered why in the world she had made that comment. Would Daniel take that to mean she thought the two of them wouldn't make a good couple or that she wasn't very interested in him? She quickly got up and headed toward one of the windows. "Does it feel warm to you? I think I'll open this so we can get some fresh air."

Daniel too was caught off guard by Claire's comment and didn't know how to respond. He decided it best to let that conversation drop, so he rose from the couch, took both of Claire's hands, and looking into her eyes said, "I'll be here tomorrow for sure. I can hardly wait to see what Mrs. Mayor has planned. I have no doubt it will be an event to remember." He chuckled as he let himself out, leaving Claire wishing the whole birthday thing was over.

SIX

Five-year-olds who usually sleep late on Saturdays break that habit on those Saturdays when they're turning six. Claire learned that at six o'clock when she was awakened by a bouncing redhead and her white fuzzy companion who had turned her bed into a trampoline.

"Come on, Mrs. Menefee. Time to get up!"

Claire looked through half-opened eyes. "What time is it?" She groaned, squinting at the clock. "Go back to bed. It's not a school day."

"I know. It is better. We have to get up so we'll be all ready for my party."

"It's eight hours from now. You need to rest so you won't have to take a nap." Claire wondered who she was trying to kid, saying a child would be napping on her birthday.

"No, come on and get up." Abby pumped Claire's limp hand while Lucky, trying to aid in the effort, licked Claire's cheek.

"I have an idea. You go back to your room and read some library books."

"You know I can't read."

"But you can read the pictures. You can make up a story to go with the pictures. Read to Lucky. He'd like that."

Abby looked at Lucky as she contemplated Claire's suggestion. She climbed off the bed and headed for the door. "Okay, but I ain't readin' him that cat book. Dogs don't like cats." Lucky followed her down the hall, appearing not to have any preferences in reading material.

Claire tried to get back to sleep by thinking of boring thoughts. But no matter how much she tried to avoid it, she kept thinking of the big birthday party. She was not looking forward to the party, but she was looking forward to Daniel's being there for support. She had thought about inviting him, but she decided having adults at a little girl's party was not necessary. She figured she and Lila could handle six or seven youngsters.

Finally, she gave up on the idea of sleeping. As she headed to the bathroom, she heard Abby's voice coming from her room. Claire peeked in to see the two companions lying on the bed snuggled together as she read her version of one of the books, and Lucky looked very engaged.

Claire went to the kitchen to get breakfast. When the coffee was done, she poured herself a cup and headed toward the back porch to check on the weather. She dropped the cup when she was startled by what appeared to be giant insects crawling through her trees. She rushed out to get a better look only to find Steve Hornsby and some friends perched in trees and attaching blue crepe paper streamers and blue balloons. Below them was Lila who, bullhorn in hand, gave directions. Although the blue did look nice, Claire was surprised at the choice of color.

When Lila saw Claire, she hurried over. "Won't it be just elegant? I'm so pleased with how things look."

"Well … I think it will be fine, but I'm rather surprised about the color. I thought maybe pink might be more appropriate."

"Pink is so girlie!"

"But this party is for a girl!"

Lila wandered off not even hearing Claire's response. She returned to giving directions, so Claire shook her head and returned to the kitchen just as Abby and Lucky came in. When Abby saw the backyard, she too rushed out to look. "Wow! This is so cool. This is going to be a great day!" After wandering around checking out the decorations, she rushed back inside. "Mrs. Menefee, did you see your yard? Isn't it beautiful? I ain't never seen a yard so pretty." Claire had to agree that yes, it did look lovely and didn't say a word about the color.

Abby was too excited to eat, but Claire insisted that she have something, so she nibbled on a piece of toast and ate almost all but the crusts. She was still eating when Sarah entered the kitchen and went immediately to the window to check out the backyard action. "Wow. Where'd they come from? They're really cute!"

"They're sure more than cute, they're beautiful!" insisted Abby. Sarah looked at her with a strange look.

"Personally, I am not sure about their color," Claire said quietly to Sarah. Sarah also gave Claire a questioning look. Claire noticed and continued, "I thought pink might have been a bit more appropriate than blue."

Sarah giggled. "Oh, you were talking about the streamers and the balloons."

"What did you think I meant?" Claire asked, taking another look out the window.

"Now I see what you are talking about. Don't go getting any ideas. Those young men are much too old for you. But I have to agree with you. They are cute."

"Oh yuck!" Abby scoffed, emphatically scrunching up her face to show disapproval. "Boys are dumb. Daddy is the only good boy." Then as an afterthought, she added, "And maybe your Mr. Daniel is okay too."

"He's not my Mr. Daniel. He's just a friend. And I invited him to come to your party this afternoon. I hope that's okay."

"Sure. Do you think he might bring a present?"

"Abby, that's rude," her sister reprimanded. "You should apologize."

Claire was not offended by her comment, knowing that on birthdays presents come first to mind. However, she was not so flattered when Abby continued with, "I'm glad he's comin' so you won't be the only old person at my party. He can keep you company." Claire momentarily visualized Daniel and her sitting in matching rockers covered with lap robes slowly rocking on the back porch as they watched children running happily through the yard. She quickly shook her head as if to rid it of that thought and finished her breakfast.

"Hi, how are you holding up? Can I bring lunch for you three?" It was a nice question to hear and a nice voice to hear it from.

"That's nice, Daniel, but I have things here. And there is always peanut butter. Plus, I'm not sure anyone is very hungry, but you're certainly welcome to join us. It won't be fancy, but we'd enjoy your company." That was a big assumption on her part since Sarah had never met Daniel and Abby was in party mode.

"I'll be over in a little while. See you soon."

Abby called from upstairs as soon as Claire hung up. When she got to Abby's room, she found that all of Abby's clothes, what there were of them, were laid out on the bed. Claire was embarrassed to think that she had been so absorbed in her own worries she had not even thought of what the birthday girl would wear.

"What do you think, Mrs. Menefee? I can't decide."

Luckily the choices had been increased by the donations from school, but still nothing stood out as particularly festive. "I don't know," said Claire in a contemplative tone. "What do you think?"

"I never had a party before. I never even been to a party before, so I don't know."

"We want you to look nice, but we also want you to be comfortable."

"I can be comfortable any day, but this is my very special day, and I just want to look special."

Together they decided on a pink pinafore with a donated white blouse. The little puffy sleeves added a feminine touch, but the favorite thing about it for Abby was the collar embroidered with butterflies.

"I love butterflies," Abby said excitedly as she looked at herself in the mirror. "I like to lie in the grass and watch them. I always lie very still and hope one will land on me."

Luckily, the well-worn, originally white tennis shoes had come out somewhat clean after Claire had washed them earlier in the week. Abby had explained she really had not seen the mud puddle she had walked through. Claire had a feeling it was more like stomped through since there also was mud up both her legs.

Claire heard the doorbell ring, but Sarah yelled that she would answer the door. Then she heard, "Mrs. Menefee, there is a clown here to see you."

That's not a very nice way to talk about Daniel, she thought as she made a fast trip past the bathroom mirror before heading down the stairs. When she turned past the open door, she was startled to see that indeed there was a clown at the door. He came complete with a red curly wig, big red nose, multi-colored shirt with baggy overalls, and huge brown shoes that turned up at the toes.

"And might you be the birthday girl?" he asked jokingly and honking a horn that was fastened to his pants.

"Oh sure, and who might you be?"

"I might be Fred Young. I'm sorry we never met. I'm the barber who keeps the men in this town looking so handsome. But today I am just Chuckles, and I am here to entertain."

"Well, Chuckles, you're a bit early. The party doesn't start until two o'clock."

"I thought Lila said twelve. So now I'll have to wander around dressed in this getup for two hours?"

Claire, who had always hated clowns, had the urge to say, "Why don't you just go home, take off the gear, and don't come back," but instead invited Chuckles to stay. As he entered the living room with his big floppy shoes slapping on the floor, Abby came running down the stairs.

"Wow! It really is a clown. I never seen a real live clown before! Are you here for my party, Mr. Clown?"

"Yes, I am, and you can call me Chuckles."

"Okay, Mr. Chuckles. My name's Abigail, but you can call me Abby. Can Mr. Chuckles have lunch with us, Mrs. Menefee? Pleeeese!"

"That would be fine. Sarah already got out some things for sandwiches. You take Chuckles into the kitchen and help him." Claire watched the two of them walk hand-in-hand through the door and thought maybe this day wouldn't be so bad after all. The doorbell rang behind her, and she was glad that this time it really was Daniel with a nicely wrapped package under his arm.

"Everything looks the same from out front. Nothing terrible seems to have happened yet." Claire just smiled, took the package from his arm, dropped it on the couch, and led him toward the kitchen. "Yikes! There's a clown in your kitchen. I hate clowns." Claire looked at him in disbelief and started to laugh. "What?" he asked.

"Oh, nothing." She smiled, leading him over to still another redhead in her house. "Chuckles, this is Daniel."

The white-gloved hand extended to Daniel, who responded with a grin, "Nice to meet you. Can I call you Chuck?" Fred looked up at Daniel with a less-than-pleased expression and then went back to eating some grapes while Abby finished slathering peanut butter on a piece of bread for the unexpected guest.

Sarah appeared from the basement, where she had unearthed an old record player of Claire's. She did a double take at finding the clown and another strange man standing in the kitchen. Claire quickly introduced Daniel to Sarah, who politely excused herself, saying she would eat later when the kitchen was not so crowded. Claire urged Daniel to make himself at home, which he did and took his lunch to the back porch. Chuckles, Abby, and Claire followed him. They all sat and took in the sight before them. The Lavelle brothers, owners of the local furniture store, were finishing putting folding chairs around the tables that had been set up around the yard. The tables were covered with blue and white checkered table cloths. A long table standing close to the house had a solid blue tablecloth and a bouquet of yellow roses.

"The yard looks beautiful, Abby. Blue must be someone's favorite color," Daniel commented.

"Well, it might be someone's, but it sure ain't mine. But that's okay; it still looks pretty."

After a brief pause Daniel continued, "I hope you don't mind that Mrs. Menefee invited me to come to you party."

"No, I'm glad you came, especially if you…" Claire gave her a quick stern look and shook her head. After a short awkward moment, Abby continued, "Especially if you like cake and ice cream…and clowns."

"Then I guess I came to the right place."

Lila was in high octane mode when she arrived with the food. "Yoo-hoo! Could someone help a lady with these heavy trays?"

Heavy trays? thought Claire. *What in the world is she bringing?*

Chuckles had gone out to help when Lila noticed him. Looking him over from head to toe, she quietly asked, "Why are you dressed like that?"

"You told me it was a party for a six-year-old."

"Oh yeah, right." She was going to have him help carry some of the food when she noticed his shoes were having trouble navigating over the uneven surface of the lawn. Instead, she delegated him to carry the paper plates and napkins.

Claire looked puzzled as she stood by the back porch door as Floyd and Lloyd Lavelle and Daniel helped carry things to the table by the porch. "What in the world has she brought for these children to eat?" she mumbled. When Lila wasn't looking, Claire peeked under the cover of one of the trays and discovered finger sandwiches, vegetables, cheese and crackers, and dainty cookies. I *can't imagine the children will think of this as party food*, she thought, and her fears began to build again.

"Move over, watch out, here comes the cake!" shouted Lila as if she were directing traffic safely through the streets of New York City. Daniel and Lloyd carefully placed it on a separate table. Claire went over to look and her faith was restored—or at least somewhat restored—in Lila. The cake was two layers, two very large layers, covered with white frosting and piped with blue trim and yellow flowers. On the top was a plastic princess, looking a lot like Cinderella, with a long blue dress and a golden crown. That definitely did look like a cake for a little girl. But the size seemed rather excessive. "Maybe children in this town really like cake. I mean really, really like cake," Claire said in a quiet voice as she stared at the cake. "But Abby will love it."

Lila scurried around, checking to make sure everything looked right. Then she assured Claire that she would be back before party time, gathered up her two helpers, and whisked out the gate to go change into "something more appropriate." With Lila, one never knew quite what that might turn out to be.

About the time the food was delivered, Abby realized that she had not seen Lucky since she had gone upstairs to pick out what to wear. She quickly found him asleep atop the clothes still strewn across the bed. She also noticed scratches on the bottom of the door. "Oh, Lucky, did I lock you in? I'm so sorry. I sure don't want you to miss all of the fun." Abby rummaged through one of her drawers and pulled out a long red ribbon. "You need to be dressed up too." With effort on her part, and lots of effort on his part to avoid it, she managed to tie it around the wiggling neck. She whisked him into her arms and bounded downstairs. It was then she noticed the package on the couch. Abby put Lucky down, looked in all directions, and then carefully picked up the box wrapped in pink paper with a large white bow. Once again she looked around before giving the box a shake. First it was a gentle jiggle, but not much of a sound was heard. Then she gave it a big hard shake and heard sort of a thud. She was about to go for a third shake when a hand firmly grabbed her around the back of her neck.

"What are you doing, you little sneak?" said Sarah, taking the box. With her arm still on the back of Abby's neck, Sarah marched her through the kitchen. "Look what the little sneak was shaking," she complained to Claire.

Claire took the package from Sarah. "Mr. Chambers brought this for you. I guess I should have let him give it to you instead of leaving it in the living room."

"Are there any rules that say the birthday girl can't open one present before the party starts?" asked Daniel, who was now finished with food duty.

"Not that I know of. I say it's up to her," agreed Claire, holding out the box.

Abby took the package and sat on the grass to open it. She carefully tried to remove the paper without tearing any. "I want to save the paper."

"Mama always did that," commented Sarah, who was just as anxious to see what was inside.

With the paper off, the lid was lifted, and a pair of white sandals was removed. Abby slowly ran her hand over the scuff-free leather and came to rest on the small butterflies that were embroidered across the top. "They're beautiful! Thank you so much!" She got up, ran toward Daniel, and hugged his legs. Then she quickly pulled off the old tennis shoes and slipped on the new shoes.

"I hope they're the right size. I just guessed," Daniel whispered.

"I think you got lucky," Claire whispered back as they watched Abby dance around the yard.

"That was very nice, Mr. Chambers. Abby has had so many pairs of hand-me-down shoes. That's a very special gift." Sarah looked longingly at her little sister as she seemed to fly with wings on her feet.

All eyes were on Abby, all except those of one small dog who had found the smell of the food much too interesting. Although Lucky was small of stature, he could jump to remarkable heights as he proved when with one strong leap he launched himself onto the end of the table. Unfortunately for him, the sound of his exuberant taste testing caught the attention of the others, whose shouts startled him. As they ran toward him, he headed down the length of the table with remnants of a cheese sandwich hanging from his mouth. Luckily for Claire, the ribbon Abby had wrapped around his neck provided just enough extra surface for her to get hold of the racing dog.

"Bad dog! Bad, bad dog!" Claire scolded, holding the pup by the scruff of his neck while Daniel and Chuckles had something to chuckle quietly about. Abby ran to get the leash so he could be better supervised. Claire surveyed the damage, and it seemed that amazingly only one tray had been touched by foot or mouth. Since there was another tray of identical sandwiches, she dumped the contents of the dog's snack tray in the trash, washed and dried the tray, and equally divided the remaining sandwiches.

"She'll never know," said Daniel, putting his hand around Claire's shoulder, "unless Chuckles tattles." She smiled and Daniel pulled her a little tighter.

When the doorbell rang at 1:45, Claire figured it was children too exited to wait. She was quite surprised to find Reverend and Mrs. Carlson instead. "Bill, Grace, what a nice surprise. Won't you come in?"

"No thanks. Lila invited us, but we thought there'd be nothing worse than having stuffy grown-ups at a children's party. We wanted to bring this for Abby. We hope she has a fun afternoon." Claire took the package and carried it to the backyard, where Abby's brothers had started to arrive. Sarah too had joined them as they sat around a table talking.

The first two guests to arrive were Vickie Thornton and Loretta Goering, teachers from school. When Claire opened the door and saw them standing there, presents in hand, she thought it awfully nice of them to take time from their weekend to attend a party and be around children again. The teachers were joined at the door by Helen Evans. Claire escorted them through the house, where they paused to admire some of the antiques Claire had collected. When the three got to the backyard, more guests had come in through the back gate.

Tim Payne, dentist, and William Swan, real estate agent and town attorney, had walked together down the alley from the end of the block where they were neighbors. John Brook, high school coach, was visiting with the McRoberts boys. Floyd and Lloyd Lavelle had returned looking much neater than earlier in the day. Parked in the alley outside the gate was the star-bedecked black car of Sheriff Butch Johnson. Irma Fisher also had joined the group. The children from the other temporary foster families had come in and were sitting politely by the McRoberts clan and John Brook.

Claire again heard the doorbell and was greeted by quite a group and those ever familiar words, "Hi, kiddo!" Rudy Milstein led the way for the new group. And an interesting group it was—Phoebe Peoples, the church organist; Marian Fossel, second grade teacher; Cliff Wilkens, school custodian; and Thomas Thomas, the new young Lutheran minister. At the rear and looking more as if she were about to face a firing squad was Pearl Hatcher, school principal.

Claire was walking them through the kitchen when again the doorbell rang. This time it was a smiling Ben Miller, one of Claire's favorite neighbors, and a not so smiling Bertha Banter, the dour city librarian. Claire was surprised to see them but really not much more surprised than seeing who already had arrived. "Ben, it's good to see you," she said, bending over and planting a gentle kiss on his cheek. "And Bertha, how nice of you to join us. The festivities are in the backyard."

"I hope there are no bugs."

"Pardon me?" Claire wasn't sure she had heard correctly.

"I hope there are no bugs. I don't like being around bugs."

Claire thought Bertha could have added "or people" to her comment. "I do have some insect repellant if it should be a problem."

"Can't stand it. Gets one all sticky or oily."

Claire chose to say nothing but instead indicated the way toward the back door. "Where in the world did Lila come up with this guest list?" Claire mumbled as she headed once more toward the backyard. She got there just as Lila arrived in all of her glory. The dress of pale blue lightweight fabric with draped neck, softly fitted shirt, and short sleeves, was, of course, much dressier than those of the other women. Still, it was tasteful, but the hat was another Lila special. The wide blue brim, edged with satin, supported waves of even paler blue netting and feather plumes that danced slightly in the gentle spring breeze.

Following Lila through the gate was Deputy Burton Taylor, who tried to sneak in like a child late to school. He quickly blended in with the others. Lila knew how to work the crowd as she waltzed around greeting the guests. She made her way to the head table, where she picked up her bullhorn from under the table. "I'm so glad all of you could attend this event to celebrate the birthday of sweet little Annette." Claire quickly corrected her. "Oh yes, of sweet little Abigail. Where are you, dear? Come up here so we can sing to you. Phoebe, could you start us?" With her arm around a beaming Abby, she joined everyone in the song. "And what would you like to tell the people, dear?" Lila asked, smiling down at her.

Without missing a beat, and since she had been asked, Abby instantly responded, "You sure can't sing very well." As color rose in the faces of both Lila and Claire, the crowd stifled giggles. Claire mouthed something to Abby. "Thank you all for coming. Thank you for the many gifts. Thank you, Mrs. Hayward, for planning this wonderful party."

The people clapped as Abby walked to the table with the gifts and looked at them longingly. Lila continued. "I think we should let Abby open presents. The rest of you please enjoy the lovely refreshments." The group again began to mill around as Lila hurried back to her people. She was quite busy dragging people from one to another, making sure everyone was meeting and mingling. It was almost as if she had some prearranged plan of who should meet whom and a time frame for everything to happen. Young Deputy Burton would have been more than happy to make sure that Vickie Thornton remembered him, but Lila made sure that happened when she physically grabbed him and pulled him toward Vickie. The two young people stood and visited for a while until, as if on a time schedule, Lila showed up with John Brook and pulled Burton away and headed him toward Loretta Goering, who was visiting with Thomas Thomas, who was then led to the food table and encouraged to enjoy the food for a while.

Helen Evans was introduced to the Lavelle brothers after Tim Payne had talked to her and was then rushed off to Phoebe Peoples. Cliff Wilkens was hurried to the side of Bertha Banter, and Ben Miller was hustled, as much as Ben could be hustled, to talk to Pearl Hatcher. When Lila grabbed

Butch Johnson and rushed him to replace Tim Payne at the side of Helen Evans, Lila muttered, "Wrong!" and traded Butch for William Swan.

Claire was so busy keeping a list of who had given what to Abby she was not fully aware of what was happening. She didn't even notice Jane Dunn walking toward her. "Is it time to move the children into our yard?" Claire looked up with a puzzled look. "Lila told me that part of the party plans for the children was to let them play on our new playground equipment. Where are all the children, by the way?

"What you see is what you get," answered Claire, moving her arm in the direction of the McRoberts and host family children that were patiently watching Abby go through her large array of presents. "I really don't know what's going on, so I guess letting them go play would be a good idea. Abby can stay to finish with these. I'll come get them when the cake is cut."

"Let's go, kids. Let's go play." The group raced each other through the gate and across the alley to the Dunns' backyard.

The only one who stayed was Sarah. "I'll finish with this. Why don't you go talk to the grown-ups?" Claire just started to say she wanted to stay with the two girls when Lila grabbed her and hustled her to Rudy Milstein and Fred Young. Talking to Rudy was always pleasant, but trying to carry on a sensible conversation while looking into a large plastic nose in the center of a face surrounded by a red wig wasn't easy. Thankfully it was not long before Lila had her by the elbow and was leading her to William Swan.

Since they felt they knew each other quite well, they decided not to "get acquainted" as had been their directive and instead watched Lila buzz from person to person. "Is this the latest thing in party games?" asked William.

"I have no idea, but this wasn't what I expected. I must say she's very interesting to watch, isn't she?"

"Interesting is a nice way to put it."

When Lila felt her introductions were complete, she returned to her bullhorn and asked everyone to sit according to the place cards. Until then, Claire hadn't noticed the cards on the tablecloths. Claire didn't have time to find hers since Lila asked her to retrieve the children so the birthday cake could be cut.

Abby made the first cut, and then Claire took over with help from Helen Evans. "Is she always like this?"

"Lila seems to be happiest when she's organizing people."

Claire and Helen found their places at the table with Daniel, William, Tim, and Rudy. Since Daniel was not on the original guest list, his addition made it somewhat crowded. As Claire ate she made a point of observing Irma Fisher. Rumor had it that Irma would buy a dress at the end of a week, wear it over the weekend, and then return it on Monday saying she had changed her mind. Claire was trying to commit this dress to memory to see if it showed up back at Felton's.

When the party ended, Abby politely thanked the guests. Lila talked to Abby before she left. "I hope you had a fun birthday party, little Abby. Now I have to head home. I am exhausted!"

No wonder, thought Claire, *you must have run two miles this afternoon.*

The Lavelle brothers stayed to take away the tables and chairs, and Claire insisted that they take the leftover food. The McRoberts children, in their typical polite way, also volunteered to help clean up. Matthew and Mark, with the guidance of Daniel, climbed up to release the streamers and the balloons. Jane came over to help clean up, but what she really wanted was the gossip about the party.

"That looked like a diverse group of people." Claire listed as many of the guests as she could remember. "I'll bet you didn't make the guest list."

"Are you kidding? I hardly even knew some of them, like that clown. Why do you think Lila chose that bunch?"

Jane thought for a minute. "I think I've got it. None of them are married! She's lining up prospective clients." Both of them sat back and laughed.

After everyone had left, Abby reexamined her gifts. She had received a variety from crayons and paints to dolls and stuffed animals. There also was the pink dress Claire had seen Gladys Felton taking out of the store window. In addition she had received quite a bit of money, which Claire thought was an unusual gift for a young child. Abby, on the other hand, was quite happy with it. "I'm going to give this to Daddy. I know he can use it."

Daniel offered to take Claire and the girls to Dairy King for hamburgers and fries. The girls jumped at the offer. Afterwards, Sarah helped Abby put her things away, and Claire got a very tired Abby to bed early. As she was tucking in Abby and Lucky, Abby had a very serious question. "Why didn't any of my school friends come to my party? Don't they like me?"

Claire leaned over and tenderly brushed a wisp of red curl off her forehead. "I think that Mrs. Hayward got the invitations all mixed up and sent them to grown-ups by mistake. I'm sure your friends would have come if they'd received invitations. I hope you still had a nice party."

"I did." Then she stated very emphatically, "We should go to see Daddy tomorrow. I want to tell him all about my party."

"We'll think about that in the morning."

"We'll go. I know we will." As Claire closed the door, she had the feeling Abby probably was right. It would be a good thing to do.

When Claire came down, she and Daniel relaxed and talked. "Lila asked me some unusual questions today," commented Daniel with a whimsical look on his face.

"Like what?"

"She wanted to know if I was getting close to retirement or if I could run my government business out of Hayward. She asked what I thought of middle age marriages. Stuff like that."

"I heard her asking others some weird questions too. I was surprised people stayed as long as they did. With her strange behavior, I would have left if I hadn't lived here. Hey, how about another piece of birthday cake? I think I can enjoy it now." Claire went to the hutch where she had set the remaining plates and napkins. She paused for a moment and then looked more intently. "That's funny. The little blown glass swans aren't here."

"They most likely just got moved with all the commotion. They'll probably turn up tomorrow."

SEVEN

Abby stuck to her guns about visiting her father. Sarah said she would like to see him too. The two older boys decided to go, but Luke and John didn't want to see him lying there unable to respond. Daniel volunteered to drive so he could get to know more of the McRoberts. Claire gave Abby only half a Dramamine since she was worried a whole pill might make her too sleepy for the visit with her father.

The children talked some about school and their friends, but overall they were quite reserved. When they reached the hospital, the staff on duty remembered the first visit of the McRoberts and was somewhat relieved that the number was smaller.

Abby insisted that she go first and rejected the offer that another sibling be with her. "No, I need to talk to Daddy alone. We'll be just fine." With those words she staunchly followed a nurse to her father's bed. She went right to his side and gently held his hand.

"Hi, Daddy. I'm sorry I didn't come sooner, but I have been busy with school. And besides, I didn't have a way to get here. It's just too far to walk. Daddy, did you remember today is my birthday? Mrs. Menefee had a big party for me yesterday, and I got lots of great things and even some money. I counted it and it's eighty dollars. Can you believe that! Eighty dollars! But

I'm gonna save it for when you come home and you can have it. I prayed that God would help to take care of us, and he is doin' a good job. I know you don't believe. I guess that's up to you. But I believe enough for both of us. So I'll keep prayin' and I know you'll be okay someday. I have to go now." Abby motioned for the nurse to come closer and asked for a boost so she could bend over to kiss her father's cheek. "I love you, Daddy." Then with absolute certainty she turned to the nurse and stated, "He can hear me. I know he can."

The other three also asked to visit their father alone. It was as if Abby's bravery had set the expected norm and none of them wanted to appear reluctant to be alone with him. There was little dialogue from the boys, but Sarah tried to present a verbal picture that things were going well and that he was not to worry about them. "You just worry about taking care of yourself and getting well."

As Daniel turned on the ignition, Abby nodded triumphantly. "Seein' Daddy was the best birthday present I could have. Thanks for bringin' me, Mr. Chambers." Daniel and Claire looked at each other with a look of guilt. With all of the excitement on Saturday, they had forgotten that Sunday actually was her birthday.

Daniel thought for a moment and then in a quiet voice said to Claire, "I've got it covered." The six of them drove for about five minutes before the car pulled into the parking lot of Duncan's Dairy Delights. The children looked in amazement at the huge ice cream cone that marked the front of the building. They piled out and walked into the store through a cut-out of a tall chocolate soda. They were seated at a large rounded red vinyl booth, and a smiling waitress brought menus. "Have anything you want," Daniel announced.

The children looked at each other in amazement, and then they returned in wide-eyed wonder to the taste-tempting menu. Claire felt either they had never been in an ice cream store before or they had been limited in what they could order. Each child selected something different from the Tin Roof sundae to the Chocolate Waterfall Supreme. Daniel and Claire decided to share the oversized banana split.

After the orders were placed, Daniel excused himself, leaving Claire to enjoy hearing the children talk about how just a trip to Dairy King to get a small cone was the closest they ever had come to going out for ice cream. Daniel returned shortly and joined the conversation about ice cream. Claire told that her favorite place for ice cream was a small family-owned store that sat on a county road but was always crowded on summer nights. Daniel said his favorite place to get ice cream was his grandparents' where they churned their own. Claire added that her father did that too, but not very often. She even remembered one time when, for variety, he had added strawberries to the ice cream. Unfortunately, he left them whole, and they froze as hard as rocks and no one could even bite into them.

When the order came, it took more than one waitress to deliver it. In fact, it looked as if all of the employees were helping. Not only did they bring the ice cream, they also stayed and sang happy birthday to a beaming Abby. As the children ate, Claire had as much fun watching and listening to them as she did eating her share of the banana split. There were lots of giggles, and extra napkins were requested to clean chins from the multi-flavored dribbles. When everyone was finished and quite full, they walked to the door, where Daniel paid the bill.

"Thank you, sir," said the waitress. "It was a pleasure serving you. You have a lovely family."

The children managed to hold their laughter until they were outside. "She thought you were our parents," smiled Sarah. "That's pretty cute." Daniel and Claire looked at each other and laughed too as they walked to the car.

When they arrived back in Hayward, Daniel and Claire decided to take a walk. The children went to play with the twins and followed Daniel and Claire. When they came to the Graves' house, Claire saw Ellen Hornsby, Helen Evans, Betty Nutting, and Elizabeth Lambert, sister of Mayor Hayward.

"It looks as if I missed a meeting of some kind," said Claire.

"Yes, it's the meeting of the Babysitters Relief Society," answered Betty. "We've been doing tag team sitting so Vernina could make a fast trip over to Livonia to see her aunt. She just got back, but we're too tired to move."

"We wanted to play with the twins," said Mark, who seldom said much of anything. "Where are they?"

"They're just waking up," answered Vernina, coming out the door. "Why don't you go get them up? I'll be there in a minute."

Claire filled them in on the hospital visit and ice cream stop. Then she and Daniel continued their walk. Sarah came out on the porch as Claire was finishing the story. As Daniel and Claire walked off, she told about the waitress mistaking them all for a family. "She thought Mrs. Menefee and Mr. Chambers were married. Isn't that cute?" She watched them fondly as they walked up the street.

Mondays were Claire's days to help in the school library. She shelved and checked out books, read to classes, and did whatever was needed. Halfway through the morning, Theresa Stevens rushed into the library to tell Claire she was needed in the office right away. Claire, of course, was worried about what could have happened, but she was sure that whatever it was would not be good. When she reached the office, Pearl Hatcher was waiting and ushered Claire into her office, closing the door behind her. Already there, sitting stiffly in a chair, was Abby. Claire sat down beside her while Pearl shuffled around to the back of her desk.

"We seem to have a situation here, Mrs. Menefee. It seemed that Abby got into a fight with another girl at recess."

"Abby?" interrupted Claire in disbelief. "What happened?"

"I can't get her to say much, but from what her teacher said, the girls got into an argument at recess, and Abby pushed her and then hit her."

"Is the other girl all right?" asked Claire.

"She is fine, but we need to get to the bottom of this."

"Where is the other girl? Shouldn't she be here also?"

"I think we have who we need right here," Pearl replied brusquely.

Claire was irritated that Abby was the only one called into the office but figured for the moment she wouldn't bring up that point. "Tell me what happened, honey." Abby sat silently and firmly, staring at the wall. "I need to know—now." Claire tried to be firm when what she really wanted to do was hold Abby in her arms and provide comfort for a little girl whose world seemingly was going through more turmoil.

Finally Abby began her story. "Melissa called me a liar." The two women waited silently, and then she continued. "She yelled at me that I had lied about invitin' her to my birthday party. She said I had said she was gonna be invited and that she really wasn't invited because I just wanted to hurt her feelings. She said I was mean. So I pushed her." There was a long pause, and the tears began to fill her eyes that had turned from anger to sorrow. "Then she said she hoped that Daddy would die. That was when I hit her."

Claire thought her heart would break, and she reached out to hug and comfort the crying girl. A quick glance at Mrs. Hatcher told Claire that even she was moved. When Abby had calmed down, Pearl spoke up. "Well, that certainly was an unkind thing for her or anyone to say, and I'm sure you are sorry that you hit her, aren't you?"

"Yes, I guess."

"I think it best if you apologize to Melissa, and then we can put this entire unfortunate event behind us."

When Claire and Abby walked home from school, they discussed the disagreement. Claire asked how many children Abby had told they would be getting invitations to her party.

"I can't remember, but it weren't very many. And I certainly didn't say it to no boys!"

"Pretend you are Melissa and you are excited because you think you're going to go to a party with some friends. And then you don't get invited after all. How does that make you feel?"

"Not too good, I guess. It must be kind of like standin' in line to get a piece of chocolate birthday cake and when it's your turn, the chocolate part is all gone and all that's left is dumb old vanilla. Or worse, there's no vanilla left either."

"So we agree Melissa was disappointed and her feelings were probably hurt too. What do you think you could do to make her feel better?"

"I already apologized, didn't I?" Abby snapped defensively.

"Yes, but I'm not sure that made her sad feelings go away. Do you like Melissa?"

"I liked her better before she said those things."

"I know, but did you like her before that?"

"Yeah, she's okay."

"I have an idea. Why don't you invite her over and the two of you can play? We could even make cookies or bake cupcakes. You two could have your own private party."

"I guess that'd be okay, but I don't want her talkin' mean about Daddy again."

"I doubt that we'll have to worry about that. Now let's go home and have lunch."

Claire wasn't sure what kind of reception she'd get when she called Melissa's house, but she knew it had to be done. She would have been relieved if no one had answered, but it was picked up after the first ring. "Mrs. Clark, this is Claire Menefee. I am taking care of Abby McRoberts and—" Claire was cut off before she could finish the sentence, and she expected the worst.

"Mrs. Menefee, Melissa told me what happened and I am so sorry. Melissa never should have said those terrible things about that poor man. I cannot imagine how upsetting it must have been to that little girl. I cannot tell you how very sorry I am."

Claire was so surprised and relieved that she didn't respond for a moment. "I appreciate your apology, but I think both of the girls were wrong. In fact, Abby feels badly about what happened and wondered if Melissa could come over some afternoon to play."

Mrs. Clark also was relieved the incident was seemingly put to rest, and the two planned a time for the get-together. Claire had barely hung up when the phone rang again. There were some uncomfortable pauses after Vernina identified herself. Then she forced herself to come right to the point.

"I noticed last night that one of my grandmother's small china dolls is missing from the set I have sitting in the living room. I know it was there yesterday morning because I was dusting so things would look nice when the ladies came over. I have looked everywhere, Claire, and I just wondered if…if you had seen it by any chance."

"Well, no. I know the dolls you're talking about, but I didn't even go in yesterday. Daniel and I just kept on walking when the kids stopped in to…" Claire suddenly realized what Vernina was suggesting. "Oh, Vernina, I don't think that either one of the girls would have taken it."

"I really don't think so either, but Sarah and Abby had admired them. I just wondered if maybe they absentmindedly picked it up and forgot to set it back down before they left, don't you know."

"I'll sure ask the girls and have them check the pockets of what they were wearing too. I'll give you a call if I learn anything."

Claire had a sick feeling in her stomach. This was the third thing that had disappeared since the McRoberts children had moved in—the silver jam spoon from the Nuttings, the blown glass swans from her dining room, and now the china doll from Vernina's house. Claire had discussed the disappearing swans with both girls, and each had claimed no knowledge of what had happened to them. Now she was going to have to ask them about other items. "Man, I didn't sign on to this job to play detective," she said to herself as she went to look through her cookie recipes.

Not wanting to spoil dinnertime, Claire decided to bring up the other two missing items after they ate. Since all of them were in the kitchen doing dishes together, she decided it was best to get it over with. She had never been one for confrontations and was always trusting when a person claimed innocence or ignorance of something.

"Girls, I have a question that maybe you could help me with. Mrs. Graves called this afternoon and said she can't find one of the little dolls from her doll collection. She wondered if either of you might have remembered seeing it in some other place in the house when you were there yesterday."

"Which one's missing? I hope it's not the one with the fancy red dress. She's my favorite," volunteered Abby.

"I don't remember them much at all. I know we had looked at them before, but this time I just walked by and went right to the twins' room upstairs," Sarah explained.

"If you happen to think of anywhere they could be, just let me know. Mrs. Graves is sad that one of them is missing."

Reality suddenly hit Sarah. "Oh gee, she doesn't think one of us took it, does she? We didn't, or at least I didn't," she added, looking suspiciously at Abby.

"Well, I sure didn't take it neither! Why does everyone always blame me for everything?"

"No one's blaming either of you. She just wanted me to ask if you had any idea if they might have been misplaced. Just forget it and let's finish these dishes so we can get homework done."

"I'll do mine in my room tonight," Sarah said with an irritated tone as she deposited the dishtowel on the table and marched out of the room.

"And I'm gonna go read to Lucky. He never blames me for nothin'! Come on, boy."

"Well, that went well," sighed Claire as she put away the rest of the dishes, "but who could blame them? I think I might have jumped to conclusions too fast. I'm sure there's a logical explanation for these disappearances."

Later that evening, Claire went up to tell the girls good night. By now Abby had become accustomed to staying in her own bed, so she went to talk to her first. "Good night, sweet Abby. I want you to know I trust you. I hope you have pleasant dreams. I'll see you in the morning." She kissed Abby on the forehead and patted Lucky. "Pleasant dreams to you too, and no barking in your sleep." Abby giggled, and Claire turned out the light.

Claire's good night message to Sarah was the same, but she was not as willing to let the subject drop. "If Mrs. Graves tells people the doll is missing and says the McRoberts kids were the last ones to see it, then people all over town will think one of us—or all of us—are thieves. That's how people treat poor people. They think they steal to get what they want. It's happened to us before."

"I wouldn't let it worry you. I'll call Vernina back tonight and tell her neither of you knows anything about the doll. I'm sure the matter will go no further. Now you finish your homework and get some sleep." Claire shut the door as she left, but she wished that she could shut out the thoughts that were going through her head. Would others who heard about this jump to the same conclusions that she and Vernina had? Unfortunately, she thought that Sarah had a point. Plus, now she was wondering about Sarah's comment about the family being blamed before. That planted a bit more doubt in Claire's mind.

When she was sure Sarah was asleep, she called Daniel. "I need some help with interrogations."

"What?" he replied with surprise.

Claire explained what happened and how the girls responded. "I feel so guilty, but yet I still kind of wonder."

"So you're human and you're facing an unusual situation. I'll bet those things will turn up in some weird place and the whole thing will be over."

The two talked for a while longer before the conversation ended with, "I wish you were here right now."

"So do I, Claire. So do I."

After Abby's daily far-too-brief nap, she and Claire went to pick up a few items. At the hardware store Claire wanted to replace the yardstick Lucky had turned into a very long chew toy. Abby jumped when she walked through the door and encountered Farley, rifle across his lap. Her apprehension didn't last very long as instead she inched closer to him.

"Hey, mister, why'd you need a gun in here anyway?" she asked, first examining the gun stock to barrel and then Farley head to toe. Farley, who was unaccustomed to people addressing him directly, didn't respond at first. She continued to stare at him and repeated her question. "I said why'd you have that gun in here?" And after a few seconds added, "Cat got your tongue?"

Farley leaned over and looked her square in the eye and quietly said, "Because they might come any time now."

In turn Abby leaned in closer and replied almost in a whisper, "Who might come?"

"The Krauts."

"The Krauts?" Abby turned back toward Claire.

"I'll explain later. Tell Farley good-bye, and let's go look for that yardstick." Since Bob wasn't around to help, Claire had to wander to find what she was looking for. She was so intent on her search she didn't notice Abby wasn't with her. She backtracked and found her sitting on the floor in front of Farley. The two seemed to be carrying on a conversation. Since things seemed to be under control, she continued her hunt and then took the yardstick to the counter where Bob was now busy sorting out a pile of nails.

"Don't tell me that nails come all mixed up like that."

"Oh no. I was carrying the new shipment to add them to the shelf when some darn mouse ran in front of me. I'm not afraid of mice, I want you to know, but that sudden movement startled me. I dropped all of the boxes and they went everywhere. It took Dad and me quite a while to pick them all up."

"You should ask that old guy over there to shoot that mouse," said a voice from in back of Claire. Abby was standing with a serious look on her face. "Daddy took a shot at a rat once. Never hit him but scared him so much we never seen him around again."

When they left the store, both spoke to Farley. "Good-bye, mister. It was nice talkin' to you," Abby said.

"What did you two talk about?" Claire probed as they headed to the drugstore.

"I don't know, just stuff. He looked kind of like my grandpa." Those words were barely out of Abby's mouth when she stopped and stared at the young woman leaving the drugstore. She watched as she got into her car and drove past them heading up Main Street.

Claire wasn't sure what the fascination was, so she ventured a guess. "Pretty, isn't she?"

"Yeah, but she looked an awful lot like Momma. She had red hair. That's where we all got ours. Who is she?"

"I don't know," shrugged Claire, realizing she had seen the woman a couple of times before in the drugstore. "I guess we could ask."

The bell over the door rang as they entered, and Abby looked around to try to figure out where the sound was coming from. "Hey, kiddo, what are you up to?" yelled Rudy from one of the aisles. "What can I do for you two lovely ladies this fine afternoon?"

"In the first place," Abby said, emphatically placing her hands on her hips, "I ain't no lady. In the second place, we want to know who that was that just left."

Rudy looked at Claire and raised his eyebrows. Then he bent over to talk to Abby. "I am sorry if I insulted you, Miss."

"Just call me Abby and tell me if you know who that was."

"Okay, Abby. That's a college friend of my nephew's. Her name is Tara Frasier. She comes over to see Ronnie every now and then. Pretty, isn't she?"

"Yeah, and I like her hair too."

"We came to look for some new coloring books or paper dolls. Abby's entertaining a friend, and we want to find something fun for them to do. We'll just go look, Rudy." Claire looked at makeup while Abby made the final decision in the children's aisle.

When the choice had been made, Abby carried two new coloring books and a box of crayons to the front counter. "For the books and crayons, that will be one dollar and ninety-five cents, and the information about the redhead is free today." Abby giggled and proudly gave Rudy two dollar bills.

Claire was somewhat surprised to hear Lila's voice on the phone since she was not used to getting calls from Mrs. Mayor. In fact, knowing the peculiar ideas that Lila sometimes came up with, she wondered if it would have been better to have ignored the ringing phone.

"Hello, dear Claire, however are you this beautiful morning?" She continued without giving Claire a chance to respond. "I am having a fun little game night Saturday, and I would love to have you join us. I'm hoping that handsome police officer friend of yours might be in town so he could come too. So can I plan on your company on Saturday?"

"Thanks for the invitation, Lila. Let me check my date book. Hold on." Claire held the phone close to the book she had been reading and rustled the pages. After about a minute she casually brought the phone back up. "What time would that be?"

"I thought seven would be good, not too early, not too late for the early risers for Sunday church. So can I count on you and … and … and what is his name again?"

"Whose name?" Claire asked, trying to appear blasé about her friendship with Daniel.

"That handsome man that arrested those two crooks. He's a sheriff or something like that."

"Oh, you must mean Mr. Chambers. Well, I'm not sure if he can attend. I certainly don't know his schedule. But if he happens to get in touch, I'll ask him."

"But you are planning on coming, aren't you, dear? The party just wouldn't be the same without you."

Claire rolled her eyes with that comment and was glad that neither girl was home to see her response. She knew full well that Daniel was planning to be in Hayward over the weekend, and she figured she probably could talk him into going to Lila's party. He still found Lila fascinating in an annoying kind of way. "Yes, I think I can make it."

"Oh good. Please let me know about Mr. Chalmers."

"That's Chambers, not Chalmers."

"Right, dear, Chambers. Anyway, I like to keep the numbers kind of eve..." Lila stopped herself mid-sentence and rephrased her comment. "I like to keep the numbers small for a fun evening." Claire once again rolled her eyes as she remembered the Haywards' Christmas party. Claire was certain half the town was in attendance. "Oh, and one more thing, Claire. Do you have any games I could borrow? What fun would a game night be if there were no games?"

What a twit! Claire thought and then answered, "I think I might have some in the basement."

"Wonderful! Could you just drop it by sometime before Saturday? Thanks so much. Now I must run. Ta-ta."

"I'm surprised that she didn't ask me to bring the refreshments too," Claire said after hanging up. "Or maybe she's asking someone else to bring those."

When Abby came home for lunch, she didn't know where Claire was until Lucky came bounding up the basement stairs when he heard her in the kitchen. Then the two went down to see what Claire was doing.

"Wow! Look at all the fun stuff!" Abby squealed as she started looking through a pile of old stuffed animals, toys, and games. Lucky too was having fun with what barely resembled an old stuffed bear that he tossed into the air and then ran after it. "Can I play with these?"

"I suppose, but they're quite dusty, and they're quite old and used too."

While Claire was deciding which game to loan, Abby unearthed a box of dolls dressed in costumes from different countries. "Melissa and I would like to play with these. Can we?"

"You mean 'may we.'"

"Oh, did you want to play too?"

Rather than trying to take a grammatical stand, Claire decided simply to decline the offer, and she took a dusty game of Parchesi upstairs while Abby carried up the box of dolls.

After dinner the three walked to the Haywards' to take the game. As they went up the walk toward the impressive building, Abby looked around trying to take in the size of what was considerably larger than the other houses in Hayward.

"How many people live here, anyway?" she asked, looking up at the second floor balcony.

"Two."

"Just two? Gee, it must get lonely in some of the rooms with no one there."

Sarah gave her a sideways glance. "That was silly. Rooms don't get lonely."

Claire was glad they had reached the door so the argument she sensed was about to happen was cut off with the ringing of the doorbell.

Chester answered the door. "Howdy, little ladies. Is it Girl Scout cookie sale time already? I'll take three boxes." Claire introduced the girls and explained why they were there. "She's going to have a what? When? Oh, come on in and you can give it to her yourself. I just can't keep up with all these things she plans." Chester ushered the visitors into the kitchen, where Lila was looking over an array of cookbooks. "Claire is here with a game she said you asked her to bring for some shindig you're planning."

"Oh, Chester, think! That was why Ben Miller and our new neighbor, Helen, brought those games over earlier. Your brother said I could borrow some from him too." Chester just shook his head, turned, and walked out of the kitchen. "Men! They just can't seem to remember a thing. Thanks for bringing this. Now help me choose a recipe."

While the two adults browsed the cookbooks, the girls wandered in amazement around the kitchen, which was very large and very modern. There was lots of counter space in addition to an island work space. A variety of highly polished pots and pans hung from a rack above the island. At one end of the kitchen, separated slightly by two large upright oak beams, was a dining area. There was a fireplace on the outside wall. The fireplace had a decorative mantel, which was currently filled with a collection of ceramic cows, pigs, and chickens. The farm theme also was carried out in the kitchen towels that hung from a rack at the end of the island. There were even sets of chicken and pig salt and pepper shakers sitting on the island along with a cream pitcher in the shape of a calf with a mooing mouth spout.

After leaving, the girls commented on the house. "I can't believe how big that kitchen was. It seemed as big as our entire kitchen, living room and our bedroom," marveled Sarah. "But if I had a kitchen like that, I would love to cook. I would want to be cooking all the time."

"She sure had some funny things," added Abby. "I don't think I would want to drink milk that came out of a cow's mouth."

Claire called Daniel after the girls had gone to bed and tried to build up his enthusiasm for Lila's party. "She called it a game night and is gathering different games to play. I know because the girls and I took one over to her this afternoon. She mentioned that other neighbors also had contributed. She specifically asked if you would be able to come also. She must have a little crush on you since she kept talking about you as my very handsome friend."

"Stop for a minute and let me get this straight. Lila is having a game night where people can play a variety of games? But she seems to have no games of her own so she has to borrow them from others? And her guest list includes people she hardly knows?"

"That about sums it up. So what do you say?"

"Who else will be there besides the queen bee herself?"

"Now that's another strange thing. On the way back from taking the game, I talked to Dorothy and Elizabeth, and I mentioned Lila's party. Neither one of them knew anything about it. Then I felt bad they had not been invited."

"I wouldn't feel too bad. Maybe they're feeling relieved they weren't included. Maybe we should be the ones feeling bad."

"So does that mean you will go?"

"I don't know how I could say no, especially to someone who has noticed my ruggedly handsome looks. Besides, I do enjoy spending time with your friends. Some of them are quite … er, interesting and colorful. You have to understand that playing games isn't one of my favorite things, but I'll go just to keep you company. I'm curious about who else might be coming. I wonder if Chuck will be there."

"Chuck?" Claire asked. "Do I know a Chuck?" Then she laughed. "Oh yeah. I wonder if he'll be dressed the same. Otherwise, I doubt I would recognize him."

They talked a while longer before the conversation ended. Just before they hung up, Daniel said, "I have one more question about the party Saturday. So you think they might play spin the bottle?"

"Go to bed! Good night!" Claire smiled as she placed the phone back in the receiver.

Daniel showed up at Claire's Saturday afternoon. Claire, however, was not at home. She had made a fast trip to the library to deposit some books she had forgotten were due. In the months she had lived in Hayward, Claire had become a faithful library customer and had not once failed to return books on time. She had to admit she wasn't sure what the consequences, or punishments, were for returning things late. Even though she outwardly professed to no longer being afraid of Bertha Banter, the ill-tempered town librarian, Claire didn't have any desire to get on Bertha's wrong side for any reason. It had taken months before she was allowed to check out books without showing some form of identification and become somewhat trusted by the librarian. She didn't want to take any chances of not keeping her library record blemish-free.

Sarah answered the door when Daniel rang the bell and invited him in. "I'd stay and visit, but I'm in the middle of doing my nails. Abby's in the backyard if you want to talk to her. She'll talk to anyone." The minute that she said those words, she began to blush. "Oh, I didn't mean it like that. I just meant most of the time she loves to talk to anyone about anything. I think you're nice to talk to too, but I really have to go now."

As Daniel walked through the dining room, he looked at the hutch where the glass swans had rested but found they had not returned. He continued on to the back porch, where he stood for a couple of minutes just watching Abby as she played in the yard. Then she suddenly dropped down to the ground on her back and appeared to be looking up into a flowering bush. She lay very still in that position for a long time. Finally, his curiosity got the best of him, and he decided to see what she was doing. Not wanting to startle her, he called from the porch. "Is anyone out here?"

"I am," she answered, sitting up and waving.

Daniel walked over and squatted down beside her. "Do you mind if I join you?"

"No, but you have to sit still and be quiet."

In a whisper he asked, "I can do that, but why?"

"I'm waiting for my butterfly."

"Your butterfly?"

"There is a big beautiful butterfly that sometimes comes and talks to me."

"It talks to you?"

"Yes, but it talks very softly. It has to be very quiet out here or I can't hear it. I don't think you'll be able to hear it either, unless it sits right on your shoulder and talks right in your ear. So sit still and wait."

The two sat close together in silence, just waiting and enjoying the warm afternoon. Daniel was beginning to get impatient when he spotted a rather large butterfly fluttering around the blossoms in the bush overhead. He could feel his muscles tensing to make sure that his body gave no involuntary movements. After landing on a few of the flowers, the butterfly fluttered around his head and then around Abby's before landing on her shoulder.

The multicolored insect was perched right in front of Daniel's eyes, and it seemed to be staring at him. In fact, had anyone been watching, it would have appeared they were having a stare-down. Daniel studied the beautiful, fragile-looking creature that had a wing span of about six inches. The main wing color was a creamy yellow with black segmenting markings. Toward the bottom of the wings, there were small sections of rust and pale blue. The body was mainly the same creamy yellow, but there was a definite black stripe down the middle of the back.

Slowly the butterfly's apparent examination of Daniel ended, and the six fragile legs moved so its head faced Abby's neck. She tilted her head toward the creature and held back a giggle as the antenna softly brushed against her neck. It was in that position for just a moment before it took off and once again resumed its fluttering around the yard. Then it gently flew over the fence into the Nuttings' yard next door.

"See, I told you I had a butterfly that talked to me."

"And you were right. But I didn't hear a thing. What did it say?"

"Are you sure you want to know?"

"Yes, I think so."

"Well,"—she hesitated—"it said you have a sad heart."

Daniel was stunned. "Did it say why?"

"No, but I think you have a sad heart too."

"Why do you think that, Abby? I think I'm a pretty happy person."

"Well, you are most of the time, on the outside. But there's just somethin' kind of sad about you too. I don't know what it is, but I thought that when I first met you. It's kind of like you're, uh...missin' somethin' in your life."

Daniel sat there dumbfounded, not knowing what to say. Here was a little girl who had no mother, whose poor family had been torn apart, whose father was fighting for his life, and she—and that alleged talking butterfly—could read him like a book. Even through her own misfortunes she saw sadness in him that even he often tried to forget. Abby continued to look at him with understanding eyes as if waiting for him to say something. Thank goodness the awkward moment was broken up with the sound of the screen door closing.

"I hope I'm not interrupting. You two look much too serious for such a lovely day."

"No, we were just visiting, weren't we?"

"We're just talkin' about butterflies. I like them very much. But I think Lucky would like to go for a walk."

"I think that's a great idea. Just make sure that leash is fastened tightly. We don't want to have to chase him down Main Street like we did last week." Abby skipped to the porch and let the door slam behind her. "I'd remind her to close it quietly, but this way I can tell when one of them is coming or going. Anyway, what were you two talking about, if you don't mind my asking?"

"It seems Abby has her own butterfly that talks to her. And a very lovely butterfly it is too. I saw it land right on her shoulder. You came just after it left. Quite an imagination that girl has." Daniel chuckled, and he tried quickly to change the subject. "So what time are we due at Lila's?"

"Seven o'clock, so we have plenty of time. What would you like to do?"

"We could go for a bike ride," Daniel said, smiling.

"I think we've discussed that before, but since we still have no bikes, that's not an option. How about a walk around town? The way things are starting to bloom it should be lovely."

They had not gone far when they met Ben, who was doing his best to improve the appearance of his yard. Even though Ben had moved into town a few years ago, he still was not used to having to do yard work. He had farmed most of his life and moved into town at the request of his late wife. Ben could easily plow or reap acres of good farm land, but pushing a lawnmower or using hedge trimmers seemed almost beyond him. The previous fall Claire had helped plant some shrubs to hide the house's foundation, and she was pleasantly surprised that Ben had managed to keep them alive, at least so far.

"Hi, Claire, Daniel. Beautiful day, isn't it?"

"Yes, and it's a great day to get in some yard work. I assume that you're going to Lila's tonight since you provided her with a game to use."

"Yeah, I thought it was a little odd, but then you know Lila." Ben laughed. "You just never know what that woman will come up with next. Bertha was invited, but she said there was no way she was going to sit around all night and pretend she was having a good time. I like games as long as I don't have to play charades. I hate that."

"Me too," said Daniel.

"And me too," added Claire. The three looked at each other and laughed. "I get dibs on having a headache if she brings it up."

"I think I will be too sore from all of this yard work," grinned Ben.

The two looked at Daniel. "I'll just have to arrest her for being too annoying."

Claire and Daniel continued on their walk when Ben called after them. "Are you staying at the Snooze Inn when you come to town?" Daniel nodded. "Why don't you just stay with me whenever you're here? I could sure use the company, and you would be much closer to Claire." She blushed a bit with those words. "You could even help me with some of this infernal yard work."

Daniel nodded as he looked over Ben's lot. "We might be able to come to some agreement on that. I think I might take you up on your offer."

They continued toward the park. As they passed the mayor's house, Mellow let out his normal loud, obnoxious barks, and both of them jumped. "Do you ever get used to that?" Daniel asked.

"Apparently not."

"I guess I shouldn't complain about that dog since he did save me. I might not be here today if it weren't for him."

There was a woman working in the yard of the next house. She looked up at the sound of Mellow's barking. She stood up and walked toward the couple. "Isn't that dog infuriating? Beautiful day, isn't it? Are you out for a walk?"

"Would you like to come?" Claire asked Helen.

"Oh, you know that old saying. 'Two's company, three's a crowd.'"

"I'm sure Daniel wouldn't mind, would you?"

Daniel really wanted to say, "Isn't there any place in this town that we can be alone?" but instead he did the gentlemanly thing and insisted she would be more than welcome. She quickly put down her trowel, brushed the mud off her knees, and joined them.

Even though Claire had spent some social times with Helen, she really had not had the time to get to know her well. Also, with the exception of Abby's birthday party, Helen knew nothing about Daniel and his connection either to Claire or to the town. Helen became quite fascinated with the story the couple told about the former occupants of her home, Tony and Rita Canella (alias Mike and Missy Brock), who had been placed in Hayward by the witness protection program.

She loved hearing about what had happened on the evening they were planning to leave town with all the funds they had embezzled. Daniel, who ironically happened to be in town for Founders' Day, had sensed something was wrong and was coming down the alley to check out things from the back of the house. In the meantime Farley, having misinterpreted something in his alleged codebook, burst through the front and got the drop on the couple. They in turn forced him to drop his rifle. Daniel then came through the back door and took control. However, a gangster that was out to find and eliminate Tony Canella had followed Daniel down the alley and crashed through the back entrance, forcing Daniel to drop his weapon.

Coming through the front door at that same time was Clara, who had been watching Farley and followed him to the Canellas' house. But to the surprise of everyone involved, Mellow had become interested in what was going on in the yard behind him. He jumped the fence, charged through the opened back, jumped on the gangster, and held him firmly in his teeth. At that point Clara pulled her squirt gun from her purse and squirted the growling dog in the eyes, causing him to release his grip.

"Wow! That is quite a story! That would make a great scene in a movie. I am sorry I missed it."

"I think Claire gladly would have traded places with you. We forgot to mention that while trying to be a good neighbor, she ended up tied to a chair in the bedroom while all of this was happening."

"On second thought, I'll just wait for the book or the movie."

"Now, I know you are from Chicago and are on sabbatical working on a book. How's that coming?"

"Okay, but writing a book takes time, especially when it involves research."

"What kind of research are you doing?" asked Daniel, thinking back to the amount of work the Canellas did to make their scheme look legitimate.

"I'm comparing the types of things important to a community: housing, food, medical care, entertainment activities, cost of living, education, and social interaction and involvement."

"So how do we stack up?" Claire asked, knowing she had some definite opinions.

"Really pretty good. There's not a lot of available housing, but yet there doesn't seem to be much of a demand. I easily found a house, and I think you said that you did also, right, Claire?"

"I did, but from what I heard I got lucky. And your house had not been empty for long, so your timing was good too."

Helen continued, "The grocery store isn't fancy in what it stocks, but yet it seems quite adequate for the needs of most families. The area that I see lacking is the entertainment and recreation. The movie theater's restricted schedule isn't too convenient, and not everyone seems to be into bowling. Couples seem to be quite content to stay around the house in the evenings, but for a single like me, I find very little to do to keep me entertained."

"You're going to Lila's party, aren't you?"

"Yes, and going to Abby's party was nice too, but I would like a chance to get out a little more. There don't seem to be a lot of single men around."

"Maybe there are more than you realize. You might meet someone interesting tonight."

"I'm not really interested in a serious relationship right now. My divorce is still too recent, but I wouldn't mind finding some men to socialize with just to get out and have some fun. For me to get serious again it probably would take someone about like Prince Charming. And what do you think the chances are of that?"

"Well," Daniel paused for effect, "from my experience the smooth talking Prince Charming types are most often those that you shouldn't trust. So it's good that you're not in a hurry to find that perfect man."

The three walked to City Park, took a couple of laps around its outskirts, and headed back. Daniel and Claire dropped off Helen at her house and continued back toward Claire's. Abby and Lucky were playing in the front yard. When Lucky spotted Claire, he pulled the leash out of Abby's hand and ran as fast as he could toward her. When he was about four feet away, he left his feet and launched himself. Luckily, Claire had good reflexes and was able to catch the little dog as he made contact with her body.

"Nice catch! I want you on my softball team."

While she held him, a wiggly Lucky covered Claire's face with very wet doggie kisses. "But a dog is a lot bigger than a softball and easier to see coming."

"But a softball certainly doesn't wiggle as much." By then Lucky, still in Claire's grasp, was stretching as far as he could to share his affection with Daniel.

"I'm sorry, Mrs. Menefee. I didn't mean to let him go. He just moved too fast and I wasn't ready. He did great on our walk, didn't bark or growl or anything bad. I'll take him now."

Claire put the white bundle on the sidewalk, and as Abby and dog walked into the house, Daniel commented, "I wonder who is the luckier of those two—that dog or Abby."

EIGHT

Claire made Daniel linger at her house before they headed off to the Haywards. "I wouldn't want to be first to arrive. I'm sure we'll get our fill of Lila the rest of the evening without giving her the opportunity to have just the two of us as her captive audience if we're the only ones there." When she deemed it safe, they again headed up Oak Street, this time hand in hand. At the corner they were somewhat surprised to see people lurking on the sidewalks out of sight of the Haywards' windows.

"Well, at least now there will be strength in numbers." Daniel laughed. As they started to cross Maple Street, Claire heard someone call her.

"Claire," said Dr. Tim Payne as he and William Swan stepped off Tim's porch, where they were hiding behind lattice work covered with some type of climbing vine. "We were beginning to think we were going to be the only ones at Lila's whatever-the-theme-is-this-time party."

"If you had the courage to come out in the open, you could have seen guests lingering all over the neighborhood. Come on, you two chickens. Let's get going."

"Every time I say yes to one of Lila's invitations I wonder why I don't just say no," said Tim.

"It might have something to do with the fact that the Haywards hold the lease on your office building and have kept your rent ridiculously low for years, or so I've heard," teased William.

By the time the four made it to the Haywards' sidewalk, many of the other hesitant guests joined them, and they approached the door together. Claire was in front, so she rang the bell, and the door opened almost immediately. Lila, who was attractively dressed in a peach-colored full skirted dress with satin latticework long sleeves, gushed as she welcomed her guests. A wide flower-bedecked headband adorned her head.

"Welcome, welcome! My, if I didn't know better I would think you were all hanging out on the street corners so you all could come together. Please, come in." With those words she spun around dramatically, causing her lightweight skirt to twirl around her. Then with one arm giving a graceful sweeping movement, she led them into the living room, where card tables and chairs had supplanted the normal living room furniture. "Come, come," she repeated, still waving her arm in the air. This time they followed her into the kitchen where nametags, lettered in different colors, also were marked with different letters and numbers.

"This can't be good," Daniel whispered to Claire.

"Compared to some situations you probably have faced in your job, this shouldn't be too bad," she whispered back.

"But I've never dealt with a Lila before."

"Be brave. Look tough and I'm sure things will be fine."

Lila floated through the crowd explaining that not everyone was there yet and that the games would begin shortly. She passed by Claire and Daniel, took each of their hands in hers, and gushed, "You two make the cutest little couple. Just, just... so perfect." Then she grabbed Daniel and turning back to Claire said, "Excuse us, dear." She hustled Daniel out of the kitchen and into the dining room, where she scanned the guests. After a moment she pulled him toward a group of three women. "This is our G-man hero, Daniel. He saved some of us from that very embarrassing incident a few months ago. I don't know what we would have done without his bravery and courage. This is Ruby, Vickie, and Loretta. Come, Vickie and Loretta, there is someone you absolutely need to meet." And Lila was off again, this time dragging the two younger women toward Ronnie from the drugstore and John Brook, the coach. After making sure that they all knew each other, which they did from Abby's birthday party, she continued with her people-shuffling activities. On the way back to the kitchen, she snatched one of the Lavelle twins and hustled him toward Claire.

"Claire, dear, I think you already know Lloyd."

"Floyd," he corrected her.

"Oh yes, sorry. Anyway, he runs a very successful furniture business here in town. I have known Lloyd ... "

"Floyd."

"Right, Floyd, and you could not find a nicer, more upright citizen. You two just get to know each other for a moment." Lila momentarily disappeared only to quickly come back with her bullhorn. In a volume almost overpowering, Lila bellowed, "Attention, my wonderful friends. Chester and I are so delighted you could join us. Thank you to those who are sharing their fun games. Now I have the evening all planned. And we will all have fun, fun, fun if you follow my directions. You need to go find the table with your color, and that will be your first game. So let's go find our places and get started."

After much shuffling and searching, Claire found her place. Her first game was Sorry, and she was playing with Floyd, Helen Evans, and William Swan. The four talked while they played, and Helen seemed quite interested in learning about one of the local furniture magnates and William. The fact that William was a widower seemed to create more attention than did the information that Floyd never had been married.

Floyd, on the other hand, was taken with Helen's statement she was not very happy with the furniture that came with her rental house and had been thinking of purchasing some more up-to-date pieces. He pulled a business card out of his pocket with the alacrity of a magician performing some slight-of-hand trick and handed it to Helen. "Give me a call anytime and I'll be happy to show you around the store, or we could check into getting pieces from our suppliers too."

Helen took his card and shoved it in her purse. Then her attention turned right back to William, who was excited since he had just picked a Sorry card and was getting out another of his pieces at the expense of one of Claire's. "Aha!" he said, giving her a gloating look.

In the living room Daniel was playing Mille Bornes with Irma Fisher, Pearl Hatcher, and Fred Young. Irma seemed quite interested in Daniel and questioned him about his job. She looked into his deep green eyes with the look of a teenager with a crush instead of a middle-aged widow when she told him that he must be very brave to do the kind of work he does.

"If you decide to move to Hayward, I am very helpful around the house. Sometimes men just don't see the many things that need to be done to keep a home looking nice." Daniel just nodded.

Pearl didn't think much of the game. "But then I personally am not very fond of the French. I find them to be quite snooty."

Fred, on the other hand, seemed to be having a wonderful time. He always seemed to have something to say or some comment to make, most of which he found quite funny even if no one else did. He seemed to be more jovial out of his clown costume, and, if one could tolerate his corny jokes, he wasn't too bad for a game partner.

Ben Miller and Cliff Wilkens were enjoying each other's company at a lively game of Chinese checkers. They hadn't met before but exchanged stories about "the good old days." Marian Fossel and Phoebe Peoples were tolerant of their conversation, although their good old days didn't go back as far as those of their table mates.

Maude Richards, who was enjoying a night away from her restaurant, Tim Payne, Tom Thomas, Rudy Milstein, and Ruby Smith, were at the Yahtzee table. Lila floated by the table joking about the names of the players.

"I had to be very careful with this little group. If I had gotten my vowels mixed up, I might have had two Toms or Tims. And if I was one to mix Bs and Ds, we wouldn't know our Rudys from our Rubys." She laughed and continued with her exaggerated gliding movement to another group.

The games were well underway when Lila's voice bellowed from the living room giving instructions for the next rotation. Everyone got up and moved to the new assigned locations. A group of younger players emerged from the kitchen and went to their new locations.

"I wonder where they've been," whispered Ben to Claire as they walked past each other.

"I'm not sure, but I did see a game of Twister in the kitchen."

"Oh my, I hope she doesn't have that in the plans for me." Ben rubbed his back as he spoke.

The evening proceeded with every round having a different mix of players. After round three there was a break for refreshments. Everything was attractively arranged on the table, and Lila stood close by to receive compliments. And of course, she got in a few plugs for her new wedding planning business.

"Please keep me in mind for any important upcoming events you might be planning. I'm sure I could make that special occasion memorable for you and your loved ones."

Claire wondered if Lila had done all of the food preparation herself since she couldn't imagine the social butterfly could pull it off all by herself. Her question was answered when Maude brought out another loaded tray. She was followed by Burton Taylor carrying a large, carefully decorated sheet cake.

"Mom said to make sure her cake wasn't close to the punch bowl. She didn't want to take the chance that any of the red punch Lila always serves would splash on the special white frosting on her chocolate cake. She made it her priority at the bakery this afternoon."

Claire was visiting with Rudy when Daniel came out of the kitchen and joined them. She looked at him and didn't think he looked too well.

"Are you all right?"

"My stomach is a bit upset. And my eyes need some time to readjust."

Claire nodded since she too had had these same symptoms when she had been at Lila's big Christmas blowout. "I bet you were just in the bathroom."

"I take it you've been in there too."

"Yes, and isn't it about the most horrible room you've ever seen? I didn't know you could find so many different red bathroom fixtures and accessories. And that red flocked wallpaper is like a bad, bad dream. Rumor has it that it is the only room in the house that Lila decorated herself."

Claire looked around and noticed there was more interaction between the men and women. When everyone was arriving, the men tended to stay together, as did the women. Now there were many more conversations between mixed groups.

Another thing that Claire noticed for the first time was that Chester did not seem to be in attendance. She distinctly remembered Lila had said that she and Chester were glad everyone could join them for the evening, but now it dawned on her that she had not seen him all evening.

After a break for food and a chance to get up and move, Lila directed people to their final round. Claire thought she was finishing the evening with Sheriff Butch Johnson, Lloyd Lavelle, and Tom Thomas. The three men did not seem to have much in common. Tom was relatively new to town compared to both Butch and Lloyd, who had both been born in or around Hayward. Their occupations were quite different, although one could make the argument that both Lloyd and Tom were in the sales business with the former pushing furniture and the latter promoting God. One common denominator was that none of these men had ever been married, and, as she studied each one in between her moves, Claire wondered why. Each was attractive and seemed to have a pleasant personality. She figured Lloyd was more attractive in his earlier years before his hairline had receded and his waistline expanded.

Lila raised the bullhorn to her lips once more and asked everyone to help take all of the games to the kitchen and fold up the card tables. Everyone looked relieved, and around the room comments were made about the fun evening. When some asked where the chairs were to be taken, Lila said to put them all in the living room and divide them into two groups. Then once more she blasted directions to her tired guests.

"I want all the women on this side and all you handsome men on the other."

Numerous comments such as, "Well, that lets me out!" were heard from the men's side. But, of course, that didn't work, as Lila organized everyone for another activity.

"Now we are going to end the evening with a game I know you all love—charades!"

Above the groans were three people who stood almost in unison saying they'd love to play, but their headaches were getting worse and they felt they should leave. Sounds of muffled laughter were heard through the group, and Ben whispered to Daniel who was seated next to him, "That was supposed to be my excuse."

"Oh pish posh," said Lila. "We need all of you for this fun. But I do have aspirin in the downstairs bathroom if anyone really needs it." This was followed by lots of shuddering and head shaking as people settled into their chairs. "Do I have a volunteer to be first? Now, now, don't be shy."

Everyone tried to avoid eye contact with Lila as people checked the time on watches, brushed lint off trousers, tightened shoelaces, and checked for chips in fingernail polish. Claire, who for a moment had a hard time deciding which she hated worse—playing the stupid game or the uncomfortable silence—raised her hand.

"Here we go. Claire will start off the fun. You pick out a title of a book, movie, or song."

Lila held a silver bowl toward her, and Claire quietly said under her breath, "Please don't make a complete fool of yourself." She breathed a brief sigh of relief when she opened the paper and read her movie title. She turned toward her teammates, made the motion for movie, and then held up seven fingers.

"*Seven Brides for Seven Brothers!*" yelled Helen.

"Right! Good job, Claire. Good job, ladies. Now we need a man."

Daniel, who was surprised Claire had volunteered, and thinking the sooner everyone played the sooner they could all go home, raised his hand. He quickly looked over at Claire, who gave him a wink. He reached his hand into the blue glass bowl that Lila had thrust at him. He swallowed hard when he looked at his pick. He did the movie motion, which was the only success he had. No matter how hard he tried, he couldn't think of any motions that helped the men guess *The Graduate*.

"Oh, too bad, dear, but time is up." Everyone groaned when Daniel told his title.

Things went faster after that. It was almost as if everyone had read Daniel's mind with the idea of getting it over with and getting out of there. Helen volunteered next, and Lila extended the silver bowl toward her. By just pointing to parts of her clothing immediately helped her team guess *Buttons and Bows*. Fred Young did no clowning around and instead got very frustrated with the men's inability to guess *The Philadelphia Story*.

Phoebe Peoples, who didn't seem to have a shy bone in her body, had a great time first standing on a chair and then startling everyone by falling on the floor. Marian Fossel yelled, "*The Rise and Fall of the Third Reich!*" The ladies all clapped.

Floyd drew again from the men's blue bowl. "Are you kidding me? I've never even heard of this book!"

"Just do your best. I'm sure one of the other men will know it."

Floyd tried to do his best even though everyone looked at him with blank stares. When the time was thankfully up, everyone—men and women—all responded with, "What?" when Lila announced his book title, *O Ye Jigs and Juleps.*

From the silver bowl came titles guessed relatively easily: *When You Wish Upon a Star, Singing in the Rain, Rear Window, Father of the Bride,* and *Vertigo.* From the blue bowl came *Requiem for a Heavyweight, Yojimbo, Suspicion,* and *Dr. Strangelove.*

The last contestant was John Brook, who as a coach did not like losing at anything. He read his title, motioned for a movie, turned, and looked as his teammates. He then made a sweeping motion toward all of them and silently counted off twelve of them. Then he turned toward the women and emphatically crossed his arms, and William Swan yelled, "*Twelve Angry Men.*" The women cheered.

"Very nice, very nice. And that concludes our game. It looks as if the women were the winners, but we're all winners for being such good sports. Please feel free to stay and enjoy more food. I know Chester and I won't be able to eat it all. I hope you made some new friends tonight. Thank you all so much for coming."

Although it wasn't exactly a mad rush to the front door, there wasn't a lot of lingering. People were polite to Lila as they left and thanked her for the unique game night idea. When Claire got to the door, her curiosity got the best of her. "I didn't see Chester here tonight. I hope he is not ill."

"How kind of you to ask! No, he and his brother, Charles, needed to go check their grain elevators for the upcoming summer months. There's no downtime in farming, you know. You two have a safe walk home. Oh, how silly of me. I guess you both don't go home tonight, do you? Well anyway, good night."

"That was a little awkward, wasn't it?" Claire said.

"About as awkward as explaining Chester's absence as having to inspect grain elevators at night."

They were almost to the street when Ben called after them. They turned and waited as he carefully walked down the front steps in the dim light. "Well, it could have been worse," Ben said.

Claire and Daniel looked at each other, wondering if his comment pertained to what they just said. "Oh, you mean game night?"

"Sure, what else would I be talking about?"

"We were talking about Chester."

"I think he was a wise man to be gone. That woman makes me nervous."

"Did you find a new lady friend tonight?" Claire asked.

"Oh, Claire, you know I'm a one woman man."

Claire thought about his response and wondered if he was referring to his late wife or if he was thinking about the time he had spent with grumpy Bertha Banter.

"Do you want to just stay with me tonight so you don't have to go back to the motel?"

"That's a tempting thought, Ben, but I think I'll head on back. But I would like to take you up on your offer on my future visits."

"Great! Make sure Claire gives you my number so you can call ahead to make sure that I have a vacancy." Ben laughed as he waved good night and headed toward his door.

Daniel put his arm around Claire's shoulder as they sat on her front porch swing.

"The Haywards are quite an interesting couple, aren't they? At least they give people something to talk about."

"I wonder what people say about us," Claire said, turning coquettishly toward Daniel. He put his hand under her chin and tilted her head so he could gently place a kiss on her lips. She willingly returned it.

"If anyone is watching, that will just add to their conversations," smiled Daniel.

Back at the mayor's house, Lila was congratulating herself on what she perceived as a successful evening. She and Maude were cleaning up the remaining food, which Lila insisted that Maude take home. Lila often wondered how Maude could stand to cook all day at the restaurant and then go home and cook for herself. She felt the leftovers would be a welcome reprieve for Maude.

Lila was straightening up the island and replaced the cow pitcher and chicken salt and pepper shakers she had moved to the kitchen counter to make room for the food. She made a quick round of the entire kitchen before asking Maude, "You didn't happen to see my pig salt and pepper shakers, did you? I had them earlier this week. I remember they were here when Claire and those girls brought over her game. They thought they were cute. Now I can't seem to find them anywhere. Hopefully they'll turn up when Chester helps me put away the dishes tomorrow. Maybe he stuck them some in weird place."

NINE

Claire was surprised when the doorbell rang Sunday morning while she was getting ready for church. "Now who in the world could that be?" she mumbled as she headed down the stairs in her bare feet. She was surprised to discover it was Daniel. "This is a nice surprise."

"Thanks, but I'm not here to see you." Claire was quite taken aback. "I guess that look on your face means Abby didn't tell you she asked me to go to church with her today."

"No, she didn't say a word."

"She asked me yesterday. She thought it would be good for me and would make my heart feel better. She said when her mother was sad, she always felt better after she went to church. I've always put a lot of credence in a mother's advice. Also, I couldn't say no to that pleading look on her face. So here I am. Where is my companion?"

"She ate breakfast and hurried upstairs. She said she'd be ready in time for church, but I haven't seen her since. I'll go check. Have you had breakfast? There's coffee, and help yourself to cereal or toast or whatever you can find."

Claire bounded up the steps faster than she had done since before Abby and Sarah had come. Watching them speed up and down the stairs had inspired her to pick up her pace too. She knocked on Abby's door.

"Yes?"

"May I come in?"

"Sure."

When Claire opened the door, she found Abby standing in front of the mirror checking out her appearance. On the bed was Lucky, who tilted his head back and forth as if he too was appraising her choice of clothes. Abby slowly turned to give Claire the full picture. For this special occasion, Abby had selected one of her birthday presents, a blue dress with white lace on the collar and sleeves. The color brought out the clear, blue color of her eyes. Her hair, which was usually braided or pulled back in a ponytail, now fell softly around her face and shoulders. In her hair was a blue satin ribbon.

"Does this look okay?"

"You look lovely. Your hair is beautiful!"

"Sarah did it for me. I want to look just right. This is a special day, you know."

Claire thought she knew the answer but decided to play dumb. "Why?"

"Because I'm taking Mr. Chambers to church. There's somethin' botherin' him, you know, and I want to help him figure out how to feel better."

Claire was very glad that she had not jumped in with an answer, for what Abby had just said once again showed the depth of her understanding into other people and their feelings. Claire had never had a hint when she was first getting to know Daniel that there was any sadness buried deep within his soul. But little Abby had seen it, had felt it, and had wanted to do something about it.

"Mr. Chambers is here already. I think he's having some breakfast."

"Good, because I'm not quite ready." Abby had picked up the white sandals with the butterflies Daniel had given her for her birthday. Then out of a drawer she pulled a sock on which she proceeded to spit.

"Yuck, what are you doing, honey?"

"I want these to look as clean and white as they did the day I got them. They have some dirt on them. I'm just gonna clean them off."

"I think it would be better if we got a cleaning rag from the closet and put some water on instead."

Abby followed Claire into the bathroom, rag in hand to finish the cleaning job. At their heels followed Lucky, who sat in the doorway. Abby was almost through wiping when she lowered the rag to examine the shoe. That was just the right move for Lucky, who lunged, grabbed the rag in his mouth, and ran down the stairs at full speed.

"You come back here right now, you naughty little dog!" yelled Abby, speeding after him.

"Wait, you put on your shoes. I'll get the dog." Claire continued the pursuit but didn't have to go far. Standing in the kitchen door was Daniel, holding one small white dog with one damp rag hanging from his mouth.

"Is this what you're looking for?"

"He was just helping us do a little cleaning."

Claire took the rag from Lucky's mouth, which was no easy task since he wasn't interested in giving it up, and Daniel set him down on the floor. Not wanting the fun to end, he ran in circles in the kitchen barking as he went. On one of his rounds, Claire opened the back door, and out he went.

"That should take care of that for a while," Claire said, brushing her hands together.

The two turned back toward the dining room when they heard, "Good morning, Mr. Chambers."

"Good morning, Abby. My, don't you look nice."

"Thank you. And you do too. Are you through eatin' so we can head to church? Momma always said it ain't polite to be late to God's house, especially when he offers a special invitation on Sunday mornings."

"Is Sarah coming with us?"

"No, she just doesn't understand how good church can make you feel. So you and I can just pray for her."

"Claire doesn't look quite ready," Daniel said, looking at Claire's bare feet.

Claire caught the somewhat disappointed look on Abby's face, thinking that Claire was going to tag along. There was no way Claire would have interfered. "You two just go on. I'm not even close to ready. I might have to just sneak into a back pew. I certainly don't want God to think I'm impolite. I'd better hurry. I'll see you two after church."

Claire scurried upstairs, but instead of finishing getting ready, she ran to the window. She was in time to see Abby and Daniel walking hand in hand toward the church. Of course, she had no idea what they were saying, but she could tell they were having quite a conversation. She wondered if

Daniel would pass on anything about their special time together, but she knew she would never pry. She respected the privacy of both these people who, in such a short time, had become so important in her life.

Claire found one of the last seats in the back row. There seemed to be the regular churchgoers, and she tried very hard not to look for Abby and her date. On the other hand, Abby had insisted on sitting toward the front. "You just feel extra close to God when you sit up front. I know he can find you anywhere you sit, but Mama always said it saved him time lookin' if you sat right in front."

Although Claire was very comfortable in the church, she always felt more comfortable and less conspicuous seated somewhere near the middle. She was quite certain Daniel wouldn't want to be plopped down right in front of Reverend Carlson and the choir. This was one of the first times she had been this close to the back since her first time in the church when she had first moved almost a year before. The downside was when singing the hymns it sounded more as if she were singing solo since there were no voices coming from behind to help blend in with hers.

However, the advantage in the back was that one could keep better track of who was in attendance. One of Claire's favorite church pastimes was trying to spot Lila. She seldom needed to look for the woman herself but instead just looked at the heads. This time, however, it was Clara who caught Claire's eye. Clara was two rows in front of her, and Clara's movements were what drew her attention. Clara would slowly lean forward then quickly lean back against the pew. Her daughter-in-law, Meredith, elbowed the older lady, and then the movement stopped.

After a few minutes the routine would begin again. Claire, who had by then tuned out most of the sermon, became intrigued and continued to watch Clara. After about the third round of these movements, Claire noticed what was in front and slightly to the left of Clara. There was a very large, floppy, lavender mesh bow that, if one did not know better, might think was suspended in the air. However, on further examination, Claire could see that the bow was attached to something resembling a wide but somewhat shallow lavender flower pot. The way the bow hung brought it down close to the cheek of the person wearing the creation. Clara evidently had discovered that with a little encouragement from her breath, she could move the bow and tickle the wearer's cheek. Then Claire detected movement in the pot, as if it were trying to help the bow rid itself of an annoyance. After a few more blows from Clara and a few more nudges from Meredith, a hand came up to wave in the general direction of the bow. This happened a few more times before the congregation stood for a hymn and Meredith traded places with Clara.

Claire always looked forward to the choir's presentations. Even though the choir was small in size, petite Grace Carlson could get a strong, unified effort from the members. Both of the Lavelle brothers were in the choir, and as they sang Claire was not sure which one was which. The Taylors, owners of the bakery, also were choir members, as was their son, Burton, when not on duty as deputy sheriff. Claire was somewhat surprised to see that Helen Evans had joined the group and was seated next to two teachers, Loretta Goering and Vickie Thornton. There were others who sang in the choir who lived in the outlying communities that Claire didn't know. But no matter what the makeup of the group, Grace got the most out of them.

The other musical part of the church was the organ and organist Phoebe Peoples, who played with gusto that matched her physical size. Phoebe seemed to have the philosophy that loud was better, and sometimes her accompaniment almost drowned out the choir. With Grace's direction the tempo was good, but when Phoebe played alone or with the congregation, it was always interesting to see how many tempo or key changes she would make. Claire felt that there was an arranger or composer in Phoebe who was trying to get out. More than once Claire had the desire to leave a metronome anonymously on the organ for her.

Claire stayed in the pew and greeted others as they began to leave. She spoke to Clara, Meredith, and Aaron as he kept a firm grip on his mother. Following a few steps back were Lila and Chester. Lila spoke to anyone with whom she could make eye contact. When she reached Claire, she greeted her like her best friend.

"Didn't you just have the best time last night? Where's your friend? Did he already go back to wherever it is he lives? And did you meet some interesting gentlemen? I felt everyone got along just divinely." Claire felt the conversation was probably over even without her responding. However, there was a slowdown in the line, so Lila, who apparently felt uncomfortable with a pause in a conversation, continued. "Did you notice how bad the flies were in here this morning? They kept flying around my head, and it was very annoying."

"Hmm, I didn't notice any. Maybe they were just in the spot where you were sitting." When Claire spotted Daniel and Abby exiting their row, she jumped in line behind Chester. "We missed you last night. I assume you and your brother found everything in order with your grain elevators."

"What? Oh, I wasn't ... " Chester started until Lila whipped her head around, giving him a stern look. "I mean I wasn't worried. It was Charles who felt we should check them. He worries too much."

Claire smiled. "I see. Well, it's good that Charles doesn't have to worry now."

"I was kind of surprised to see you alone this morning," said Reverend Carlson as Claire shook his hand.

"Oh, Bill, you know you are never alone when you're in church."

"Of course you're right, but you know what I mean."

"Little Abby had a date for church, and I didn't want to interfere. I had better skedaddle, or they might think I am hanging around spying on them. See you later."

Claire hurried down the steps and quickly walked back to her house. She wanted to be completely out of sight when Abby and Daniel walked home. She took a quick peek before she walked through the door and saw them just walking down the steps. Inside she was greeted with, "Hello, Mrs. Menefee. How was church?"

"It was good. I really wish you would come with us sometime. Or if you didn't want to go to the regular church service, you could go to the sixth grade Sunday school class. The kids seem to enjoy it. It's taught by John Brook, the high school coach. He's pretty cute."

"Maybe I'll think about it, sometime. Oh, the hospital called."

Claire thought Sarah might have mentioned that first. "Is there any change in you father?"

"No, they said they were just updating me, but it was the same thing they've said before. He's still in a coma, and they get no response from him. It's just so discouraging."

"But the positive way of looking at it is that things aren't worse. Remember, when the accident first happened, they didn't think he'd even survive."

Just then the door opened, and in came a beaming Abby, pulling Daniel behind her.

"We're home and we had a good time. And Mr. Chambers is taking me to dinner and we'd like you two to come too."

Sarah glanced at Claire with a questioning look. Claire wasn't sure if she was wondering if she had to go or if she should go since this seemed to be such a special time for her sister. Then Claire and Sarah looked at Daniel, who was standing behind Abby. He nodded vigorously to both of them.

"I think I'd like that. How about you, Sarah?"

"I think I would too," she said. "I'll go change."

"It doesn't have to be fancy," Daniel yelled as she ran up the stairs. "We're just going to Maude's."

When Daniel said that, it dawned on Claire that the girls had never been to Maude's. She'd been there many times, but she'd never taken the girls. She had the feeling that going out for meals was a rare occurrence for their family.

The three sat down in the living room and were immediately joined by Lucky, who jumped into Abby's lap. "So how was church?" Claire asked.

"You know. You were there too, silly." Abby giggled.

"I know, but did you enjoy the service?"

"Yeah, I did. But do you know what?"

"What?"

"That organ playing lady could use some lessons. Sometimes I think she gets confused."

"I think she gets so involved in the music that she tries to add her own style."

"Well, I don't like it, but I do like that choir. Do you think they'd let me sing with them?"

"I don't know. You should ask Mrs. Carlson. How did you enjoy the service, Mr. Chambers?" Claire asked.

"It was fine, but I especially liked the company."

"But you were supposed to like the church part," said Abby in a disappointed tone.

"I did, but I also enjoyed being with you."

Abby jumped up from the chair, dumping poor surprised Lucky on the floor. She faced Daniel with hands on hips. "We've got to work on that church part. That's the important part, you know."

"I think I'll feed Lucky some lunch before we go," said Claire.

Claire was glad to leave, for she felt Abby was getting ready to deliver her own sermon, and she knew that would be a serious moment. But with the six-year-old standing there sternly shaking her finger in Daniel's face, Claire was having trouble stifling a smile. It just seemed so backwards. Usually it was the grown-ups who were trying to convince the children of the virtue of attending church. But in this situation it was just the opposite.

Sarah popped through the door as Claire waited on the back porch for Lucky, who was having a great time chasing a squirrel that taunted him as it ran back and forth along the top of the fence. "I'm ready. How do I look?"

That comment pretty much confirmed what Claire thought about how special this trip to a local restaurant was. Looking at Sarah as she turned slowly in her yellow dress, Claire was fully aware not only of how pretty she was but also of how she was well on her way to becoming a young woman. She wondered if she would soon need to have a conversation with Sarah about the birds and bees. But then the only thing she needed to say was, "You look very lovely. Now let's go eat."

The four walked hand in hand across the courthouse square. If a stranger had seen them, he would have thought that they were a family. At Maude's they hit the end of the breakfast crowd and the beginning of the lunch bunch. Abby asked if they could have the table by the window. As soon as it was ready, she scurried over to claim a chair that let her see both the other diners as well as the sidewalk outside. Sarah sat across the table from her, and Claire sat facing inward. That left Daniel to enjoy the view of the flowers blooming in the square.

When the menus arrived, Abby held hers up and studied it as if she actually could read what was written. After a couple of minutes, she proudly said, "I'll have French fries." Daniel smiled then leaned over and helped her add to her order. "I'll have fried chicken too."

Sarah leaned over and whispered in Claire's ear. "Would it be all right if I have a steak? I'll have the smallest one."

"Honey, you have whatever you want."

Maude came to take their order. "Now, what can I get for you folks?" Once she had recorded everything, she stuffed her order tablet in her apron pocket and rushed off to another table.

Sitting where she did, Claire took a chance to check out the other customers. She waved to Helen, who was sitting between the Lavelle brothers at a table toward the back. Loretta Goering and Vickie Thornton were with John Brook. Claire had the urge to take Sarah over for an introduction but decided this was not the best time. Ruby Smith was at a table with William Swan and Tim Payne. An attractive though somewhat flashy redhead also was at the table. Although she had never met this woman, she had heard Tim frequently dated a redhead from the area. Claire thought how the population of redheads had increased drastically since the McRoberts had come to town. However, as she studied this woman, she was quite certain her color had help from a bottle.

No sooner had she passed judgment on that redhead than Abby, who was looking out the window, yelled, "Look, Sarah! Look at that lady! Doesn't she look like Mama? I told you there was a lady who looked like her."

"Shh, Abby, and please don't point," said Claire in a quiet voice but to little avail.

Sarah turned to see a lady step off the curb and get into her car. She studied her for a few moments, turning her head as if to look at her from different angles. "She does look a lot like her. Who is she?"

"All I know is her name is Tara Frasier and she's a college friend of Ronnie's who works in the drugstore."

Sarah continued to watch as she backed out of her parking space and drove slowly past Maude's. "I wonder if that's how Mama looked when she was that age," wondered Sarah out loud.

"Do you have any pictures of your mother?"

"Dad has some somewhere, but I don't know where he keeps them." She paused for a moment. "I guess if things don't work out, I'll have to go through all of his things. I guess I'll have to make some decisions about lots of things."

"Maybe, but let's look at the positive. It's a good sign your dad hasn't gotten worse." Looking up, Claire added, "And I take this as a good sign too," as Maude showed up with a large tray she set on a stand by their table.

Three of the four were about to start eating when the fourth one said, "Thank you, God, for this good food and these nice people who have taken good care of us. Please watch over our daddy and keep all of our brothers safe. Please help Mr. Chambers to feel happier. Amen."

The other three joined in the "amen," and they all began to eat. Claire continued to look around the room and out of the corner of her eye caught movement as Burton Taylor rushed by to join John Brook at the table with the two attractive young teachers. Coming in with much less speed was her neighbor Ben Miller following Bertha Banter. Claire waved at them after they were seated. Ben responded with a wave, and Bertha just scowled.

She spotted Fred Young at a corner table with Irma Fisher and Phoebe Peoples. Claire had never been to Maude's at midday on a Sunday and wondered if this was a singles gathering place. She questioned whether these match-ups were a normal occurrence or whether Lila's Saturday night party had brought some of these people together.

"This is so cool!" marveled Abby. "And we don't even have to help wash the dishes." Then she turned to Claire and quietly asked, "We don't have to, do we?"

"Of course not, you goof!" Sarah snapped at her.

Claire gave Sarah a stern look, but she didn't even notice since she was eagerly attacking her steak. The gusto with which the girls ate made Claire wonder if she had not been feeding them enough. Or maybe they just didn't care for her cooking and were too polite to say anything. She almost had the urge not to eat any of her own dinner and just take it home in a doggie bag to divide up for the girls for later.

Daniel too seemed to notice how the girls were making quick work of their meals. He looked back and forth between them. Then he looked across the table at Claire and mouthed, "Wow!" He and Claire were still eating when both Sarah and Abby finished. "How about dessert, ladies?"

Sarah, trying to be polite, answered with, "I'm pretty full, thank you anyway."

Abby, on the other hand, was her truthful self. "I don't know. What do they got?"

"You mean what do they have," Claire asked, hoping that Abby would hear the correct grammar.

"That's what I said. What do they got for dessert?"

Maude happened to be walking past and in response rattled off the day's choices for desserts. Abby didn't hesitate.

"I want that chocolate cake thing."

"And do you want that ala mode?"

"I don't think so. That sounds pretty weird."

"That just means it comes with ice cream."

"Then why didn't you just say that so people will understand?"

Maude smiled and turned to Sarah. "And how about you, dear?"

The steak, baked potato, green beans, salad, and rolls must have settled rapidly in her stomach, for the sounds of the desserts now appealed to Sarah. "I'd like the cherry pie and with the ala … ala … the ice cream stuff, please."

Maude, who always moved in fast forward mode, hustled off to place their dessert orders and take care of other customers. Daniel looked at Claire and smiled. "I guess she figured we didn't need dessert, and she would definitely be right about me. Did you want something?"

"Absolutely not. I couldn't eat another thing." But turning down Maude's desserts was not easy. In fact, turning down goodies along Main Street was a challenge. Not only did Maude offer a variety of fattening delights, but two doors south was the Taylors' bakery. And two doors beyond that was the drugstore with its tempting soda fountain. Claire's mouth watered as she watched the consumption of pie and cake, but the pressure around her waistband reminded her she'd made the right decision.

They had just left Maude's when Sarah asked about the candy by the cash register. "I didn't notice a price on those mints. Were they free?" After Claire answered in the affirmative, Sarah asked, "Can I go get one?"

"Me too?"

"Go ahead. I'm sure that you both need a little something else to eat."

The girls turned and hurried back in, momentarily returning sucking on peppermints. Even with candy in their mouths, they managed to thank Daniel for the dinner. He assured them it was his pleasure. Claire was one hundred percent sure he meant every word. The four joked and laughed as they walked back across the square. Several good memories went through her head of the fun times she and Dennis had enjoyed with their children while they were growing up, but at the same time she was saddened to think of what Daniel had missed by what he had lost.

As soon as the girls hit the front door, they were up the stairs to change clothes and then down again to go visit with their brothers. Lucky, who had been ecstatic with their arrival, now sat dejectedly watching the front door.

"Come here, boy," Daniel said, patting the couch next to him.

Lucky turned his head and looked at him as if contemplating the offer. Then he charged toward the couch, but instead of aiming at the spot Daniel had patted, he plopped himself down between Daniel and Claire. There really was not much space there, but he wiggled back and forth and nestled in, resting his head on Claire's lap.

"Nice chaperone you have there, lady."

"Yes, he's the current man around the house after all." The second she said those words, Claire wanted to take them back. She thought it sounded as if she were hinting that she was interested in having a new man in that position. She felt the blush in her cheeks and turned her face down toward Lucky, rubbing his neck and ears. "Good boy."

Daniel put his arm around Claire and rubbed her shoulders and neck. "This has been quite a day. Those girls are so much fun. I'm certainly sorry their father had that accident, but I think they've been really good for you. They seem to have rekindled your maternal instincts. They also have reminded me of why young people have children, not people in their fifties. I had forgotten about all the little things that go on with kids this age. Thankfully, they're really good kids. Their father has done a good job. Speaking of their father, I have to go to Des Moines this afternoon to check on someone. Can I take anything to the hospital for the kids?"

"I doubt it. I think they're all in limbo, not wanting to give up but not wanting to get their hopes too high about a recovery." Claire ended talk about Mr. McRoberts and hoped Daniel would talk about his time with Abby, but he didn't seem inclined to bring it up, so she didn't either. "When will you be able to come back?"

"I don't know. When dealing with clients that someone wants to kill, I never quite know what might come up from one day to the next. But you know that I put Hayward on my agenda whenever possible. I'll call you."

"You'd better. I hate to keep paying the phone bill if no one ever calls."

Daniel wrapped his arms around her, hugged her gently for a few seconds, and then kissed her three times. "One for you, one for Sarah, one for Abby."

"How come they get the same number I do?"

"Okay, two more for you. Then I have to go." After those additional kisses, he and Claire heard giggles coming from the dining room. Abby and Sarah were standing and softly laughing. "'Bye girls, see you later," he said, waving.

As he headed toward his car, he heard a voice calling his name. He looked up to see Ben Miller hurrying, or at least moving as fast as Ben could move, toward him, waving something in his hand.

"Here, Daniel. Here are keys for the house and the garage in the alley. I usually don't even lock the doors, but just in case here they are. And please stay whenever you can. I would love some company."

He dropped the keys in Daniel's hand, which he then shook vigorously, causing the keys to painfully press into Daniel's palm. Daniel tried to hide a grimace as he thanked Ben and climbed into his car and was off.

That night Claire went into each girl's room to tell her good night.

"Mr. Chambers kissed you. Ooooh! Yucky! Creepy! How could you stand that?" asked Abby with a nauseated look.

"It's a grown-up thing. You'll understand someday."

"No way! That's just gross! I'm never kissin' no boy—ever!"

"Okay, that sounds good. You remember that for at least the next fifteen years."

"I'll remember it for the next fifty years!"

"Good night, Abby."

"Good night, Mrs. Menefee."

Next, Claire went down the hall to check on Sarah.

"Mr. Chambers kissed you today. That is so romantic! He's so dreamy!

You are so lucky he likes you so much. I hope I can find someone that loves me like that someday."

"You will, dear Sarah, but don't be in any big hurry. Sometimes it takes a long time before the right one comes along. Good night, Sarah."

"Good night, Mrs. Menefee."

Across the street as Maude was straightening up for the night, she was looking all around the cash register. "I know that was here this morning. I just put more toothpicks in this morning. I hope it didn't accidentally get broken and someone just cleaned it up without telling me. I loved little Herky the Hawkeye. The hole in the top of his head made him the perfect toothpick holder. I'll just ask the waitresses tomorrow. Maybe one of them will know."

TEN

The quilting group was anxious to hear about Lila's game night. Perhaps the most anxious was Gloria Gibson, wife of Scoop Gibson, publisher of the weekly town newspaper. She had told her husband she would take notes about the party so he could follow up on any good stories. Claire and Phoebe Peoples were the only regulars of the group who were at Lila's, and that Tuesday Phoebe was unable to attend, so Claire became the sole source of information. She was bombarded with questions almost before she could even sit down.

"Did you really play games all night?'

"Was Chester there too?"

"Who all was there?"

"Did you meet any new men?"

"Did your government friend get to go with you?"

"Did any romances seem to bloom?"

"Just tell us everything!"

Claire felt everyone was starved for gossip or, as they liked to refer to it, newsworthy information. She wasn't crazy about gossiping, but then everything she told them would be the truth as she saw it. Plus, there really wasn't much to tell except who was there.

"Yeah, go ahead and spill it. I was invited, you know, but I figured Lila would just try to match me up with that crazy coot that lives next door. Plus, I could do better than the old fuddy duddies in this town if I wanted to find me a new man. But who wants to go to the trouble?" With that comment Clara emphatically crossed her arms and leaned back in her chair. "So go ahead and tell us who Lila tried to sucker into her matchmaking web."

"The only man I didn't know was the new Lutheran minister."

"Well, that one won't do anyone any good. Most ministers aren't the marrying kind. They're much too interested in caring for their flocks to care for a wife too. Plus, aren't most of them celebrate?" Clara interrupted.

"You mean celibate, Mother, and no, I don't think they are," Meredith spoke as most eyes turned toward Grace Carlson.

"Why is everyone looking at me? Please, go on with your story."

"Anyway, he's a nice-looking man. In fact, all of the gentlemen there were nice looking."

"She must be thinking of running for mayor." Clara scoffed, turning toward Meredith but loudly enough so everyone could hear. "That sounds like a politician's comment."

"John Brook from the high school was there."

This name was followed with many comments. "Now there is a cute one." "He is one handsome man." "He would be quite a catch."

"Rudy and Ronnie were there, and so was Burton Taylor, who seemed to be keeping an eye on Vickie Thornton."

"I had heard he has quite the crush on her," someone chimed in.

"William Swan and Dr. Payne were there."

"Did that slutty-looking redhead come with him?" Vernina asked, and then she immediately added, "I'm sorry. That wasn't very nice, but she is, don't you know."

"No, she wasn't, but I did see them together at Maude's Sunday. The Lavelle brothers were there."

"Were they dressed alike? They still do that sometimes," Betty asked.

"Thank goodness, no. It was hard enough to tell the difference without that. Ben and Cliff Wilkens came and seemed to have a great time talking to each other. I don't think they paid much attention to any of the ladies. And let's see, what is that man's name? He's the barber?"

"Fred Young!" many answered in unison.

"Oh my goodness!" said Vernina. "What did you think of him?"

After a brief pause, and remembering her mother's advice not to say anything if she couldn't say anything nice, Claire answered, "He was nice."

"He's nuts!" Clara said boldly. "I'll bet everyone here could tell a story about that crazy clown."

Luckily, for the sake of a juicy discussion, Grace had left the group to take care of church business, which left them to talk almost guilt free.

"One Saturday he dressed as a priest and went to a college football game. He wandered around where folks were tailgating, and everyone gave him food. He bragged about that for years."

"Then there was the time he borrowed one of Joe Brewster's cows and rode the poor thing up and down Main Street."

"Another time I saw him sitting on a busy corner in Des Moines with some monkey he'd gotten from somewhere. He was an organ grinder, and that flea-bitten monkey was dancing all around carrying a tin cup for contributions."

"When he said he was going to be a clown, everyone kind of laughed because we all thought that he was pretty much a clown already. And then he goes and shows up with that whole clown getup. He really did go to some clown school. I think it was somewhere in Florida."

Claire had the feeling there were other stories to share, but she politely shut them off with, "He does sound like a colorful fellow. Now do you want to know about the women who were there?" Heads nodded as she began to tell about the distaff side of the party. She listed as many as she could remember, starting with the youngest and working her way up to the oldest. She didn't comment about all of the female guests, but she did say, "Maude was there, but she kept disappearing to go into the kitchen to check on the food. I'm not sure how much relaxing she really got to do."

Claire continued naming Irma Fisher. The minute she said that name, the group responded almost in unison, "What was she wearing?" They all laughed.

"Now did you tell us about all of the men that were there?" Dorothy asked, winking at Claire.

"And yes, Daniel came too."

"What did he think of the whole affair?" someone asked.

Claire wasn't sure she liked the choice of words but just quickly answered the question. "He actually enjoyed himself. I thought I might have to twist his arm to go, but he said he thought it might be interesting. We both had a good time."

Fortunately, Claire had made a positive comment right then, for at that very moment Hayward's "hostess with the mostest" came sweeping into the room in some weird-looking, bright reddish-orange, tent style dress that gave the appearance of a Middle Eastern whirling dervish and a matching hat that somewhat resembled a sunbonnet.

"I'll bet you all were talking about my little gathering, now, weren't you?" Lila asked, pointing her finger at different members of the group and pretty sure she would be pleased with the response. "Was our little Claire telling you all about it?"

Claire had to clench her jaws hard to keep from jumping up, standing next to Lila who was at least four or five inches shorter than "little Claire" and pounding her on the top of her sun bonneted head. Instead, she sat on her hands and forced a smile.

"I'm so sorry that I could not have included everyone in the fun, but my little old house would only hold so many people. I'm sure the rest of you understand."

Clara, in typical form, could not keep her thoughts to herself. "I thought about coming but decided to do something more fun like go knock down the wasps' nest in the backyard." This was followed by a slap on Clara's wrist by her daughter-in-law.

Claire was trying to decide if Lila was hard of hearing or just totally self-absorbed when she instantly replied, "The backyard! What a wonderful idea! I could have set up some tables in the backyard. That way more people could have come. I'll have to think about that next time."

Eyes instantly dropped to the floor out of fear that Lila might start issuing invitations right then and there. Needles once again started to fly in and out of fabric that would make up the next quilt. Lila, apparently pondering the yard idea, wandered out the door and up the stairs the same way she had entered.

Abby's lunch with her friend Melissa went well, and the peanut butter and jelly sandwiches were eaten with as much gusto as if they had been prime rib. Claire would much rather have had something else since peanut butter had never been a favorite and she ate it only in dire, near-starving situations. However, since she had forgotten to go to the grocery store and there were no other choices, she ate half a sandwich with a smile on her face and then quickly ate some carrot sticks and apple slices to get rid of the taste.

After lunch the girls hurried downstairs to play with an old dollhouse. Claire, with help from Abby, had refurbished the house, adding some new furniture as well as new little dolls to live in the house. Claire was pleased with the final outcome, but the radiant look on Abby's face when the project was completed was the best reward. At one time during the process, Abby had commented about the amount of furniture. When Claire thought back to the day she and the others had gone to the tiny house where the McRoberts were living, she could understand Abby's surprise by the apparent affluence of the make-believe people.

Claire took Lucky into the backyard, where she planned to work in the flower beds. The little dog sat on the grass and watched intently. Claire started digging holes to relocate some of the bedding plants she previously had planted. As Claire pushed the soil into piles, Lucky cocked his head from one side to the other. He then decided the activity looked like fun and walked into the bed and began to dig too. This was the first time Claire ever had seen him dig, and she was quite tickled by this new discovery. Nonetheless, she knew this was not an activity to be acknowledged in a positive way. With a firm, "No! No digging!" Claire picked up Lucky and set him back onto the grass.

He was not to be deterred that easily, and two more times the digging and the removal took place. After the third time, Lucky seemed to get the message or else just lost interest and wandered off to sniff and explore in other areas. While Lucky napped in the warm sunshine, Claire finished the transplanting and took her equipment back to the garage. When she returned, she was shocked to see that her little white dog was not exactly white anymore. He stood knee deep in the dark brown soil, and scattered around him were the colorful remnants of plants that Claire had so carefully relocated. He turned his head and looked at her with that half grinning look on his gritty face as if to say, "Look, I helped with the planting too."

Unfortunately for Lucky, Claire was not the least bit pleased. "Naughty dog! Naughty, naughty dog! Look what you've done!"

Somewhat ironically, he actually turned his head and looked around as if surveying the scene. He didn't seem too concerned until Claire started toward him with a look he seldom had seen since coming to live at 101 Oak Street. He turned and skedaddled in the opposite direction as fast as he could go. Also unfortunately for Lucky, Claire's very loud, displeased voice had been heard by the girls in the basement. They had run upstairs to see what the hubbub was about and stood right in Lucky's path as he tried to evade Claire.

"Oh yuck," said Melissa as Abby scooped up the surprised dog.

"Oh heck, it ain't nothin' but dirt. My brothers get dirtier than this." With great strength she was able to hold Lucky until Claire lifted him from her arms.

"Abby, please get some money from my purse and go to the hardware store to see if they have dog shampoo. If they don't, go to the drugstore for some strong people shampoo. And please hurry."

The two little girls looked at each other with big grins and looked as if they had just been invited to go on a great fun-filled adventure. With money in hand, they went running across the square and headed for the door of the hardware store. They were about to cross Main Street when Melissa came to a halt.

"What's the matter?" Abby asked.

"Look, it's that scary man."

"Oh, he ain't scary. He's just old and kind of different. Did you ever talk to him?"

"No!"

"You should; then you wouldn't be scared no more. Come on." With some reluctance Melissa allowed herself to be pulled across the street. "Howdy, mister, how're you doin' today?" And then to Melissa Abby whispered, "Now you say somethin.'"

"Hello, mister," Melissa yelled.

"He ain't deaf, just shy," corrected Abby.

"We're gonna buy shampoo for my dog. He got into the flower garden and got all muddy. We've gotta clean him up. See you later."

After paying for the shampoo, the girls walked out and again spoke to Farley.

"We got the shampoo. We're gonna go wash up a dog. You could come watch if you want to, mister. It might be kind of funny."

"Bye, mister," they both yelled back as they headed across the square and left Farley flipping through his dog-eared codebook looking up "shampoo, dog, and mud."

"Hmmm," was his only contemplative reply.

After procuring the shampoo, the girls insisted that they get to help with the dog washing. Claire wasn't too sure just how helpful they would be but could think of no logical reason why they shouldn't.

Luckily for Claire but not for Lucky, the previous owners had left a large metal wash tub in the rafters of the garage. When Claire had first seen it, her immediate thought was, *That would be great for bobbing for apples.* Never would she have imagined she would be using it to wash a muddy addition to her family. Even though it was a warm day, she took pity on the dog and brought hot water from the kitchen to mix with the cold water from the garden hose. Before putting the struggling dog into the tub, Claire brushed then sprayed off as much dirt as possible.

Then Claire reeled in the dog's leash. She grabbed the struggling dog, trying not to spread the mud from Lucky to her. "Stand back!" she warned. "He's going to be doing lots of splashing." The two girls looked at each other and with giggles moved even closer to the tub. With one hand Claire kept a tight reign on Lucky's leash while with the other she tried to pour on shampoo.

"We can help," insisted Abby. She took the shampoo from Claire's hand and handed it to Melissa. "Here, you be in charge of this. I'll talk to Lucky."

Abby moved in front of Lucky where, squatting on her knees, she firmly but gently placed her hands on both sides of his squirming wet head. She bent over and looked him square in the face. "You're fine. You know this was your fault. If you had done what you were told, you wouldn't be here right now. Now you sit still so Mrs. Menefee can get you clean."

Much to Claire's surprise, the wriggling subsided to an occasional fidget. And the motion seemed to stop altogether when Abby's face moved even closer and her blue eyes locked on Lucky's big brown ones.

"You know this is for your own good. And this really hurts Mrs. Menefee more than it hurts you."

Boy, is that true, thought Claire as she shifted her weight, trying to get into a more comfortable position as she continued to work the lather.

Abby continued, "You know we love you or we wouldn't care how you looked." Claire had a feeling she was listening to a replay of reprimands Abby had heard in the McRoberts' household.

The washing, rinsing, washing, rinsing process continued until Lucky returned to his more normal white self. When Claire was satisfied he was as clean as he was going to get, she moved her hand from his collar back to his leash. Lucky took this as the signal he was now free to try to dry himself. He shook hard and long, sending water flying in all directions and drenching the two captors and their accomplice. This sent the girls off with fits of laughter as they also tried to shake themselves off.

Claire was about to release him from his soaking captivity when she had a second thought. She had seen Lucky's reaction to a bath and remembered how his version of air drying was to run around wiping himself off on whatever surface he could find. Fearing that he might actually head back to the flower bed where the entire disaster had begun, she let him jump out of the tub but confined his movement to the sidewalk while she sent the still laughing girls to get old towels from the basement.

As she sat in the warm sun trying to absorb as much moisture as she could, she thought back to Abby and how she had quieted the uncomfortable, nervous animal. "She calms a scared dog, she talks to butterflies, she sees goodness in people that others cannot see, and she could tell that Daniel was seeking something when not even he knew he was. What kind of a six-year-old is this?"

She might have thought about it longer, but her thoughts were disturbed by the sound of a siren passing in front of her house.

Claire and Lucky were enjoying their walk as they followed Abby and Melissa at a block's distance while Abby walked Melissa home at the end of their play time. They met Clara and Meredith as they were walking home from the library.

"I see you're going to be doing some reading," Claire said to Clara.

"No, I'm just getting these books so I can improve my posture by walking around with them on my head," she mocked in reply.

"I'm sorry," Meredith mouthed to Claire, who just smiled.

"I heard a siren a while ago. Any idea what's going on?" Claire knew it really was none of her business, but sirens were so rare in Hayward she was concerned.

"Boy, did you ask the right person. I can tell you all about what that crazy old coot did this time. He got agitated about something in that stupid codebook—something about a dog or mud. He took off for the filling station and scared the guys who were filling up their cars, so Jen called the sheriff. They should just put that old fool away."

Claire looked a bit puzzled, so Meredith offered what she knew. "The sheriff was dropping Farley off at the Simpsons' house when we were leaving. Sheriff Johnson said Farley told him his codebook said dogs meant a convoy and mud meant gasoline. So he thought a German convoy was going to be filling up at the gas station, and he needed to stop them before they came right into town."

"Oh dear. I hope no one was hurt."

"No, but I guess it shook up some people."

"Of course it would," Clara said, interrupting. "Just watching him wave that rifle around with that wild look on his face would scare anyone—except me. I'm out of here to go put these books on my head."

Clara shuffled off and left Claire and Meredith to discuss the trials and tribulations of dealing with aging parents. Their conversation was cut off when Abby came skipping down the street, and then one adult, one child, and one dog headed home together.

Abby was in bed and looked as if she could fall asleep at any moment, but she wasn't quite ready for Claire to leave. "Mrs. Menefee, can I ask you something?" Claire nodded. "Do you think I could call you Mrs. M instead? It's easier, you know."

"I think that would be fine."

"And one more thing, Mr. Farley, what's wrong with him?"

Claire sought the proper words to explain in a way that it would make sense to her. "He was in a war, and lots of his friends got hurt and he felt it was his fault. He still feels bad about it."

"No wonder he always looks so sad. Does he have any friends?"

"I don't know. That's a good question."

"Everyone needs friends. I think I'll be his friend. Then maybe he won't be so lonely."

Remembrances of some of Farley's odd antics rushed through Claire's head. She was pretty sure he was harmless, but she also knew some of his ill-conceived ideas had led him in weird directions. Yet she didn't really think it would be unsafe for Abby to show the man some kindness.

"I think it would be nice if you would be his friend and visit with him at the store. But it probably wouldn't be good to go anywhere with him."

"Of course not … I ain't stupid. Who wants to go check out some dumb old gas station anyway? I just want to be his friend."

"Good for you. Now go to sleep. Thanks for helping me wash Lucky today."

"It's okay. He was just scared and cold, you know."

"I know. Good night, sweetie."

Eleven

The manila envelope was delivered by Jim Dunn, the postmaster, who said it was therapeutic to get out of the rat race of the post office and interact with his postal patrons.

"Here you go, Claire. I don't know what's in there, but I'm sure delivering lots of these. It must be some type of special promotion or something. Anyway, I hope it is something good. See ya later."

Claire looked at the envelope with curiosity. "Hmmm, I wonder who it's from." Then she chuckled. "Why do people try to figure out who sent a letter by looking at the envelope instead of just opening it? It's like a little guessing game we play with ourselves. No more wondering." She ripped the envelope open and read the enclosed letter.

"You have been chosen at random to be the guest of the Hayward Theater at a special showing of the hit movie *Magnificent Obsession*, never before seen in Hayward. This special event will be on Wednesday, June 6, at 7:00 p.m. Tickets will be held for you at the ticket booth. We hope you will join us for this event."

"Well, that's interesting. I wonder what that's all about. Someone's probably trying to sell something and will do a presentation before the movie. But that was a good movie, although it is a rather old one. I wonder why they chose it. Probably got it cheap. Anyway, it might be fun."

Claire took the letter and paper-clipped it to the June calendar page and then flipped back to May. "I can't believe that May is almost over and so is school. What am I going to do with two girls during the summer? Maybe they won't be here all summer. Hopefully their dad will be home before summer's over. But what if he doesn't make it through the summer? Oh my, then we'll have a different problem. Don't even think about that. Think positively like Abby does." She shook her head as if to shake out the negative thoughts.

"Now, on to those cookies." The end of the year school-wide potluck was that night. Claire already had started cooking her barbeque meatballs in a crock pot, but she had promised the girls she would make some soft cookies from her grandmother's recipe. Abby liked the chocolate ones while Sarah preferred the vanilla. Personally, Claire's favorites were the marbled ones made with both chocolate and vanilla dough.

As she pushed the dough off the spoon onto the cookie sheet, she adjusted the size of the dollop by pinching off and eating any extra from those that were too big. "I'll just count this as lunch. After all, there are eggs and milk in here." She smiled and loaded another spoonful as the back door opened and then slammed shut.

"Hi, Mrs. M. I'm home. What's for lunch? I'm starving!"

"There's a ham sandwich all ready for you in the fridge. There's also a glass of milk."

"And do I get cookies too?"

"Only if you eat some carrots."

"I ain't no rabbit, you know."

"You mean 'I'm not a rabbit.'"

"That's what I said, 'I ain't no rabbit.'"

Claire decided not to argue the point any more since the timer was going off with its annoying buzzing. She slipped a second baking sheet into the oven and started to move the hot cookies to a cooling rack.

"Those sure look yummy. I'll bet Mr. Farley would like some nice warm cookies. I'd better go now before they cool off too much."

"Nice try, but Farley will have another chance later to have warm cookies. Right now he's probably hoping that you finish your lunch, carrots included."

The sandwich and milk disappeared quickly, but the carrot sticks were not met with great enthusiasm. Abby thought of as many diversions as she could to put off the inevitable. "Look, I could direct the church choir with one of these. Maybe Mrs. Carlson should try it. I'll bet that choir could see better if she was wavin' one of these." Abby gave a dramatic demonstration of how that might look. Then she was on to another idea.

"Luke and John used to pretend carrots were guns and point them at each other makin' shootin' noises. Bang, bang! But Gram said God didn't grow no carrots to use as guns and she'd make 'em stop.

"Wouldn't it be funny if I had teeth this long?" Claire looked over to see two carrots protruding from her mouth like two fangs. Abby giggled. "But it would be hard to eat corn on the cob with those. Or maybe I could use 'em as chopsticks."

"Enough, Abby, just eat them."

With a disgusted look on her face, she bit down on the well-handled vegetables. When she finally managed to swallow the last bite, she again pleaded the case for some warm cookies for Farley.

"He might be home having lunch now. Look out and see if you see him."

Abby returned so fast it hardly seemed she had had time to make it to the front door let alone make a round trip. "He's there, just sittin' all lonely. Can I go when the next cookies are done, please?"

When the timer once again sounded its noisy alert, Claire carefully lifted four chocolate and two vanilla cookies and set them on the plate Abby was dutifully holding.

"Do you think he should eat so many? It might give him a bellyache."

"I thought you might like a couple too. Some people don't like to eat alone, you know."

"Right. I knew that. Thanks, Mrs. M."

"Remember, Abby, you may visit with Mr. Farley at the store, but you are not to go anywhere with him. Do you understand?"

"Yeah, I know. 'Bye."

Abby left with such speed Claire wondered what the chances were that the cookies would stay on the plate until they reached the hardware store.

"Oh well, worse things have happened than someone eating cookies that have spent a second or two on the ground." She turned back to load another tray, sampling cookie dough as she worked.

When the cookies were all done and safely sitting on the cooling racks, Claire could no longer resist peeking across the street. She didn't want Abby to know she was spying, so she tried to hide behind one of the porch pillars. From what she could see, Abby was sitting on the sidewalk facing the store. She imagined she was looking at Farley, but Claire could not see him at all. She had been watching only a minute or two when Abby got up, leaned forward, and then turned to head for home. Claire hurried back into the house in hopes Abby had not noticed her.

When Abby returned, she went immediately to the kitchen, where Claire was washing cookie equipment. Abby walked over and longingly looked at the cookies.

"Only one and it has to be with a glass of milk." Abby made her choice and sat by the table slowly eating. "How was your visit?"

"I think it was okay. He said he liked the cookies, but that was about all he said. I asked him some questions, but he didn't answer much. So I just talked about school and my friends and springtime. Oh, I told him about my butterfly. I think he smiled when I told him it talks to me, but I'm not sure if he believed me."

Claire couldn't help but think that probably no one would believe it and wondered how many people Abby had told about this unusual insect-to-child relationship. She had hoped it would remain an in-house secret.

Abby had a faraway look in her eyes as she tilted her head slowly from one side to the other and screwed up her pink little lips as if she were thinking very hard. After a few minutes she said, "I think he needs a friend his own age. Aren't there no old people in town who'd like to play with him?"

Claire wasn't sure how to answer that. She was pleased Abby did not categorize her as a town oldie, and she knew that Abby had seen other older people around. But the qualifier of wanting to play with Farley definitely limited the field. In fact, she couldn't think of anyone who would volunteer to humor him by chasing all over town looking for invading armies or even searching out a spy or two. She wanted to choose her words carefully so she didn't give Abby the impression that Farley was not mentally well, which everyone in town seemed to think. So as she carefully began to store the cooled cookies in Tupperware containers, she tried to explain about Farley in six-year-old terms.

"Remember how I told you that he was in a war? Well, in his mind, for some reason that no one really understands, he thinks he's still fighting that war. He still thinks his enemies will be coming to attack the town. That's why he always carries a gun. He wants to make sure he protects the people who live here. You and I know we don't have to worry about that, but he just doesn't understand. So all he seems to want to do is sit and watch out for trouble. I don't think there are many other people who would want to play that with him, do you?"

"Yeah!"

"Who?"

"My brothers. They're always wanting to play war."

Claire saw a disaster in the making and jumped on that idea right away. "It's an interesting thought, but I don't think that would be too good an idea. If you get other people running around Farley acting as if they are in a battle, he would probably get even more worked up, and he might actually hurt someone who was just playing because he might think they are his enemy. So I think playing war games is not the best plan."

"Okay, how about music. Does he like music?"

"I have no idea. I never thought about it."

"Mama always said music could make almost anyone feel better. She always sang a lot. I can almost kind of hear her voice sometimes." She closed her eyes, and momentarily a smile slowly crept over her face as if the sweet memories were stirring in her mind.

Sarah and Abby were both excited for the end-of-school potluck and got dressed in record time. Claire carefully wrapped the crock pot filled with meatballs for transport. After a quick trip with Lucky to the backyard, they shut him in the house and headed toward the school.

The gym was a hive of activity, and Abby ran to stake out a place to set their plates. She chose the table where the Hornsbys, Graves, and Dunns already were seated. Sarah was much more involved in visiting with her friends and would have liked to sit with them until Claire gave her that look that reminded her this was to be a family event, so she parted with a wave and headed toward Abby and Claire.

As was typical of potlucks, there certainly was no shortage of food. Anything one could imagine, plus many other dishes too, was laid out on long tables. Many of the children were the first in line to load up their plates, but the McRoberts children politely stayed with their adults as the line formed. As Matthew and Mark piled their plates so high Claire wondered how they could possibly get back to the tables without spilling, she was again reminded of how much growing, active boys could eat. "I'm glad I got the girls," she said quietly to herself.

"I'm sorry, did you say something?" Jane Dunn asked.

"Oh, I just said that I was glad I got the girls to come." Claire smiled.

Luke and John appeared to be good eaters too, as they also put so much food on their plates that the plates were not even visible. "I cannot believe how much these boys eat," said Jane. "I still think they are making up for years of not always having enough to eat. It's a good thing I like to cook."

When the adults returned to the table, they discovered that all of the places had been rearranged. The McRoberts clan was sitting three on a side across from each other and was busily engaged not only in eating but in talking and laughing. The adults sat at the end of the table and spent a lot of time watching the children.

"It looks like a family reunion," Jane said.

"After all, that's exactly what it is," added Ellen.

"I wish I had brought the twins after all instead of letting Katie babysit," commented Vernina sadly.

"Once school is out, they can spend lots more time with each other," Claire assured her. "Plus, I'm not sure you would have much fun if you had them with you."

When the eating was over, the children were allowed to go play with equipment that Mr. Regal, the P.E. teacher, had taken outside. That left the adults to sit in the now quiet gym and listen to Pearl Hatcher give her standard, less-than-convincing speech about what a good year it had been, how the parents had been so supportive, and about how she and all the teachers were sad to see the year end and were looking forward to September when school would start once again. Claire knew that was pretty much a lie, not only from her own experience but also from what she knew about Pearl. She was surprised the woman was not standing pompoms in hand leading a cheer for the end of the year. But then she decided that Pearl probably didn't have enough enthusiasm or energy even for that.

After her table mates had gathered up their belongings, they all walked out together and sat to watch the children as the sun began to slip slowly down in the western sky.

"The kids really seem to like Mr. Regal. Carly and Joey liked Mr. Brownlee too, and they hated it when he had to leave, but this new teacher has worked out well for them, don't you know," commented Vernina.

"He sure is cute too. I wonder if he's married. Maybe someone should give his name to Lila and she could check him out," smiled Jane.

"Please, let's be kind to the nice man. I don't think he needs Lila in his life."

The four laughed as they rounded up their respective children and headed home in the quickly disappearing sunlight. When Claire and the girls got to the door, they were not greeted by the regularly perky puppy. Instead, Lucky slowly walked over to sniff their feet.

"It looks as if you need to go to bed too. You look pooped," Claire said, bending over to pet his soft white head.

Claire set the dishes on the kitchen counter as the girls quickly headed up to get ready for bed. She was surprised when she turned around to find a lower cabinet door opened and one of the cookie containers sitting on the floor.

"That's odd. I was sure I had put that away before we left." When she bent over to put it away, not only did she see it was opened, but it appeared that quite a few of the cookies were missing. Claire looked at the container and then at Lucky, whose ears and entire body were drooping even more than usual. "Oh, you naughty little dog. You've been a busy boy. No wonder you're not acting like your usual frisky self."

Claire headed upstairs to check on the girls when from Sarah's room she heard, "Hey, who put this cookie under my pillow?" Claire went in to find her holding up a chocolate cookie.

"I think Lucky went on a cookie caper while we were gone. I found one of the cabinets open and one of the cookie containers opened. I guess he thought this would be a good hiding place for his loot."

"That was pretty clever, wasn't it?" Claire was glad that Lucky, who hadn't felt well enough to follow her up the stairs, wasn't there to see the two of them laughing at his heist.

Their laughing stopped when they were joined by Abby. "Who stuck this cookie in my pajamas?" she asked, holding them up with a cookie stuck to her pajama bottoms. The others laughed again and left Abby with a puzzled look on her face. Claire explained Lucky's cookie caper, and Abby joined in the laughter.

Claire collected the cookies and told the girls good night. Then she walked downstairs where Lucky lay lethargically with a full-looking stomach. "I have a feeling you're feeling quite sick. I think you'll be spending the rest of the evening on the back porch, just in case. But let's take a few laps around the yard for right now."

While they walked, Claire thought about the evening and how much fun it was to again spend time with some other families. While she was reminiscing, Lucky was busy eating grass to try to settle his stomach from his cookie spree. Claire was glad that she had the girls to share the humor of this event. She could tell others about it, but it would never be as funny to anyone who had not been there to witness it.

Cleaning day was never a favorite time for Claire. The same old routine over and over for so many years was drudgery. Sometimes she would play music and try to dance around doing the many unpopular tasks. Other times she would try to listen to the television or radio, but that only worked for the room where the set was. There had been a couple of weeks when she tried to do a different job every day, but that didn't last. It seemed more that she was making each day unpleasant. So after a routine trip to the grocery store, which, of course, involved visiting with folks, she just gritted her teeth and got to work as quickly and efficiently as she could.

Although the girls were basically responsible for the upkeep of their rooms, Claire did run the dust mop around on the floors since she had it in her hands for other upstairs areas. As she reached under Abby's bed, she

Mary Ann Seymour

noticed the wastebasket was tipped over, so she nonchalantly straightened it up and headed into Sarah's room. Things looked pretty good in there with nothing on the floor to hinder her sweeping. But once again she found the wastebasket lying on its side.

"Now what are the odds of that?" Claire said, setting it upright.

Even though it was not in use, she went into the fourth bedroom to dust and stopped right inside the doorway. With hands on her hips, she stared at the wastebasket once more tipped over.

"Okay, what is going on here?"

She dropped her dust mop and dusting cloth and hurried toward her own bedroom. On the way past the bathroom, she looked in, and sure enough, that trash can as well as its contents were on the floor. Upon entering her own room she stopped and gaped.

"There has got to be an explanation!" She stood studying the situation for a few moments before turning. "Downstairs!"

She rushed down the flight of stairs almost as fast as the girls could have done it and rushed into the downstairs bathroom. She really was not surprised at what she saw but was even more puzzled than before. Then she went toward the kitchen trash can, which stood as straight and upright as ever.

"Okay, what's your story?" she asked, facing it. "And just what do you know about all of this?"

Lucky, who had been sleeping in the warmth of the afternoon sun, had come in from the porch to see what was going on. He sat on the floor and looked curiously at Claire, tipping his head from side to side as if trying to figure out why she was shaking her finger at the kitchen trash.

While Claire returned to the bathroom to set the can back up, Lucky waddled back to the back door, where he stood waiting for someone to let him out. When Claire finished, she walked past him to open the door.

"Those cookies have done nothing for your figure. You're looking quite pudgy. And when you get to be my age, you'll have to be even more careful about indulging in goodies like that. You and I will have to take a nice long walk tomorrow morning to try to work some of that off." Lucky sauntered through the open door and descended the stairs in a slow, deliberate manner. "I wonder how many of those you ate. It's a wonder that the chocolate ones didn't kill you. Did you know better than to eat any of those, or did you just get lucky, Lucky? I guess we'll never know."

At dinner that evening, Claire told the girls about the wastebasket mystery.

"Well, I certainly didn't do it!" Sarah stated emphatically.

"Well, don't blame me! How come the littlest one always gets blamed? It's not fair!"

"No one is blaming anyone," Claire said, trying to calm everyone. "I was just hoping one of you might have some logical explanation for what happened. It is just so strange."

Looking at the other two in turn, Sarah asked, "If it wasn't Abby and it wasn't you and it definitely wasn't me, then what else could have caused it?"

Slowly all eyes turned toward Lucky, who was sitting in his usual spot next to Abby's chair in hopes some tidbits might secretly fall his way. He looked up at them with innocent, big dark eyes and wagged his tail hoping that all of those people looking at him meant he was going to get a taste of something other than dog food.

"But why would he do that?" Sarah continued.

"Maybe he felt like he was going to barf and he knew better than to do it right on the floor." Abby laughed.

"I used to have a dog that loved to pull tissues out of the trash and tear them up, but I didn't find signs of anything like that."

"When I was little, we had a puppy that loved paper too. Whenever he could, he'd get a hold of the end of the toilet paper roll and take off with it. He'd run with it through the house until he had used up the whole roll or until someone came home and caught him. It looked pretty funny to us kids, but Mama tried to act like she didn't think it was funny. She would scold him every time. But I could see she was trying to keep from smiling."

Later that evening as the girls were getting ready for bed, Sarah yelled from the bathroom. "I know! I know what happened!" She came running out waving a cookie in her hand.

Claire looked at her and jokingly said, "Planning on a bedtime snack?"

With a disgusted look on her face, Sarah huffed. "No, of course not."

"Okay, I give up. What happened?"

"I found this cookie wedged behind the clothes hamper. I think Lucky hid cookies all around the house. He must have eaten as many as his tummy could hold and then hid more for later. I'll bet he dropped some in the wastebaskets and then had to turn them over to get those cookies out."

"I'll bet you're right. Good thinking, detective McRoberts."

Sarah grinned. "Gee, it would take a smart dog to be able to do that, don't you think?"

"I sure do."

Abby dropped to her knees and threw her arms around the neck of Lucky, who had been sitting listening to the discussion of his crime wave. "Oh, Lucky, I always knew you were a smart dog. Not every dog would have thought to save some for another day. I am so glad you're my dog!"

"Excuse me?" Claire said with false indignation.

"Oh, I mean our dog." Abby added a kiss to his furry head.

"That's better. Now that the mystery is solved, it's serious bedtime. Come on, you little thief, let's take one more trip outside, and then you can join Abby. Good night, little ladies." After a kiss to each forehead, Claire and Light Fingered Lucky trotted down the stairs and out the back door.

Claire was looking forward to having lunch and playing cards at the Andrews.' Claire thought this would be a nice social getaway. She had hoped Abby could play at Melissa's after school, but a longstanding dentist appointment foiled those plans. Meredith had invited Abby to join them, knowing that if she wanted Claire she would have to include Abby. So Claire had arranged for Sarah to stop on the way home from school to pick up Abby if the card game was not yet over.

Claire wasn't really worried about Abby going with her. She just was not sure how she and Clara would get along. She was sure Clara would have no trouble putting Abby in her place if she felt like it. She didn't want the little girl to have her feelings hurt. To pave the way, she had explained that Clara could sometimes be very crotchety and even say mean things. She had reminded Abby they were guests in the Andrews' house and to try not to say or do anything that might make Clara upset.

Also, Claire heard via the town grapevine that numerous items had turned up missing since the McRoberts children had come to town. So part of the pre-luncheon lecture included keeping hands off the many nice items in the Andrews' home.

It had been agreed that the two would meet on the corner in front of the mayor's house after the morning kindergarten class was over. Claire got there a minute or two before Abby did, but she could see her coming from a couple of blocks away. She recognized the bouncy way she walked, which caused her braids to swing back and forth. When she spotted Claire, she waved and started skipping toward her.

"Hi, Mrs. M. Do I still look all right? I tried to not play hard at recess 'cause I didn't want to get messed up. I've never been to a luncheon before, did you know that?"

"Yes, dear, I think that you mentioned that a few times."

"Do you think we should go so we won't be late? Bein' late is bein' rude. That's somethin' Daddy always says. So we all try to be on time so we won't be rude and so he won't get mad."

"But isn't it hard to get eight children ready on time?"

"Yeah, sometimes, but Daddy usually has a system. If it's the kind of gettin' ready that we are used to doin,' we all have a job to do and a little kid to help." Claire wondered if Abby considered herself one of the big or little kids. "If it's a kind a gettin' ready that we're not used to doin,' then Daddy writes down plans and times for everyone to follow. But he can't write mine, you know, 'cause I can't read, so he just draws pictures for me. Then we all do our jobs and aren't late. It works great. Daddy calls it the McRoberts' way, workin' together and gettin' things done on time."

"That's quite a system. Maybe he can teach it to me."

Abby looked up at her skeptically. "Okay, but I really don't think you need it. You seem to be doin' pretty good by yourself."

"You may ring the doorbell."

After pushing the button, Abby stood and listened in silence. Aaron had invested in a door chime system that played a different short selection every time it rang. ""Now that's darn pretty. Can I push it—" The door opened and Meredith welcomed them.

"Abby is intrigued with your door chimes. Could she push the bell one more time?"

"In fact, I think you should push it twice." With each push, she stood with her head cocked, listening carefully.

"Wow, that's really somethin.' It's almost like angels are sittin' right here on your front porch playin' to welcome people."

"Speaking of welcoming you, please come on in. Some of the other ladies are already here." Abby's chest puffed out, and she stood a bit taller at being referred to as a lady. She walked in next to Claire and looked around at the heads that turned in her direction. Already seated were Grace Carlson, Betty Nutting, Ellen Hornsby, and Francine Simpson. Clara was sitting in her rocking chair, scowling at the newcomers.

Meredith introduced everyone, mainly for Abby's sake. "And I think you know Mrs. Carlson, the minister's wife."

"And the choir director." Abby smiled.

"We're still waiting for two more. Please have a seat."

Abby looked up at Claire, who guided her toward an overstuffed chair that both could fit into. Their seats had barely touched the cushion when the doorbell rang again. "That's sure pretty," Abby whispered to Claire. "You should get some of them fancy doorbells."

Meredith ushered in her last two guests, Elizabeth Lambert and Helen Evans. Once more she introduced Abby to them. "Yes, ma'am, I know Mrs. Lambert. She lives across the street with the pretty house with the little guard room at the front door. And I think I met Mrs. Evans somewhere, but if I didn't, it's nice to meet you."

Claire was as proud of Abby as if she were her daughter. She made a mental note to tell her father what a nice job he had done teaching his children good manners. She just prayed she would have that chance.

After everyone had visited for a while, there was a momentary lull in the conversation. Abby, being one who found it hard to keep a burning question from being asked, turned to Grace. "Mrs. Carlson, ma'am, I like listenin' to your choir, and I wonder if you ever let children sing in the choir. I really like to sing, and I'd really like to if I could."

Grace seemed quite surprised. "Well … no one has ever asked before. I guess I would have to think about it. You do know that we don't just get up there Sunday morning and sing together. We practice during the week."

"I would surely hope so. I don't think you would sound so good if you didn't practice, now, would you."

"No, I guess we wouldn't. I'll talk it over with Bill and see what he says."

"Thank you, ma'am. I hope he says yes." Abby grinned her biggest grin.

"Lunch is ready," Meredith called, and the group moved to the dining room. She let everyone choose where to sit except for Clara, whom she directed to sit next to her.

"Why do they get to choose and I don't? Or do you think it's too tough a decision for an old lady? How about if I go in the backyard with the rest of the varmints?" Clara leaned over the plate of chicken salad attractively nestled on a lettuce leaf. "I thought we were having peanut butter and jelly sandwiches, or did you think it would stick to my partial?" She folded her arms and stood firmly while everyone else sat down. "Hey! How come she gets peanut butter and jelly?" she said loudly, pointing at Abby's plate. "What kind of a gyp joint is this?"

"I told you I was making the sandwich for Abby because I knew she didn't like chicken salad. But I know you do like it, so that is your plate."

"Not eating it!"

"Fine. The rest of us will go ahead and eat." Meredith sat down and dramatically placed her napkin in her lap.

"Excuse me, please," a small voice said. "I would be very happy to share my sandwich."

"See, at least the children know how to treat the elderly."

"Thank you, dear, but that's really not necessary."

"I know, but I really want to."

"Hey, kid. How about you and me split and go out to the backyard to eat? I'll even show you my gun."

Helen Evans gasped at the prospect of this seemingly unstable woman fooling around with firearms. Dorothy patted her arm and whispered, "It's okay. It's just a squirt gun."

Claire, trying to be the peacemaker, jumped in with, "I think that's a good idea. It's a lovely day, and I'll bet Abby would enjoy seeing your backyard."

"Maybe my butterfly will come too."

"You have a butterfly?" Elizabeth asked.

"Yes, I do, and it's beautiful and it—"

Claire cut her off before she said any more. She quickly stood, picked up Abby's plate and glass of milk, and headed to the door. "I'll take this out for you." She got Abby and Clara situated at the picnic table and returned to the dining room. "They're fine now." With that, the tension ended, and they started to eat.

While the grown-ups were carrying on their conversation, the conversation in the back of the house was very different.

"Why do you carry a squirt gun in your purse?"

"'Cause no one will get me a real one."

"Why would you need a gun? Do you go huntin' and stuff?"

"Yeah, I hunt birds and bad guys."

"Huntin' birds sounds mean."

"Oh, I don't hurt them. It just throws them off course a bit. It's like big raindrops hitting them. And shooting at them improves my aim for when I hunt the bad guys. And I got me a bad guy once too. If it hadn't been for me and that G-man friend of Claire's, he would have gotten away. Hey, hold on a minute."

Clara pushed herself up from the table and shuffled across the patio. She reached inside a bucket of gardening tools and pulled out another squirt gun. Then she went to the hose and filled it. Shuffling back, she held it outstretched toward Abby.

"Here you go, practice with this. If you don't want to shoot at the birds, just pick another target. The tree or the side of the garage is good because the wet spots show how your aim was. I keep asking my son to paint a target on the garage, but he keeps putting it off—seems to think it's more important that he go to that blame golf course and swat some innocent little ball all over the grass. Now that's a waste of time, if you ask me."

Abby took the gun and shot at many things in the yard. After emptying it, she would go back to the table, take some bites, refill the gun, and start over again. After Clara ate her sandwich, she emptied her gun and moved to the lawn chair by the table. Abby had so much fun she didn't notice when Clara fell asleep. It wasn't until the snoring began that Abby discovered she had dozed off. She set the squirt gun on the table, quietly opened the back door, and entered the room where the ladies were playing cards.

"Shhh! She's sleeping."

"Then it's a good thing Sarah should be here any time now," said Claire.

"Would you like a cookie or two? I never got those out to you and Clara." Abby had just picked a cookie when the doorbell rang.

"Yes, ma'am, thank you very much. Would you mind if I took one for my sister too? She's been workin' hard learnin' all day, and I think she's probably hungry." Abby took four cookies from the plate, holding two in each hand. "Thank you for invitin' me to lunch. I had a very nice time. I enjoyed meetin' your mother and havin' target practice with her. She's a darn good shot too." The rest of the group stifled giggles and looked toward Sarah, who joined her in the dining room. "We can find our way out, but would you mind if I rang that doorbell one more time?"

As the girls walked through the living room, Claire could hear Abby's voice still resonating with excitement. "Here, these two cookies are for you, and did you hear that great doorbell? I get to ring it once more. I wonder what it will play this time." The ladies returned to their card game to the strains of "Take Me Out to the Ballgame."

As the card game was winding down, Helen got up the nerve to ask what she had been wondering about for days. "You all may think this is silly, but do you have trouble telling Floyd and Lloyd apart?"

"I know I do," volunteered Claire.

"I don't anymore, but I did until I really got to know them." Betty went on to explain. "Floyd used to have a small mole on the left side of his nose, but he had it removed. If you look closely you can see a tiny scar. So I think 'Floyd has a flaw.'"

"Also, I've noticed Lloyd's eyelashes are longer and curl up more than Floyd's," said Francine.

"I get it," interrupted Helen. "Lloyd's longer lashes!"

"I think their laughs are different too, but I really can't describe them."

"I think Floyd is the one who kind of snorts when he laughs, isn't he?" asked Grace. "Anyway, what made you wonder?"

"I think they've both asked me out, but I'm really not sure. I know I went out with them twice, and I think it was a different one each time, but

I'm not positive. Or else they were playing a trick and wanted me to think there were two of them, but it might have been the same one both times. I was too embarrassed to ask. And whoever I went out with the other night asked me to go bowling—"

"Lloyd!" the ladies all said in unison.

"He loves to bowl and thinks he's quite good," said Francine.

"Now, if he asks you to go fishing, you can bet it's Floyd. That's his sport," added Betty.

"Not that it's any of our business, but I heard that you've been out with Fred Young a couple of times," smiled Meredith.

Helen paused a bit before answering. "He is, ah, rather interesting. I did learn quite a bit about clown school, but the cowboy clothes he wore I found a bit strange. He did take me to a nice barbeque place and said he was just dressing for the occasion. Another time we went on a picnic, which was nice, but he said it also was a bird watching experience. He brought binoculars, and we kept track of what kinds of birds we saw. That was okay, but when he insisted I try to duplicate the bird calls he made, I figured we probably were not a match made in heaven."

Meredith loved to entertain, but she hated to clean up, so she decided that it was best to just get right with it and get everything back in its proper place. She made a quick trip through the living room to make sure everything was taken care of, but as she walked past the curio cabinet, she stopped. She turned and looked around the room, bent over and checked the floor and bottom shelf. She even looked behind the chairs.

"Now where do you suppose that little bird went? I'll bet Mother took it again. She's always sneaking one of these out into the backyard to use as target practice. That gold finch seems to be her favorite. I'll have to ask her about it when she wakes up."

At dinner Abby and Claire talked about the luncheon. "That wasn't quite what I expected a luncheon would be. I didn't think there'd be shootin.'"

"Normally there wouldn't be, but you have to understand that Clara is kind of... different."

"I think she's cool. I like her. I think we should do more things with her. I wonder if she would like to do some things with Farley. I'll bet she would like him if she just got to know him better."

Claire smiled. "Maybe so, Abby, maybe so."

TWELVE

The end of the school year came with cheers of jubilation from the children and moans from their parents. Claire hoped there would be enough to keep the girls from being bored. For at least a few days she figured the girls would wallow in their free, unstructured time.

However, the children already had plans for the day after school was out—they were arranging a trip to Des Moines to see their father. The boys also were hoping for some other fun activity like going to the new water park or taking in an Iowa Cubs baseball game. A baseball game sounded like fun to Claire too, but Sarah didn't want to have anything to do with that. The girls preferred a picnic in a park or a visit to the botanical gardens, where Abby thought she might be able to see some butterflies.

The other guardians agreed the children were due for a visit to their father, but only Claire and Ellen Hornsby were available to drive. Ellen's seventeen-year-old son, Steve, said if they were going to a baseball game he wanted to come too. Steve even volunteered to drive, but Ellen quickly put her foot down on that suggestion. Then her daughter, Katie, said if Steve was going she should be able to go too. Of course, seven-year-old Johnny was not about to be left out. Suddenly the group from the Hornsbys' house had grown from one driver and two McRoberts children to one driver, three Hornsby kids, and two McRoberts.

That still left Luke, John, Sarah, and Abby. But when Jeff Dunn found out that Johnny was going, he started lobbying to be able to join the group. Once Jane had given in and said that Jeff could go, she told ten-year-old Jenny she could go too.

Word traveled fast in Hayward and especially in the neighborhood, and when Ryan heard Johnny and Jeff were going, he wanted a good reason why he couldn't go. "Plus, I've helped a lot taking care of the twins. I think I need a break." Vernina felt she couldn't argue with that, although she really wanted to say she had worked for ten years taking care of three children and wondered when she would be getting a break.

One would have thought that would be enough of a crowd heading out to the ballgame, but siblings, being what they are, don't ever seem to be happy if one has more than the other. When Maggie found out about the trip, she said she wanted to go to Des Moines to the game too.

When Bud Hornsby learned about the plans, he was quick to offer to take his wife's place behind the steering wheel. Jim Dunn, who always had been a big fan of the Chicago Cubs, said it wouldn't be right to not have enough drivers and changed his schedule at the post office.

To complicate matters, Helen got wind of the trip. She said she wanted to go to Des Moines anyway to get some specialty cooking items. Plus, being from Chicago, she thought it would be good to support the local branch of her beloved Chicago Cubs. That brought the number of drivers to four. With the Dunns' station wagon, the other two cars would not be overcrowded. It was decided Claire would ride with Helen, thus leaving her free to ride back with Daniel, whom the girls had begged to meet them in Des Moines. The plan was that all the cars would meet at the hospital. Helen would then go to the food store, leaving the remaining children with Jim and Bud in the park across the street from the hospital.

Everything was under control until Helen's car developed trouble and Bud didn't have what was needed to make the repairs on such short notice, leaving the group one car short.

"I think I might be able to find another car, but it would mean another driver. Let me get on it and see what I can do." Helen hung up the phone where she and Claire had been hoping to form plan B. She hurried into the bathroom, refreshed her makeup and hair, and headed out the door headed toward the square. She turned into Lavelle's Furniture store. As soon as she entered, she looked around. She spotted a head moving past a tall bookcase. She studied the person for a moment before approaching him, hoping she would be able to tell which one it was.

The head turned around and smiled. "Well hello! To what do I owe this special surprise?"

Helen turned on the charm and shook his outstretched hand while studying his face. She crossed the fingers on the other hand. "If I'm not mistaken, you told me to let you know if you could ever do anything for me." She was so hoping that it was this twin who had told her this on one of her previous dates. Unfortunately, she had no idea whether that had been Floyd or Lloyd.

He looked a little surprised but responded, "So what can I do for you?"

Helen explained about the trip to Des Moines. She tried to really play up the disappointment that would befall the children if the trip had to be cancelled. She slowly shook her head and tried to look as if she too would be terribly saddened if they couldn't go.

Whichever Lavelle it was smiled and didn't hesitate to come to Helen's aid. "My brother will be working in the store tomorrow, so I'd be more than happy to drive you and the others." Helen was hopeful that he'd use his brother's name, but no such luck. "I'm not sure I should tell my brother though since I'm sure that it will make him jealous."

"Oh, thank you so very much! You are our hero!" Helen reached over and planted a gentle kiss on his cheek while trying to check out the length and curliness of his eyelashes and looking for a small scar on his nose at the same time.

Helen turned and waved as she left the store. She was hopeful that on Saturday someone else would be able to recognize which Lavelle he was. She walked quickly past the local beauty shop, Hairs to You, and the office building that housed the offices of both Dr. Leonard Nutting and Dr. Tim Payne, the dentist. She thought about stopping at the market to buy chicken and other things for Saturday's lunch, but instead she went into Maude's, where she placed an order to pick up on Saturday.

Except for those going with Mr. Lavelle, the rest of the group assembled in Claire's backyard. Bud and Jim were anxious to get going since they both had to stop on the way out of town to get gas.

"When you live here and walk to work every day, you kind of forget you need a fuller tank of gas to get you to some places," Jim said almost apologetically.

"We'd better get loaded," said Bud, who was known for opening and closing his dealership at exactly the times on his front door. "However, if someone comes in waving cash at me and wants to order a new Thunderbird, I'd throw open the door and put on a new pot of coffee," was a comment that many people in Hayward had heard from Bud.

Everything seemed to be going smoothly until Katie realized there would be other girls going and insisted that she was sick of being around only boys and lobbied to go in any car except the one with her dad, her disgusting brothers, and the two oldest McRoberts boys. She was then placed in the Dunns' station wagon, which was fine with her. This caused her to take the assigned place of Maggie Graves, who was then relegated to the Lavelle group. This was agreeable to everyone else except Jenny Dunn, who cried, saying she wanted to ride with Maggie. Jim was about to invite her to stay home when Luke suggested trading Maggie for Katie. That solution sounded rational to everyone but Ryan Graves, Maggie's brother, who protested he could never get away from her and that she had been bugging him his entire life. Maggie vehemently fired back saying she certainly didn't want to look at his ugly face all the way to Des Moines. Thankfully, Jim stepped in and said that Maggie and Jenny could sit in the rear seat of the station wagon and since they would be facing backwards, the only face Maggie would have to look at would be that of his lovely daughter.

With those two cars finally loaded, they pulled slowly out of the driveway. "See you at the hospital." Bud waved,

"Come on, Abby, Mrs. Evans will be here any time."

"I just have to look for something." Her eyes scanned the sky and the bushes. Then as if by some divine plan, the beautiful multicolored butterfly fluttered gracefully across the yard and landed on a branch in front of Abby.

"I knew you would come. I just knew you would." She paused as if listening. She nodded and smiled. "I think so too." She listened again. "Yeah, I'll tell him. I'd talk more, but I need to go. See you later." The butterfly tilted its wings as it lifted and disappeared into the trees.

"If I didn't know better, I'd think it is waving good-bye to her," Claire said as she watched from the doorway. She really wanted to ask about the conversation but figured Abby would tell her if she wanted her to know.

Mr. Lavelle and Helen pulled up in front of the house. Claire, Sarah, Abby, and Katie Hornsby came off the porch, loaded with gear for the picnic and the game. Claire was glad that the arguments over who was going to ride with whom had been settled before Helen and the mystery Lavelle arrived. She thought the two of them might back out if there was a prospect of bickering all the way to Des Moines.

"Good morning, ladies. What lovely passengers I am privileged to have in my car today." His smile was warm and sincere, but Katie and Sarah looked at each other with somewhat disgusted looks. He helped load the gear into the trunk and opened the doors for everyone. It was hard to tell who was more disappointed, Abby or Mr. Lavelle, when it was decided that Abby would sit in the front seat between Helen and the driver.

Finally everyone was situated and the adventure began. At first the driver made many irrelevant comments. It seemed as if he was still somewhat uncomfortable with so many relative strangers riding in his car. After a few miles he stopped rambling on, and there were some comfortable moments of quiet. The silence was broken with a round of snoring from the middle of the front seat. Abby's dose of Dramamine had kicked in.

Twin Lavelle and Helen chatted as the girls talked to each other in very quiet tones. Claire felt rather left out but didn't let it bother her. As Helen talked she turned somewhat sideways, trying hard to study the driver's face. Even though he did a good job of staying focused on the road, he became very aware of the scrutiny.

"Have you heard any good jokes lately?" She addressed her question to him but said it loudly enough for those in the backseat to hear also.

Lavelle smiled. "I imagine I have, but I've never been good at remembering jokes, even the really good ones. I can remember the catalog numbers and prices of different pieces of furniture, but remembering jokes has never been my strength. Now you should ask my brother. He can tell some real side splitters!"

In desperation Helen turned to those in the back. "Do any of you know any good jokes?"

The girls just looked at each other and rolled their eyes as if to say, "How corny can this get?"

Claire responded. "I'm in the same position as our driver. I never can remember a joke. Dennis, my late husband, could always come up with a good joke that he had heard sometime in his life. He couldn't remember what I would send him to the store for, but jokes he never forgot. I have been wondering how your parents came up with the names Floyd and Lloyd. Are they family names?"

A slight smile crept across Helen's face when Claire asked that question. She bent a little closer, again giving the impression she was interested in him and not just his explanation.

"Well, it seems that my mother's name was Lillian. She said she always thought it was fun to write all those Ls. And my father's name was Filbert, which was usually shortened to Fil, like F-I-L, which was really confusing when people wrote his name since most folks assumed it was P-H-I-L. Anyway, Mother made really fancy capital Fs and decided that her child's name should start with one of those letters. When we turned out to be twins, she was tickled that she got to use both letters, and she thought of rhyming names that started with those letters. So I got one of them and my brother got the other."

Helen waited in anticipation, but no more information came. Abby continued to sleep in the front, and Claire found herself nodding off too. And then, as if by ESP, Abby sat up just as the car pulled up in front of the park. "I think Daddy can feel we're coming. I'm so excited!"

Sarah sadly looked toward Claire, neither one of them wanting to be the one to say something but both feeling that they should. Finally Claire said, "Sweetie, you need to remember there probably hasn't been much change since the last time you were here. If there had been, I'm sure the hospital would have told us the good news."

"Come on. Let's go see!" As soon as she was out of the car, she grabbed Sarah's hand, and they ran toward where their brothers were waiting.

While the other children played catch, the McRoberts clan, accompanied by Claire, headed across the street to the hospital.

Claire had called ahead to warn the staff about the children's visit. By now the number of children no longer shocked the nurses, and they almost seemed pleased to see them. The oldest children went first, which was an irritant to Abby, who could hardly stand the wait. The boys seemed to have more trouble thinking of things to tell their father. They all mentioned going to a baseball game. John even said that if he caught a foul ball, he would bring it to the hospital to show him. They all also mentioned that school was over, and they each smiled with that comment.

Sarah, still acting like the little mother of the group, tried her best to summarize what had happened since their last visit. She told him she had finished the sixth grade and would be going to junior high next year and confided that she was rather scared about that. She managed to laugh a bit when she told the story about Lucky eating and hiding the cookies. She tried to assure him they all were fine and were lucky to have been taken in by such generous families. She tried to not let her voice give away the fact that tears were trickling down her cheeks as she patted his hand and told him she was sure he would soon be better and be able to come home.

It seemed like an eternity for Abby as she had to wait her turn. She bounced up and down on the couch, paced the floor, and looked out the window at the park where she could see Steve tossing balls to Jeff, Ryan, and Johnny. She watched Maggie and Jenny swinging in the playground area. Finally, it was her turn. Sarah asked if she wanted someone to go with her to their father's bedside.

"Heck no. We'll be fine."

She turned toward the long, sterile-looking hallway so fast that her braids flew straight out on both sides. When she found the room, she tip-toed over to his side and gently picked up his hand and kissed it. "Hi, Daddy. I sure miss you. I'll bet you're missin' us too. I did great in school. Next year in first grade I'll learn more about readin' and writin.' I would have written to you this year, but I didn't know how.

"I get to do lots of fun things with Mrs. Menefee. She's the nice lady that Sarah and I stay with. She has a crazy dog too, and I love him lots. Not as much as I love you. And I got to go to a ladies' luncheon with Mrs. M. It was great. And this nice lady showed me how to shoot, and I got to shoot too." Abby wasn't positive, but she thought she felt her father's hand twitch a bit when she said that.

"Oh, don't worry. They're just squirt guns. And I have a friend named Melissa, and we play together and we like each other a lot even though I beat her up once. And I have a very special friend. It's a butterfly, and it talks to me and tells me that everything will be okay with you, and it said that Mama is okay and that we're not supposed to worry about her.

"Oh, and one more thing, and don't get mad when I say this, but I have been goin' to church with Mrs. M. and it makes me feel really good and I always pray for you when I go. Of course, I pray for you every day and night, even when I'm not in church. But Mrs. M. has this nice friend who used to be really sad in his heart. Well, he didn't tell me that he was sad in his heart, but I just knew he was, and so I took him to church with me and now he is not so sad anymore. Isn't that great, Daddy? Maybe when you come home and are feelin' better you can come to church with me too. Okay, Daddy?"

Abby waited for some kind of response but none came. "I better go, Daddy. I love you so much, and I miss you so much too." She squeezed his hand and bent over and kissed it. This time, without a doubt, she felt a soft squeeze in return. "Thanks, Daddy. I knew you were in there somewhere."

Abby wanted to run down the hallway, but actually remembering from having been told so many times at school that it's not polite to run through the halls, she walked as fast as she could to join the others in the waiting visit.

"He's there! He's there!" They all looked at each other, trying to understand what she was talking about.

"Of course he's there. We all just saw him," said Mark impatiently.

"No! I mean he's back in his brain. He moved my hand. He did it two times. Isn't that great?"

No one else had any response from their father, so they all figured Abby was imagining it. Everyone was ready to leave the hospital, so they let her comments ride.

"I'm hungry! Let's go eat," said Matthew, taking Abby's hand and heading toward the elevator.

When they reached the park, Daniel had joined the group that anxiously awaited their return so they could start eating their lunches. As soon as they finished, they reassembled in the cars with the three girls riding with Daniel this time. It had been decided that Helen and Mr. Lavelle would just meet them at the stadium after Helen finished her shopping.

The weather was perfect for a baseball game. The parking lot at the stadium looked as if many others thought it was a great baseball day. The group assembled close to the ticket booth and waited rather impatiently for Helen and Mr. Lavelle. Finally, they came hurrying up the sidewalk and joined the rest.

"I was beginning to think you had gotten lost," said Claire.

"No, I just had a lot of stops to make," Helen explained.

"She is one fast shopper. She was in and out really fast considering all of the items she got. She had me just stay in the car each time. Said it would be easier that way since she knew just what she wanted. I think she was afraid I would wander around and get lost in the stores."

Daniel returned with the other men, tickets in hand. As he stopped to speak to Mr. Lavelle, Helen listened carefully in hopes they would introduce each other but, alas, no luck. "Howdy. We met at Lila's game night. Good to see you again."

"Sure, good to see you again. Daniel, wasn't it?"

"Right. Here are the tickets for you and Helen. We got lucky. There were quite a few seats together in one of the upper sections down the third base line. We better go and follow the others."

The group of nineteen trudged up flights of stairs to reach their seats. Considering they were far from the field, they still had a good view of the action. Claire was glad that she was seated behind the Hornsby group that had come well equipped with their mitts for the game.

Katie also had come prepared but with totally different equipment. She pulled binoculars from the bag she carried. Claire figured that she must be a diehard baseball fan but was surprised when Katie said, "Not really. I just want to watch for really cute guys. We came once last year and sat close to the field and found some real hunks."

Lavelle explained the finer points of the game to Helen. Claire wasn't sure if she had asked for them, but she certainly was getting a lesson on baseball. Daniel, on the other hand, was quite involved in the game. The men and boys were caught up in the action, but the girls had other interests. Katie was taking turns with Sarah using the binoculars. Maggie and Jenny had brought some small dolls and were sharing them with Abby. By the end of the fifth inning, the call of the hawkers got to the children, and the cries of, "Popcorn, get your popcorn here!" "Peanuts, fresh salted peanuts!" and "Hot dogs, get 'em while they're hot!" affected their minds as much as their stomachs.

The food was a treat to all of the children, but for the McRoberts it was like a dream come true. In fact, the entire event must have seemed like that to them. Even Sarah and Abby who initially had said no to the idea of a baseball game actually were watching the game. Katie, on the other hand, still looked not only at the players but also at the crowd.

"Oh my gosh! I don't believe it!" she shouted.

Everyone turned and in unison responded, "What?"

"It's Miss Banter and Mr. Miller!"

"Let me see!" they all yelled. Now, had Katie been a shrewd business-woman, she would have sold chances to use the binoculars. Instead she passed them on to the others.

"Man, that's really something!"

"Wonder what they're doing here?"

"How can he stand to be around her? He's so nice and she's so—" Johnny's comment was cut off with a nudge from his dad. The binoculars continued to circulate as if no one believed what the others were telling and everyone needed a chance to see for himself.

Steve's mouth dropped open. "Hey! You'll never believe this. She actually is smiling."

"Let me see!" shouted everyone except Helen and Daniel, who had not yet formed a negative opinion of the town's librarian.

After everyone had a turn, attentions went back to the game. With the binoculars back in Katie's hands, she adjusted the focus.

"Wow! There's Dr. Payne and that redhead." Excitement over seeing a redhead didn't excite most of the group since six of them also had thick golden-orange locks. "Boy, she sure is pretty. I wish I looked like her."

Helen managed to refrain from grabbing the binoculars from Katie's hand. She needed some guidance to find the couple, but once she did, she could see why Katie had spotted them so easily. Not only did her hair make her stand out, but the bright purple jacket that looked as if it was covered with hundreds of sequins seemed somewhat out of place.

She looked longingly at the couple noticing the way he looked at and smiled at her. She turned toward the unnamed Lavelle who turned and smiled admiringly at her too, but still it wasn't that same "You-knock-me-out" kind of look she had just seen on Tim's face.

She smiled in return at her date, who reached over and patted her hand.

Claire had enjoyed the game, but still it was a relief to tell them all good-bye as they left the game. Now she and Daniel had a chance to be alone, something that did not happen a lot with the girls always in the house. Since neither one of them had been tempted by the lure of hot dogs and cotton candy, they decided to stop at a nice restaurant before heading for home.

Talking to an adult during a meal was a treat for Claire as they discussed everything from politics to hobbies. They both were relieved to find that their viewpoints on many issues were not far apart. Still, for the most part, their conversation remained on a casual level.

At least that's how it was until over dessert Daniel, while still looking at his cherry pie ala mode, asked, "Have you ever thought about getting married again?"

Claire was somewhat surprised, although she had felt that the question would arise at some point. She already had an answer. "I've thought about it, but I'm not sure I would ever want to leave Hayward. I've found such peacefulness there. I don't know that I would want to go anywhere else. And it certainly would have to be to just the right person. How about you?"

"I would like to—sometime. But I'm not sure when that would be. I'm not even close to retiring, and with my job I have to travel quite a bit. And let's face it, my job can be risky. I'd have to have a serious talk about that with myself and with any future wife. I think I'd really like to try it again under happier circumstances than the first time around."

"You know, though, you can never guarantee happy circumstances. A good marriage has to be able to weather those bad times. Often that makes the marriage even stronger and the couple more committed."

"You're right, but I think the grief we felt over Davy's illness and death was only intensified when we looked at each other because we kept thinking of him. I would hope if I tried again, any bad times wouldn't be so emotionally devastating."

Daniel's eyes had rarely looked up during the conversation, but finally he looked at Claire. "If I did marry I would have to be deeply, head over heels in love, and I would really have to like the woman too. She would have to be my best friend."

Claire stared at Daniel for a moment and then dropped her eyes. She wondered if he was telling her he was falling in love with her or warning her that if that feeling didn't happen soon, he was moving on without any commitment. Sensing the conversation was getting awkward, she changed subjects.

"Something special seems to be going on between Tim and his lady friend. And what about Ben and Bertha? Maybe Lila has put some magical spell on them to help boost her crazy wedding planner business."

"Maybe." He smiled.

Claire was sweeping the walk when Abby came running to the house. "It was great! We told Farley all about the baseball game, and you know what?"

"No, what?"

"He smiled, not a little smile but a big one, and he started telling us about playing baseball when he was little. He talked about his friends and about where they played. We all sat and listened, and we even asked him questions he answered. And he really had a good time. And do you know what?"

"No, what?"

"Guess!"

"I have no idea. You tell me."

"He even put his gun down and never even paid any attention to it when he was talking. Isn't that great?"

"Yes, that is good." Claire's voice sounded happy but the worried look on her face showed her concern about a rifle lying on the sidewalk with children gathered around even though the gun wasn't loaded. "Who else was there besides you and Farley?"

"Matthew and Mark. I told them about Farley and what had happened to him and how sad he was. And they said they knew what it was like to be sad after someone died. We all feel like that, you know, but anyway they said they wanted to meet him, so when I saw him sitting out in front of the hardware store this morning, I called them and we met over there."

Claire had mixed feelings about what Abby had told her. She was glad that these children seemed to have connected with Farley when adults didn't seem to be able to, but worrying about one McRoberts spending time with him was one thing. Thinking about two more kids with him, and bigger kids at that, made her a bit uneasy. Knowing some of the unusual things Farley had done made her hope that the Hornsbys might want to have a talk with the boys. Claire felt she needed to reemphasize to Abby never to go anywhere with Farley without first checking with her.

She would have done it right then had not Ben Miller walked by. "Hey, Ben. How are you doing? Beautiful weather we're having."

"Yup, and perfect weather for baseball." Claire wondered if he had heard that he and Bertha had been spied on Saturday, so she said nothing as he continued. "I heard that some of you were taking the McRoberts kids to a Cubs game, and I thought that sounded like a great idea. I hadn't been to a game in years. I thought about asking if I could tag along until I heard how many people were going. So I just figured I would find someone to go with. I remembered that some time ago Bertha told me she used to play in a women's league. Can you picture that? Well, anyway, I called her, and she hemmed and hawed and finally said she would go. And I think she had a good time." Ben paused, as if remembering the day, and chuckled. "She even smiled and actually laughed once or twice. I couldn't believe what a different person she was. She explained some things about the game that I never knew."

"Maybe you should take her again sometime."

"Yeah, maybe I will. I think she'd like that."

Claire was leaving for quilting group when the phone rang. She thought about not answering it but decided she would make it a quick conversation.

"Mrs. Menefee, this is the charge nurse at the hospital calling about the condition of Thomas McRoberts."

Claire felt her heart skip a beat, and her mouth got instantly dry. "Yes?" she said in a nearly silent voice.

"I just wanted to tell you that since the children's last visit, we have seen a slight improvement in Mr. McRoberts. I need to emphasize it is only very slight, but there appears to be more response when we talk to him and work with him. Before it was almost like his body had no life. Now there seems to be, I don't know, maybe just a slight spark, a spark of hope. I thought you might like to know."

"That is good news."

"But I also have to be honest and say it definitely doesn't mean that he's out of the woods. Things still could go bad, we just never know. But since Saturday, he's just looked better."

"Thank you so much for the call. We appreciate everything you're doing for him." Claire hung up and stood by the phone debating whether or not to mention it to the children. She wanted to be honest, but she didn't want to build up false hopes. "I think I'll just keep that to myself for now," she said as she hurried out the door.

Claire's being late to quilting gave many ladies the chance to air a common concern.

"I really hate to mention it, but I seem to have misplaced my grandmother's pearl-handled pie server. I was wondering if I left it here at the last potluck. I looked in the kitchen but didn't see it. Does anyone remember seeing it anywhere?" Ellen surveyed the faces but found only shaking heads.

"I can't find my silver jam spoon. I don't think I brought it for the last brunch, but now I'm wondering if its here somewhere." Dorothy was pretty sure that had not happened, but she was still searching for an answer.

Once the dam was opened, others started recounting their missing items: miniature china doll, goldfinch figurine, thimble from Jane Dunn's collection. Francine Simpson said that a new set of miniature screwdrivers had disappeared from the hardware store.

"I heard that Rudy has had things taken from the drugstore too," commented Phoebe Peoples.

The ladies sat solemnly looking at each other. All of these disappearances happened since the McRoberts children came to town. The silence was uncomfortable, but everyone became even more uneasy when Claire walked in.

"Gee, you all are sure quiet. Either you're all in deep thought, or there must be some kind of a problem."

No one said anything when finally Phoebe broke the silence. "We just realized that many folks are missing items and can't figure out where they could have gone."

Claire felt uncomfortable as all eyes focused on her. Then her memory clicked in. "Now that you mention it, I have missed a couple of things too, but I think I'm just getting forgetful."

Grace Carlson, who had just emerged from the tunnel that led to the parsonage, got in on enough of the conversation to redirect it back to the purpose of the gathering.

"Good morning, ladies. How's that new quilt coming?"

Busy fingers got to work and questioning mouths spoke no more.

On the way home, Claire got to thinking about all the missing items. The timing of the disappearances was not good. From what she knew, the first thing was missed shortly after the McRoberts children came. She figured the others must have been since then or she would have heard about them before. She came to an abrupt halt as she turned up her walk. "If I'm thinking these children are somehow responsible, then the other women must be thinking the same thing. That must be why things got so awkwardly quiet the moment I walked in." She stood frozen as thoughts rushed through her head. "I'll just have to talk to the girls about it."

The conversation was brief but uncomfortable as over lunch Claire brought up the subject of the missing things.

"So you're accusing us of taking them?" Sarah asked with bewilderment in her voice.

"No, I'm just telling you about them and asking if you have any idea what might have happened to them."

"Well, I certainly didn't take them!" Sarah stood up, stomped her foot, and marched out.

"I didn't take nothin' either! How come people always blame me when bad things happen? That always happened at home too. I didn't do nothin' wrong!" The crying started as Abby ran off.

"That went quite well, I'd say." Claire sat and thought about the situation and how she would have felt had the shoe been on the other foot. "If they're innocent, they sure do have the right to be mad at me and at the others too. But what if… what if one of them did take some of the things? What if their brothers took them? Oh my gosh, what if they're all involved?" That thought was just too horrible. "Come on, Claire, that's just ridiculous. What would boys want with all that girly stuff?" She shook her head vehemently as if to toss any such ideas completely away. "No! None of them had anything to do with this. I just know it!" But just in case, Claire crossed her fingers and said a little prayer.

Later that afternoon, Sarah came to the back porch, where Claire was trying hard to concentrate on the book she had in her hands. "May I talk to you, in private?"

Claire looked around and saw no one but Lucky, who was lying on his back, legs in the air, enjoying the warm sunshine on his belly. "I think it's safe. The dog won't talk. He can keep a secret."

Sarah didn't seem to find her joke funny as she pulled up a chair and scooted it very close to Claire. "I need to tell you something," she spoke in a voice almost a whisper.

"Fine, but could you please talk just a bit louder? I'm not very good at reading lips."

"Come on, Mrs. M., this is serious." Sarah looked at her with sad blue eyes, so Claire moved her hand in front of her face as if to change any semblance of playfulness on her face to a look of seriousness. "After you accused us—"

"I wasn't accusing you. I merely asked you about the disappearances." This time Claire was on the defensive.

"Okay, whatever. Anyway, I got to thinking about what you said and I, well, I … I thought of something. Daddy has this little flashlight he keeps in the truck. Abby always thought it was neat and wanted to play with it. Daddy told her he kept it there for emergencies, but she took it twice and hid it in her bed so she could play with it at night. Then there was the time that Luke got this yoyo and it had all these fancy colors that sparkled in the sun. Well, she took it and said she didn't. She promised she didn't take it, but we found it stuffed in one of her socks. Boy, was Daddy mad, not just because she took it but because she lied about it."

"Sometimes young children do take things before they learn that it's wrong. I hope she knows better now."

"Yeah, me too. But sometimes, when you don't have much, like Abby, and you see nice things you think the only way you can get them is to take them. Anyway, I just thought you should know." She got up and slowly walked back into the house. Lucky lazily lifted his head to watch her departure.

"You're sworn to secrecy on that little story. Do you understand?"

Then almost as if to say that he did, the dog gave a little jerk with his head and went back to sleep.

It wasn't long before her reading was once more interrupted with a "Pssst, pssst."

Claire looked toward the door and saw a solemn face surrounded by red pigtails. "Is Sarah out here?"

Claire shook her head while motioning to come on out, and Abby sat down beside her. Lucky, never being one to pass up the chance to sit with his favorite person, was in Abby's lap almost before her seat hit the chair.

"How are you doing, Abby?"

"Not too good, Mrs. M. I been thinkin' about what you said and I, I…" Claire was certain she was going to hear a confession. "I thought of some things you should know. Dad caught Sarah a couple of times wearin' Mama's weddin' ring. She really liked it because it was so pretty and because she was sure that Mama wouldn't care. And you know, Mama didn't need it anymore anyway. So she just took it and put it in her room. Daddy told her she couldn't have it. Said when she grew up, it would probably be hers, but she was too young to wear it now. Sarah said that was silly and took it and wore it anyway. She wore it to school one day, and Daddy came home early and found it on her. He was really mad, so he took it and hid it somewhere. That made Sarah mad, so she looked and looked for it. I don't know where, but she up and found it. I don't think she ever wore it again. I think she still has it, but I don't know where she keeps it."

"My, that's quite a story. Why are you telling me this?"

"I guess because I wonder if maybe she did take some of those things. I hope not, but I wonder."

"I bet that was hard for you to tell me, wasn't it?"

"Yes, but I don't want Sarah to get into trouble. I love her." Her voice cracked and trailed off with those words. Lucky looked up sympathetically and licked her cheek that was damp from the tears that trickled down it.

That night after the girls were in bed and Claire was sure that they wouldn't reappear for some trumped up reason, she called Daniel and explained what had happened. "I feel just terrible. I'm not accusing them of anything, really. It's just that the timing seems more than coincidental. And I think everyone in that quilting group thinks someone in the McRoberts family is responsible. Even Sarah and Abby suspect each other. Oh, Daniel, what should I do?"

"How about if I bring over some FBI interrogators and they can get the truth out of them?"

"Daniel, this is not something to joke about."

"I know, but I think you should believe the girls when they told you they didn't do it. There are lots of other explanations for the disappearances."

"Oh yeah? Like what?"

There was silence on the other end. Finally, "I'm not sure right now, but I know there have to be. I'll bet it will end up that most of those things were just misplaced. Oh, I have another idea."

"And what would that be?"

"Remember when you told me about that monkey that lived by you when you were growing up and how it would open its cage and get into people's yards and steal things? Have there been any mysterious monkey sightings around Hayward?"

"No, of course not. That's a dumb idea."

"Still, I think there's some other explanation. Don't worry about it anymore. You sound tired. Get a good night's sleep. You know no matter how bad things appear at night they always seem better in the morning. Good night, Claire."

"Good night, Daniel."

With letter in hand Claire stood with others outside of the Hayward movie theater. She recognized most of those in the group, and she identified them for Helen. Fred Young talked to and evidently annoyed Pearl Hatcher, judging by the look on her face. But then it was hard to tell since Pearl almost always had that annoyed look. Marian Fossel, one of the teachers, chatted with Cliff Wilkens. Claire wondered if she was reminding Cliff to keep an eye out for ants in her room since the previous summer a colony had made its home in a chair in her room. In fact, the school district seemed to be very well represented. Vickie Thornton and Loretta Goering were surrounded by a gaggle of admiring men including Deputy Burton Taylor, John Brook, the new P.E. teacher Phil Regal, and Sheriff Butch Johnson.

Rudy and Ron Milstein talked to Ruby Smith from the bank. Claire didn't mean to be eavesdropping but got a rather sick feeling as Rudy mentioned there had been items mysteriously disappearing from the drugstore. Maude Richards, who evidently had arranged for a much needed night away from her restaurant, overheard what Rudy said and added that she had been having to refill her supply of free mints more often. Now Claire tried to recall how many times she had taken the girls into Maude's with her and told them each time that, yes, they could have a mint. Just how many had they been taking?

Tom Thomas, the new Lutheran minister, was having a serious conversation with Phoebe Peoples. Claire hoped he wasn't trying to lure her away from the Methodist church to be the organist at his church. Claire had heard via the Hayward grapevine that the previous organist had resigned due to severe arthritis in her hands. Apparently, her cheapskate husband had refused many years ago to invest in a milking machine for their five cows, and she had been milking them by hand, which in combination with all the organ practice caused more pain than she was willing to face. In addition to resigning as the organist, she was diverting the egg money to hire someone to do the milking.

William Swan enjoyed a joke with Tim Payne, who had just walked from his dental office at the other end of the block. Joining the two after Tim's arrival was Irma Fisher, who had checked her appearance and straightened her dress while looking at the window of the Lavelle Furniture store. Claire wondered if it was a new dress she was wearing, and, if so, would she have the gall to try to return it to Felton's clothing store after the evening was over. With so many present to witness her appearance, Claire figured this navy dress with the white lace trim and tiny pearl buttons would be hers to keep.

Helen stared admiringly at both William and Tim while Claire told some story about some dress somewhere and continued to identify the theatergoers.

"Now I get it!" Claire suddenly realized each one she knew was either single, divorced, or widowed. "I have a feeling Lila is behind this," she mumbled to herself.

"Did you say something?" Helen asked.

Claire smiled. "I just said I hope we don't have to sit behind this." She nodded toward a stark white hat with the most immense brim that Claire ever had seen.

"You almost need sunglasses for that," whispered Helen.

"I wonder if it glows in dark," Claire joked. But the joking stopped as Lila rushed toward them.

"Won't this be just the most enjoyable evening?" Without missing a beat she continued. Claire often had wondered if she did this because she was afraid of the answers she might get or if she simply was a fast talker. "The movie is wonderful. Chester and I saw it when it first came out. It was just marvelous, marvelous. You two step up to the window now and get your tickets. I have things to do. Ta-ta."

"That's one interesting woman," Helen commented.

Since her grandmother's saying "If you can't say anything nice, then don't say anything" immediately came to mind, Claire just grabbed Helen's elbow and steered her toward the window, where much to their surprise they received a ticket with a seat number. They looked at each other in amazement.

Claire looked at Helen's ticket. "I wonder who you will be sitting by."

"Yeah, you too. This could be interesting."

"Or a disaster. Come on, let's go find out."

The two passed between the heavy velvet curtains that were pulled back from the doorways to the seating area and proceeded down the center aisle. Claire came to her row first and squeezed past two people she didn't recognize. When she got to her seat, she was pleased to see it was in the middle, which provided for good viewing of the screen and the crowd. She sat down wondering who would be seated by her. While she waited, she watched Helen and noticed a relieved look on her face. As she sat down, Claire recognized one of the Lavelle brothers. She wondered if it was Lloyd who, she had learned Sunday, was the one who had volunteered to drive to Des Moines. She also wondered in the dim light if Helen would be able to tell which one he was.

Out of the corner of her eye, Claire saw movement. She looked over and flashed a big smile. William Swan flopped down in the seat next to her. "Looks like you're my date for the night." He smiled back.

"I'm rather surprised to see you at Lila's big matchmaking shindig."

"I had no idea when I got the letter. I just figured it was a promotion of some business that might be opening in the area. But when I got here and checked out the crowd, I caught on. No offense, but I'm really not interested in Lila's matchmaking."

"No offense taken. Neither am I. Since we're here and I've heard this is supposed to be pretty good, we might as well enjoy ourselves. I might even treat you to some popcorn if you promise not to talk during the movie," Claire offered.

"Wait, I think I'm supposed to treat you." William pulled something out of his shirt pocket. "I was given this voucher to be used at the concession stand at intermission."

"Good old Lila. She thought of everything!"

THIRTEEN

Excessive noise never had been a problem since the girls had come to live with Claire. There had been some noisy times when the two girls were arguing or when Abby was squealing when playing with Lucky. In general, they had been quiet, polite houseguests. But suddenly the quiet was even quieter than usual.

Claire knocked and peeked into both bedrooms only to find them empty. Claire remembered Sarah had commented she had finished all of her books and needed to go get some more. Sarah, like many others in the town, was not comfortable around the librarian, Bertha Banter.

"Please will you go with me, Mrs. M.?" Sarah had pleaded. "That librarian doesn't like me. In fact, she kind of scares me."

Claire knew just how she felt, for even though she had been using the library since she moved to town, she still dreaded encountering Bertha. Her sour-looking face and cranky demeanor made the library anything other than an inviting place. Claire had found it interesting that even though Bertha seemed to play no favorites, the men in town appeared to be more intimidated by the little curmudgeon. She knew of many men who would send their wives to check out their reading material instead of dealing with Miss Banter themselves.

Claire was sure the girls hadn't taken off for the library. They always had been good about telling her where they were going and asking before they went any farther than the Dunns' backyard. She figured they probably were in the yard. However, the only things moving in the yard were the birds and multicolored butterflies that flitted among the trees and flowering shrubs. She continued to the large garage the girls had turned into a nicely equipped craft room. No luck there either.

Claire walked out into the alley and listened for sounds of children playing. All she heard were the birds chirping contentedly in the warm morning sunshine. Using her old loud teacher's voice, she yelled down the alley, "Abby! Sarah!" She waited for a moment before she tried again. "Abby! Sarah!" The only response was from a cardinal that cocked its head and then twittered back at Claire. She smiled up at the little bird. "If you find them before I do, tell them to hurry home, please."

As Claire walked back into the house, she saw the closed basement door. "Why didn't I check there first?" she asked herself, thinking of the many hours Abby had spent there looking through a variety of items Claire had stored there. Sarah hadn't shown interest in the lure of the boxed treasures, but for Abby they were as enticing as a toy store.

As Claire descended, the first thing she noticed was Lucky lying on something red and white and fuzzy. Then she saw a guilty-looking Sarah sitting amid open boxes of Christmas ornaments. Abby was sitting there too. However, she didn't look one bit in the wrong since Claire had never objected to her exploring the basement mysteries and treasures as long as they were repacked when she was finished. Claire figured it was a safe and cheap form of entertainment.

"We're sorry, Mrs. M. We should have asked first."

"It's okay. Abby and I have kind of an understanding about basement things, right, Abby?"

Abby didn't respond but seemed completely mesmerized as she handled the glittering ornaments as if she had just unearthed the queen's royal jewels. "These are beautiful. Did you really put these on a tree?"

"Yes. Decorating the tree is a fun part of the Christmas season." Claire almost asked the girls about how they celebrated Christmas but stopped out of fear of the kind of answer she might get. She immediately learned she didn't have to ask the question, as Sarah sadly offered an explanation.

"Mama loved Christmas and said that next to Easter it was the most wonderful time of the year. Daddy never liked it very much. He said Mama spent too much time and money trying to make it perfect when it would never be perfect. He said it was a waste of money to buy all those things to put on a tree when the way it looked growing in the forest was good enough. Mama also liked to have candles at Christmastime, but after she died he wouldn't let us use those. He said burning candles was just an easy way to burn down the whole house."

Claire was getting the impression that when Mrs. McRoberts died more than just a mother died. It seemed that much of the family's spirit died too. Christmas for Claire had always been a special family time. Her heart was thinking of the depression that must have hung over this family at the holidays.

"Let's have a Christmas party. Let's have it next week." Abby jumped up and down with excitement.

"Christmas is in December, silly," replied Sarah sarcastically.

"I don't care. That will make it even more of a special surprise. Can we, Mrs. M.?" Claire didn't even have a chance to respond before Abby continued with her case. "We can put up a tree, and Sarah and me and all of our brothers can help decorate it except Timmy and Tommy because they're too little and they might drop things and break them and they will think the ornaments are toys and play with them. And we can hang up stockings and—"

Sarah interrupted. "Why would we hang up stockings? Santa won't come in June."

"Well, we can pretend. And we can make presents for the others and make paper to wrap them in, and we could bake cookies and sing songs. It'll be fun. Can we, Mrs. M.?"

Just the thought of dragging out Christmas stuff made Claire tired, but she didn't want to nix the idea, at least not without giving it a fair amount of thought. "I'll think about it." Abby stared intently at Claire as if she expected an answer right then. "Give me a little time." She turned and walked back upstairs, partly because she did need to think over the idea and partly because she knew if she stayed the pleading look on Abby's face would win her over.

When she reached the kitchen, she heard footsteps behind her and figured it was Abby. Instead it was Sarah. "Mrs. M., can we talk about Abby's idea?"

As they sat down at the kitchen table, Claire was impressed by the grown-up approach Sarah used. Then she remembered Sarah had been treated as a second adult in their household and probably was used to acting as an intermediary in family arguments.

"When Abby first said something about a Christmas party, I thought it was a dumb idea. But I watched her face and she was so excited. And I thought about what she said. I think Daddy really doesn't hate Christmas. I think he just feels that way because he can never give us the nice things that other daddies can, and since he doesn't want to admit that to any of us, he tries not to celebrate it at all. It was bad enough when Mama was alive, but without her it's been even worse. Last year we didn't have a tree except for the one out in back that we hung a few little ornaments on. When Abby saw all of your pretty things, I think she thought for once this would be her chance to decorate a tree the way it should be. I guess the only problem would be finding a tree this time of year." She paused and smiled. "I don't remember seeing any Christmas tree lots here in Hayward."

Claire let out a big sigh. "Let's go explore."

As the two of them came down the stairs, Abby looked up in anticipation of a decision. A look of confusion appeared on her face when Claire said nothing but buzzed past her and started rummaging through the pile of boxes. After moving some of them, Claire found what she was looking for.

"Aha! Here's what we need."

Sarah looked at Abby and shrugged. The girls got closer to see what the mystery box contained. After tearing off the tape that tightly sealed it, Claire lifted the lid, revealing something green. The girls crowded closer as she pulled out some unfamiliar green things.

"It looks like a bush," Abby said. "I didn't know you could grow a bush in a box."

"It's better than a bush, or at least it will be."

The girls helped remove the green branches of different sizes. "Abby, do you know what this is going to be?" Sarah asked excitedly.

"I'm not sure. It just looks like someone cut up a tree."

"That's right. And I think we're going to put it together again, right, Mrs. M.?"

"That's right, but before we get too far, let's think a bit more about this party, like when will it be?"

"Tomorrow!" squealed Abby, jumping up and down waving green branches in her hands.

"I don't think we can be ready by tomorrow. This is Tuesday, so how about Saturday? I think we could get everything ready by then." There were reasons for Claire's choice of that day. It would allow time for some simple planning and preparation; plus she wouldn't have to have Christmas decorations up for too long. Up on Wednesday, down on Sunday—maybe not too many people would go by her house and judge her insane in that period of time.

"Perfect! Let's put the tree together right now!" pleaded Abby.

"First we need to make some plans. We'll all need to help. Let's go upstairs and make a list."

"And let's have hot chocolate too," chimed in Abby.

"That's ridiculous!" chided Sarah. "It must be eighty-five degrees. No one drinks hot chocolate when it's that hot."

"But Grandma used to make it at Christmastime!"

Rather than letting an argument develop, Claire redirected the conversation to the job at hand, the list. "Let's think of what we need to do, and Sarah can make the list," she said, shoving a pencil and pad of paper toward her. The list started growing almost faster than Sarah could write.

"Bake cookies."

"Make presents."

"Make wrapping paper and wrap presents."

"Decorate the tree and the house."

"Hang stockings."

"Write invitations."

Claire couldn't be quiet after that. "Invitations? I thought this party was for just your brothers and you."

"Yeah—"

"Yes," Sarah corrected her.

"Yes, but invitations are still fun to get."

The ideas stopped, much to Claire's relief. Those things would keep the girls busy for the next three days, and as she looked at the list, she felt they could handle most of them with little or no supervision. Most of the supplies they already had.

Next, they prioritized and decided they would decorate the tree that evening. Sarah said it would be more fun to do it at night since it would look prettier with the lights on. Abby agreed, but she said she didn't think it was fair her brothers couldn't help since they never had been able to put so many fancy ornaments on a tree before. Before she knew it, Claire had given the okay, and the girls were calling to invite Matthew, Mark, Luke, and John to join in the tree trimming.

"We should have their invitations ready when they come," said Abby.

"First we still need to put the tree together," reminded Sarah.

The girls were off in a flash carrying armloads of branches into the living room. When all the pieces were there, Claire showed the girls how they should be assembled.

"We can do this by ourselves," Abby said adamantly.

Claire started to insist it was too much for just the two of them, but Sarah took her by the arm and headed her toward the kitchen. "This was our idea, so we'll do it. You go read a book or something."

"You should do something like bake a big chocolate cake and go to the store and get some ice cream to go with it." Abby giggled.

"I think I'll stick with the book reading if you're sure you can handle this yourselves. I'll be on the porch if you need me." She had trouble keeping her mind on her reading, especially when she heard lots of giggling coming from the living room. She tried to ignore it, but her curiosity finally got the best of her, and she tiptoed back to peek into the living room. There she saw Abby rolling on the floor with hysterical laughter.

Sarah was laughing so hard that tears were rolling down her cheeks, but she couldn't roll on the floor, for she was supporting the craziest-looking Christmas tree ever. Claire moved in to get a closer look. Instead of building a tree with the biggest branches on the bottom and work up to the smallest at top, the girls had pretty much reversed the order. There were some branches in odd places, but in general the tree had an inverted look.

For a moment Claire stood laughing with them then said, "Wait. Stay just like that!" She ran to the hall closet and rummaged through a collection of items on the top shelf. Finally she found what she was looking for and hurried back, Polaroid camera in hand. "Abby, go stand by Sarah. Smile."

The flash went off, and the unfinished picture shot out the bottom of the camera. "Wow, is that one of them cameras that makes the pictures right away?" Abby asked, squeezing in closer. Sarah, wanting to seem like she actually had seen one before, casually walked to Claire's other side. "Where's the picture?" Abby asked impatiently.

"It takes about three minutes before the picture shows up really well. You should be seeing it any time now."

As the image became clearer, the girls watched in amazement. When it was finally done, Abby shook her head. "Wow! That is somethin.'"

Sarah too was astounded. "Gee, I wonder what they'll think of next."

"I agree, it's pretty amazing, but I want to look at the picture of the tree." The three laughed again at the weird-looking thing leaning on the couch. "I don't think that's going to work."

"I think we need do-overs," said Abby as they started to disassemble and rearrange the branches. When it was done, they gave their approval to the improved tree.

"That looks better, but it's sure not as interesting," commented Sarah. "I'm glad I won't have to keep holding it up."

With the tree finally assembled, the girls then moved on to the invitations for their brothers. Abby dug out an assortment of art supplies. With the addition of glitter, the project became rather messy but gave the kitchen a sparkly touch. The finished invitations varied from the conservative ones done by Sarah to Abby's that were done in every art medium she could find.

"Let's take these right now!" Abby squealed with delight, waving hers around and sending glitter to further outreaches of the kitchen.

"Not until we clean up," advised Sarah.

After everything was put away, the girls took off through the back door, leaving Claire in a still slightly sparkly kitchen. Next, she went into the basement to eliminate some decorations she felt didn't need to be included in the project. Had it actually been Christmas, she wouldn't have been so selective, but now she wanted to allow the girls to have a holiday feeling without overdoing it.

She was lost in her thoughts when she heard the back door slam shut and footsteps run across the floor. Then she heard the voices calling her, so she pulled herself off the floor and climbed back up the stairs while allowing her knees to adjust to moving again. At the top, she was met by two very beaming faces. "So what did they think?"

"They think it's neat!" Abby jumped up and down, holding Claire's hands in hers.

Claire's head was beginning to spin at the thought of six children traipsing through her living room. But who could have said no to those four sparkling eyes that beamed at her at that moment?

By seven thirty the selected ornaments had been carried into the living room. Claire would have liked to have skipped putting lights on the tree but had to agree that it wouldn't be right to omit them. "That's why we are doing this at night," Sarah had reminded her. The girls had distributed some of Claire's other decorations—Santas on the hutch, fat candles on the end tables, and a wreath on the door that Claire was sure would convince the neighbors she had completely lost her mind.

Much to Claire's surprise, the boys all came to the front door instead of the back as they normally did. They were all very well behaved, and there wasn't even any arguing as they hung the decorations. They all seemed so in awe that they spent more time comparing ornaments than bickering over them. When it was all done, Abby ran to turn off the lights, and all six stood in silence. Then one by one they all quietly sat down and just stared.

For the first time Claire felt that this had been a mistake. What if now they would never be satisfied with the Christmases their father could provide for them? What if this tree became the standard by which future trees would be compared? Had she actually done a disservice to the family? She felt she needed to say something that might help. "It is pretty, isn't it?" she said quietly as she sat on the floor between Sarah and Abby. "But did you know the first Christmas trees had only white candles on them? And I have seen some lovely trees that are very simply decorated. Some of my favorites are those outside just covered with pure white snow."

"It really is pretty," young John said, "and the lights really make your hair sparkle too, Mrs. Menefee." Claire caught the look between Sarah and Abby and realized some of the glitter from the afternoon's activities must still be in her hair.

The silence in the room continued until suddenly Abby jumped up and ran to the hall closet and returned with the camera. "Will you please take a picture of all of us?" The children arranged themselves in front of the tree, and Claire pressed the button. "Wait 'til you see this!" she said proudly, knowing something that her brothers didn't. The boys were as impressed as the girls had been as the image slowly appeared.

"We should take this to show Dad," Luke said.

"Let's take another one on Saturday so the twins can be in it too," suggested Mark. "Would that be all right, Mrs. Menefee?"

Claire silently walked into the kitchen, leaving the children to talk freely without her. After about twenty minutes, the children walked into the kitchen, thanked her, and told her good night. She was surprised they would leave without being prompted. She later learned Sarah had laid out the time frame beforehand so the evening wouldn't go too late. Once more, Sarah was playing the role of the grown-up for the family.

Abby hopped into the chair beside Claire and gave her the smile that Claire had come to know as her "wanting something" smile. "Yes?"

"We were talking, all of us, I mean, and we want to invite some other people to the party, and it wouldn't be any more work because we would all help and do everything."

Claire was somewhat doubtful about that, but she was more interested in whom they had in mind. She imagined it would be their friends. However, she was not prepared for the updated guest list.

"We want Farley. The boys like him, and so do I, and we think he's lonely and needs friends. I want Clara because she's funny and needs some new friends too." Claire knew how that combination would liven up the gathering in more ways than one but said nothing. "I think it would be nice to invite that Mrs. Evans since she's new and doesn't know many people either."

Sarah continued, "The boys would like to ask Mr. Miller. He reminds us of Grandpa. He spends a lot of time talking to Matthew and Mark, and they think he misses being around his grandchildren."

"And I thought that since we're pretendin' it's Christmas and that it's really supposed to be Jesus's birthday maybe the minister and his wife would like to come. That was my idea. No one else thought of that," Abby added proudly.

"And, of course, we want Mr. Chambers to come," added Sarah.

"It's your party, so it's totally up to you who you invite. But if for some reason they don't want to come, please don't be hurt. They might feel they would be imposing on a family party." Abby rushed toward the cabinet with the art supplies to start on the new invitations. "Not tonight. It's too late. You can work on those tomorrow. Now it's off to bed, ladies."

"I'll beat you!" they said in unison and raced off through the living room and up the stairs.

All the party plans were going well. Everyone the girls had invited said they would attend. Of course, it probably helped that Claire called all of the adults, or at least their families in the case of Farley and Clara, and explained that they were specially selected guests.

Abby and Sarah thought of simple things they could make for their brothers and for each other. For the adults they decided to make an assortment of cookies as well as some fudge and candy-coated pretzels and nuts. The kitchen looked as if more than two elves had been at work. Claire was close by in case she was needed, but as promised, the girls did the baking. They did let her help with the fudge since that was a new cooking experience for Sarah. Claire also made sure more than usual was left in the pan as the three of them, spoons in hands, indulged in the sweet, warm, gooey leftovers.

Daniel called on Thursday night, which had become a weekly occurrence, and Abby insisted she get to talk to him first. "We're having a Christmas party Saturday. Yeah, that's what I said, a Christmas party. We hope you'll come. Our house looks pretty, and the tree is up and a wreath is on the door, and we made cards and baked cookies, and Mrs. M. even showed us how to make fudge. Oh, phooey, I just spoiled the surprise, but anyway we want you to come. I know that Mrs. M. always wants you to come. And remember, Mr. Miller said you can stay with him and he's coming too. So you'll be able to come, won't you?"

There was a moment of silence on the other end as Daniel made sure Abby actually had stopped talking. "Now let me see. I have to check my very full calendar. Hmmm. I don't think I have any bad guys to take care of this weekend, so unless something comes up, I think I can make it."

Abby yelled her news into the phone. "He says he can come. Here, you talk to him now."

"I think you need a new calendar," Daniel said with a smile Claire could almost see through the phone. "My calendars always have Christmas in December. Is this some kind of Iowa custom?"

"Of course not, silly. This was the girls' idea after they discovered my Christmas boxes in the basement. They've worked really hard to make this special."

"Is there anything I need to bring, like Santa and some reindeer? Hey, maybe that clown guy from the barbershop has a Santa costume."

"No thank you!" Then she added, "I know what would be fun if you have the chance. The girls are hanging stockings for all of the kids. It would be a nice surprise if you could find some inexpensive little things for those." She reminded Daniel of the ages of the eight McRoberts children.

"I'll do my best. I'll plan on coming Friday evening. I'll talk to Ben about staying with him."

Daniel paused for a moment. "There is no tactful way to ask this, but I need to prepare myself. Is Lila coming?"

"No, thank goodness. As far as I know she doesn't even know about it. We want this to be a party for real children and not for someone who's never grown up and still thinks she's the center of attention."

"I'd better go to make a shopping list. I'll see you Friday."

When the doorbell rang Friday evening, Claire assumed it would be Daniel and instead of answering the door in her normal manner only cracked the door and without looking out said in her best damsel-in-distress voice, "My oh my, who would that be knocking on my door at this time of night? I'm afraid."

The door was pushed open, almost hitting Claire in the face. "Oh, don't be silly. Dale and I are just bringing this for your party tomorrow." Lila motioned for Dale Taylor to follow her through the dining room into the kitchen with a befuddled Claire trailing behind.

"There must be some mistake. We didn't order a cake."

"I know, dear, but it's a courtesy of my party planning business. I heard you were having this party, and I figured you wouldn't be able to make anything special and festive, so my business took care of that for you. Absolutely no need to thank me, dear."

Thanking Lila was about the furthest thing from her mind as Dale set the sheet cake down on the kitchen table. In fact, she might have said something she probably would later have regretted had not the girls come in through the back door and stood looking in amazement at the white frosted cake that was decorated with a large green wreath with tiny silver candy balls and a red bow at the bottom.

"Wow! Is that for our party? It's beautiful!" Abby stared in wonder.

Claire swallowed her anger and was quick to give Lila the credit for what was meant as an act of kindness. She knew Lila was trying to build up publicity, but to do this basically for the McRoberts children was a kind gesture.

"Now before I leave, do you have everything under control for tomorrow—plates, napkins, punch cups? I do make a delightful fruit punch. It's red and would look just lovely with the cake."

"Mrs. M., we didn't even think of punch. Could she do it, please?" asked Sarah, which kind of surprised Claire.

Those pleading eyes, oh those pleading eyes! Claire wondered if the girls would be staying with her long enough for her to learn not to be such a sucker for those eyes. "Okay, Lila, if you're sure you have time. But I insist on paying you."

"We'll talk about that later. Right now I need to go make my shopping list. Your party is at two thirty, so it will be here at twenty minutes after. Ta-ta, see you tomorrow."

As Lila and Dale walked out, they passed Daniel, who was just about to ring the bell. Lila gushed when she saw him and patted his face as if he were a small child she was complimenting on the chubbiness of his cheeks. "Oh, I'm so glad you're here. I assume you'll be here for the party. It wouldn't be right for Claire to celebrate Christmas without you." Lila laughed and put her hand to her mouth as if she had misstated. "Oh, silly me, it really isn't Christmas, is it? I'm sure you'll enjoy the beautiful cake Dale and I made for the party." Dale rolled his eyes since Lila made it sound as if she had been in the kitchen stirring, baking, and decorating elbow to elbow with him. "I also could make a wedding cake if you know anyone who needs one, winky, winky." She actually added winks before she ushered Dale off the porch and down the walk.

"Boy, I'm sure glad that I came in time for that," Daniel said sarcastically.

"In time for what?" asked Claire, who had just come through the open doorway.

"Oh, never mind. So take me to see this festive cake."

Sarah was dressed in a red velvet dress that had been one of the contributions from the school families. Abby planned to wear a red plaid jumper and white blouse. The jumper was a hand-me-down from Sarah, and both the girls liked it because their father had told them the plaid was very similar to the McRoberts' clan tartan. The jumper and blouse lay on the bed, but there was no sign of Abby.

Claire found her in the backyard sitting quietly on the grass, knees bent, hands across her knees, and one pretty butterfly perched on her motionless hands. The two truly appeared to be looking in each others' eyes. She could tell Abby was talking, and for a brief, unbelievable moment, Claire actually wished for binoculars to see if the butterfly was talking too. The moment was so sweet that she hated to interrupt, but she was afraid Abby wouldn't get dressed in time, so she quietly walked toward the two. She was a few steps away when the butterfly fluttered off, and Abby waved as it departed.

"You two seemed to be having a nice talk."

"Oh yes! I was telling it all about the party and how it would be so much fun. I told it I wish Mama knew that we were having the party. And do you know what?"

"No, what?"

"It said Mama knows already. Can you believe that?"

Her intellectual side wanted to blurt out, "Of course not, no one would believe that!" but her emotional side decided to avoid the question. "You had better skedaddle. You'll have guests coming soon."

As Abby skipped toward the back door, she turned to Claire. "Isn't this going to be the best party ever?"

Claire just crossed her fingers.

Farley was the first to arrive, escorted by his son. Claire had been somewhat worried it might be an issue for Farley not to bring his rifle, but he actually seemed calm as Abby took him by the hand and led him to a comfy arm-chair. "I saved this seat just for you!" she proudly told him.

Ben Miller rang the bell just as Clara was dropped off by Aaron. Ben, always being a gentleman, went to the sidewalk to meet her and offered her his arm. "I may be old, but I'm not helpless!" she grumbled. However, unbeknownst to her, he kept his arm behind her as she slowly took each step.

Abby served as hostess and led them to the couch. Clara looked across the room at Farley and scowled. She whispered to Ben, "Do you think they made him check his gun at the door? If he tries anything, let me know. I brought my gun just in case." She patted the purse she held securely in her lap.

After all the McRoberts children were there, they checked the contents of their stockings. Daniel had done a good job. There were small cars, marbles, yoyos, baseball cards, jacks, decks of cards, hair ribbons, hair clips, fingernail polish, and even toys appropriate for the two-year-old twins. The children spread out their loot on the floor to examine it, and before anyone knew it, Farley was on the floor playing with them. With this unexpected move, Clara started to reach for her water pistol, but Ben grabbed her hand.

"It's okay," he whispered.

"We'll see about that!"

The doorbell rang again, and Abby again was quick to answer it. "I'm sorry I'm late," apologized Helen. "I got tied up with a long distance phone call." Claire was sure the children didn't mind her tardiness when they noticed she came bearing gifts.

"You certainly didn't need to bring anything," Claire said, somewhat embarrassed.

"They're hardly anything. But I just couldn't celebrate Christmas without gifts—no matter what time of year it is."

Farley was quite engaged talking with the children about the things they found in their stockings and was telling stories about things he used to get as a child. Also, he looked with interest at some of the items he was not familiar with, and the children explained them to him. The McRoberts children seemed to be quite taken with him while the adults in the room were still in shock over what they were watching.

Clara, of course, spoke her mind. "The old fool thinks like a child. No wonder he gets along with them." Everyone politely ignored her comment.

The girls stood up together, and after a bit of giggling, Sarah started. "We're so glad you're all here. We'd first like to sing some songs."

Abby started with "Jingle Bells" and then went to "Rudolph." "I was going to have Mrs. Carlson start this next song, but they couldn't come, so I'll start 'Silent Night.' Sarah said it was Mama's favorite song."

When the singing was over, the girls passed out the gifts. The boys didn't look too pleased with the treasure boxes the girls had made from cigar boxes they had gotten from Rudy at the drugstore. The children were excited with the comic books and magazines from Helen. She even brought two small board books for the twins. The adults, in turn, seemed pleased with their cookies and fudge, presented on paper plates that had been painted in green and red.

Clara was so pleased with hers that she started eating right away. "Good thing I came here since they never give me anything to eat at that place I live."

"Oh, don't eat that now, Clara," Abby said. "We have a surprise dessert we want all of you to see."

Claire walked the cake around so everyone could see it before it was cut. "Lila had Dale make it for the party. Wasn't that a nice thought?"

"Nice, smice. I'm surprised she didn't have him write 'Lila's Party Planning' with big red frosting right in the middle of the wreath. And you'll probably get the bill on Monday," Clara grumbled.

"She also brought some yummy punch for us. Who would like some?"

"You taste it first, and if you don't keel over, I might have some."

"Excuse me, please," Mark interrupted in a quiet voice, "but do you think we could take that picture of all of us before we eat because we might not look so good after that."

"You gather your brothers and sisters in front of the tree while I get the camera."

Taking a picture of eight active children wasn't easy, especially when two of them were tired two-year-olds whose afternoon nap had been cut short. Claire took three more pictures in hopes at least one of them might catch everyone looking at the camera. Then, as if eight children weren't enough, Daniel suggested that everyone get in a picture. Claire glared at him, but he just smiled and took the camera from her so she could be in it.

Organizing the adults was almost worse than the children. Clara said she didn't feel she should look at the camera since she was keeping her eye on Farley. She whispered to Ben, "I'm not too sure about that Helen person either. She's probably a crook, you know."

After lots of maneuvering and complaining, everyone was arranged and more or less smiled at the camera. Daniel took another quick shot just to make sure. The developing pictures were placed on the table, and the children anxiously waited for all the images to fully appear.

"It's quite amazing," Ben said to Daniel. "It's a heck of a lot different than my first camera. Kind of makes you wonder what they'll come up with next, doesn't it?"

The children took their food to the backyard while the adults sat in the living room and compared their Christmas stories. Everyone, even Farley and Clara, seemed to enjoy listening to the stories of the others. It was amazing to Claire just how different those two were during this time. The veil of depression seemed to disappear from Farley, and Clara's sarcasm dissolved like the ice cube in her punch cup on that hot June day.

Everyone agreed the party had been a big success, and Claire thought if Lila ever did get her party planning business going maybe Sarah could work for her. It had been fun having the house decorated, and it was somewhat sad taking things down following church. But the big surprise on Sunday was when Sarah decided to go to church with the other three.

After lunch everyone helped take off ornaments and place them back in the boxes. The girls returned the candles and the wreath to the basement, and then the girls were dismissed. Sarah hurried upstairs to read the magazines Helen had brought, and Abby disappeared through the back door. Claire wondered if she was searching for the butterfly so she could report on the party.

Daniel helped Claire wrap and pack the Santas in her collection. They were about halfway through when she paused. "Oh no. I haven't seen the tiny Santa holding a little snow globe, have you?" Daniel shook his head. "I was sure the girls put it out, but I hope I'm mistaken. I'll have to ask them about it later." In the back of her mind, however, was the fact that this was yet one more item to have mysteriously disappeared since the McRoberts' arrival.

FOURTEEN

"Can't you please go with us?" whined Sarah. "I just can't face her alone."

"You're getting ready to start junior high and you're scared to go to the library?" She didn't want to share that half of the town was also hesitant to go into the library. "I know you can do it. You've been with me many times, and nothing happened, did it?"

"No, but I didn't like the way she looked at me. Besides, didn't you say that you just finished the book you were reading?"

Drat! thought Claire. *She got me with that one.*

"All three of us can go together, and Abby can pick out some more books for the summer reading program. I'm sure she can't do a good job of that herself."

"For one thing, I think she is quite capable of picking out her own books." Claire paused, racking her brain for another point to make for her case. Thinking of none, she continued, "Okay, but after this you'll need to go by yourself. Go find Abby."

"She's probably out back trying to find that butterfly. Mrs. M., don't you think you should talk to her about that? She really thinks that butterfly talks to her. I don't think it's very good for her to believe that."

"I don't think it's much of a problem. Didn't you ever have pretend friends you talked to when you were little?"

"No, not really. Daddy didn't like anything like that. He said it was a waste of a good brain to deal with pretend things."

"I guess I'm different from your father. I think an imagination is a great thing for children. I can still remember the names of my make-believe friends. One was named Sharlin and another was Boatsie. And then there was Eggie Rattle."

"Eggie Rattle?" Sarah said in disbelief.

"I know, it's weird. One Thanksgiving my father drove me all around our town looking for Boatsie and Sharlin's house. We never found their black house with a yellow roof. My brother thought that looking for that house was the dumbest idea he'd ever heard, but my father was very patient and supported me in that search. I don't think I was hurt by my imaginary pals, and I don't think Abby and her butterfly is a problem either. Now, if you want to make that library trip, you need to round up your sister."

Lucky bounded through the door when Sarah returned with Abby following. Abby had an uncharacteristically worried look on her face. "Is something wrong?" Claire asked.

"There is, but I don't know what it is."

Remembering that young children often knew when things were not right but couldn't always put their feelings into words, Claire probed. "Can you tell me what you mean?"

"Well, my butterfly told me to be strong and brave but not to worry. It said things would turn out okay. Then it flew off and didn't tell me anything else."

Claire looked at Sarah, who had an "I-told-you-so" look on her face. Claire gently asked. "Abby, honey, are you really sure that's what the butterfly told you?"

Sarah interrupted, "Yeah, don't you know butterflies don't make any sounds at all, and they certainly don't talk. That's just dumb!"

"It's not dumb! That's what it told me. I heard it. You just think I made that up because I'm little and don't know any better."

"I even think that butterfly is some kind of an angel God sent to me."

Sarah looked at Claire with a look of exasperation. Claire stood silent for a moment, not having any idea what to say next as Abby stood defiantly, arms crossed as if to take on anyone who might challenge her.

"Well, I'm not sure about that. Maybe we could discuss it with Reverend Carlson. I think he would be our best expert." Extensive knowledge about angels was far out of Claire's league, so she figured that for the moment she would delay the discussion until she had a chance to talk to Bill. Also, she knew Abby adored him and hoped he would be able to explain to her that the notion of a butterfly being an angel didn't make much sense. "Right now, let's gather up the books and get going to the library."

"Maybe we even can find some books about butterflies and angels, and then you'll see that I'm right." Abby's voice was unwavering.

The girls walked behind Claire as they went through the door of the library located at the south end of the square. They breathed a sigh of relief when they realized Miss Banter wasn't peering over her extraordinarily large desk that loomed in front of the door. Sarah quickly and quietly took off for the teen section. Claire headed toward the picture book section, but Abby grabbed her sleeve.

"Let's go find the butterfly books," she whispered.

The two turned the corner heading for the card catalog and jumped when they almost ran into Miss Banter, who was not at all startled since she had heard them approaching. On the other hand, they had no idea she was there since she moved through her domain on thick, noise-muffling, rubber-soled shoes. Claire was not sure whether she wore them because they were comfortable or because she liked being able to move around the library without the patrons knowing where she was.

"We're just headed to the card catalog."

"Well, one must be very careful using it. One must make certain that the cards are not bent or smudged."

She glowered down at little Abby, who raised both hands toward Bertha's face. "See, I washed 'em right before we came."

"Hmmm. It is too bad more people do not follow that procedure before entering the library. They are unaware of how fragile some of my library materials are." She went shuffling off, mumbling to herself about how inconsiderate library visitors could be.

Claire just shook her head and pulled open the B drawer. She jotted down the call numbers for books about butterflies and was ready to go find them when a small voice whispered, "Now look up angels." Claire took a deep breath, hoping in a way there would be none. She did get lucky, as all of those listed were novels with the word *angel* in the titles. Abby was disappointed but accepted the fact stating that most people obviously did not have as much experience with angels as she did.

While Claire and Abby were looking, Sarah was busy doing her own thing. Once she had successfully passed by the desk and found no Miss Banter glowering at her, she relaxed in the quiet stacks of the library. She carefully removed books from the shelves, looking for those that caught her attention. If she decided not to take one, she just as carefully replaced it in the space it had come from. Although she had looked at quite a few, she so far had found only one to check out. She started to return another book to the shelf when she heard, "You there, you are not to reshelve those books yourself!" Miss Banter's grouchy admonition echoed up and down the aisle. "That is a library rule, and if you cannot follow the rules, you may not use the library!" Sarah was so startled she jumped, dropping the book to the hard floor.

"Now look what you have done." As Sarah nervously bent over to pick up the dropped volume, the scolding continued. "Books are not like rubber balls. They cannot be dropped without damage. And they do not merely bounce back up to their places on the shelves. I must insist that if you want to continue to utilize my fine facility and use my materials you must be more careful and follow the established rules."

Bertha's harsh voice had extended all the way to the 595 section in the nonfiction area. Just as she finished her diatribe, Claire was standing right behind her. "That was totally unnecessary. I'm sure that dropping the book was an accident. If Sarah made a mistake, there was no need to yell at her. And what makes you think this is your library? The wording outside, chiseled in stone, I might add, says Hayward Public Library, not Bertha Banter's library. It's no wonder people don't want to come in here. You're nothing but a mean, crotchety woman." She paused for a split second to calm herself and did not see the look of total bewilderment on the librarian's face.

"Are you through, Sarah?" Sarah stood, tears brimming in her eyes, and said nothing. "You just take your time. Abby and I are not quite done. We'll meet you at the checkout desk, where I'm sure Miss Banter will be more than happy to help us." Claire turned her head toward the still startled woman, who in turn took a step back and headed toward the front of the library.

Abby and Claire went back to selecting books while Sarah finished by just grabbing something off the shelf without even looking at what it was. Rather than immediately going to the front desk, she wandered until she found a spot where she could see the desk without being seen by Miss Banter. As soon as the other two emerged from the stacks, she quickly hustled in step behind them.

"Please check all of these out to me," Claire said, handing up everyone's books.

"It is library policy that we don't ... "

"Well, today let's just bend that policy and put all of them on my card." The unyielding look on Claire's face was one the girls had never seen. Apparently it was new to Miss Banter too, as she took the books, opened each one, and stamped them in her typically rhythmic manner. Then she handed them back without even looking at Claire.

"Good day. I'm sure the girls will be using the library many times, and I imagine that future visits will be more pleasant experiences, don't you, Miss Banter?"

Claire got no response. She really didn't expect one. The three of them turned and headed out the door. As soon as the door closed behind them, Sarah exhaled loudly, as if she had been holding her breath through the entire checkout procedure.

Abby, on the other hand, couldn't wait to talk. "Way to go, Mrs. M. I've never heard you talk so loud." She beamed up at her in an admiring way.

However, Claire was not proud of what she had done and felt she owed the girls an explanation and an apology. "That was not a good thing I just did. I let my temper get the best of me. I'm sorry I acted that way. I should have spoken to her in a less angry way. I should apologize when I've calmed down. Maybe I'll write her a note." Claire personally didn't care for the woman, but she tried to soften her harsh exterior in the girls' eyes. "Really, she's just trying to do what's best for the library. It's her responsibility to help keep all the materials in good shape so everyone can enjoy them."

"But why does she have to be so mean?" whined Sarah as they descended the marble stairs.

"I think she's lonely. I think she just needs some good friends." Abby, the optimist, was at it again.

"Mr. Miller is her friend. Remember, we saw them at the baseball game."

"Yeah, I know, but I think she needs lots of friends. I'll have to think about that."

Claire inwardly shuddered at those words. She loved Abby's desire to befriend everyone, but she was apprehensive about what plan this miniature social director would hatch next.

Abby spent lots of time just sitting with Farley in front of the hardware store. Many times Matthew or Mark or both of them were there too. The boys especially loved hearing Farley's retelling of his war experiences. Abby, although patient with those, preferred his reminiscing about his childhood. She even recently had honed in on his mention of playing baseball. The boys liked that too and frequently, when the discussion was over, would round up some friends and head to the city park to play. Abby was irritated that they wouldn't let her or any girls play.

Claire volunteered to play catch in the backyard but put her foot down at having batting practice there. Abby frequently tried to talk Sarah into playing with her but usually got a big "No!" On those rare occasions when Sarah did agree, she would play for a while but get quickly discouraged by Abby's lack of catching and throwing skills. Abby, in return, did not always welcome Sarah's coaching techniques since they always sounded to her like criticisms rather than suggestions. Abby tried to build up interest with her neighbors Jenny Dunn and Libby and Maggie Graves. Maggie was somewhat interested, but the other two said they didn't know anything about baseball.

Abby wished she had someone who could teach her and her friends. One evening she asked if she could call Daniel. Claire was curious but respected their special relationship and didn't feel she needed to know about all their conversations. However, she stood close to the kitchen door drying the same plate over and over.

"Hi, Mr. Chambers. This is Abby. I have a question for you. Do you know how to play baseball?"

"Yes, I played in high school."

"Were you any good?"

Daniel chuckled. "I thought I was and so did my parents, but I don't know if anyone else thought so. Why?"

"I was wondering if you could teach me and some of my friends to play. The boys won't let me play, and so I thought if you could help my friends learn, then I would have someone to play with."

"I imagine I could, but you need to remember I never know for sure when I'll be in Hayward. It might be a couple of weeks or more between my visits. That might not be enough to get you playing this summer."

"Okay, I guess that'll have to do. Thanks. 'Bye."

Claire peeked through the door and saw a dejected Abby slouched on the couch.

She put down the dishtowel and extremely dry plate and sat beside her. "That's not the happiest face I've ever seen. What's wrong?"

"I'm trying to find someone to teach me how to play baseball. Mr. Chambers said he would, but he can't come very often." Abby wasn't the only one disappointed about that. "I guess I'll have to find someone else."

The two sat silently when Claire suddenly remembered what Ben had said about Bertha. "Oh!"

"What? Did you think of someone?"

At that moment she wished she hadn't remembered and definitely wasn't sure she should mention it. But the look on Abby's face was so hopeful she told anyway. "Well, I kind of did, but I doubt it would work out. Mr. Miller told me that Miss Banter likes baseball. In fact, she used to play when she was younger."

"Gee, Miss Banter played baseball? That's perfect! She needs friends, and we need someone to help us learn how to play."

"That sounds like a good idea, but I don't know how she'd feel about it."

"There's one way to find out. I'll ask her." Abby jumped up and down with excitement.

"I think we might need an advocate."

"A what?"

"An advocate, someone who can be on your side to help your idea work." Claire knew that wasn't the exact definition but figured it was close enough.

"So who can we get? Wait! I know ... Mr. Miller! Let's go ask him right now!"

Claire got up and walked slowly into the kitchen. Her tongue slowly moved across her lips as she looked longingly at the apple pie she had baked that afternoon. "It never hurts to add a little incentive."

The two walked to Ben's house, where they found him relaxing on his porch. "Good evening, ladies. How're you two doing?"

"Fine, Mr. Miller."

Ben was trying hard not to stare at the pie when Claire explained about the baseball coaching job and needing his help.

Ben could stand it no longer. "Would that pie be for me or for her? I'm thinking with a question like that it had better be for her."

"We really meant it for you, but you do what you think is best."

"Your timing couldn't be better. We planned a picnic for tomorrow. I think I'll take the pie for when I pop the question."

Claire faked a startled look. "Ben Miller, you old romantic!"

Ben looked puzzled for a moment; then he laughed. "Now wait a minute. I didn't mean *that* question! I meant the one you were talking about. Getting married again ... no way, at least not anytime soon."

During her time in Hayward, Claire had been a faithful walker covering many, many miles. Since the girls had moved in, her walking had decreased. With school over and Sarah at home more, Claire could walk more often.

She walked quickly toward the park, passing the house rented by Helen, who was working in the yard. "You've done a good job of bringing this yard back to life."

"This has been a change and a challenge for me, for sure. In Chicago I lived in a nice condominium complex and an apartment where all the grounds were cared for. My neighbors have been very helpful in telling me what to prune and the best kinds of fertilizers. Won't you come in for some tea or lemonade?"

"That's a tempting offer, but I'm determined to get in a good walk."

"Would you mind if I joined you? I could use some exercise too. It's been some time since I walked at anything other than a stroll. I usually don't find it necessary to be in too big a hurry around here."

"I'd love some adult company for a change. How's your book coming?"

"Pretty good. There are some definite differences, some good, some not so good. I'm really enjoying myself here. In fact, I like it much more than I thought I would. I figured I'd come in, spend some time to get a good feel for the town, and then move to another small place or two to compare. Now I'm in no hurry to leave."

"Do you think you might want to stay here permanently?"

"I might, if the right situation came along."

"Well, I can recommend it highly." They reached the park and circled the baseball field where some boys, including Matthew and Mark, were playing. "Little Abby and some of her friends wanted to play too, but the boys told them no. Said they didn't know how. So now they're hoping to get Bertha Banter to help them learn."

"Miss Banter, you mean that grumpy librarian? I can't imagine her ever wanting to get anywhere close to children. I was in the library one day, and she didn't have one kind thing to say to any of the children that were there."

"I'm pretty sure she'll turn them down, but we found out she played a lot when she was younger. Seems there actually was a women's league where she lived. I just can't picture her on a baseball field unless she was the umpire and was putting everyone else in his place with her calls."

"Are the girls actually going to ask her themselves? I wouldn't have the courage to do that."

"No, Ben Miller is. Do you remember Ben, lives a few houses from me? Nice gentleman, widower. He's taken Bertha out a few times. He thought maybe she was lonely and that was why she was always so unpleasant. Personally, I can't see that it has made much difference, but he keeps trying. Plus, I think he just enjoys keeping company with someone his own age."

"I hope it works out for the girls. I'd volunteer, but I can't throw a ball to save me. And my catching is not much better."

"How are you at throwing pancakes and catching shmoos?" Claire smiled as she remembered her initiation as the newcomer almost one year before.

"What?"

"You'll find out when you come to the big Fourth of July celebration here at the park."

"Oh, I won't be here. I have a doctor's appointment back in Chicago and then plan to spend the Fourth with some friends."

"I hope it's nothing serious."

"No, it's just that I have frequent counseling sessions to attend. When my husband decided I no longer fit his requirements for a wife, I kind of went off the deep end, lots of anger and depression. I'm much better now, but I do go back for... an occasional tune-up to keep me on the right track."

As the two walked, Claire answered Helen's questions about some of the townsfolk. Yes, Lila was quite a character who had more hats than anyone could possibly need. Yes, she was extremely flamboyant and dramatic but did take the job of being the first lady very seriously and did many community service projects throughout the year.

Yes, there were many people related to the Haywards. In the town itself were Mayor Chester's brother, Charles, and his wife, who lived directly to the west of the mayoral mansion. Dorothy was just about as opposite from Lila as anyone could be with her homemade clothes that Lila viewed as dowdy and her interest in unusual foreign dishes that no one else in the family had a taste.

Yes, the bank president, Clarence Lambert, also was related to the Haywards. He was married to Chester and Charles's sister, Elizabeth. They lived across the street from Claire on the north side of the street. Claire described Elizabeth as the moderate member of the family.

And yes, the Hayward family did own much of the town, which they had since the family had founded it in the middle of the nineteenth century. They owned Farmers' Union Bank, Hayward Market, Hayward Drugs, Hayward Theater, and many other buildings that were rented for different businesses. The family had been instrumental in the construction of the very imposing edifice that housed the Hayward Library. They also had built the original church in town, the Methodist church, and had been the main benefactors to build and rebuild its current updated condition. They chose the original location to be at the north end of the square, which really was a rectangle, so anyone coming to town would see it. Later, at the other end of the square, the Hayward House was built. It was said that the first

Hayward occupants chose that location so they could sit up on the little incline and look down at the rest of the town.

Then Helen asked about Farley. "I heard that he had some kind of trauma in the war, is that right?" Claire explained the situation as it had been told to her. Helen pondered the story for a quite moment. "That's really sad. The poor man. And the poor family too. Have they tried to get help for him, I mean professional help of any kind?"

"I don't know. I never asked."

"I know it's none of my business, but they might want to look into it. Modern psychiatry can do wonders these days."

"I don't know about that. I could be wrong, but I doubt that the people here put much credence in psychiatrists."

"I can tell you if not for a wonderful psychiatrist I probably would not be standing here today." Claire was quite taken aback by that statement and tried not to look surprised wondering if she was out walking with a suicidal person. "He gave me the courage to continue with my job and my research for my book. Otherwise, I wouldn't have been able to go back to work after that hateful divorce." Claire breathed an inward sigh of relief. "I really would hope Farley's family might look into some type of counseling. They might find there are other veterans with similar issues."

After dropping off Helen, Claire mulled over Helen's suggestion. "Psychiatrist for Farley? Nah, I don't think so. Lila maybe, but not Farley."

As she passed Ben's house, she heard, "She said yes! She said yes!" Abby bounded down his steps. "Mr. Miller talked to her, and she said she'd do it. I am just so excited!"

Claire looked toward the porch, where Ben was rocking. "So what did you use as bribery?"

"At first she said, 'Absolutely not!' but then I mentioned a few things like how I was on the board that does her review every year, as are you and Dorothy and Ellen. I also mentioned community service is very important to the Hayward family, and it would be a real feather in her cap to do something like this. She said she was too old, couldn't run, couldn't hit, couldn't throw, couldn't catch anymore. I told her the girls were quite young and knew nothing and any tips she could share with them would be appreciated." He smiled and started rocking again. "And it didn't hurt that I finally agreed to drive her to the annual state librarians' conference next month. I'd kept putting her off on an answer."

"Ben Miller, you are a sweetheart as well as a martyr."

"Thank you, Mr. Miller." Abby threw her arms around his neck and kissed him on the cheek. "I'm going to tell Farley the news!"

FIFTEEN

"A talking butterfly, you say? And not only does it talk, but it's also an angel?" Reverend Carlson took off his glasses and leaned back in his chair, pondering what he'd heard. "No, can't say I've ever heard of that. So what do you think, Claire?"

"I don't know, Bill. That's why I'm here."

"I know it's been many years since I was one, but as I recall children do have quite the imagination, and usually that doesn't seem to leave them marred for life."

"I know that, but the part about the angel kind of bothered me."

"Why?"

"I'm not really sure. I guess it just seemed kind of…sacrilegious. I believe that God speaks to people differently, but I never thought of his words coming via a butterfly."

"I must admit it seems rather unorthodox, but who am I to question. Maybe this so-called friendship is just something Abby has created to give her someone nonjudgmental to talk to about her feelings and her fears about her father and her future." Bill noticed a somewhat hurt look on Claire's face. "Oh, I certainly don't mean to imply you are judgmental. It's just that often it's good to verbalize our thoughts and if no one hears them then we don't have to explain or be held accountable. She's probably just made up this whole butterfly thing."

"Oh, did I mention I have seen the butterfly, and it actually flutters around her head and then perches on her and looks right at her?"

Bill's eyebrows raised above the tops of his glasses as his eyes widened. "Perches right on her, you say?" Claire nodded. "Hmmm. Maybe I should come over and get to know this little insect. It might give me some ideas for a sermon." This time Claire just frowned. "Seriously, maybe there is something special going on here. I have learned that some occurrences that make no sense just have no explanation. I guess I wouldn't do a thing if I were you."

"But what do I tell her if she asks me if I think it's an angel?"

"Be honest. Tell her you don't know and that some things just cannot be explained. Let her believe it if she wants to. By the way, do you know anything this tiny winged angel has told her?"

"The last thing I've heard was something about her needing to be strong and brave but that things would turn out okay."

"And has anything tragic happened lately and then turned out okay?"

Claire thought for a moment. "Well, I hardly would call it a tragedy, but Abby and some of her friends wanted to learn how to play baseball, so Abby tried to find a coach for the girls, and Ben talked Bertha into doing it."

"Bertha Banter coaching a girls' baseball team?" Bill raised his hands toward heaven. "Hallelujah! I believe a miracle truly has occurred!"

As soon as Abby rushed through the back door, she pushed a baseball mitt in front of Claire's face. "Isn't it cool?"

Claire gently pushed it away from her nose. "Yes, I'd say it is, but where did you get it?" she asked with some concern about just where Abby might have picked it up.

"Guess, just guess."

"I have no idea."

"You will just never believe it, but Miss Banter bought four of them. She said not to tell, that it would just be our little secret. But then she said it would be okay to tell our family so they wouldn't think we'd stolen them or something."

Claire definitely could associate with that statement. "Tell me about practice while I fix lunch." Lucky also sat attentively cocking his head from side to side, although Claire figured he was less interested in the baseball story than in what might fall his way during the lunch preparations.

"She told us the best way to catch a ball and how to pinch the glove around it. Then she said the weirdest thing. She said, 'Always keep your eye on the ball and don't be watchin' the cute boys on the bleachers.' Why would anyone want to watch boys anyway? Yuck!

"First, we just tossed balls back and forth to each other. Then she made us roll them to each other and pick them up. That was harder. Then she has this old bat, and we practiced holdin' it and just swingin.' 'Swing straight, swing through. Swing straight, swing through,' she kept on sayin,' and she made us say it over and over too. She said next time we might even get to try hittin' the ball. And do you know what else?"

"No, what?" Claire bent over and looked into Abby's beaming face.

"She brought a big thermos jug of Kool-Aid. Wasn't that nice of her? And she told us we all did a good job. I can hardly wait until the next practice. It was just so much fun!"

Had it been night, Claire would have run outside to see if there was a full moon. Baseball mitts. Kool-Aid. Kind, encouraging words. Could this possibly be the same Bertha Banter that struck fear in hearts of even the bravest men in Hayward?

Sarah seemed to have a built-in alarm clock that told her when it was time to eat. She had no more than stepped one foot inside the kitchen when Abby started retelling the story. Sarah really didn't want to hear it but sensed that it was important to her sister, so she sat and listened.

"What are you girls planning for the afternoon?" Claire asked, setting the lunch on the table.

"I'm going to give myself a manicure and try another color of polish Mrs. Evans gave me. She sure did pick out some cool colors."

"I think I'll go to the library and look for some books about baseball."

"Would you like me to go with you?" Claire offered.

Abby looked insulted. "No, why would I? I can go there by myself."

Sarah brought the debate to an end. "I think you two might be forgetting something." She received puzzled looks. "Why do you think Miss Banter could have practice this morning?"

"Oh yeah." Claire laughed. "The library is closed today."

Claire was in the front yard doing never-ending weeding. It always amazed her how weeds could flourish in any kind of soil or weather conditions while most flowers and vegetables needed a gardener's nurturing touch. She was in mid-tug on a stubborn one when the squealing of brakes caught her attention, and she looked up to see Dr. Nutting hop over the side of his car and rush, bag in hand, into the drugstore. She figured he was in too much of a hurry to just be checking on the availability of some new drug. The sound of the siren and then the appearance of an ambulance confirmed her fears. It sped around the square and double parked in front of the drugstore. The attendants rushed in, leaving the lights flashing. Pulling herself up, she looked back once more to see the rear doors of the ambulance open and a gurney removed.

Claire naturally was curious, but she had been brought up to believe the curiosity over someone else's misfortune was not polite. She remembered a time when she was little that the company that made fire extinguishers caught on fire. The plant filled up an entire block. The blare of sirens rang through the town, and smoke was everywhere. All of her neighbors drove or walked to watch the blaze. But not her family! Her father calmly had said, as he always did, it was not their business and they should not get in the way. If it was important enough, they could read about it in the paper.

She tried to keep weeding but kept looking over her shoulder in case she should see more activity. Shortly, one ambulance attendant came out pulling a gurney as the second attendant pushed. The doors were closed, and with lights flashing and siren blaring, the ambulance finished its drive around the square and headed out of town. Claire's curiosity returned, but so did her upbringing. She went into the house, knowing full well that whatever had happened would be public information before long. *The speed of Western Union has nothing on the way news travels through this town*, she thought.

However, as soon as she finished washing her hands, she headed back to the porch and started to pick up the gardening tools she had left, not quite by accident. It was then that she saw a small congregation of neighbors clustered in the square. Her curiosity got the best of her, and she crossed the street to join the group. As she slowly walked across the grass, she could see that the object of their attention was Hazel Rudolph, who worked part time in the drugstore. Hazel, sitting with her face buried in her hands, sobbed and sobbed despite the comforting arms of the friends around her. Claire's immediate thought was that something had happened to either Rudy or Ronnie.

"What happened?" Claire whispered to Vernina.

"It's Farley. He had a heart attack."

"Oh no! Was it fatal?"

"Hazel said he was alive when they put him in the ambulance. That's about all I know." No one said anything else, and the group dispersed with solemn looks on the shaking heads.

Sarah and Abby joined Claire as she walked home. "What happened?" they asked, both with troubled looks.

"We'll talk about it when we get in the house."

Lucky, who originally greeted them with the usual excited tail wagging, soon sensed that something was wrong and quickly settled down. The three sat in the living room with Abby sitting on the couch by Claire. Sarah sat in a chair with her legs pulled up tightly in front of her as if to bar any bad news from reaching her. Lucky sat on the rug in the middle of the room so he could look back and forth between them.

"It seems Farley had a heart attack. They took him by ambulance to the hospital in Livonia. That's about all that I know."

Abby scooted across the couch and cuddled up next to Claire. "Oh, poor Farley!" she said in a breaking voice. Lucky hopped up on the couch, sympathetically laid his head on Abby's lap, and looked up at Claire with sad brown eyes as if he knew they were dealing with distressing news. They all sat without saying a word. Claire was certain the girls were once again thinking of their father. She wondered if they had the same thoughts as she had tucked away in the recesses of her mind, *Was he ever going to be back to his old self again?*

Sarah sighed as she straightened her legs and got out of her chair. "I think I'll go read a book." She went up the stairs more slowly than Claire had ever seen her move.

Abby still sat on the couch, almost as if in shock. In the short time that she had known him, Abby had grown close to Farley, or at least as close as one could get to someone who often is not communicative. However, she seemed to sense there was a soul deep within that thick veil of depression and paranoia, a soul that was well worth trying to reach and bring back to the surface.

After about five minutes, Abby sat up straight, patted Lucky's head, and got off the couch. Without saying a word, she headed out through the kitchen while Lucky tagged along faithfully behind her. Claire sat and sorrowfully watched her go. Then she closed her eyes and clasped her hands. "God, please watch over Farley in this critical time. Give his family faith and the courage to face whatever may be ahead. And please don't let Abby and her brothers suffer another loss right now. Amen."

She barely had murmured the "amen" when Abby came back hurrying back into the room. "That's what he meant!" Claire looked at her without having any idea what she was talking about. "That's what my butterfly must have meant when he said I would need to be strong and brave. And he also said I shouldn't worry because everything would turn out all right. Isn't that good news? Everything will be all right. I'm going to see if I can find it. Come on, Lucky, let's go."

The pitter patter of six feet hurried through the kitchen, and the sound of the back door slamming soon followed. Claire sat in stunned disbelief, the alleged message from the mysterious butterfly running through her head. "No, that's ridiculous! There are no such things as talking butterflies. And even if there were, they couldn't predict the future." She felt as if she was trying to convince herself, but what had happened was making her a bit less skeptical. Nevertheless, she was going to keep those thoughts to herself for fear everyone would think she was crazy. People would just smile if a six-year-old told them a butterfly talked to her, but for a fifty-year-old woman to say it was something else. On this subject she definitely would not let her opinions leave the house.

The girls had planned a picnic for Friday evening when they heard that Daniel would be coming. Claire had pulled her old grill out of the garage. She loved the flavor of food cooked on a grill but never had been crazy about doing the grilling herself. However, she definitely did not want the girls doing it. She did let, or rather insist, that they snap the ends off the green beans, for that was a job she disliked even more than grilling.

While buying the food at the grocery store earlier in the day, she had heard the latest scuttlebutt about Farley. Bryan offered what he knew, or at least what he had heard from Frank Felton, owner of the clothing store, who had heard it from Rudy, who was working at the drugstore at the time.

"Seems that Farley wasn't feeling quite right when he got up that morning. He didn't want to go back to bed, and he just grumbled around the house. Francine had planned on working at her flower shop all day, and Katie Hornsby was goin' to babysit Carly and Joey. So there wasn't much choice but to have him go with one of them to either the flower or hardware store. I guess he got kind of upset about having to go with Francine. He always did say her store was too girly for real men, don't you know. Anyway, he ended up goin' with Bob.

"Everything went okay. They ordered lunch from Maude's, got barbequed pork sandwiches. Sometimes she makes it so spicy it gives me heartburn, and I can eat just about anything, don't you know. Anyway, Farley began feeling worse shortly after lunch. Bob called the drugstore and told Rudy his symptoms, and Rudy said to send him over and he'd give him something to help. Farley had barely walked through the door when he collapsed. Rudy called Doc Nutting first and then called the ambulance.

"I guess they got him stabilized not long after they got him to the hospital, but he's not out of the woods yet, don't you know. Francine closed the flower store for a few days, and Bob was going to close the hardware store, but Steve Hornsby, who sometimes fills in, said he'd keep it open while Bob was at the hospital. And that's about all I know."

Claire stood almost mesmerized by the story. Again visions of Thomas McRoberts lying comatose with tubes coming and going from different parts of his body rushed through her head. Finally, she brought herself back to the present. "I am so sorry to hear that. I can't imagine that he would be a very easy patient to deal with either."

"No, in fact the last time he was in for something or other, they couldn't keep him quiet. Kept saying the hospital workers were the enemy and he had to get out of there. He ranted about that old codebook. Had a fit until

Bob brought it to the hospital, and just having that with him seemed to calm him down, don't you know. I heard that once he got to feeling better he looked up almost every word he heard to make sure there were no enemy activities going on around him."

"Hopefully it won't be long until he gets irritable again since that probably would mean he's feeling better. Thanks for the information, Bryan."

Claire was putting the groceries away when Abby rushed through the back door with a basket of strawberries she had been invited to pick from the Lamberts' garden across the street. She grilled Claire for any information she might have learned at the store. She hung on every word that Claire said. When she finished, Abby quickly added, "Then someone had better get that codebook to him fast!"

"I'm sure they'll take it to him. I'm positive that would be the best thing for everyone involved."

The girls were relegated to the backyard where they pulled strings off the fresh green beans and snapped off the ends. While the girls were not enjoying their pre-dinner task, Lucky was having a heyday. He had found one of Sarah's old socks under her bed, and Claire had tied a knot in it to make a new toy for him. He ran around the yard growling and shaking his head back and forth while gripping it tightly in his jaws. The fun was somewhat diminished because no one paid any attention to him to take hold of the other end to make a great tug-of-war.

Claire's job was cleaning the grill. It wasn't too bad, but since it had not been used for a couple of years, some small creepy creatures had made cozy little homes in the shelter of the covered grill. "Oooo." Claire shuddered as she wiped away those she could reach and then replaced barbeque tools and oven mitts back into the storage compartment above the grill. To the creatures still deep inside the grill, she warned, "You better get out while the getting's good. I'm leaving the rest of you to Daniel. He deals with mean critters all the time."

Claire jumped and shrieked as she felt something creeping up the back of her neck and into her hair. She waved her hands frantically, but instead of finding some little creature, she encountered fingers. She turned around to find a smiling Daniel looking at her mischievously.

"You scared me!"

"Oh, I'm so sorry," he replied without one bit of remorse in his voice. "Did I hear my name connected to my fine clientele?"

"Yes, I'm leaving you in charge of chasing out any remaining tenants in this old grill."

Daniel took at quick look at the girls, who had seen him sneak up behind Claire and giggled as he startled her. Now he was glad to see they had returned to their bean snapping. He took advantage of the moment and placed a quick kiss squarely on Claire's lips. He was surprised to hear more giggles behind him, but he ignored them. Taking the rags from her outstretched hand, he asked, "So what's new in this quiet little burg? Has Lila had any luck in her matchmaking enterprise?"

"No news about Lila, but the bad news is that Farley had a heart attack."

"Gee, I'm so sorry to hear that. How bad was it?"

"I'm really not sure. I did hear that his condition had stabilized, but that's about all I know."

Daniel did some minimal wiping and declared the grill good enough for use. "Anything left in there will just get burned off. What delicacy am I cooking tonight?"

"The girls begged for steak. It wasn't my original plan, but when Sarah said she and Abby had only had steak once or twice in their lives, I gave in. Plus, I did have two in the freezer from when Bryan was running a great sale a couple of weeks ago."

"Sounds good, one for me and you three can share the other one."

"That wasn't quite what we had in mind, but I'm sure we can come to some compromise," she said, tweaking his cheeks as she headed back into the house.

Daniel started to follow but was intercepted by Lucky, who had lost interest in the sock and had searched out a ball instead. He dropped it at Daniel's feet and looked up hopefully. It was a look only the hard-hearted could refuse. He bent over, tousled Lucky's soft head, and picked up the ball. With a flick of his wrist, the game was on.

When Lucky returned, he decided to make up his own rules, and instead of relinquishing the ball, he held it tightly in his teeth as Daniel tried to remove it from his mouth. When he did release it, Daniel threw it again. This time instead of just holding it stubbornly he took a step away from Daniel each time he reached for the ball. All of this was done with a strange growling noise that seemed to emanate from deep within Lucky's throat. Daniel's first instinct was to just walk away since obviously Lucky didn't understand the proper procedure for playing fetch. But on second thought, Daniel decided to see who would tire of the game first and was determined he could outlast this small competitor.

After finishing the remnants of the bean project, the girls set the picnic table, and Claire worked on other dinner preparations inside. Finally, she came out and grabbed the ball right out of Daniel's hand as he brought it back to throw it again. "Game's over. I call it a tie. You need to get the fire started if we want to eat before dark."

"Party pooper!" Daniel yelled as Claire walked away. Had she looked back she would have seen that Lucky had a disappointed look on his face too.

The cookout was a big success with everyone, especially Lucky, who was quick to pounce on a piece of meat Abby accidentally dropped. The steak was supplemented with the green beans that Claire felt could have cooked a bit longer, fruit salad made mainly with strawberries from the Lamberts, pan fried potatoes, and cloverleaf rolls. The rolls had been an afterthought, and Claire had sent the girls hurrying across the square to Taylor's Bakery. After they left, she got a queasy feeling and hoped she would not hear that anything had disappeared from the bakery on that day. To finish off the meal was chocolate layer cake with fudge frosting, also a request of the girls, probably because they enjoyed eating the frosting that remained after the cake had been iced.

Everyone helped with the cleanup. The girls cleared off the table, and Daniel brought in the tools he'd used in the grilling. Claire looked in surprise when he laid the potholders on the counter. "Why didn't you just use the mitts that were on the top of the grill?"

"There weren't any mitts on top of the grill."

"Oh, I'm sure there were."

"Oh, I'm sure there weren't," he said a bit defensively.

The standoff might have continued, but instead they both headed out into the yard. The minute they were down the steps it was apparent that

Daniel was correct. There was nothing on top of the grill. Claire started looking around on the ground and even wondered if they had fallen and Lucky had taken them for a new plaything.

"Is this what you are looking for?" Daniel had opened the top storage section of the grill and was holding a pair of severely scorched cooking mitts.

"Well, that's not quite how I remember them looking, but yes, I imagine those are they." The sheepish look on her face slowly turned into a smile, and they both laughed.

"Well, now I know what to get you for your birthday. Hey, by the way, when is your birthday?"

"I don't do birthdays anymore. I gave those up many years ago."

After dinner the four played Old Maid and Go Fish around the kitchen table. When it got dark, they went outside so the girls could try to catch fireflies. Having spent most of her life in northern Colorado, the little lightning bugs were still a novelty. And even though both Sarah and Abby had been around them all their lives, the insects' intermittent lights were still fascinating to them. The fact they didn't know exactly what caused the tiny bodies to light up only added to their charm.

Meanwhile, across the street, Irene Taylor was cleaning up after a busier than usual Friday while Dale was in the back getting things ready for an early Saturday start. Her forehead glistened with perspiration not just from the heat from the summer evening but also from the heat that never seemed to dissipate in the bakery. As she looked around the top of the counter, she did a mental inventory of what remained and what had been sold.

"Dale," she bellowed so he could hear her over the sound of the heavy duty mixer. "Did you sell both of those bags of chocolate drop cookies with the firefly decorations?"

"What?" he yelled back.

"The bags of chocolate firefly cookies, did you sell them?"

"I sold one to that really pretty redhead that hangs around the drugstore a lot."

"To whom?"

Dale decided to shorten the description of the buyer. "To that lady that hangs around the drugstore."

"What about the other one?" she shouted.

"You don't need to yell, I'm right here," he said, wiping flour on his long apron that had started the day in pristine condition. "I don't know. I just know that I sold one. Come on, let's finish up and go home. Morning will be here before we know it."

Morning came early, not only for the Taylors but also for the girls on Abby's team. Bertha had told them they could practice on Saturday but that she wanted to do it early before it got too hot. Abby downed a quick breakfast, grabbed her mitt, and was out the door in record time. She skipped to Ben Miller's house and knocked on the door. Ben groggily opened the door, a cup of coffee in his hand.

"Is Mr. Chambers ready?" she asked cheerfully.

"Yes, I am," he answered, emerging from behind Ben and patting his shoulder as he passed. "Maybe you would like to come with us. I'm sure Bertha would enjoy your company."

"You two just run along and have fun. Maybe I'll stroll down after I wake up … in an hour or two."

Abby turned and continued to skip. "Come on, Mr. Chambers. I don't want to be late."

"I think we'll be fine, plus I'm way beyond my skipping years."

They chatted as they walked with Abby doing most of the chatting. But Daniel did have something he wanted to ask. "Have you and your butterfly had any more visits lately?"

Abby thought for a while. "No, it has been awhile. But the last time it told me something interesting. It said something was going to happen and I would need to be brave and strong, but things would be okay. I didn't understand then, but now I think it was about Farley. Somehow that butterfly just knew that was going to happen."

"But the butterfly said things would be okay?"

"Yup!"

"And you think they will?"

"Sure. That butterfly really is an angel, you know."

Daniel stared at her with a questioning look. "An angel you say?"

"Yes, I'm pretty sure."

Daniel took a deep breath before he proceeded. "But Abby, from what I've heard, Farley isn't out of danger yet. Honey, he might not get well again."

"I know."

"But I thought you were sure that things would be all right."

"They will."

Daniel stopped and turned to look squarely in her face. "I'm lost. If Farley gets well and comes home, that's good. Right?" Abby nodded. "Then how do you think it will be all right if he doesn't get well and come back?"

"Now, I've thought about this a lot, and you should know this too. Part of livin' is dyin.' If he don't come back to us, that means he's gone to God and is in heaven. And that's good, right?" This time it was Daniel that nodded. "And that would mean his mind isn't confused and he's at peace and people around here won't be talkin' about him behind his back. In heaven they don't do that, you know. So either he comes back to his family that loves him, or he joins God's family in heaven and is surrounded by God's love there. So you see, either way it works out all right."

Daniel stood in amazement staring at this petite fount of wisdom. Then he felt a tug at his hand. "Mr. Chambers, come on, we've got to go, or we'll be late!"

"Practice was great! And it was a good thing Mr. Chambers came too, because he got to help. He got this funny-lookin' rubber thing out of her car and carried it to the field, and then we got to put the ball on top of it and practice hittin' it. And if we weren't hittin' it, we got to practice catchin' it and throwin' it back toward the rubber thing. It was so much fun!"

"And how was Miss Banter today?"

"Oh, she was okay, but she didn't smile a lot. She said that practice was a serious business and that if we wanted to get better we needed to concentrate and not goof off."

"Miss Banter actually said 'Goof off'?"

Daniel answered. "Those were not her exact words."

"But she did kind of laugh once when Mr. Chambers was supposed to show us how to hit the ball and he took a big swing and missed."

"I didn't know she laughed at that."

"It was funny."

"Some of us didn't think so."

"Are we gonna play catch?"

"I'll be there in a minute. Let me just sit and cool off and talk to Claire for a few minutes."

"Okay. Come on, Lucky. Let's me and you go play ball." And the race to the back door was on.

"Seriously, how was practice?" Claire asked, sitting on the couch, leaving plenty of room for Daniel to sit beside her. Much to her dismay he instead sat in the wingback chair across from her.

"Not bad. Miss Banter really did have some good pointers for the girls, and I felt she treated them fairly. I thought she was quite grumpy toward me though. With a few more practices, I think they could have a fun game if they could find some other players who would take it easy with them."

"Like their parents and you and me?"

"Yeah, that's kind of what I had in mind. But there's something else I want to tell you."

Daniel explained the conversation about Farley, and Claire found herself inching closer and closer to the front of the couch as they talked. When he finished, all she could say was, "Wow." Then after a moment she added, "It sounds like she'll be at ease with whatever happens. Unfortunately, I'm pretty sure that not everyone would feel the same way with either outcome."

"We can talk about this later, but now a little leaguer is waiting for me. Want to come play?"

"No thanks, but I might watch from the porch. Then if I feel like laughing, no one will hear, and no one's feelings will get hurt."

SIXTEEN

Mail in Hayward was usually quite different from what Claire had been used to in the Denver area. Although she did receive cards and letters from old friends, there seldom was advertising. About the only advertising she ever did see was in the weekly newspaper, *The Banner*. But in Monday's mail was a delicate white envelope devoid of a stamp and handwritten: "The Fourth of July picnic is just around the corner. I sure hope you will be there for all the fun. I look forward to seeing you and spending some time with you." It was signed, "A Secret Admirer."

"Oh, that Daniel," she said out loud, but as she looked at the letter more closely, she realized it wasn't his handwriting. She examined the envelope more closely but got no clues as to who the sender could have been. *It's a mystery. I imagine I'll just have to wait until the picnic to find out.*

She was about to walk back into the house when she heard running feet and a car door slam. She turned toward the square in time to see Sheriff Butch Johnson tear away from his usual parking place in front of Maude's with lights flashing and siren blaring. It sped past her house and then turned west on Maple. She assured herself that if it were anything important she would hear about it at the meeting of the Tuesday morning quilting group.

Just as she turned to go in, both the girls came out all excited. "What was that?" Sarah asked. "We heard it, but we didn't see anything."

"It was the sheriff. He took off in a big hurry."

"Why?" Abby asked.

Claire tilted her head and looked down her nose at the little questioning face. "Do I look as if I am involved in police business?"

"No, I just thought you might have seen a bad guy go by or somethin.'"

Momentarily Claire thought of telling the girls that the sheriff was on a campaign to track down the culprits who had been stealing things from all over town but decided against it. "Nope, the sheriff was the only one who went by. Maybe someone was speeding, or there might have been an accident out on the highway. If it's anything important, I'm sure we'll hear all about it later."

Attending the quilting group was usually much more informative than reading Scoop Gibson's newspaper. She was glad she was one of the first to arrive on Tuesday, and since Clara and Meredith were not there yet, it didn't take long for those who were there to quickly start telling what they knew.

Phoebe Peoples started the ball rolling. "Did you see the sheriff go tearing out of town yesterday morning?" Heads nodded. "Did you hear why?"

From those who had heard the story, or at least some version of it, there were slight titters of laughter. Claire breathed a slight sigh of relief since this seemed to indicate no one was ill or seriously hurt or there had not been a crime committed or serious property damage. But she anxiously waited to hear the rest of what Phoebe looked like she was bursting to relate.

"Well, I heard this from my neighbor, who heard it from her cousin, whose brother told her he had heard ... " From the way this was beginning, Claire already doubted the validity, but that didn't stop her from listening with interest. " ... that Clara stole a car and was headed out on the highway. She was going pretty slowly by the time the sheriff caught up with her, and he was able to pull in front of her and stop her."

This didn't sound like the feisty Clara that Claire knew. Instead she visualized Clara stepping on the gas to ram any car that might be trying to get in her way.

Phoebe continued. "Butch took away her keys, helped her into his car, and took her home."

Heads shook all around and the comments followed.

"I have never seen Clara drive around here."

"I didn't even know she knew how to drive."

"I wonder if she even has a driver's license."

"I'm glad I wasn't on that road yesterday. The thought of her behind the wheel is too scary for me!"

Comments ceased when footsteps were heard on the stairs, and hands got busy with the current quilting project. It was a good thing too since the footsteps were those of Clara and Meredith. All the quilters acted as innocent as possible and, except for the obligatory casual greetings, kept their heads down and tried to look engaged in their sewing. Clara plopped herself down in a chair, and Meredith seated herself next to her.

The conversation soon began again, but this time it had nothing to do with the car chase of the previous day. Claire was sure everyone was as curious as she was about the true story and not the fourth-hand version she had just heard. However, like everyone else, she certainly didn't want to be the one to ask Meredith for the details. And after all, maybe the story had stretched so far in the retelling that it might not have involved Clara at all.

Someone in the group asked if anyone had an update about Farley's current condition, but instead of an answer, Clara started muttering. Betty Nutting, who was sitting the closest to her, asked, "I'm sorry, I didn't hear you. What did you say?"

"Taxi service!" She looked around at the circle of faces that looked at her curiously. "Taxis! You know, those things that take poor old people places when no one else can be bothered."

"Mother, I told you I would take you tomorrow," Meredith said very defensively.

"Tomorrow, tomorrow! Lois might be dead by tomorrow!"

"She is not going to be dead by tomorrow. She's in good health and would love to see you, but she will have to wait until then."

"By then she'll probably have totally lost her memory and won't even know who I am." Clara folded her arms for emphasis.

"She will not have forgotten you any more by tomorrow than she would have by yesterday. Now, let's talk about something else."

The conversation returned to Farley. Betty, who had the closest connection through her doctor husband, told what he had said after his last visit to the hospital. "Leonard said he is doing okay. They keep him sedated much of the time so he can rest and not get so agitated. It helped when Aaron brought his codebook, and Farley insisted it be kept on the stand right beside his bed."

"Old fool," came the all too familiar grumbling voice. "Most sane people would ask to have a Bible next to their bed, but oh no, not him. Someone should just take that dumb old codebook and burn it and make him get over the past."

Betty told about what kind of damage might have been done by the heart attack and what further treatment might be needed. Everyone was interested, that was everyone except Clara, who kept muttering under her breath. "This place needs a taxi service. How do they expect anyone to get anywhere without it?"

Although others might have thought about it, Claire was the first to verbalize an offer. "I could take you, Clara. I have nothing to do this afternoon."

Meredith jumped in, "That's really nice, Claire, but I'll just take her tomorrow. I'm sure that will be okay for Lois's schedule, which I doubt varies much from day to day. Clara doesn't need to go before then."

"I don't think she was talking to you. I can answer questions addressed to me. I'm not deaf and dumb." Clara glared at Meredith. Then she turned to Claire. "What time this afternoon?"

"What would be good for you? Do you usually nap in the afternoon?"

"Nap? Nap? Do you think I have one foot in the grave or what?"

"No, of course not, I just wanted to let you know I can go whenever you would like. Maybe Lois naps and we should consider that."

Clara looked as if she were thinking over that possibility. "Hmmm. How about three o'clock? She should be awake by then and ready for tea time. She's English, you know."

Eyes rolled, and Claire figured that Clara's last comment probably was far removed from the truth, so before anyone could say anything she answered. "Three o'clock will be fine. I'll be by to pick you up then."

"Since that's settled, I'm out of here. I'll just go sit in the park and hope the birds and squirrels don't attack me while I'm waiting for this hens' group to break up." She slowly arose and shuffled toward the stairs. The group sat silently listening for the habitual creak whenever anyone stepped on the top tread.

"I'm so sorry. I just…"

"No need to apologize, Meredith," Grace said, waving her hand as if to wave off her words, "but can you tell us exactly what did happen with Clara and the car?"

"Well, for the last few days, she has had this bee in her bonnet to go visit Lois. And she's right; it has been a long time since she's seen her old friend. But I had just started a painting project and told her I couldn't go until tomorrow. And, as you all know, she doesn't take kindly to things not going her way. So she took the keys from the hall table, went to the garage, and somehow managed to back the car out without doing any more damage than bending the rearview mirror and nicking the side of the garage. Then she headed out of town. Luckily, I saw her from the upstairs window. I yelled at her, but, of course, it did absolutely no good. I didn't know what else to do, so I called Maude's hoping the sheriff would be there, and thankfully he was."

Around the circle were comments like "Where else would he be?" "Does he ever go anywhere else?" "Doesn't he ever have anything better to do?" and "I wonder how much coffee that man drinks in one day."

Meredith continued, "I told him that Clara had just stolen the car and probably was headed to Livonia."

"Does she have a driver's license?" someone asked.

"She hasn't for years. I was surprised that she even knew how to start the car and shift the gears. Anyhow, another reason I couldn't take her until Wednesday was that Bud Hornsby had ordered something or other for the car and I wasn't supposed to drive it until he could put in the new part. He was going to do it tomorrow morning. I didn't tell Mother that part since I wasn't going to go until the painting was finished anyway.

"I could hear the siren on the sheriff's car leave town, and I just prayed he would get to her before she hurt herself or someone else. Thankfully, just as Bud had predicted, the car didn't make it very far before it stalled. She made it about a mile past the Dairy King. Then Butch put her in his car and locked the door while he went to check on the car to see if there was any damage. When he saw the broken mirror, he was afraid that she had sideswiped someone or something, which she had, but that wasn't all that important right then.

"He drove to the gas station to get Jen Jensen and called me to say she was safe. Then the three of them drove back, and the two men pushed the car off the road so it would not endanger traffic. Butch was going to bring her home when Aaron drove by. I had called him at the golf course, and he was headed home. When Aaron walked in with one fuming old lady, I was so thankful to see she was all right that for a moment I forgot how angry I was with her.

"We didn't know what to do. You can hardly send someone her age to her room as punishment, and you can hardly ground her since she doesn't go much of anywhere anyway. The only punishment we could think of was taking away her gun. She put up quite a struggle, but I finally managed to wrestle the purse from her grip. She's really quite strong for her age. We hid the gun and told her she might get it back at a later time if she could behave herself."

When Meredith had finished her story, there were words of sympathy and support. Claire had heard these many times before and agreed with them completely. She knew Meredith wished her husband would agree to moving his mother to the nursing home in Livonia, but he would not hear of it. "We are her family, and we cannot dump her just because she is old and sometimes hard to get along with." However, Aaron usually was gone during the day and was not around to put up with her many shenanigans. He came home only in the evenings, and by then she usually had run out of momentum and was either peacefully watching television or was already in bed after a long day of being exasperating.

After the group broke up, Claire walked over to the park with Meredith where they discovered Clara peacefully sitting, her head tilted forward as she napped while the birds and squirrels foraged for bits of crackers that lay around her feet. Meredith whispered, "She usually has crackers in her purse in case she gets hungry."

"That was nice of her to share, and it kept the animals from attacking her too."

Meredith smiled. "I don't think she would have to worry about that. She would be too tough." She walked around in front of the bench and quietly spoke Clara's name. After a few times, Clara raised her head and groggily looked around.

"I thought you would never come. I thought I would die of boredom. Let's go home and eat so I can get going to see Lois." Meredith reached out to help her, but Clara only swatted away her hand. "I may be old, but I'm not helpless!" She teetered unsteadily when she first rose, but Clara did not see Meredith's hand placed with precaution behind her back. As they started across the park on the way to their house, Clara looked back at Claire and yelled. "Go take a nap, missy. I don't want to take any chances of you falling asleep at the wheel."

✹

The ride to Livonia was filled with much criticism of Claire's driving.

"Slow down. Do you think this is a race car?"

"It's too hot in here! I think I'll melt into a puddle."

"Can't you drive any faster? Lois might die of old age before we ever get there."

"You're too close to the side of the road. Are you trying to scare an old lady?"

"What did you do now? I'm freezing. Did you bring any blankets?"

"Don't take those curves so fast. You might roll this heap!"

Claire found her grip on the wheel getting increasingly tighter. By the time they reached the nursing home, her hands were so cramped she barely could release them from the wheel. She had the desire to find a parking place at the far edge of the parking lot just to make Clara walk. Claire felt it would be good exercise for her. However, she did not want to hear any more complaining, so instead she parked in the drop-off area by the door. After entering the lobby, Clara assured Claire she knew the way to Lois's room and told her to wait while she and Lois visited.

Claire parked the car and then reentered the building, but this time she headed down the hall that led to the hospital that was attached to the nursing home. When she reached the desk, she inquired about Farley's room number.

"My, he's a popular gentleman this afternoon. Another lady was just asking about him."

When Claire reached the door to his room, she felt she should wait until the previous visitor was finished, but she decided to take a peek to see who it was. There was Clara, standing at the head of Farley's bed. She started to step back into the hall to give Clara some privacy, but then she remembered the comment about throwing away the codebook. So she again edged forward enough to keep a watchful eye on what might happen.

Most of the time Clara just stood there, but at times she appeared to be talking to him. When Clara moved slightly, Claire could see that Farley was either sleeping or was pretending to be. But he lay so still she became convinced he indeed was sound asleep. She continued to watch in amazement as Clara took one of Farley's hands in hers. With her other hand, she stroked his dry, wrinkled skin. After that she gently stroked his cheek in a way that a loving wife might do for her husband.

Claire quickly pulled back behind the door of the next room when Clara appeared to turn around to leave, but when she didn't emerge from the doorway, Claire tiptoed back to her previous vantage point. Clara was going through the items on top of the bedside stand. Then she bent over and looked under the bed. Next she opened the door of the stand. She bent over and came up holding what appeared to be a dark brown or black rectangle.

"Oh, the codebook!" Claire meant to think it, but the words actually quietly escaped her lips. She was certain Clara would have heard, but luckily she didn't as she held the book and opened her purse. Claire wasn't sure what to do next. She didn't want to confront Clara if she tried to remove it from the room, but she soon realized she didn't need to worry. Instead of stuffing it into her purse, Clara removed a dainty white handkerchief and tenderly wiped off the book. Then she laid it on the top of the stand, checking to make sure it would be within Farley's reach should he want it. Finally, in one final act of caring, she bent over and kissed him on the forehead. After another pat on his hand, she turned toward the door.

This time Claire knew she had to move fast. She ducked into the room across the hall, much to the surprise of the patient who looked up with startled eyes. "Hello," she said, thinking quickly. "My mother is thinking of moving into the nursing home next door because of the closeness of this medical facility. I thought the best way to find out about it was to talk to some of the patients. So how do you like it here?"

Still kind of surprised, the man thought and began to answer. "The workers are nice, but they sure do have cold hands. But then this place is kind of cold anyway. Could you please hand me that afghan on the chair? The place is really clean, but they do keep me awake with all the cleaning machines they run up and down the hall at all hours. Let's see. Oh, the food is not the best, not like home cooking. And boy, do they have the Jell-O, every kind of Jell-O you could imagine. And they seem to stick anything they find lying around the kitchen in that Jell-O. And then there's the broccoli. I didn't know there was that much broccoli in the world! Oh, and here's something that irritates me. I'll be asleep at night, and those darn nurses come around waking me up and asking if I need a sleeping pill. Now isn't that just crazy? Can't they see I'm already asleep?"

By then Claire was quite sure that Clara had shuffled back to the nursing home section. "Thanks for your help. Gotta go!"

"Wait! I have a few more things I could tell you!"

But it was too late since she already was almost running toward the outside hospital door in hopes that she could make it back through the front door and to the lobby before Clara realized she wasn't there. Luckily, by the time she got there, Clara was nowhere to be found. She sat down, sighed, and grabbed a magazine from the end table. She opened it but never even looked at it. Instead she just thought about the tender scene she had just witnessed. Then her mind drifted to thoughts of Thomas McRoberts, and she wondered what his future would be as well as the future of the children.

The words, "Well, let's go," brought her back to reality. She stood up and replaced the magazine. "Thinking of going into farming now, are you?" It was only then that Claire noticed what she had picked off the table. The colorful cover of *Successful Farming* was facing her. "Great magazine, been around for over fifty years, but I don't think it's your thing. Come on, let's blow this joint."

Clara seemed to be revitalized as they walked to the car. "How was your visit with Lois?"

"Fine. She was fine. Said everything was fine. Said she misses her old friends. Said the food's not bad, but lots of Jell-O and too much broccoli."

Claire told Clara that she had gone to see Farley, but he had been asleep, so she had not even stepped into his room. Clara said nothing, nor did she even seem to look concerned about what Claire had said. In fact, Clara's comments about the Jell-O and broccoli were the last things she said until the car pulled up in front of the Andrews' house. Instead her words were replaced with the soft humming of "Amazing Grace" and "It is Well with

My Soul" all the way home. When they arrived, she surprisingly seemed accepting of Claire's help getting out of the car. And when she mumbled a soft but sincere "thank you for taking me" as she walked up the steps, Claire thought the visit had worked some kind of magic. Claire wondered how long the change would last.

SEVENTEEN

The sound was so thunderous that it rattled the windows and awakened Claire from a deep sleep. For a few seconds she thought it was some strange early morning thunderstorm. Then she laughed as she remembered her first July Fourth in Hayward and having the same reaction to that noise. Later that day, she had learned that Ronnie took great pleasure in awakening the town with the loudest firecrackers he could find. She put her head back on her pillow in hopes of getting back to sleep, but then the door flew open and in ran Abby and Lucky.

"What was that noise?"

"That was merely an early start to Independence Day."

"Well, it scared me."

"I'm sorry. Come on and get in bed." As Abby climbed onto the bed, Lucky hopped up too and snuggled between them. "Maybe the two, I mean the three of us can get back to sleep."

It didn't take Abby and Lucky long to doze off, but Claire just lay there thinking back a year. She remembered the Hayward town band that had practiced for the Fourth of July parade in the courthouse basement, and the noise that emanated from that building sounded like beginning elementary school students or even more like a herd of wounded moose. She got a bit embarrassed remembering the events at the picnic and how terrible she had been at the pancake flipping, potato carrying race, and the three-legged race with Betty Nutting. She remembered standing bewildered when Rudy asked if she had a partner for "shmoos" and then the fun she had tossing the water-filled balloon back and forth.

And of course, who could think of a Hayward event without thinking of the huge selection of food in every category? Last year she had been warned to hold back on her eating the week before the picnic. Now she truly understood why and had lived by that advice. Her mouth watered just pondering the choices that probably would be available later that day.

The day would end at the park with a fireworks display, just as it would in thousands of other communities, towns, and cities across the country. She never had been a fan of the noise, but she had not wanted to offend her new neighbors by not staying for the finale. She had stuffed pieces of Kleenex in her ears to try to stifle the sound. This year she had planned ahead and had Rudy order her the best sound-muffling earplugs he could find.

As the thought of the booming sounds of the fireworks rushed through her head, she wondered how Lucky would cope. She might have to rethink her plans and come home early so he would not get upset. Looking at him now, it was hard to think that much of anything could disturb him lying on his back, against Abby, with his four little legs pointing toward the ceiling. His pink tongue lazily hung sideways from his wide-open mouth.

She gave up on going back to sleep, but with her first movement, Lucky awakened too and scampered off the bed. He stood in the doorway, chin jutting forward with an anxious look on his face and then turning circles he indicated his need to go out. "How can you go so quickly from being sound asleep to not being able to wait one more minute?" She threw on her robe and followed Lucky down the stairs.

While he was out doing his thing, Claire groggily started her coffee. While she waited she watched Lucky run around the backyard. Sometimes he decided he needed to bark while he played. Claire often thought it was as if he was talking to himself, which she did all the time. "What are the odds I would find a dog with that same annoying habit?" Lucky ran out of enthusiasm for his laps around the yard at the same time that Sarah appeared in the kitchen. She laid two outfits on the table. "Which one is better for today? I can't decide."

Claire looked at the choices. The color choice was good since both included red, white, and blue. One had a sleeveless white shirt with a red flower on the collar. That was next to a pair of cutoff jean shorts. In fact, it looked as if Sarah had cut them off herself and, in Claire's opinion, had cut off way too much. The other outfit had navy shorts of a much more modest length, but the shirt Sarah had selected to go with it looked more as if it was Abby's size. This was one of the first decisions Claire had needed to make from a parent's, and maybe from a father's, point of view.

She tried to look as if she were heavily weighing the possibilities when in actuality her decision had been made the moment the clothes hit the table. "Since you'll be wearing them for a long time, you're going to want something comfortable. If you're going to do some of the games at the park, you'll want to be able to move well, so you don't want anything too tight. And remember, it will be hot, so I'd go with the cotton shirt and shorts. Those should keep you much cooler." Sarah looked disappointed as she picked up the clothes and walked out of the kitchen.

"I wonder what she'll actually pick," Claire said to Lucky, who tilted his head back and forth, trying to understand. "I'm pretty sure I know what her father would have said. I can hardly wait until he gets home, and then he can make those decisions and she can be upset with him and not me."

As Claire joined the rest of the neighborhood in setting up chairs or sitting by the curb, she was not surprised, although she was disappointed, to see Sarah wearing the tight red t-shirt and short cutoff shorts. "How can she comfortably sit in those?" she mumbled.

"Were you talking to me?" Betty asked.

"Not really. I was just thinking out loud about what Sarah is wearing." She nodded toward a group of girls standing in front of the Graves' house.

"Her outfit seems to fit in with what the rest of them are wearing. But how can they stand things that tight? I would be tugging at those shorts all the time."

"But don't you think they're rather…" Claire paused, looking for the right word,

"suggestive?"

"I guess, but I wonder what our parents thought of what we wore when we hit those teen years. I imagine every generation does a bit of rebelling in clothing styles. I wouldn't worry about it. Besides, you're not her mother, after all."

"Oh, I know that, but believe me, these last couple of months it sure has felt like I was."

Just then the nonmelodious strains of the community band could be heard as they began to play, and the parade was underway. The Cub Scouts and Boy Scouts turned the corner in front of the bank building and headed north on Main, then turned west in front of the Methodist church, and then south on Oak right in front of Claire's house. Everyone stood respectfully, hands over their hearts, as the color guard passed. Next came the band playing what Claire thought might be "Stars and Stripes Forever." The spectators clapped and a few shuddered visibly after they passed. The cheerleaders from the high school followed the band, trying to march in time to the music, which was no easy task. Their red, white, and blue uniforms and pompoms accentuated the patriotic theme. Five little baton twirlers followed the cheerleaders.

Next came a dozen or so veterans, some of whom could still squeeze into their uniforms. Last year Farley had been a proud member of this group, and it was sad that he was not there. Applause greeted these men and one woman as they continued on the route. There were a few more young men in this group than there had been the previous year. Claire figured they were Vietnam vets. She was glad these returned soldiers were more welcomed here than in many other parts of the country.

Just as last year, Mayor and Mrs. Hayward followed behind them in a Ford convertible. He wore a short sleeved white shirt with a red tie. Lila was dressed in a short sleeved dress in a red floral print. Claire also had a vague recollection of the red linen suit and the hat Lila had worn the previous year, a large red straw number with a long scarf that went across the top and tied under her chin, giving the impression that she was ready for a road race more than for a gentle drive for a few blocks at five miles an hour. This time she had chosen a white straw skimmer that made her look as if she belonged in a barbershop quartet. Both Mr. and Mrs. Mayor waved to the crowd, Chester looking as if he enjoyed being around his constituents while Lila looked as if she were sitting on something sharp.

The stilt-walking Uncle Sam, dressed in the traditional patriotic outfit, was back and again threw pieces of red and white peppermint candy as he strode very efficiently from one side of the street to the other. He got a good round of applause, which was probably for both the talent and the candy. When he came closer, Claire looked closely and was quite sure that it was Fred Young. "I'll bet he learned that trick at clown school," she mumbled to herself.

There were two 4-H floats. One had young children holding bouquets of red and white flowers. The other one had older children along with two lambs, a pig, and a calf that let out a loud bawl with every jerk of the flatbed that carried it. Children on bicycles decorated with crepe paper streamers followed the float. Playing cards had been inserted in many of the wheels. Next came the pet parade. A few unfortunate dogs and one pig had been dressed up in various getups but seemed to be taking it all in stride.

Behind the dogs and children were the sheriff and his deputy, Burton Taylor, riding and waving from his shiny black car with a big gold star on the side. The sheriff's car served as a buffer between animals and a variety of tractors. Some were very old and looked as if they should not still be running. Others were new and looked as if they had just been driven off the lot for the parade. The crowd clapped its approval as the tractors passed, for they marked the end of the parade.

The spectators folded up their chairs while those who had been seated on the grass unfolded themselves and headed off either to homes or to the park to try to get a good spot for the picnic later in the day. Claire met Sarah as they both reached the steps at the same time.

"I know, I know. I'm going to change before I go to the park. I just wanted to try these clothes too." Claire decided that enough had been said and walked through the door as Sarah held it for her.

Shortly before three o'clock, Claire headed down Oak toward the park and had just passed the mayor's big white house when she was startled by the sound of the dog lunging at the fence. She could see his head appear and disappear as he jumped, trying his best to get over the fence. "Darn dog!" she muttered.

Many cars passed as Claire headed south. As she got closer to the park, both sides of the street were lined with cars. She spotted Leonard's Thunderbird convertible. She smiled as she thought of the first time she had seen Leonard, who had lost one leg during World War II, get into his car. In what seemed like one smooth, continuous movement, he would throw his leg over the side of the car, swing in the rest of his body, and bring his crutch onto the passenger seat. When getting out, he did use the door, but his method of entry was the fastest she ever had seen.

Claire found Betty and Leonard at the same location in the park as last year. She tucked her oatmeal chocolate chip cake under the tree in the shade and plopped herself down in the empty chair next to Betty.

"Are you more at ease than you were last year?"

"Definitely! Last year I felt that everyone was out to get me. Oh, that sounded a bit harsh, didn't it? What I meant was that everyone wanted to check me out. It feels good not to be in the spotlight so much."

Claire was still chatting with Betty when she saw movement to her left. She looked up and saw Fred Young smiling down at her. He was dressed in knickers, puffy white shirt, tricorn, and powdered wig. He removed his hat and swung it in front of him as he bowed at the waist.

"And a good day to you two fair damsels. I trust you are not suffering too much from the heat on this fine summer day. I have been looking for you, fair Claire. I was hoping to spend some time in your charming presence." With that he opened up the folding chair he carried.

Claire was somewhat dumbfounded and didn't know how to respond. All she could think of was that not only did this man dress like a clown, he really was one. She thought his costume was appropriate for the day, but his greeting and his plan to spend time with her certainly was not what she had planned. Then she remembered the mysterious letter she had received and figured that Fred must have been the sender.

After listening to him talk incessantly about many inane topics, Claire came up with the excuse that she needed to go check to make sure that Abby and Sarah had made it to the park. She honestly wasn't worried about either of them. Sarah had left long ago to meet some friends. Abby was coming with the Dunns. She excused herself and assured Fred that she did not need him to escort her around the park.

She headed toward the baseball field, where the children were having a game. Much to her surprise and pleasure, Abby and some girls were playing with the boys. Luke and John were two of the boys. The girls had been divided between the two teams. Claire sat on the bleachers and along with most other spectators cheered for both sides. But she did cheer extra loudly for Abby, who not only made a couple of good plays in the outfield, which was overfilled with players, but also got a hit and ran safely to first base.

When the game was over, Claire found Abby and congratulated her on a good game. "It was so much fun. We didn't think the boys were going to let us play at first, but then Miss Banter's nephew who was that vampire guy—"

"I think you mean the umpire," Claire corrected.

"Yeah, anyway, he was going to be in charge of the game, and he said it was only fair that girls should get to play too. He even said it would be fairer if there were girls on both teams. I can hardly wait to play again."

Abby had just finished talking when Claire heard some muffled announcement coming from the center of the park. "I think the children's races are getting ready to start. I think you should try those. As fast as you run, you would be good in the races."

With a simple, "Okay," she was off like a flash. As Claire walked back toward a place to watch the races, she was joined by Floyd Lavelle, or at least she was pretty sure it was Floyd. He asked her if she was enjoying the day and if she planned on taking part in some of the events. Without giving her much of a chance to say anything, he talked about the events he thought he might try. He also invited her to be on his Wild and Whacky Croquet team.

"I appreciate the invitation, but I think I'll need to watch that a few more years before I understand the rules. Last year I couldn't begin to figure out what was going on. It just looked too confusing."

"Okay, but you'll be missing out on lots of fun. Guess I'd better go find another teammate. Oh, if you're needing any new furniture pieces, be sure to drop by over the next three days. We'll be continuing our big July Fourth sale. There are good deals in every department."

With those advertising words, he hurried off. But no sooner had Floyd left than his twin appeared at her side. "Going my way?" he asked with a wink.

Since Claire really would have liked to have time to visit with friends of her own choosing, she had the urge to check to see which way he was going before she answered his question. "I thought I would watch the kids' races. Those are always fun."

"I think I'll mosey over there with you, if you don't mind." Lloyd cleared his throat a couple of times, and she had the feeling he wanted to ask her something. She thought she would help him out and hurry up the inevitable, whatever it was.

"I'm sorry, did you say something?"

"Er, uh, I … I was just wondering if you've seen Helen. I've kind of been looking for her."

"She had to go to Chicago for a few days. She should be back by the weekend, I think." Looking at his dejected look, she added, "Helen is nice, isn't she? I know I have enjoyed getting to know her."

"I have too. But I have to tell you, I'm pretty confused right now. You see, I got this letter last week from someone who said she was looking forward to seeing me at the picnic. It was signed 'your secret admirer,' and I just figured it was her. Now I have no idea."

Claire didn't let on that she too had received the same letter. Instead she tried to buoy his spirits. "I think that makes it even more interesting. I guess that means there's someone out there who might be looking for you. Maybe you just need to wander through the crowd so she can find you."

"Good idea. See you later."

Claire shook her head. "I think Lila has been a busy little cupid again. That probably explains all of the attention I've been getting this afternoon. I wonder just how many of those letters she sent." She also wondered if she would have any more would-be suitors trying to keep her company.

After the children's races finished, it was time for the adult games. Claire did them all and was much more at ease than last year. She and Betty defended their three-legged race title, but as before struggled with the pancake flipping race. Rudy again asked her to join him for the tossing of the shmoos. He also asked if she was the sender of his secret admirer letter.

"Oh, Rudy, I'm definitely an admirer, but it's certainly no secret. I got one of those letters too. I don't want to burst your romantic bubble, but I have a feeling Lila is behind them."

"I guess I'm not surprised. But it was fun having so many unattached women talking to me today. So maybe her idea wasn't so bad after all."

The shmoo tossing ended without either Claire or Rudy getting too wet, although on such a hot day it would have felt good. He escorted her back to her chair by the Nuttings.

"Having fun?" Betty asked.

"If nothing else, it has been interesting." She started to explain when a shadow fell across her lap and she felt someone tap her gently on the shoulder. *Oh my, I wonder who it could be this time*, she thought, almost afraid to look. When she turned, she looked up into twinkling eyes and a sparkling smile. "Daniel!" She jumped out of the chair and took his hands.

"I was just wondering," he said, feigning shyness, "if you could be the one who sent me this letter."

"Oh no, not you too!" laughed Claire.

Claire, Daniel, and Lucky swung back and forth on the front porch swing enjoying the temporary quietness of the evening. Daniel moaned and patted his stomach. "It's a good thing I don't go to more of these Hayward events. My waistline couldn't take it. These folks sure do know how to put on a spread. And that roast pork was incredible!" Lucky seemed to be enjoying it too as he licked a spot on Daniel's pants where he had dropped some of the pork.

They rocked some more in silence. "Are you sure you don't mind coming back here early before the fireworks?"

"You mean leaving that swarming crowd with yelling children, crawling ants, and swarming mosquitoes to spend some quiet time alone with you? It was a tough decision, but I think I can live with it. Besides, Lucky probably needs some company when the fireworks start."

"We probably could see the fireworks from my bedroom." As soon as she'd said it, she could feel the blush and was glad it was too dark for Daniel to notice.

"Hey! That sounds like a great idea!" he said, knowing full well that she hadn't intended it the way it came out. "On second thought, Lucky probably wouldn't be too happy up there."

"Yes, you're right. For his sake we should just stay right here and enjoy the evening."

Daniel reached over, picked up Lucky from his cozy spot between them, and set him on his other side. He then put his arm around Claire, pulled her close, and kissed her. The moment their lips touched, the first round of fireworks rocketed into the air, lighting up the nighttime sky. "Wow," he said, "that was quite a kiss!"

"Is the invitation for a home-cooked breakfast still open?" asked Daniel after knocking at the back door.

"I imagine, but let's see how good you are at breaking these eggs. That will determine whether you get them scrambled or fried."

With great expertise and artistic flair, he broke them into the waiting skillet.

"Nice job. I think you've done that before."

"Yes," he said, grabbing a wooden spoon and the milk bottle from the counter, "but I like them scrambled better." With that he stirred the eggs and milk together and continued stirring and cooking until the eggs were yellow and fluffy. He then piled them onto the plates Claire handed him. "My work here is done." Then he sat down, picked up the fork, and smiled at Claire.

"The attention from so many men was flattering but misguided. I hope no one was too terribly disappointed last night," Claire said as she set a plate of scrambled eggs, bacon, and toast in front of Daniel.

"For all you know, there might really have been some romantic connections made thanks to those letters. I think I got lucky finding my admirer."

"But that was no great secret, was it?" She sat down with her plate to join him. "But something else was odd last night. There were lots of people who made a point of mentioning they were missing items from their homes or yards. No one came right out and accused anyone by name, but I got the distinct feeling they were intimating that one or more of the McRoberts children were involved."

"And what do you think?"

"I really don't think it's them. I just have the feeling they're too honest to be picking up things that don't belong to them."

"What have the girls said when you talked to them about it?"

"To be honest, I didn't get the response I expected. At first they both denied it, but later they both came to me concerned that the other one actually might be involved. They both like you and trust you. Why don't you talk to them and see if you can find out anything?"

"In other words you want me to grill them like I might some of my big time criminals—bright lights, toothpicks under their fingernails, listening to Guy Lombardo music, that kind of thing?"

"Of course not, but I'd like to see how they react when you start talking about the disappearances."

"I don't know, Claire. I'm so far from being their parent I don't think I should interfere."

"If you haven't noticed, I'm not exactly their mother either. But right now I think we're about the closest people to parents they have. Someone has to be asking more questions and trying to find the answers before the entire town turns on them."

Daniel looked at her and sighed. "You know, I wouldn't do this for just anyone."

"I know." She leaned over and kissed him on the cheek.

After being up so late the night before, neither girl was up very early. Sarah was the first to appear in the kitchen. She groggily grabbed the orange juice and milk from the refrigerator and set them on the counter. After pouring a glass of juice and adding milk to some cereal, she headed for the table. It was then she noticed Daniel and nearly spilled the juice.

"Oh my gosh! You scared me! Why didn't you say something?"

"I was just marveling at how quietly you did all that. I didn't hear a sound, not even when you opened and closed the refrigerator. I was thinking what a great spy you would be. Did you have fun last night? I know I did. We didn't get to see all of the fireworks since the trees blocked out some of them, but it seemed to be a good display."

"It was good."

"There sure was a lot of great food. What was your favorite?"

While munching a bite of cereal, Sarah thought. "I think the home-made ice cream was the best. My grandpa was going to make it once when I was little. But when he went to get the freezer, he couldn't find it, so we never got any. He said that one of their neighbors probably had stolen it, but I don't know if that was true or not."

"That's tough when favorite things get taken. I had a jackknife when I was a kid. My grandpa gave it to me. It disappeared one day, and I was sure one of my friends, or at least someone I thought was a friend, had taken it. He always denied it, but to this day I'm pretty sure he was the one."

"Too bad."

"Claire said some things have disappeared from around town too. No one seems to know where they could have gone."

"She told me that too. I think people believe that either Abby or I took them. I sure as heck know I didn't, and I don't think she did either. You're a law guy. If you want to, you can search my room, and I'll bet Abby would let you search hers too. I don't think it's fair to think we did it just because we're new in town and poor and don't have much. Just 'cause someone's poor doesn't mean they're dishonest."

"You're sure right about that."

Seeming anxious to change the subject, Sarah asked, "Where's Claire, still asleep?"

"No, she left right before you came down, said she needed to tell Mrs. Dunn something. I don't know why she didn't just phone her. Must be a girl kind of thing." Sarah smiled at that comment but just kept eating.

The dreaded discussion with Abby came later that morning. She was alone in the backyard on her back watching the clouds float by.

"May I join you?" he asked as he rolled onto his back. "See anything interesting?"

"Oh yes. Look there. That's a big bus. Do you see it? And over there's a rose. What can you find?"

"Let me see. Oh, how about that one? I think that's a big bowl of vanilla ice cream. Speaking of ice cream, did you get any of that homemade ice cream last night?"

"No, but I did have a piece of chocolate cake, a brownie, and a piece of cherry pie."

Then he got back to the ice cream topic. "That ice cream would have been really good on that chocolate cake."

"Or on the cherry pie too."

"Right. In fact, I think homemade ice cream is good on just about everything."

"How about spaghetti and liver and onions?" Abby giggled.

"Well, there might be some exceptions. Sarah and I were talking about that ice cream, and she mentioned that your grandfather used to have an ice cream freezer he thought someone stole."

"I don't know. I don't remember that."

"Oh look, that one looks like a sailboat!" Then Daniel quickly got back to the subject. "Speaking of things being stolen, Claire mentioned that lots of things have disappeared around the town and that it's really quite a mystery. Do you have any ideas who might be involved?"

"Heck no, I don't know no thieves. I wouldn't want to have any friends that would take things. Stealin' is naughty. Mama and Daddy always taught us that. Daddy says if you can't afford to buy things, then you just can't have them no matter how much you might want them. Daddy said that sometimes it's all right to trade someone for stuff but that everyone has to agree that it's a fair trade. Did you ever trade for anything?"

Not expecting this, he had to take some time to think back a few years. "When I was about your age, one of my neighbors, he was littler than I was, got a very fancy silver belt buckle from his grandfather. I thought it was about the best thing I'd ever seen. I wanted it very badly, so one day when my mother was baking cookies, I told him I would trade him six cookies for his belt buckle. You have to remember that he was little and those fresh warm cookies sounded like much more fun than some dumb old belt buckle. So we made the trade. That night when I started getting ready for bed, my mother discovered what I'd done. She made me march over to the neighbor's house in my pajamas and return that silver buckle."

"Hmmm. That wasn't a very fair trade then, was it?"

"It sounded fair to me at the time, but you're right. There wasn't one thing fair about it. It was kind of like stealing, in a way. Anyway, if you hear anything about those disappearances, make sure you tell Claire, okay?"

"Okay. Now we have to be quiet. I'm kind of waitin' for my butterfly. It's been awhile since it's been here, you know. Maybe you should go inside so you don't scare it away."

Daniel quietly, although definitely not quickly, pushed himself up and went into the kitchen, where Claire sat pretending to look through recipes.

"Anything?"

"No, not really. Just like with Sarah, nothing she said gave me any indication they were guilty, but neither could I say positively they're not involved. But I think you should go with your woman's intuition and continue to believe they had nothing to do with any of those things. By the way, I was invited to search their rooms. Do you want me to?"

Part of her wanted to say yes, but she just couldn't show distrust in front of the girls. "No, I think I'll just stick to my belief they've been raised to know right from wrong."

Daniel bent over and wrapped his arms around her. "Those girls don't know how lucky they are to have you right now." And with a kiss on the cheek added, "And so am I."

EIGHTEEN

"You sure missed a good time last week," Claire told Helen as they stood by the meat counter making their selections. "And believe me, your absence was definitely noted by a few gentlemen."

"Oh, like who?"

"Lloyd and Floyd both. I heard Tom Thomas asking about you. And there were a couple of men I didn't know I heard asking Lila if she knew where you were." Claire didn't mention that Lila was so thrilled by the inquiries that she looked like the cat that had just been promised a big bowl of cream.

"That's kind of flattering, isn't it?"

"I would certainly think so. How was your trip?"

"It was good. It's nice to get a mental health boost once in a while. But I was really surprised how anxious I was to get back here. I didn't realize until I left how much I feel at home here. It does, however, lack in the grocery department," she said and with a disgusted look on her face tossed a package of pork chops back into the refrigerated case.

"I know what you mean. But I have done a pretty good job of getting by on what Bryan stocks. But then I'm not the gourmet cook you are. Have you met Dorothy Hayward yet? She's the only one I know who tries fancier things. I'll bet you two would enjoy each other. You should ask Lila to introduce you." Helen scrunched up her face. "Or I could see if Elizabeth could introduce you to her sister-in-law."

As soon as Claire got home, she called Elizabeth and made the suggestion. Claire had just finished putting the groceries away when the phone rang. "Wow, that was fast. I'm glad she thought it was a good idea too. Thanks, Elizabeth." She smiled as she hung up the phone. "Good. That should be good for both of them."

"Both of whom?"

Not realizing anyone was there, Claire jumped when she heard the voice. "You startled me! I didn't know you were there."

"Sorry. Both of whom?" Sarah asked again.

"I thought Mrs. Evans might have a lot in common with the mayor's brother's wife. So I called Mrs. Lambert, and she thought it was a good idea too, so she is going to get them together."

"That's nice. What's there to eat?"

Claire smiled as she reminded Sarah she could fix her own lunch.

"Well, someone has got to talk to her about it. We cannot ignore this anymore."

"But are we sure there could be no other explanations?"

"I certainly don't have any. Does anyone else?

The rest of the quilters were silent.

"Then who is going to do it?"

All the ladies avoided eye contact with each other.

Grace finally volunteered. "I guess I could talk to her, but I'm not convinced that the girls are responsible."

"I don't know what you all are babbling about," said Clara in her usual irritated tone. "That little girl didn't do it. She didn't do anything wrong. She's honest as the day is long. And I'll bet her sister had nothing to do with it either. You just mark my words about this!"

"Then who do you suspect?" Phoebe asked in an equally unpleasant tone.

"I don't know, but she didn't do it. Maybe it's the new guy who's been helping out at the post office while that Steve Williams is on vacation. Or maybe it's Williams himself. Have you ever noticed his shifty, beady eyes? That's a dead giveaway that there's evil there."

"That's absolutely ridiculous, Mother. Now be quiet."

"Well, she didn't do it," Clara mumbled one more time.

Once more the conversation quickly changed as Claire came through the doorway. "Good morning, ladies. Did I miss any good gossip?"

"Gossip, no. Mean talk, yes." Clara looked around the circle. "These female vigilantes have decided the McRoberts gang has been pilfering the town's precious treasures. I say they're dead wrong and they should all have their mouths washed out with soap."

Claire wasn't really surprised. She knew many people thought this, but she had hoped that the members of this group, the ladies who knew her well, wouldn't think the girls were responsible. She felt all eyes staring at her and quickly gathered her thoughts. She didn't want to say anything that might alienate her friends.

"I've talked to the girls together and alone, and I honestly don't think they know anything about these missing items. I even had a U.S. Marshall question them."

Before she could continue, Clara, her enthusiasm intensified, leaned forward. "Did he grill them really good? Shine a bright light in their eyes? Shove toothpicks under their fingernails?"

"No, of course not. He just talked to each individually, and he's convinced they had nothing to do with this. He deals with liars and crooks all the time, and he said he was sure they weren't lying to him."

"Good enough for me. I thought we were here to quilt." Claire was never so glad to hear Clara talk as she was right then. "Or maybe some of you would like to hear about what was going on behind the picnic pavilion during the fireworks."

Many of the women looked interested, but Phoebe quickly spoke up. "No, you're right. We're here to get some work done and not spread gossip or point accusatory fingers."

Claire was curious, and she was sure many others were too. She wondered if she had missed out on something interesting by leaving the Fourth of July shindig early. But as she thought back to her time alone with Daniel, she was pretty sure that whatever had gone on in the park could not have been any more enjoyable to her than the time she had on her own front porch.

Her thoughts were interrupted when a lavender swirl swished through the doorway. Lila, dressed in a full skirted lightweight dress, swooped in to greet the group. "Good morning, dear ladies. I'm sorry I cannot stay, but I just came over to do a quick check of the kitchen. I need to make sure it's all stocked and ready to go, if need be." With one hand holding out her skirt, she made another twirl, giving the impression that the cute little purple bird attached to the band of her small lavender and white hat was trying to take off as its wings fluttered with her circular movement. She then headed toward the church's kitchen at the end of the basement. As she left, the ladies could hear her singing something that sounded like "Love is in the air everywhere I look around."

"I liked that song until now," Clara stated emphatically.

Much to Claire's relief, the conversation changed dramatically when Ellen asked Francine how Farley was doing.

"He's making good progress, and we hope he'll be home later this week. The nursing staff said they started to see big improvements about a week and a half ago. They said he started talking about being visited one afternoon by an angel that comforted him by stroking his hand and kissing him on the head."

Claire knew she dared not look at Clara, but, on the other hand, she could hardly avoid it when Clara loudly proclaimed, "Angel? Angel? You must be kidding. It would be more likely that he would be visited by the—"

Meredith quickly placed her hand over the older lady's mouth before she could finish the sentence. "An angel you say?" Meredith started in a louder voice to cover up Clara's final word, but then her voice quieted. "That's very interesting."

"Bill has told me of times when those close to death believe they were visited by or talked to some kind of spirit," Grace volunteered.

"My mother told of a similar experience, although she was not the one who was dying. My dad was not well and lingered in the hospital for months, and many times the doctors told her he would not make it until the next day. She said that when she went home from the hospital, she felt there was something or someone there with her. She said it wasn't a scary but a comforting feeling, a feeling of support, so she would not have to face the crisis alone."

Elizabeth added her experience. "I tried to give blood once. I lay down on the cot, they stuck the needle in my arm, and the next thing I knew I saw bright lights and heard a choir of children singing. Then I heard a voice say, 'Well, at least she's breathing again.' I was so far out that I even lost bladder control. Oh, I guess you didn't need to hear that part, did you? Anyway, the bright lights and the singing kind of scared me. It made me wonder just how far out I really was."

Others around the circle told stories they had experienced or heard of, and hardly any work actually got done on the quilting project. The group adjourned, and Elizabeth walked home with Claire to offer moral support. "I don't believe for one moment that those two sweet girls are responsible for the thefts. There has got to be another explanation we're all missing."

"I don't suppose a monkey has moved into Hayward within the past few months, has it?"

Elizabeth gave her a weird look. "Not that I know of. Why?"

Claire repeated the story about the monkey that lived by her years ago and stole things in the neighborhood.

"Hey, maybe the monkey that Fred Young used for his organ grinder gig really was his. Have you heard that story?"

"Yes, he's quite an interesting character. But I somehow doubt that he has a monkey responsible for this."

"We'll figure it out. Don't worry about it, promise?"

"Okay, promise." But that really didn't stop her worrying.

Just to prove she did indeed trust the girls, Claire sent them to the drugstore with a list and some money for something from the soda counter. The bell above the door jingled their arrival. Abby always had been fascinated with the bell, so she went out and reentered not once but twice. Rudy came hurrying from the back of the store. He looked around somewhat surprised.

"Hey, kiddoes, what are you up to?"

"We're fine. How are you today, Mr. Milstein?"

"I'm impressed by your manners, as usual, but I thought I heard more people come in."

"It was just me. I think that bell is so cool. I think I'll put one over my bedroom door."

"That's a goofy idea," Sarah said with disgust. "No one ever goes into your room but you."

"Yeah, but it still would be cool."

"What can I do for you ladies today?"

"Mrs. Menefee sent us to pick up some things—"

Abby excitedly interrupted, "And we get to sit at the counter and order something too."

"Then step right up and let me work my ice cream magic. Then, if you like, I'll work on that list."

After ordering her banana split, Abby twirled round and round on the red vinyl stool. "Don't make yourself sick doing that," warned Sarah.

"Oh, I won't. Remember I told you I went around the most times on the merry-go-round at school without getting sick?"

"Quite something to be proud of," Sarah said sarcastically.

Even after Rudy delivered the banana split and Sarah's sundae with double scoops and double hot fudge, Abby continued to spin between bites. On one of her spins, she stopped and whispered to Sarah.

"Looks who's coming up the aisle."

Not wanting to stare, she turned to take a quick look.

As she walked by the stools, Abby couldn't resist. She whirled around. "Hi."

"Hi," the somewhat startled redhead replied.

"I'm Abby. This is my sister, Sarah. Who are you?"

Sarah thought she would slide off the stool with embarrassment and at that moment wished she had a place to hide. "Abby, that's not very polite. I apologize for my sister."

"It's all right. My name is Tara. And I love the color of your hair."

Abby giggled. "And I love the color of yours too. And you know what else?"

"No, what?'"

"You look just like our mother. Well, you don't look just like her because you're younger, you know. But you look lots like her. And she was pretty just like you."

Tara didn't catch the *was* in Abby's sentence. She replied with, "Thank you very much. And tell your mother she has two very pretty daughters."

"Thanks, and I would, but I can't because she's dead now."

Tara's hand flew up to her mouth as if she had said something terrible. "Oh, I am so sorry. I shouldn't have said that."

Without missing a beat, Abby soothed the waters. "We're sorry too, but it's really nice of you to say that we're pretty."

Tara smiled sympathetically. "It was nice to meet you girls. I need to hurry. I'm running a little late."

"Nice lady."

"Yes, she is, but I wish you wouldn't do that to people. It's embarrassing."

"She didn't seem embarrassed."

"I wasn't talking about her. I was talking about me!"

The bell above the door jingled again. It was Helen who came in and walked over to talk to the girls. This time it was Sarah who asked the questions. "I heard you went to Chicago. Did you have a good trip?"

"It was all right, but it was sure good to get back."

"I've never been to a big city like that. It must be lots different than here."

"It is. There are lots of stores and museums. There's a huge park right by the lake, and hundreds of boats dock there. There's even a big amusement park. There are thousands of people and lots of traffic. It can get pretty noisy. Usually it's not as clean as it is here. There's always lots of rushing around."

Sarah seemed to have stopped listening after thousands of people. "It sounds wonderful. I hope I can go sometime."

"Maybe you could go with me on one of my quick trips. We can talk to Claire about it. I'd better go grab what I need. See you girls later."

By then Rudy was back with a sack filled with Claire's items. Sarah handed him the money, and he walked to the cash register for change. As the girls were finishing, Ronnie appeared from the back. "Howdy, girls, how are you this fine day? Did my uncle get your orders just right? I think

I'm better with the ice cream scoop than he is." He purposely said it loud enough that Rudy could hear as he returned with Sarah's change.

"I'm not so sure about that, but I do know you might put us out of business with your generous portions of whipped cream, nuts, and cherries." The girls grinned as they listened to the make-believe argument. When they finished, they thanked Rudy and hopped down from the stools. As they walked out, Rudy yelled after them, "Don't be wearing out my bell, you hear?" Abby giggled as she and Sarah raced home.

"I can't thank you enough! Dorothy and I are having so much fun comparing recipes and thinking of new cooking ideas. In fact, we've decided to have a dinner party and try out some new things." Claire shuddered as thoughts of Dorothy's curried Thanksgiving turkey came to mind. "I want to make sure we plan it for a day your friend Daniel can come. It's going to be a couples' dinner." Helen listed a couple of possibilities.

"I'll try to get in touch with him tonight, and I'll let you know tomorrow."

Claire had barely hung up the phone when it rang and startled her. "Maybe it's Daniel. Maybe he's clairvoyant," she mumbled to herself.

"Mrs. Menefee, this is the charge nurse at the hospital calling about Thomas McRoberts."

Claire tried to stay calm. She had received a call like this before, and it had not been good news. She said a little prayer, hoping that this call would be positive.

"Mr. McRoberts took a turn for the worse this morning. His vital signs aren't strong. We're worried that ... " She paused as if to rephrase what she was about to say. "I, I mean the staff, feels it would probably be a good idea for the children to come see him."

Claire had the feeling the nurse wanted to add "as soon as possible" to her statement but refrained. Her hands started to shake as she hung up and started making calls to the other guardians. Since Matthew and Mark were out of town for a baseball game, it was decided they would all go together in the morning. Claire hoped it wouldn't be too late.

Sarah received the news with tears and fears. Abby had the same reaction as she ran into the backyard. Claire thought she might need some additional comfort and a shoulder to cry on, but as she headed out, she stopped cold. Abby was sitting on the ground close to a pink flowering bush, and on her hand was a butterfly, her butterfly.

Abby studied the butterfly as it slightly moved its wings as if trying to maintain its balance while perched on her small hand. She appeared to be listening to whatever the insect was telling her, or at least in what she believed it was saying. Occasionally, she nodded her head while also wiping away tears. As Claire watched, she was surprised that Abby didn't seem to say anything, she merely sat and listened, something that she was not known for. When Abby brought the butterfly up to her cheek, the two seemed to touch briefly, and then on beautiful, silent wings, it flew off to the pink bush to sip nectar from the sweet blooms. Abby watched it until it flew over the fence into the Nuttings' yard; then she got up and skipped back toward the house with an entirely different demeanor.

Claire was quite surprised by the remarkable turnaround in both facial expressions and body language. She wanted very much to know what had happened during the past few minutes and hoped Abby would volunteer information. She tried to play innocent and make it look as if she had just arrived in the doorway as Abby met her coming from the opposite direction.

"Hi, sweetie. I came to see how you're doing, but that smile on your face tells me you're feeling better than a few minutes ago."

"I feel great now. I'm hungry."

"Dinner won't be ready for quite a while, but you could go ahead and set the table." As Abby got silverware from the drawer, Claire continued with some gentle probing. "I'm so glad you're feeling better, but I don't understand what happened that cheered you up so quickly. Want to share any of your secrets?"

Over the clatter of knives, forks, and spoons, Abby gave a brief six-year-old explanation. "My butterfly just told me that Daddy would be just fine. Can I at least have a snack?"

At that moment, Sarah, whose eyes were red and puffy from crying, walked into the kitchen. "Oh, Abby, how can you even think about eating at a time like this?"

"It will be fine, don't worry."

"Didn't Mrs. M. just tell you that Daddy has gotten worse?"

"Of course, but my butterfly was waiting for me when I came downstairs, and it said Daddy would be okay. Can I have some cookies?"

"How about some cheese and crackers instead?"

In a voice that rose in intensity and volume with each word, Sarah had her own response. "No cheese, no crackers, and no more about that stupid butterfly! They don't talk, they don't give advice, and they are not angels! Just stop that nonsense!" With that she turned and ran out of the room. They could hear her footsteps overhead as she ran up the stairs and into her room, slamming the door behind her.

"That's too bad."

"What's too bad, Abby?"

"That she doesn't believe me about the butterfly. You believe me, don't you, Mrs. M.?"

Claire paused and swallowed hard. "I have to admit that the idea of a talking butterfly is very hard for me to understand too. But I also have never seen one sit on a person like that one sits on you or gets as close to a face as it does. But I do believe in you, and since I hope you will never lie to me, then, yes, I guess I believe there is something special going on between you two. Did the butterfly tell you anything else?"

"It said it would just take a little longer for Daddy, but he would be okay, just like Farley was. And it was right about that too, wasn't it? No one believed me then either. Oh yeah, it also told me that Mama said hello. Can I have those crackers now?"

"In a minute, but let's check the table first. Which side is the knife supposed to go on?"

Abby sang something Claire had made up to try to help her remember how to set the table the right way. "The knife goes on the right, the knife goes on the right, the spoon and the knife hold the plate in tight, the knife goes on the right."

"You got the song right, but you didn't get the right right. You put them on the left side instead."

"Oh phooey, I always get that mixed up."

"I do sometimes too, but it'll get easier as you get older. Right now you fix the silverware, and I'll get you something to eat. But it won't be much. I don't want you to spoil your dinner."

The children were unusually quiet on the trip to the hospital. Abby was the only upbeat one and probably would have talked all the way there were it not for the dose of Dramamine Claire administered an hour before they left. She usually did not give it to her so early, but Claire thought it would be better if it took effect sooner so she didn't annoy the other riders with her talk about the message from the butterfly. At first Abby had said she wasn't going to go since she knew her dad would be getting out of the hospital before long while the five older children were going because they were fearful this might be their last chance to see him. She finally consented when Claire convinced her that he might worry if everyone showed up except her. Claire felt rather guilty about using this tactic because if Mr. McRoberts still was in a worsened condition she doubted he would have any idea who was or wasn't visiting.

Instead of the wide-eyed looks of apprehension, the staff genuinely seemed pleased to see all of them. Matthew and Mark went separately into their father's room while Sarah took Luke and John one at a time for what she figured probably would be their last visit. Then she went in alone and spent quite a bit of time with him.

"Oh, Daddy, I'm so scared. If something happens and you don't come home, that means I'll be in charge, and I don't know how to do that. I barely made it through sixth grade math, so how could I take care of money and stuff? Oh, how would there even be any money anyway? I'd probably have to quit school and get a job, and do people even have jobs that twelve-year-olds can do? Oh, Daddy, what am I going to do?"

As she spoke those last words, her eyes dropped, and as they did, she saw slight movement in one of her father's hands. Ever so slowly his index finger pointed upward. Sarah's eyes followed the direction of the pointing finger, and she was surprised to see a white aura high above his bed. Before she realized it, she found herself speaking toward that light.

"Oh, God, I need you. We all need you. Please help Daddy get well. I don't know what we all would do if he didn't. And if you can't help him get well, please help me take care of the rest of the children. I will need your help because I don't have any idea how to be a parent. I am so scared and I need your help."

Had she been asked to explain it, she would have had trouble putting it in words, but as she finished her brief prayer, she felt a change go through her entire body. It was as if the entire burden had been lifted from her shoulders, and a sense of relief came over her. When she looked up again, the strange light was gone. She looked down at her father's hand, which was once again lying flat against the blanket that covered his thin, pale body.

She stood for a few minutes in silence trying to comprehend what had just happened. Slowly, a look of relief came over her face. She leaned over and whispered in his ear. "I love you, Daddy."

Abby had asked to be last, plus that gave her more time to wake up from her long in-transit nap. Her demeanor as she strode down the quiet hall was much different from that of her siblings. Her head was held high, and her arms swung with confidence. As soon as she turned the corner into her father's room, she started talking. She pushed a chair up next to the bed and kneeled on it so her head would be more level with his.

"Hi, Daddy. It's good to see you again. But you know what? I almost didn't come. Oh, don't feel bad because I said that. It's just that everyone else thought they needed to come because one of the nurses called Mrs. M. and told her they were worried about you and thought you might not hold on much longer. But I know that's not true. And do you know how I knew? Remember the beautiful butterfly I told you about? Well, it told me. It said you would be all right and it would just take more time. But then I decided I needed to come anyway to cheer you up since everyone else was going to come in here and be all sad. So here I am.

"I'm having a great time this summer. Of course, it would be lots better if you were with us. But I'm busy. I swim at this pool and go to the library. I get to run errands for Mrs. M. and play with Lucky. He's the dog. And you'll never guess what! I'm learning how to play baseball! The old lady who runs the library is teachin' me. She's pretty grumpy in the library, but at practice she's not too bad. I can hardly wait until you can see how I can catch the ball. My hittin's not too good, but you can help me when you feel better."

Abby stopped talking and for a few minutes just stood and looked at her father. Then after studying him closely she spoke. "You're looking too skinny. When you get out of here, I'll take you to the bakery in town. I'll buy you brownies and cream puffs. And if we get there early enough in the morning, we can get a loaf of bread and eat it while it's still warm. It's the best!

"I better go now, Daddy, so you can rest so you can get better faster. I love you. You're the best daddy ever!" After a kiss on the cheek and a squeeze of his hand, she climbed down from the chair, pushed it back away from the bed, and walked to the door. There she turned around, smiled, and waved.

NINTEEN

Claire had put away the groceries and washed the new head of lettuce, which she had just wrapped in a clean tea towel, when the doorbell rang. Instead of setting down the towel and lettuce, she absentmindedly carried them to the front door. When she opened it, no one was there, but lying in front of the door carefully wrapped in green floral paper was one long-stemmed red rose. She looked in all directions but saw no one other than William Swan at the far end of the block mowing his lawn.

She picked up the rose and noticed a card was underneath. She bent again to pick it up and read it as she straightened up. "Your arrival last year added beauty to Hayward, just as I hope this rose will add beauty to your home." Claire turned the card over to see if it was signed, but instead of a signature she discovered the message continued. "But unlike this rose whose beauty will fade in a few days, yours continues to stay fresh." She turned it over a couple of times hoping there was a clue about the sender, but she found nothing to help solve the mystery.

It was then she felt water dripping on her foot and looked down to discover the head of lettuce waiting in the towel. By now the water that was in the washed lettuce had saturated the middle of the towel. So she carefully gathered the dry corners, leaving the lettuce in center of the towel, and stepped off the porch. With the corners gripped tightly, she started to swing the towel in big circles. The water from the towel and lettuce flew everywhere, leaving dark spots on the walk and porch. Then Claire changed the direction of the towel. Instead of smoothly switching directions, the bottom of the towel ripped, and the head of lettuce flew through the air.

Claire quickly looked around to see if anyone saw what had happened. Thankfully, William still seemed to be the only one stirring outside on the hot, steamy day. Claire followed the path of the round green missile and started to laugh. Then she began to remove lettuce leaves from where they had been impaled on branches of the bushes in front of the porch. "I don't remember my grandmother saying this was part of her way to drain the lettuce." Once she had extracted lettuce sections and wayward leaves and put them in what remained of the towel, she gathered them up and headed up the steps of the porch. She picked up the rose that she'd quickly set on the porch and headed into the house.

Abby was coming down the stairs as Claire came through the door. "Oh, pretty rose! Where'd you get it? And what's all that green stuff?"

"Oh, I was just out picking some fresh lettuce from the lettuce bushes in front."

Abby looked puzzled for a moment. "I think we always growed ours in the ground. I didn't know you could grow it on bushes." When Claire smiled she caught on. "Oh, you're just kiddin' me, aren't you? But where did the rose come from?"

"I don't know. There was a card, but it had no name. It's a mystery."

"I bet it's from Mr. Chambers. I think he loves you."

"I don't think so, Abby." Claire wasn't quite sure if she was responding negatively to the part about who had sent the rose or to what Abby had said about Daniel loving her. "Maybe the mystery rose person will let me know sometime."

Sarah came into the room in time to hear the last part of the conversation "A mystery person left you a rose? How terribly romantic! I'll bet anything it was Mr. Chambers. He's in love with you, you know."

As if trying to avoid hearing that suggestion again, Claire drew the attention to the flower itself. "If I don't get this into water soon, no one will want to take credit for it."

"What's in that wet rag?"

"Lunch," Claire replied, walking toward the kitchen.

"Yuck! I don't think I'm hungry," Sarah said, scrunching up her face.

"It certainly is a sweet, romantic thing to say," said Betty, holding the small white card in her hand as she and Claire gently swung back and forth on Claire's front porch. "And you have no idea who could have sent it?"

"No, but I'm quite sure that it wasn't Leonard."

Betty looked quite shocked. "I should certainly hope not, but why did you say that?"

"Look at the handwriting. It's quite neat, and you know what people say about a doctor's handwriting."

Betty chuckled. "That is doubly true with Leonard. His writing is atrocious! I'll bet you could ask Francine if someone bought it at her store. There's no place else close by to buy roses."

"I don't know," Claire joked. "Does she have to honor a client-merchant confidentiality like lawyers or doctors do?"

Betty continued speculating. "Maybe someone around here has a secret garden where he's figured how to grow long stem roses."

To emphasize her point, Claire shook her finger in the air. "You know what else I thought of? I wonder if this is one more of Lila's crazy ideas to stir up romance. I wonder how much money she's spent on her enterprise so far. The dinner, the theater tickets, the letters before the Fourth of July picnic. And then if I'm not the only one to get a rose, the amount could really add up. She would have to do lots of wedding or party planning to make up for what she's spent so far. I wonder if any of it is working."

"I don't know, but it seems to me that there is much more dating going on lately. I seem to see unmarried couples more often than I used to, not just here but also in Livonia and Abbot Springs. And she definitely has been working on you. Do you have anything to report?"

"Not a single thing. But I think whatever has happened between Daniel and me probably would have happened without, or should I say in spite of, Lila playing cupid. He thinks she's nuts. He seems to enjoy everyone else in the town, but I'm not sure how many more of Lila's events he wants to be involved with."

"I can't say that I blame him. Just between you and me, Leonard can hardly stand to be around her. He often has commented about how glad he is that she is so healthy. In fact, all of the Haywards seem to be blessed with good health."

"Speaking of health, how is Farley?"

"Pretty good. Leonard told Bob he should stay home and rest as much as possible, but Farley fretted so much about not keeping guard on Main Street that they compromised. He can go to the store in the mornings but has to rest at home in the afternoon."

"That reminds me of something Helen said. She confided in me—oops, I guess I shouldn't say any more."

Betty's eyes widened with Claire's comment. "Do you think maybe you could rephrase things in such a way that you really would not be telling me anything you shouldn't?"

"That might work. Let's see. She asked if anyone had ever checked into the possibility of getting Farley into some kind of therapy to help him deal with whatever issues he's struggling with. She said she knows many people who regularly go to counseling sessions for different problems. She, rather they, seemed to swear by their therapists. Do you know if the Simpsons ever thought about that?"

"I don't know for sure, but I kind of doubt it. Folks around here seem to think that their problems are theirs to deal with and don't cotton to dragging outsiders into them. I think many people would look at going to a psychiatrist as a waste of time and money. I will, however, mention it to Leonard and see if he thinks it might be worth talking about with Bob and Francine."

"I hate to be a gossip, but do you know anything about what Clara was talking about at the quilting group, the part about what was going on behind the pavilion during the fireworks?"

"I don't know the truth, but rumor has it that Phoebe and Cliff Wilkens were doing a bit of smooching back there."

"Nice, quiet Cliff Wilkens? And Phoebe? I can't believe it! They just seem to be such opposites. I can't imagine them together at all."

"But maybe Lila was right when she said, 'Love is in the air.'"

"Well, you might know that better than I," Betty teased as she smiled at Claire, who blushed slightly and then quickly changed the subject.

The weather was beautiful, not as overwhelmingly sticky as it had been the past week. Claire was reading in the backyard when she felt something lightly touch her hair. With a quick flick of her wrist, she brushed it away, or at least she thought she brushed it away. She felt it again and once more waved at her head but to no avail. The she felt something soft touch her neck. She shivered and again tried to brush it away. Then she felt a different sensation on her neck, a sensation she had not felt in years. She sighed and closed her eyes.

"Let me think. Fred? William? Ben?"

"Gee, I certainly hope not. Just what goes on in this town when I'm not here?"

"You'd be amazed! The quiet façade is just a cover. You should drop by during the week sometime and check out the action."

Daniel bent over and kissed her on the forehead. "Seriously, anything new around town?" He sat on the grass next to her chair.

Claire looked at him curiously. "Why, should there be? Is there something going on that you know about and we don't?"

"Not at all. It's just that with Lila and some other interesting people around here, I never know what stories I might hear."

"The only real update is that Farley seems to be doing well."

"Glad to hear it."

"More things seem to be missing throughout the town, and although no one has accused the girls directly, people still look at them suspiciously."

"Looks can't hurt them."

"You obviously don't know girls. Will you be able to go to church with us tomorrow?"

"I was planning on it, why?"

"I can't tell. It's not my surprise. You might just have to wait until then to find out."

"You definitely have piqued my curiosity. Now, about tonight, I didn't bring my tux—"

Claire looked at him in amazement. "Do you really have a tux, or were you just kidding?"

Daniel feigned a hurt look. "So what are you saying? You don't think I'm suave enough to own a tux?"

"Not at all, Marshall Chambers. You indeed are both suave and debonair. But I just picture you more in cowboy boots."

"Well, I do indeed have a tux. Haven't worn it for a few years, but I imagine that it still fits. The last time I wore it was to my nieces' weddings. It's great for those wedding kind of occasions."

Daniel gave her a look she couldn't interpret, so rather than putting her foot in her mouth, she just went back to his original question about the dress for the evening. "Did you bring a suit?"

"Yes."

"Too bad, you won't need it. A nice shirt with a good pair of slacks will be just fine."

"Then I assume that I will not need to provide you with a corsage."

"One should never assume that a lady would not welcome flowers—of any kind."

"But I think something else might be more romantic. My style would be roses, or better yet, one single long-stemmed rose."

Claire looked at Daniel in disbelief. "Then it was you!"

"Then it was me what?"

"Come on, don't play dumb. You know it was you who sent the lovely rose with the romantic note attached. That was very sweet."

"That would have been very sweet had I been the one, but I wasn't." Claire looked as if she didn't believe him at all. "Honestly, I didn't do it."

"Then I'm back to the original mystery. I have no idea who could have done it."

Thoughts about the mysterious rose were interrupted when Abby came rushing out of the back porch, ran across the yard, and jumped in Daniel's lap. "Hi, Mr. Chambers. I'm so excited that you're here. Did you hear about Farley? Isn't that great news? See, I told you things would work out okay. My butterfly angel was sure right about that. You are comin' to church tomorrow, aren't you? You just have to come. It wouldn't be right without you!"

"Hi, Abby, it's good to see you too. I'm very glad to hear about Farley, and yes, I'm planning on going to church. But what's so special about tomorrow?"

"I'm not tellin,'" she said, closing her eyes, crossing her arms, and shaking her head. "And don't try to get Mrs. M. or Sarah to tell either. They're sworn to secrecy."

❦

The meeting of the Hayward Women's Club had just ended at the Catholic church behind the library. Three women walked across the street to visit with Meredith, who was working in her yard. Francine, coming home for lunch from her flower shop, joined them. Then Helen, who had been washing her windows, grew curious and walked over to see what was happening.

"I'm not one to point fingers, but I can't help but think the McRoberts children must be involved with these disappearances," one woman said.

Another chimed in, "We never had trouble like this before."

Clara, whose hearing was still sharp, heard the conversation from where she was sitting in the shade. "They didn't do it," she yelled.

"I don't like to think of that possibility either. In fact, I feel guilty when I do, but I can't think of any other possibilities," Francine confided.

"I guess I'm lucky. As far as I know, I haven't had anything disappear," said Helen.

"What do you think we should do?" asked the woman who had first brought up the subject.

In a louder voice so as not to be ignored, Clara yelled, "They didn't do it! Leave them alone!"

Busybody number two suggested, "Maybe we should go to the sheriff with our suspicions."

"But that's all there are, right?" offered Helen. "I don't think that's much to go on. No one has proof of anything. Maybe we all just need to wait and see if any other things disappear."

The first woman turned on Helen. "Well! That's easy for you to say since you don't have anything missing!"

"And just what are you missing?" asked Francine.

The woman stumbled with her words but finally said, "Nothing, but I've heard that many others have."

"Then maybe they should be the ones to take action," Francine replied.

The woman bristled and said nothing except to her companions. "Let's go, Nellie, Gertie. It's almost lunch time."

As the three headed off, Clara just had to get in the last word. "They didn't do it! Leave them alone!"

"You clean up very nicely, Mr. Chambers," Claire said when he came to pick her up for the dinner. The green plaid shirt brought out the deep color of his eyes. She smiled, thinking back to when she first met Daniel and had referred to him as "Daniel Dreamboat."

"And you're looking quite lovely yourself, Mrs. Menefee." Claire's purple flower print dress had a matching lavender sweater she brought just in case it actually did cool off. "I always used to pick up my dates in my car, but it seemed silly to do that for a one-block drive. But if you like, I could get it out of Ben's garage."

"By the time you found a parking place, we might have to walk farther than this."

"Are you telling me there'll be quite a crowd?"

"I don't know. But I imagine when you get two gourmet cooks together they'll want to show off for as many people as possible."

The two walked hand in hand down Oak Street and turned west on Maple to the other Haywards' house just across the alley from the mayor's house. Although lacking the grandeur of the big white pillared house, it was still one of the largest houses in town.

When Daniel rang the bell, they were serenaded with the beginning strains of "Meet Me in St. Louie, Louie." Claire chuckled when she heard that. It reminded her of the story she'd heard about how Lila and Chester had met at the Iowa State Fair when Lila was entered in the hog calling contest. Daniel looked at her with a puzzled look.

"I'll tell you later," she said as the door was opened by a smiling Charles.

"Good evening. Claire, isn't it?" After Claire introduced the men, Charles nodded. "Oh, I should have known that. You're the G-man, right?"

"U.S. Marshall, really, but the same employer. It's nice to meet you."

"Please come in. The cooks are scurrying around doing their thing in the kitchen. Everyone else is out in back. Please just make yourself at home."

Claire wasn't sure who the other dinner guests might be. She hadn't mentioned it to any of her neighbors, and they had said nothing to her, so she figured they had not been invited. As they walked into the yard, Claire looked around and had the feeling that Lila had perused the guest list and made some suggestions. To a great degree it looked like the same people—single and unattached—who had been at her party a few months before. But one big difference this time seemed to be that there were definite couples.

Claire left Daniel talking to Tim Payne and his redheaded companion while she went to say hello to Helen and Dorothy. She found them in the kitchen up to their ears in pots, pans, and dishes. And working right next to them, apron tied around his waist, was one of the Lavelles, but from the back Claire had no idea which one it was.

"Do you need any help?" she asked, being quite sure of the answer.

"Oh, hi. No, we're doing just fine," Helen said, although Claire had the feeling that given the chance Mr. Lavelle would have accepted the offer, handed over the apron, and high-tailed it out of the kitchen.

Claire returned to Daniel, who was talking baseball with Tim while his date looked totally bored. Claire gracefully extracted Daniel from the conversation and made the rounds of the other couples. Burton Taylor looked as if he had died and gone to heaven as he stood proudly next to Vickie Thornton. Claire remembered the box lunch auction last fall when Burton was one of the high bidders for the lunch brought by Vickie, but he was outbid and ended up having lunch with his old principal, Pearl Hatcher.

Coach Brook was with Loretta Goering, the other popular single teacher. Reverend Thomas Thomas was standing next to Ruby Smith, from the bank, and both looked quite pleased with each other's company.

Claire was somewhat surprised although pleased to see Maude Richards was there. "She deserves to get out of that restaurant once in a while," she whispered to Daniel. When she realized she was with Butch Johnson, she said, "Aaah!"

"What did you say?" Daniel asked.

"Oh, nothing really. It's just that I've often wondered why the sheriff spent so much time hanging out at Maude's. I thought it was just because he liked the coffee. Maybe there was more to it."

"Oh, you women. You're always trying to be matchmakers. I'd just stick to the coffee theory until you find out differently."

Cliff Wilkens and Phoebe chatted with Fred Young, who appeared to be alone. Claire wondered if he was there to entertain, maybe to do some tricks he learned at clown college. Then Irma Fisher came out and attached herself to Fred's right arm. Claire studied her dress, taking mental notes, and decided that on Tuesday or Wednesday she would pop into Felton's clothing store to see if it would be hanging back on the rack.

Daniel and Claire were visiting with Cliff and Phoebe when a new couple joined the group. Ben and Bertha looked around for some friendly faces. And in Bertha's case, not many partygoers looked anxious to visit. Some quickly closed up their conversation circles and pretended they didn't even see the newcomers. The minute Daniel saw them he motioned them over.

"Good evening, Miss Banter, Ben," Daniel said, and the other three made similar welcoming comments. "Beautiful evening, isn't it?"

"I find it quite stifling, and I'm concerned about mosquitoes. They have been known to carry diseases, you know. I hope we won't be having food outside. Protein attracts wasps."

As they talked Bertha removed a small bottle of insect repellent from her purse and rubbed some on her arms and neck. Everyone except gallant Ben took a step back to avoid the strong odor.

Claire thought she heard an insect buzzing somewhere close by and wondered if she should ask Bertha if she had enough repellant to share. She tried to ignore the buzzing, but the sound persisted and got increasingly louder. She turned slowly, afraid she might see some humongous bug getting ready to attack. Instead she saw a slight movement through the cracks in the fence. Then she heard, "Pssst, Claire, pssst."

She moved toward the fence trying to give the impression she was admiring the roses that climbed the fence. As she got closer she could see an eyeball peeking at her. At that point she was not sure, but what she might have preferred to find was a large, stinging insect. Instead she pretended to smell one of the multicolored blooms.

"Did you want something, Lila?" she whispered. As she looked through the cracks, it appeared Lila was not wearing a hat. Since she had never seen her without something covering the top of her head, Claire really wanted to pull over one of the lawn chairs and stand on it in order to check it out.

"How are things going? Does everyone look happy? I was so excited to hear it was a date dinner, and I could hardly wait to see who came. I can't say I'm surprised, are you? Aren't there just some cute, cute couples here?"

Lila continued talking about something, but Claire stopped listening when she noticed that Daniel was giving her a questioning look. "I need to go and mingle, Lila."

"I can hardly wait to talk to Dorothy…"

Claire walked away mid-sentence and joined Daniel and the others. Her timing was perfect, as Helen called the guests to dinner. Most were escorted to the huge dining room table complete with china, crystal, silver, and name cards on a white linen tablecloth. The remainder were led into the living room, where card tables also were adorned with similar place settings.

After everyone except the two hostesses and Lloyd were seated, Thomas Thomas said grace, and then Helen, Dorothy, and Lloyd sprang into action. They delivered the appetizer, gazpacho. People looked a bit surprised, but no one said anything as they poked at the soup. No one seemed to want to be the first to sample the cold mixture of tomato, pepper, cucumber, and onion.

Bertha didn't even pick up her spoon and said to Ben, although it was heard by those around her, "This looks more like it should belong on hot dogs or hamburger."

The rest of the diners at least sampled theirs, and some ate it all. Phoebe ate hers the fastest, but that didn't surprise anyone since she had the reputation for being a hearty eater, as her robust figure could attest.

John Brook also ate his with gusto and added, "I wish the football team would eat more vegetables."

Cliff Wilkens whispered to Claire, "I'm glad they don't serve this for school lunches, or the kids would dump it all in the garbage."

Lloyd hurried in and quickly removed the remainder of the appetizer. He did it with such flair Claire wondered if at one time he had been a waiter or if he had taken dramatic move lessons from Lila. Next Dorothy and Helen hurried in with the salad course, greens with sautéed mushrooms and toasted hazelnuts. This was more widely accepted, and very little was returned to the kitchen.

"To cleanse the pallet," Helen said as she distributed the small crystal dishes that held delicate servings of lime and basil sorbet. Ben quietly asked if he had slept through the main course, which brought some subdued laughter from those who heard. Following that, the main course appeared. It truly was a work of art.

Three very long string beans were threaded through the hollowed out middle of a carrot coin. Claire wondered how many carrots the cooks had to use before they got enough that didn't break while stuffing in the beans. There were puffy-looking brown and white things that Claire figured were some fancy kind of twice-baked potatoes. On top were long, thin strands of cheese that gave the appearance of scraggly hair. The meat was a lovely nut-encrusted leg of lamb. Most people seemed excited about that, but Claire, who had never had lamb of any kind, was a bit apprehensive. Her grandmother had always said that lamb tasted wooly, so Claire was not looking forward to this part of the meal. She wondered if anyone would like to trade their beans, carrots, and potato for her lamb. She was glad when three containers of warm dinner rolls were placed on the long table.

Finally, after all the food had been distributed, the hostesses and Lloyd were able to sit and enjoy the meal. Everyone "ooohed" and "aaahed," and Helen and Dorothy basked in the praise. Claire was glad Elizabeth had gotten them together. They were soul mates, at least in the kitchen.

The meal was topped off with what Helen called chococan miniatures served with caramel sauce and a mint leaf for effect. They were delicious, but as far as Claire could tell, they were pretty much chocolate cupcakes with ground-up pecans thrown into the batter. Coffee, as well as hot and cold tea, was offered.

It was almost dark by the time dinner was completed. The very full guests were ushered back outside, where Chinese lanterns hanging around the patio were glowing in the dimming light. Charles, who had been quite subdued throughout dinner, started a record player he set on the picnic table. He then went inside and brought Dorothy out of the kitchen, despite her protestations. He escorted her to the center of the patio and started dancing to some big band music. That was the start of a long evening of dancing by everyone. Ben even managed to get Bertha doing the fox trot across the patio.

A few times during the dancing, Claire was quite certain she saw movement through the fence between the Hayward houses, but she definitely didn't want to check for sure. She was having too nice a time being in Daniel's arms. And from the look on the other faces, everyone seemed to feel the same way about their dates and dance partners. Claire wondered what kind of aphrodisiac had been slipped into the meal. "It must have been in those wicked little chocolate cupcakes," she mumbled out loud.

"I'm sorry, I didn't hear you," Daniel replied.

"I was just thinking about that yummy chocolate dessert." She was surprised that he had not heard her the first time, considering how close he was holding her. But she didn't mind at all.

The final dance of the evening was to "Deep Purple." The remaining guests called it a night and complimented Helen and the Haywards for a lovely evening. Even Lloyd, who seemed to trail a step or two behind Helen throughout the evening, received compliments on his help. As Daniel and Claire walked home, he put his hand around her shoulder, supposedly to help keep her lavender sweater from slipping off. He lingered as long as he felt proper at her door.

"I'm glad you don't have to go back to the Snooze Inn, aren't you?"

"Absolutely! This is much closer to where I really want to be, and you know it too." He tweaked her cheek and turned to leave. "See you in the morning for church."

Claire tried not to let her face show the disappointment she felt. But then he turned around. "Oh, I think I forgot something, didn't I?" He hopped back up the stairs, threw his arms around her, pulling her close to him, and planted a big kiss on her relieved face, a kiss that tingled all the way to her toes.

TWENTY

Abby was up and dressed before everyone else Sunday morning and waited impatiently for Claire and Sarah. When Sarah came into the kitchen, Abby handed her a wide white satin ribbon. "Please?" was all she said. Her sister tenderly pulled the sides of her hair back and fastened them with the ribbon, which she tied into a bow. Abby ate very little for breakfast while tapping on the table in an uncharacteristically nervous manner. When a familiar figure appeared at the back door, she was off her chair and to the door in a split second.

"I thought you'd never get here. I was beginnin' to wonder if you forgot."

"Sorry, I overslept. I was up quite late last night." Both girls turned and looked at Claire and tried to hide giggles. "So what's the big surprise?"

"I can't tell you yet. You'll just have to wait." Abby turned to look at the clock. "Can I go now, please?"

"Okay. We'll see you in church."

On a dead run, Abby raced from the kitchen, her white ruffled dress giving the impression of a puffy cloud being blown by a strong wind. Daniel and Claire lingered over coffee on the porch while Sarah returned to reading a book that had become her current constant companion. Shortly before ten o'clock, the three left the house and headed toward the church, where the bell rang as a reminder that there were ten minutes before the service would begin.

As had become the tradition since Sarah had started accompanying Claire and Abby to the Sunday service, Claire let Sarah lead the way to where she wanted to sit. Claire knew it would not be long before Sarah decided she would rather sit in the balcony where most of the teenagers gathered, but for now she was thankful for the time sitting next to her.

Phoebe set the tone for the service by playing "Take Time to Be Holy." Sometimes Phoebe's playing was anything but quiet and mood setting, but this selection kept the congregation in a peaceful, prayerful atmosphere. The lighting of the altar candles was the signal the service was about to start, and a little redheaded girl who looked very angelic in her white ruffled dress served as the acolyte.

"So that was the secret," Daniel whispered to Claire, who simply smiled and patted his hand.

With a striking change in the volume of her playing, Phoebe beat out a short introduction and then began the full-fledged, full-bodied playing of "Onward Christian Soldiers" as the congregation stood and the choir processed down the center aisle. The members then filed into the choir loft. Claire preferred the look of the choir when they were in their robes, but during the hot summer months, they wore regular Sunday-go-to-meeting clothes. That made for a very colorful array in the front of the church.

The sermon was entitled "Accusations in the Wind" and included the story about men who were accused unjustly just because they were strangers. Claire had the distinct feeling Grace had told Bill of the accusations that had been made against the McRoberts girls. She thought he did a good job of talking about not judging people based merely by their stations in life.

When the sermon was over, the choir rose to sing its anthem, "Great Is Thy Faithfulness" (Lyrics by Reverend Thomas O. Chisholm, Music by William M. Runyan, Hope Publishing Company, 1923.). But in addition to the regular choir members, there was also a short, redheaded soloist. Normally, a soloist would sing the verses with the choir singing the chorus or refrain. Instead, the full choir began the first verse. Then on the refrain Abby stepped forward and in a voice clear, loud, and true sang, "Great is thy faithfulness! Great is thy faithfulness! Morning by morning new mercies I see. All I have needed Thy hand hath provided; Great is thy faithfulness, Lord, unto me!"

Once again the choir sang the second verse and Abby sang the refrain. However, for the third verse, she alone sang, "Pardon for sin and a peace that endureth. Thine own dear presence to cheer and to guide; Strength for today and bright hope for tomorrow, Blessings all mine, with ten thousand beside!" When she sang the words "Strength for today and bright hope for tomorrow," she looked upward, raised her hands toward heaven, and smiled.

The full choir sang part of the third and final refrain alone, except Abby finished it with a slower tempo. "All I have needed Thy hand hath provided; Great is thy faithfulness, Lord, unto me!" As soon as the song ended, Claire heard lots of sniffling from those seated close to her. Daniel took a handkerchief from his pocket and handed it to her, and she noticed that he too had to wipe a tear from his eye. Claire looked at Sarah, who was sniffling and crying. But accompanying her tears was a sweet smile of both pride and understanding.

At the end of the service, the choir recessed down the aisle following Reverend Carlson, who walked hand in hand with Abby. Claire, Sarah, and Daniel stayed in the pew and accepted congratulations on Abby's performance. Claire was, of course, extremely pleased with Abby's singing. In fact, Daniel told her she beamed like a proud parent. At the same time, however, she felt a twinge of guilt and sadness that Abby's parents were not there to witness it. She looked upward and whispered, "Did you hear that, Mrs. McRoberts?"

When the crowd had subsided, the three of them walked to where Reverend Carlson always stood. On this occasion he had someone next to him to smile and shake hands. When Abby saw them, she ran over and grabbed Claire's and Daniel's hands. "Did you like it?"

Daniel swept her up in his arms and gave her a puzzled look. "Like what?" he asked with a serious tone.

"Oh, you know, silly. My song!"

"Oh, that. Hmmm. Yes, it was good. It was very good." He gave her a big hug, which she returned.

"Abby, it was wonderful!" Claire squeezed her hand.

As Daniel put her down, Abby looked toward Sarah.

"I am so proud of you. You were so good! You were so wonderful!" And then struggling to get out the words added, "I wish Daddy could have heard you."

"I'll just have to sing it for him when he comes home," she replied, refusing to have any sad thoughts interrupt the joyous moment.

They continued to visit with Bill Carlson, but when Grace joined them, Claire asked, "Did you pick that hymn or did Abby?"

"When she asked me many weeks ago about singing with us, I invited her over to discuss it. I asked her what she would like to sing. She said she really didn't care, but she didn't want to do 'Jesus Loves Me.' She said kids always sing that, and she wanted something different. Then she said she would like something that was about being thankful for the blessings she and her brothers and sister had received after their father's accident. So that is why we decided on 'Great Is Thy Faithfulness.'"

"It was a wonderful choice. The words are good not just for this occasion but for all of us to think about every day."

After Abby had changed clothes—at Claire's insistence since she didn't think grass stains would look good on a white dress—Abby and Daniel went into the backyard to play catch with the baseball and glove that Daniel had brought, he said, for Claire. Inside Claire worked on dinner but kept a frequent eye on the backyard. One time she looked out to see both of them lying on the grass looking up toward the tree above them. She was dying to know what they were talking about but figured one of them would tell her if they really wanted to let her in on their conversation.

Sarah appeared in the kitchen and walked toward the back door. "What in the world are they doing now?"

"I don't know. Why don't you go out and join them?"

"You must be kidding. I'd rather peel potatoes."

"Well, that works out very well." Claire handed over the peeler she held.

Outside, Daniel and Abby were having a theological discussion, or rather Abby was quizzing Daniel. "So how are you feelin' now that you've been goin' to church again?"

"I feel pretty good."

"I knew you did. I could see it in your face."

"But I feel better for lots of reasons. I've enjoyed getting to know you and your sister."

"And Mrs. M. too?"

"Yes, her too. Coming here to see all of you gives me something to look forward to. You know, I haven't had a real family for a long, long time. And even though I know you're not really my family, it feels a lot like you are when I'm here."

"Why don't you just move here and stay here all the time?"

"I wish I could."

"Mrs. M. wishes you could too. She gets all goofy actin' when she knows you're comin.'"

"She does?"

"Yeah, she smiles a lot and laughs a lot and makes sure her hair and makeup look extra good."

"That's nice."

"Don't move! Here it comes!" Abby slowly sat up and stretched out her arm. After circling her head a couple of times, the big, fragile-looking butterfly landed gently on her hand. She brought her hand slowly back toward her head and looked intently at the insect.

"Hi there. How are you? I haven't seen you for a while." Then she stopped talking and sat silently as if listening to a voice only she could hear. "I'm glad you liked it. Oh, I thought she probably could." She waited again. "Yes, I am. I know, I believe you." A puzzled look came over Abby's face. "Okay," she slowly replied to whatever she heard, or thought she heard. Then in reverse order the butterfly lifted from her hand, circled her head the opposite direction two times, and ascended gracefully toward the sky until it was no longer in sight.

"That seemed like a nice visit."

"It always is when my little butterfly angel comes."

"What did it tell you, or is it a secret?"

"It ain't no secret at all. It said it liked my song and that Mama heard it and liked it too. Then it reminded me to be brave until Daddy comes home. And that was about it. Let's play some more catch. Oh, Mr. Chambers, what are—ack-u-sores?"

"Ackusores?"

"Yeah, my butterfly said something about that."

"Sorry, I don't know what that would be." Daniel was just pulling himself up off the ground when the outside fun came to an end with a call to Abby to set the table.

"I'll race you to the kitchen."

Abby was halfway to the door before he was totally upright.

Abby quickly washed her hands and grabbed silverware. She walked toward the table but paused. "Phooey! Why can't I remember this?"

Without even turning around to see what she was questioning, Claire replied, "Forks on the left and knife and spoon on the right." But when she started setting food on the table, she had to laugh, for Abby had once more reversed the place setting. She had noticed on other occasions that Abby confused her left and right, but Claire was not worried, for she had that same problem herself for many years and even in adulthood occasionally got confused with those terms. Dennis, her late husband, often had teased her about her problem, saying if strangers ever stopped to ask her for directions she would end up getting them going in totally the wrong direction.

Daniel left shortly after dinner. He was not many miles away from Hayward when he took one hand off the steering wheel and hit himself in the head. "Oh! It wasn't ackusores Abby was trying to say. It was accusers!"

The ride to Sam Peterson's farm seemed short to Claire, but to Sarah and Abby it seemed to take forever. After going to the drug store to buy some magazines, the girls had returned to the house on a dead run.

"We need to go to our house!" said Sarah, all out of breath. "We want to look for something!"

"What are you looking for?"

"A picture."

"Of what?"

"We'll tell you when we find it."

"I can't promise, but I'll call Sam Peterson and see if he'll let us in."

Sam had said he would meet them at the old house at seven thirty that evening. The girls had been restless all afternoon but had not divulged any more to Claire about the mysterious picture. On the ride, Abby started giggling all of the sudden.

"Okay, what's so funny?" Sarah asked.

"I was just thinking of that hat the lady was wearing."

"You mean Mrs. Hayward's?"

"Yeah, I thought she was going to run right into me when she came out of the drugstore. That big red floppy hat almost covered up her eyes."

"And did you notice the decorations that went all the way around it? It looked like she had taken old fishing lures and put them on a long red string and wound them round and round the hat."

Both the girls giggled at Sarah's description. Claire knew she should remind them about manners and not laughing at other people, but she just couldn't do it. She knew how many times she personally had thought Lila's hats were ridiculous or at the least extreme. She was glad when she spotted the dirt road that was the turnoff to get to the house where the McRoberts family had lived.

"There's Mr. Peterson waiting for us, girls. I hope it doesn't take long to find what you're looking for. We don't want to make him wait long for us."

"No, I'm pretty sure I remember where it should be."

"Howdy, ma'am, girls. The door's all unlocked for you. If it's all right with you, I'll just give you this extra key. That way you can come whenever you want. Just go ahead and lock up when you're done. Evenin.'"

Claire hoped the girls had not heard the comment about coming any-time they wanted now that she was the keeper of the key, but when she turned around, she discovered they already had disappeared into the house. She followed through the squeaky front door and into the dusty house. "There will have to be some good cleaning done before they move back in here," she said to herself. She paused, proud of herself to have said that in such a positive way without much doubt in her mind that they all would be returning here. She sure did hope she was right.

She listened and followed the faint sound of voices and found the girls in one of the bedrooms going through an old trunk. "Was this your dad's room?"

"Oh no, he didn't have a room. He just slept on the couch by the front door," Sarah answered without even looking up.

Pictures and papers had been scattered on the floor around the girls.

Claire gingerly brushed dust away from a spot on the floor and sat down beside them to look at what had been discarded. There were pictures of the children and copies of birth certificates. There were old report cards from previous schools held together with a rubber band. Claire had just picked up a cardboard tube and removed the lid when Sarah's voice changed her focus.

"Here it is, Abby. Look!"

"Wow, that's really something!"

The girls stared at the picture for a few moments and then realized Claire was sitting there watching. "Look at this, Mrs. M." Sarah passed her the picture. Claire looked down and had a feeling of déjà vu.

"This looks like someone I've seen, but I can't quite place it."

"The redhead that hangs around the drugstore, doesn't it look just like her?"

Claire studied the old black and white picture carefully, tilting her head from side to side to get a better look in the dim light. "I don't know that it looks just like her, but there definitely is a strong similarity from what I remember. But I haven't seen her for a while."

"Well we have, just this afternoon!" Abby raised her voice a bit to make her point.

"Okay, we all agree there is a similarity. Whose picture is this?"

"Our mother!" the girls said in unison.

Claire looked back and forth from the picture to the two faces that looked up at her with excitement. "My, that is quite an interesting coincidence, isn't it? Your mother was a very pretty young woman. No wonder she had two such beautiful daughters."

She gave the girls more time to look through some of the contents of the trunk, but with the fading light it was getting too hard to see clearly. So they loaded everything except that special picture back in the trunk, closed the lid, and headed outside. It wasn't until Claire started to lock the door that she realized she was still holding the cardboard tube in her hand. She thought about going back inside, but since the girls were already in the car, she decided to take good care of whatever it was until they made another trip back—whenever that might be.

TWENTY-ONE

Since Bill Carlson's delivery of the sermon about not judging others merely by their backgrounds or lots in life, Claire had not heard as many innuendoes about the girls being responsible for the mystery disappearances around the town. She didn't know if folks had decided they had jumped to conclusions too quickly without any real proof or if they just didn't want to verbalize their suspicions for fear of being thought of badly. She knew the accusations had not lessened because the disappearances had stopped, because people were still noticing that items were missing. And the things that had disappeared were usually not of great intrinsic value. For the most part, they were knick-knacks that had little worth for anyone except the owners.

Abby headed to the door with her buddy Lucky dancing excitedly on the leash. "Are you ready, Mrs. M.? Lucky and I are all set to go."

"Be right there, just tying my shoes." In a minute Claire came down the steps to the joy of a dog that literally jumped up and down, anxious to get going.

The three went south on Oak, heading for a fun morning at the park. Abby had brought not only Lucky but in a bag had stuffed two baseball mitts—both hers and Claire's—and two balls. As they passed the fence behind the Hayward house, that oh-so-familiar but still scary raucous barking started. Claire and Abby both were startled, but Lucky was not deterred. He headed for the fence, ready to take on the much bigger dog and pulling Abby off balance and off her feet as he went. With a bit of help from Claire, she was able to pull him back to the sidewalk, even though he strained against the leash.

Claire didn't know if it was the excitement of the dog incident or all the laughing the two of them did once things were back in control, but Abby declared she had to go to the bathroom and no, she couldn't wait. Claire tried to talk her out of it, but the dancing gyrations that went with the request made her believe they truly were dealing with a bathroom emergency. They were right in front of Helen's house, so she figured that Helen would be willing to let Abby quickly use her facilities.

It took a couple of minutes for Helen to answer her door, and Claire wondered if she actually would come in time. When the door did open after what seemed like a very long time to Abby, Claire explained the situation.

"Absolutely! Come in. It's down the hall, first door on the left."

As Claire tied Lucky to the front porch, Abby ran down the hall, and Helen invited Claire to sit down for a cup of coffee. The coffee had barely been touched when Abby came back with a relieved look on her face.

"Feel better now?" Claire asked.

"Oh yes!" she answered, nodding emphatically. "And do you want to know somethin' interestin'? Mrs. Evans has pig salt and pepper shakers just like Mrs. Mayor does. And you know what else? She has a little glass swan just like that one of yours that got lost. Isn't that funny?"

Claire would never be able to explain the feeling she got in her stomach at that moment. At first she couldn't believe what she was hearing, but when she looked at Helen's face, she knew the truth. Then Helen slowly dropped her head into her hands.

"You know how I always get my right and left mixed up? Well, instead of turnin' left like Mrs. Evans told me, I turned right. Or was it the other way around?" Abby paused and thought about it for a moment. "Anyway, when I opened the door, it wasn't the bathroom at all. It was a bedroom, and on top of a table were the pigs and the swan."

Praying that Helen would not turn out to have the mean streak that Tony Canella did when Claire unfortunately ventured into this same house earlier in the year and ended up in big trouble, she spoke to Abby as calmly as she could, "Show me what you found."

Abby skipped down the hall and pointed past the now opened door into a very familiar-looking bedroom. Claire got a shiver down her spine as she walked past the chair that truly had been her downfall. There, in front of her, was a silver jam spoon, a glass swan, a miniature china doll, a small china goldfinch, Claire's missing Santa, Herky the Hawkeye toothpick holder, and many other items that presumably had been lifted from different places throughout the town.

Claire took Abby by the hand and led her back to the front porch, where Lucky was waiting impatiently to continue the walk. "I think I'll stay here with Mrs. Evans for a while. I want you to go back home for now, and I'll be home shortly. And cross the street here so you won't have to fight with Lucky going past the mayor's house." Abby looked disappointed, but Lucky didn't realize his outing had been cut short. Claire watched them get safely across the street and then walked sadly back inside.

"Why, Helen?"

Helen couldn't look at Claire but just sadly shook her head. "I don't know. I truly don't know. It's a problem I have. That's why I have been in therapy. I am so sorry, so, so sorry." Sobs followed the words.

Claire wasn't sure what should be her next step. She would have liked to have made everything magically reappear in its rightful spot, but she knew that was impossible. And the items had been illegally removed from homes, after all. She decided she had no other choice but to call the sheriff, which she did from the phone in the kitchen. She kept an eye on Helen, not necessarily because she was afraid she might bolt but because she could still remember her terror in the bedroom and didn't want to take any chances.

"Hi, Maude. This is Claire. Is the sheriff there?" She would have been surprised if he had not been. "Hello, Sheriff. Could you please come over to Lois Teller's old house? We have a little situation here I'd like to talk to you about. And Butch, no siren or lights, please."

Sheriff Johnson proved to be a tactful, caring lawman. He privately met with everyone whose property Claire, Helen, or he could identify. Everyone agreed not to press charges since Helen had made it perfectly clear she would leave town and never return. While inventorying the stolen goods, large amounts of cooking supplies, mainly the gourmet non-run-of-the-mill items, were also discovered. Since Helen had no idea which stores in Des Moines she had lifted them from, there was no way they could be returned. Instead they were turned over to Bryan, who also had noticed some mysterious shortages in his grocery stock.

The candy dish that had disappeared from the hostess desk at Maude's was returned. Surprisingly, there was still some candy in it. Herky the toothpick holder sat next to it.

Claire was quite sure the items Helen had given the children at the "Christmas in June" party had been lifted from under Rudy's nose at the drugstore. She was willing to pay for them, but Rudy refused, saying if he'd known it was Christmas again so soon he would have sent presents to the children himself.

Claire and some of her neighbors, who had gotten to know and enjoy Helen, expressed sadness at seeing her leave.

Lila, on the other hand, was her typical self, complaining that she and her husband were probably in great danger from this mentally unsound woman who undoubtedly was extremely jealous of the Haywards' lifestyle and that probably was what pushed her over the edge. Claire wanted to say that more than likely it was having to live next door to that infernal dog that caused Helen's problems. But she managed to hold her tongue on that point.

It had been a summer of interesting mail for Claire, and it somehow seemed fitting that she received still another unusual letter with the return address of Arthur Fitzgibbons, MD. She read it to herself and then took it to the Tuesday quilting group, where she shared it with the others.

Dear Mrs. Menefee,

I am writing at the request of my patient, Helen Evans, as she wants to offer her sincere apologies for the bad choices she made while residing in your community. She asked that I explain some things to you.

Helen has been a patient of mine since she and her husband

started to have problems. When Mr. Evans began to turn his attention to a younger woman, Helen was devastated. She did not know what to do, how to act or react, how to fight back. She felt something that was hers had been unfairly taken away. It was then that she began to take things, anything that caught her fancy. She subconsciously thought she was somehow getting back at him by taking things that didn't belong to her. Somehow to her that seemed fair.

Things at her university job steadily deteriorated as her depression worsened, and she was asked to take a leave of absence until her mental health state improved. This did provide her the opportunity to work on the book she had wanted to research and write. I felt this would be a good move for her, to get her away from seeing her ex-husband and his new wife, who worked in the same building on the same floor as Helen did. The memories of marriage were just too overwhelming at that time.

However, when she moved to your town, she saw only happy couples. There didn't appear to be any other divorced people in the entire area. The widows and widowers seemed content but also seemed open to starting new relationships. Although I am certain it didn't show outwardly, this weighed on Helen tremendously, and the kleptomania started again.

Helen also mentioned something about a displaced family and how she would have liked to have had the chance to help take care of some of the children, but because she was new she wasn't asked. To have omitted her from this project was, of course, understandable, but to her it was just one more sign of being inept and incapable of holding on to a relationship.

Helen wanted me to make sure to be clear that she does not blame anyone except herself for her regression. In fact, to the contrary, she has wonderful things to say about all of you. She especially wanted to thank the Lavelle brothers, as well as some other gentlemen in the town who treated her with the utmost respect. In addition, to a Mr. Lloyd Lavelle, she wanted to say that he was a wonderful companion and a great dishwasher, whatever that might mean. Helen hopes the townspeople of Hayward will not harbor ill feelings about her. She holds all of you fondly in her memories.

—Arthur Fitzgibbons, MD

The ladies sat quietly for a moment or two until Clara broke the ice. "I told you those girls didn't do it, but oh no. No one believed me. And if anyone had asked me, I could have told them that Evans woman was a crook!"

TWENTY-TWO

Claire's house resembled an ants' nest with people of all sizes scurrying around. The entire family—two sons and one daughter with their spouses and children—had come for the weekend. Even though the different families had been farmed out to various neighbors for sleeping arrangements, they spent most of their time in her house or backyard. She loved having them all around her, but at the moment everyone's hovering and hurrying around was beginning to unnerve her.

She had encouraged Laura, her seven months' pregnant daughter, to sit in the living room and put up her feet. She thought that was a good way to get at least one person out of the way. Also, she had assigned daughters-in-law Jill and Beth to Sarah and Abby respectively. That way they could make sure the girls had their hair done right and their matching sky blue satin dresses buttoned up the back. Her sons and son-in-law had been put in charge of the children and the dog with the directions to keep them busy but clean.

That gave Claire the chance to get herself ready in relative calm, at least for a few moments. She had already done her makeup, with the advice of the three daughters, and she carefully slipped her skirt over her carefully combed hair. After adding the jacket, she looked at herself in the full length mirror, turning in different directions to see as much of herself as she could.

"Not too bad for an old dame." She smiled. But that smile was followed by bittersweet tears that slowly formed in her eyes. "Things will never be the same after today. I always hoped this day would come, so why am I crying? Now stop being silly, pull yourself together, and get downstairs."

By some magical timing, everyone had gathered in the living room as she slowly walked down the stairs. Halfway down, she stood and surveyed her family as they all looked up at her admiringly. And right there in the middle of the group stood two small but extraordinarily beautiful, redheaded freckled-faced girls that right then seemed just as much a part of her family as anyone else in that room. Even Lucky sat still as he looked up at her, cocking his head from one side to the other, as if judging in her appearance too.

"Oh, Mom, you look beautiful."

"I've never seen you look more radiant."

"I didn't realize my mother was such a knockout!"

Claire stood for a moment enjoying the compliments. Then it was her turn. She walked over to Abby and Sarah and put her arms around them. "You girls look absolutely gorgeous. I could stand here admiring you all day, but we had better get going. We certainly would not want to be late today of all days."

"Mom, where's Daniel?"

"Oh, he called and said he was running late. He said he'll meet you at the church," Jay explained.

As the procession left the house, Claire had an amazing sense of fulfillment. The couples walked hand in hand while the children walked politely beside them. Even little James did a good job of keeping up as Jay held one of his small, chubby hands. The girls in the blue dresses led the way, which in some ways made Claire feel as if she were in some kind of royal procession. When they reached the door of the church, the group split up.

"You all go ahead and be seated. I'll go downstairs with the girls." When they reached the basement, Claire asked, "Are you excited?"

"Yes, and a little nervous," Sarah confided.

"Not me. I'm not nervous at all."

"Good. I know you will do a good job. Now you go on in there, and I'll see you upstairs in a little while." She bent over and kissed both of them on the forehead. The girls headed down the hall. As they left and Claire turned around, it seemed only fitting that down the stairs came Lila in all her glory.

Lila put her hands on Claire's shoulders, turning her slightly to the right and then to the left as if to check out the full picture. "Oh, darling, you look just lovely!"

"Thank you, Lila." At quite a loss for words, Claire stuttered slightly, "And you...well, I must say you have chosen a beautiful color for today." What she really wanted to say was, "Where in the world did you find that getup?"

It was not just a gentle, subdued shade of orange. It was an orange so bright that an orange would have paled in contrast and a pumpkin would have been jealous of the intensity of the color. But it was not just the color that was unique. The suit was one of a kind, or at least in Claire's opinion it should have been. The hip-length fitted jacket was not too outspoken with its diagonal satin cording attached to look like the rays of the sun at the waistline with more cording pointing inward from the points on the collar. The silver buttons outlined in rhinestones were, however, an unnecessary and garish touch. But even with that, the jacket could not compare with the skirt for being way out of touch with the mode of dress in Hayward. The tight straight skirt did not have a normal hemline that went straight across the bottom. Instead it was angled up from the sides toward the middle of the front, and from this unusual hemline hung long satin fringe that went to Lila's ankles.

Of course, it would not be a complete outfit if Lila did not have a hat, and this one was made to go with the dress. The basic high crowned hat had a brim that Claire guessed to be three to four inches wide. Wound around the crown were pieces of the fringe that were held together in the front with a wide rhinestone pin.

"Won't this just be a wonderful event? I am just so happy for you. I must hurry. I have so many last minute things to do, you know. See you later, lovely lady. Ta-ta."

"Ta-ta!" Claire momentarily was repulsed by Lila's "lovely lady" comment, but she couldn't help but smile as she watched Lila shuffle away. She couldn't take very big steps due to the tightness of the skirt, and a shuffle was the best way to describe how she moved. But what really lightened the moment for Claire was the thought that if the fringe along the bottom had been green, Lila would have looked like an inverted carrot.

"Whatever happened to the belief that no one should outshine the bride at her wedding?" Claire mumbled to herself. Then she looked at her watch. "I thought he would be here by now. I guess I could go up to look for him." She started up the stairs at the same time a figure came down.

Daniel gave her a quick kiss. Then he stepped back to give her the once over. Her very pale blue suit was fitted just enough to show off her figure, which was still quite good for a woman in her fifties. "Hubba hubba!"

"I thought you would be here sooner. I was beginning to worry."

"Nothing to worry about. I just kind of got tied up a while at the hospital. Are you ready for all of this?"

"I think so. And Daniel, you will not believe how beautiful the girls look. It will be such a great surprise!"

He followed her up the stairs and to the back of the church, where they surveyed the crowd and the church. "That Lila does know how to throw a party. It looks darn good in here."

"And even more surprising is that it's tastefully done."

The church was filled with familiar heads and some that Claire did not recognize. In one of the back pews sat a spiffed-up Ben Miller with a stiff-looking Bertha Banter. Between the two was a very thin man that Ben talked to frequently.

"Shall we go?" Daniel asked.

With her arm in his, Claire walked proudly up the aisle. At the front they chose to sit on the left, the bride's side, instead of the right side, which traditionally held the family and friends of the groom. Shortly after they were seated, Phoebe, who had been playing subdued music, revved it up a notch and started the strains of "The Wedding March" just as a very serious Ronnie Milstein and his uncle Rudy followed Bill Carson in from the side of the church and faced the congregation.

Spreading white rose petals that she picked from a white straw basket, Abby was the first up the aisle. She was followed by Sarah, who held a small bouquet of pink carnations and miniature white roses. Next in line was a young lady unfamiliar to most of the congregation but whom Claire had met at the rehearsal and knew was the best friend of the bride. Finally, the bride, Tara Frasier, on the arm of her father, walked down the aisle toward the beaming bridegroom. Most of those in the congregation probably thought it just a coincidence that three of those standing in front of the church had the same color red hair because most of those from Hayward knew the members of the McRoberts family, and the bride was not one of them.

During the ceremony, Claire tried to focus on Ronnie and Tara, but her attention frequently wandered to Abby and Sarah. She knew she was biased, but she still marveled at how beautiful they both looked. For a brief moment when her gaze veered toward Abby, Claire stared in wonder. The sun was beaming through one of the west windows of the church, outlining her in an incredibly bright white light. *If I didn't know better, I'd believe there is another angel right here*, she thought. She reached over to get Daniel's attention, but the light faded just as fast as it had appeared as the sun was blocked by a cloud.

At the end of the ceremony, the couple walked quickly down the aisle followed by the rest of the small wedding party. They then went down the stairs where the reception would be held. Claire and Daniel lingered at the back of the church and allowed the rest of the group to leave before them. The last to leave their seats were Bertha and Ben, who together helped the other man get up and walk to join Claire and Daniel.

"It is so very good to see you again, Mr. McRoberts."

"Please call me Tom, Mrs. Menefee."

"Only if you call me Claire."

"Okay, now that you two have that straightened out, shall we go downstairs?"

When Bertha and Ben were out of the way at the bottom of the stairs, Tom got a firm grip of the stair railing while Daniel got a strong grip on him. Slowly they descended the stairs. It had been planned that Tom would get to the basement well after everyone else. Claire felt it would not be good to cause an uproar in the middle of someone else's wedding reception.

When they got to the basement, Daniel stayed close to Tom but let him walk by himself to a chair Claire had found. They had barely gotten him seated when the initial squeal was heard.

"Daddy!" Abby was the first to see him and ran to him, with Sarah close on her heels. Then the boys, who saw the commotion, realized what was going on and joined in the welcoming. Tears, hugs, kisses, and more hugs, kisses, and tears went on until everyone had calmed down. Claire, Daniel, and Ben gathered enough chairs for the McRoberts clan to sit and visit. Then they walked over to visit with Claire's family, who had gathered in a section of the basement along with many townsfolk who came over to introduce themselves.

After Ronnie and his new bride, Tara Frasier Milstein, had done the obligatory cake cutting and feeding, people lined up for cake and punch. Lila, acting as if she were the mother of the bride and not just the organizer of the wedding, directed people to the serving line as she tried hard to remember to take small steps in her carrot outfit. Chester, who was used to working a crowd, also did a good job of getting people moving through the food line.

Irene Taylor, whose bakery had baked and decorated the cake, cut and served it. Maude, who had closed the restaurant for the afternoon, poured the punch, leaving her companion for the wedding, Sheriff Butch Johnson, sitting with his deputy, Burton, and Vickie Thornton. Also in that young group were John Brook and Loretta Goering.

Phoebe, who acted as if she had worked up quite the appetite from the organ playing, managed to be one of the first in the food line and had an admiring Cliff Wilkens following right after her. Bertha declined any cake or punch but said that she wouldn't mind a few nuts if Ben could just put some on his plate to share. Fred Young and Irma Fisher joined Bertha and Ben. When Claire looked over to check on what Irma was wearing, she was certain she had seen her wear the navy blue dress with lace trim and pearl buttons before.

The bachelor section grew when Rudy joined William Swan and Tim Payne who, rumor had it, had been dumped by his redheaded girlfriend. Rumor also said she had found a rich oil speculator whose bank account and spending habits were bigger than Dr. Payne's. The general feeling throughout the town was that he was much better off without her. When Lila heard the news, she began looking for a replacement for the redhead. When she realized that Ruby Smith from the bank had not brought Thomas Thomas with her to the wedding, she thought that might be a good place to start.

Lloyd and Floyd were with Rudy, William, and Tim, but Floyd didn't have the same sparkle in his eyes that he had a few weeks ago. Lila was open to thinking about a new match for Floyd too but didn't think it would be as easy as finding one for Tim.

Clara somehow managed to carry two plates of cake, two cups of punch, and her purse to a chair at the side of the room, where a very quiet Farley sat. She set them down on a chair that was between the two. He looked up at her when she set down the food, and although he didn't actually smile at her, he almost looked relieved that someone was sitting with him.

Lila flitted from guest to guest in her small shuffling move. She had swooped through Claire's family group a couple of times, where they had explained to her more than once that it accidentally worked out that the wedding happened on the same weekend they had planned a family get-together. The entire group had been invited to attend since the girls were going to be in the wedding and since there would not be very many people on the bride's side of the church.

When the group saw Lila headed over again, they wondered if they were going have to explain for a third time. Instead she shuffled over to where Claire and Daniel were talking together. Stopping squarely in front of them, she pinched Daniel's cheek with her left hand and Claire's with her right hand. "Maybe it will be you two next time," she said, winking at Daniel. It would have been hard to tell who blushed more as Lila continued on to annoy someone else.

Ben and Bertha checked out with Claire before they left. "I'll go on home, so when Mr. McRoberts gets tired I'll be there. So you two just take your time and stay as long as you want." Bertha actually almost smiled when she nodded good-bye.

Claire's family group left soon after Ben and Bertha did, but Claire and Daniel stayed to visit and field questions about why the girls were chosen to be in the wedding, especially since no one in town seemed to even know who the bride was except for Ronnie and Rudy.

The day the girls had insisted on going back to the house to find the old picture of their mother, Claire had picked up, although she didn't know it at the time, a family genealogy chart for their mother's side of the family. As it turned out, there probably was a reason for the resemblance between Mrs. McRoberts and Tara Frasier. They were cousins. But because the families had experienced such upheaval and numerous moves, the different branches of the families had lost contact with each other, especially following the death of both Mrs. McRoberts' and Tara's mothers.

When Tara, who had moved often because of her father's military career, found out she had relatives in town, she was so excited she decided to include the girls in the wedding. She already had developed a soft spot in her heart for both of them since they got so excited every time they saw her.

Because she had moved so often, she had no strong ties to any place she could call home. She met Ronnie in school while she was working on her nursing degree, which she recently had completed. She was lucky enough to have secured a job in the hospital in Livonia and already had met Tom McRoberts.

Daniel and Claire joined the McRoberts family group, where the boys were getting restless to leave and take off their uncomfortable clothes. Although he was starting to get quite tired from all of the activity, Tom was anxious to go see Timmy and Tommy, whom he had not seen in months. He was slowly getting up to leave when Lila and Chester came bubbling over. Claire groaned under her breath.

"Please. Sit down for a moment," Lila gushed. "I can't tell you how pleased and relieved Chester and I are that you are doing so much better and are out of the hospital. The entire town has enjoyed your wonderful, well-behaved children."

So far, so good, Claire thought.

"Chester and I have a little something for you and your family." She elbowed her husband. "Okay, Chester. Give them to him."

Chester rummaged through his pocket and came out with his hand closed. He moved his hand toward Tom and then opened it. Tom looked down and then back up at the Haywards with a look of puzzlement. "They're the keys to the house behind us."

Chester was ready to continue, but Lila took over. "We loved having old Lois Teller as a neighbor, but when she moved out, it was almost as if that house had a curse. First there were the embezzlers. Then there was the klepto. Chester and I just cannot stand to think who might move in and rent that house next, so instead we bought it from Lois's family, and we would like to have you and your family have it."

Claire didn't know who was more stunned—the entire McRoberts family, who no longer would be crammed into that tiny old farmhouse; Daniel, who dealt with people who tried to take advantage of others and even endanger them and who just wasn't used to seeing such magnanimous gestures; or Claire, who heretofore thought of Lila as shallow and self-centered. Mouths hung open all around.

Tom stumbled, trying to find words to properly express thanks from his family and himself. But he didn't have to worry as each child, without being prompted, stood and either hugged or shook hands with the Haywards. Although it probably went unnoticed by the others, Claire saw both Chester's and Lila's eyes start to glisten.

"Oh, and one more thing. Well, maybe two more things. If it's all right with you, we've arranged for Tara to come check on you two to three times a week, once she returns from her honeymoon, until you are feeling lots better. And if you're interested when you feel up to it, would you be interested in doing the maintenance work at the courthouse and city hall as well as the other properties we own in town? Of course, that wouldn't be until you're feeling up to it. We can talk more about that later."

"We'll go and leave you alone now," said Chester.

"The keys, Chester," Lila said, elbowing him.

"Oh yeah." He dropped them in the very thin upturned, outstretched hand.

The boys left with their father to help him get back to Ben's house. The girls stayed because they wanted to wait for the bouquet tossing. There was much teasing of Cliff when Phoebe used her size to elbow the others out of the way and snatch the flying flowers. Shortly after that, the newlyweds left to a shower of birdseed provided by Bob Simpson's hardware store. When the girls left after the couple drove away, they both kissed Claire and softly said, "I love you, Mrs. M."

Things were relatively quiet as Claire and Daniel walked home to join her family, whose laughter could be heard from her backyard. Lucky appeared to be joining the fun, as his occasional barking blended with the laughter. They walked hand in hand, not saying much but both seemingly deep in their own thoughts. They had just turned up Claire's sidewalk when Daniel softly said, "Stop."

Claire did as he told her but didn't know what was going on. "What's the matter?" she whispered.

"It's there—the butterfly—on your shoulder right now," he whispered back.

Claire stood as still as she could and tried to slow her breathing and heart rate. She realized she was listening very carefully. She thought it was just foolish until she heard it in a very small but still firm voice:

"God's in his heaven and all's right with the world."

QUESTIONS FOR DISCUSSION

Reverend and Mrs. Carlson took it upon themselves to place the McRoberts children with local families, bypassing any social services placement. Was this the right thing to do, or should they have followed state legal guidelines for such a situation?

Did Abby really feel responses from her father's hand on the hospital visits, or did she imagine it because she wanted to believe that he could hear her?

Clara interacted differently with different people. Why do you think her behavior with Abby was positive when it was negative with so many others?

How would you describe and explain Clara's relationship with Farley?

Most adults would agree that butterflies don't talk. What explanation could be offered for why Abby thought one talked to her, especially considering some of the things the butterfly allegedly told her?

With what we know about Daniel and his job, do you think he and Claire have a future together?

Considering Abby's spiritual strength and the change in Sarah's attitude, will Mr. McRoberts also change how he feels about the church and religion?

Were you surprised about who ended up getting married? Whom did you guess would get married in the story, or did you think that Lila's business would have no customers?

There were many characters in *Butterfly Messages*. Did any of them remind you of people you have known?

Who was your favorite character and why?